I0819799

LEWIS OF MODERN YORK

Novels published by Midnight Fire Media

Your Own Fate
Night on Earth
Dreams Belong to the Night
ShadowWalk
Alarums of Reality
Afterglow Dust
Black Dragon
Falling
Thunder road - Ice and Fire
Season of the Witch

Anthology: Red Shadow and Other Stories

The Janus Clan series:

The Defenseless
The Slaves
Birds Flying in the Dark
At the End of the Rainbow

Poetry:

Amos Keppler: Complete Poems 1989 – 2003
Secrets - Descriptions of what cannot be described

(A few of the) novels to be published:

Afterglow Rain
The Werewolf of Locus Bradle
Fangs and Claws of the Earth
Forsaken
Resurrection Dreams

For a «complete» list of current and current future Amos Keppler and Midnight Fire Media projects see the back of the book and the Midnight Fire/Midnight Fire Media web pages.

Lewis of Modern York

by

Amos Keppler

Midnight Fire Media
2019

Midnight Fire Media

http://midnight-fire.net/mfm
For more about Lewis of Modern York and The Janus Clan:
http://midnight-fire.net/lomy

E-Mail:
Amos13@midnight-fire.net
manofhood@yahoo.com

Cover, text, design, premedia, art and photos Amos Keppler

ISBN 978-82-91693-24-8

«We, the most distant dwellers upon the earth, the last of the free, have been shielded... by our remoteness and by the obscurity which has shrouded our name...

Beyond us lies no nation, nothing but waves and rocks».

- Calgacus, Northern Chieftain of the Picts

«The long habit of living indisposeth us for dying» - Sir Thomas Browne

Chapter 1

The metal construct that had once resided in the airless void tumbled towards the Earth as a giant ball of fire. The event drew everyone's attention to itself, making everyone look at the sky.

Carla Wolf slumbered on the train to Times Square. She woke up with a faint recollection of blood and fire, and the stench of dead bodies. It stirred behind her eyelids even after she had opened her eyes fully. The writing on the wall flashed before her eyes. An old lady crouched in her seat. A young woman with dark glasses looked like she was more asleep than awake. A group of young males dressed in dark leather made their presence known in quite a few ways. Everything and everyone in the coach imposed itself on Carla. She dried the sweat from her brow and pushed the dark hair from her eyes.

Most of the seats were taken, but not all. No one needed to stand this late afternoon. Another young woman, about Carla's age clutched her handbag. A young male with only a tiny jacket covering his upper body stared at her and Carla with desire in his eyes. It was crowded, or seemed that way to her overworked senses. The train approached the station. The murky surroundings, with electricity turning itself off and on constantly turned bright, though not exactly shiny.

The train was loud in her ears long after it had stopped and she had left it behind. She left the station, even as it stayed with her, twisting her gut.

The crowded subway gave way to the crowded Times Square the busy Saturday afternoon. Various images of her surroundings, both old and recent warred within her, on this day, the very heat of summer, late July 1979.

She spotted Lewis Talbot under the billboards. His tall, skinny body and hairless face stood out among dozens of others. He waved excitedly. Her heart jumped a beat. She returned the wave.

He rushed forward to meet her. She speeded up a little, discreetly, making sure they didn't embrace in the middle of the road, but at the edge of the sidewalk. He pushed at her, almost making her fall, as he grabbed her and kissed her lips, eager like the boy he was. The aftershave stank in her nostrils.

– My Lady…

With her eyes closed she easily saw him clothed in armor, a bloody sword in his hands.

It was him. It wasn't him. It was him.

My Lady, he grinned, with both respect and disrespect, both exuberance of a youth and the somberness of an older, experienced man. Both joy and sadness stuck in her throat.

She returned the kiss, beyond passionate, unable, unwilling to hold herself back.

He looked breathless at her, worship and desire glowing beneath the skin, the dark brown eyes.

She let him hold her hand and pull her with him further down the street. The wind caught her hair. He hurried up, and she hurried up with him.

A group of young men in gang colors chuckled as they passed them.

– Is your kid brother being difficult, sweetie? One of them asked.

It was an insult, no matter what they were in truth implying. She froze, and he did, too, but to her relief he kept walking, and the gang members didn't bother pushing him further.

Further down the street, at the opposite sidewalk five police officers gathered. They seemed to have their attention firmly on the gang members, and the gang members eagerly returned the interest.

Carla shivered a bit, imagining that all their attention was focused on her.

– Sometimes there are riders, she mumbled.

– What was that? Lewis wondered.

She shook her head, giving him a sweet smile.

– You're weird, he said. – I like weird.

She shivered in delight when he kissed her on the neck. Her hand touched, probed the face in front of her, both so familiar and unfamiliar, as she kept watching him. The language of his subconscious movements spoke to her far more than his voice did.

Everyone present spoke to her louder than words. She rubbed her left temple.

Soldiers screamed and howled outside Eboracum, outside Jórvík, outside Old York, fighting and dying by the blood-colored wall.

– That, among other things makes you a very interesting boy, she said softly.

That patronizing act of kindness and flirting made the fifteen-year-old boy blush hard.

– You're good at handling men, aren't you? He breathed into her ear, a taint of aggression in his voice. – I've watched you, how you discard them like yesterday's laundry.

– It's easy when you know how, she shrugged.

– But not me, he wondered, – me, you're honoring with your grace.

– I like you, she said, this time completely without irony, turning her head and staring deeply into his eyes.

He blushed again.

Her attention drifted and fanned the wall ahead, as they turned a corner, and she noticed its irregularities, its alternate realities.

Something rubbed her off, something she couldn't quite grasp…

They reached a window display. She froze. He kept moving forward. A blue… lamp of sorts glowed in a powerful light when he passed it, but it lit in a far more powerful light when she hurried to catch up with him, when she grabbed him and dragged him with her.

– Did you see that? He exclaimed. – That was some display.

– Some display, she agreed, fighting to keep the shaking from her voice.

– Perhaps we should ask if it is for sale? It must be a device reacting to movement or something. It would certainly be great to have in a living room somewhere.

– No, it wouldn't. She shook her head decisively. – It was gross. It gave me the creeps.

She kissed him, kissed him hard. He chuckled, clearly flattered. She breathed a sigh in relief when he turned his full attention to her, and away from what they were leaving behind, the fastest she could without giving her anxiety away.

They left the heavily frequented places and headed into the alleys and backstreets. The surroundings kept shifting and buzzing around her. Fairly modern buildings sometimes gave way to far older structures. She smelled smoke and couldn't always tell whether or not it was real or imagined, if it was actually here, in New York City in late July 1979.

She heard the old, haunting music first, before the sound of guitars and heavier drums reached her from the building with the open windows ahead. It pulled her in. She pulled Lewis with her. They laughed together as they crossed the threshold to the somewhat downtrodden tavern ahead.

The room wasn't packed, but already more than half full. They selected a table in one of its deepest corners. He kissed her quickly and rushed to the bar. She heard the entire conversation without exerting herself.

– C'mon, Abbie, Lewis urged the man behind the desk. – Be nice.

– Are you aware of how much trouble, and I mean *trouble* I can get into with this? It's quite the long list.

– We need a place to crash tonight, Lewis insisted. – *She* needs a place to stay. She has just arrived in the city and has nowhere else to go.

He returned with two pints of Guiness in his hands, and a very large grin on his face.

– Abbie has agreed to let you stay in the attic for a while. He could hardly wait to break the news to her. – He's an old softie at heart.

– Thank you, she said. – You're sweet.

He sat down close to her on the couch, and they drank.

– So, is the famous stout to the Irish woman's satisfaction?

– It is, she replied with large, almond eyes.

He performed the Irish's accent almost to perfection.

There was a catching in her throat and she had to work hard to conceal it from him.

– Abbie is a little outside mainstream himself, Lewis commented. – That makes him not exactly unappreciative of others in similar circumstances.

This was obviously a dive, or one with a few redeeming qualities and clearly lacking a stamp of government approval. All kinds of scents lingered in the air, adding to Carla's already stimulated senses.

– Cheers for being outside mainstream, he said, looking boldly into her eyes.

Two glasses met and parted, and they drank, drank deep.

– This tastes great, she nodded, even the taste giving her a whiff of other places.

– It can't beat American beers, a man at the neighborhood table grunted.

– I can safely say, sir, she said brazenly, – that it beats any American «beer» soundly.

– How can you tell? The man mumbled, not willing to meet the bright eyes.

– I've tasted ales all over America and the world. I know a bit about beer.

There was something in the way she pronounced «ales» unnerving them all.

– Then you must have started as a toddler, the man grumbled, even more unintelligible.

There was laughter in the room, good-hearted, adding to the already cheerful mood. Glimpses of laughing and celebrating people gained briefly the upper hand in her visions, her memories.

Everybody had more beer. There was no cashier. Abbie took the cash and put it directly in his pocket, ready to run with the rest of them if there was the slightest sign of the police showing up. There was just one barrel of Guiness. Another was brought in just as that one was about to run dry. It was very well timed and more than suggested long practice.

– You're smiling, the man that had earlier stated his fondness for American beer said. – And what a smile it is.

– This is a place where outlaws or potential outlaws gather. She closed her eyes briefly again. – I love that.

And in that brief closing of eyes she saw merry men and women dance in the forest, feasting on meat and ale. There were riders chasing them, but they could hardly ever touch the merry and fierce people of the deep forest.

Present musicians gathered spontaneously and formed a band, playing percussion, guitars, flutes and violins. They didn't find common ground immediately, but eventually they did. The guy with the portable cassette player turned it off, and the silence of the live music slowly embraced them all.

When the woman rose on her feet and began her slow and wild dance, it didn't really surprise them or most of those present at all. Movement was slow, deliberate, casual, but beneath the exterior it, she was Wild.

– I'm She Who Dances in the Forest, she cried softly, – follow me inside.

And they were pulled, but didn't resist the pull, but eagerly joined in on her dance, and she welcomed them with a happy laughter.

– I dance on the rooftops under the moon, listening to the thunder's music, she sang, she hummed, she burned into their souls. – The sun is gone, but I don't miss it. The moon cast all my great shadows.

She was listening, not being consciously aware of it until she observed how those watching her noticed it. She reached out, for the trembling in the ground.

The noise, that from the city, its Machine obscured, even blocked her senses. Bile rose in her throat, but she kept reaching.

And then, after what felt like forever, she sensed the stronger, far more powerful tremble in the ground, heard, felt the potent flapping of wings vibrating the air.

A man grabbed her and lifted her up. She laughed and kissed him. Everybody in the room looked at her. Almost every man present, and also some of the women looked at her with desire and longing in their eyes.

One man wouldn't let go of her.

– You would want to let go of me, now, she told him, a chill briefly entering her voice.

She didn't struggle, making no physical effort to free herself.

He did, did let go of her, a startled and frightened look appearing in the depth of his eyes.

She returned to Lewis. It seemed like the most natural act in the world to everybody. She pulled him with her out on the dusty dance floor, and they danced, turned and turned, tightly entwined.

– They will stay away, she whispered into his ears, whispered while staring into his eyes. – They know I'm yours.

The desire rose in him, hard and potent. Anyone could see that, but to her, with her enhanced senses it was like a slap in the face, a shock to her entire system, and desire doubled, tripled in her as well.

They turned in their dance, turned and turned and turned, until the first choir of a gasp rose from both their throats. They turned and turned and turned, until the surroundings, the people and the room faded around them, and they were alone in the attic bedroom. She touched a faded painting of a green rose on the wall. He touched her from behind, pushing her at the wall, making her gasp with a constantly open mouth. She turned around and returned his crude affection. He was quite lacking in finesse, but quite persistent, practically relentless. It made the glow within her spread slowly from the one point to her entire body.

– Sometimes the years pass by so slowly, she whispered.

The green rose glowed so strangely. She didn't just feel the glow in herself, but in him, and the walls, and in flesh many places, and the rose glowing in green. He began undressing her, eager, clumsy, relentless. She undressed him with comforting touches, whispering calming sounds in his ears. They were on the bed at the center of the room, a million miles away. What she felt rocking the Earth wasn't drums, wasn't even thunder, but far more basic than even that. He squeezed her left breast and the building shook. He pushed and pulled inside her, and it was as if a serpent rolled across the land. They kissed and twin volcanoes spit hot breath into the air.

Sleep, when it finally came cast darkness across half the planet, and Carla Wolf smiled to the moon hovering above them on the darkened sky.

2

Sometimes there were riders.

Carla Wolf woke up in the small, downtrodden Manhattan apartment, still hearing the sound of hooves from a thousand horses crossing the plain.

She saw a little girl stand bloody and pale, among piles of corpses. That same girl waited, dressed in her best clothes for the lone rider approaching her, dismounting his horse and kneeling in the dust, the wet grass before her.

The morning light flooded the room, and she smiled to the sun above. Lewis was sleeping soundly. She caressed his head. He didn't stir. She left the bed and walked to the bathroom. He woke to the sound of her vomiting into the toilet bowl, she knew he did, felt first his stir, then his blazing mind become aware, well under way to its full capacity.

They made breakfast together. He clearly didn't mind and that, too, pleased her.

– You aren't pumped up, are you? He asked curiously, more than a bit anxious.

She smiled, shaking her head over his youthful lack of compassion.

– No, I just dislike waking up in cities, that's all. She dried her jaw of remaining vomit.

– So why don't you leave?

– No. She shook her head hard. – I want to feel it, feel the wrongness. I won't run away.

– Who won't you run away from? He asked. – Is it someone of blood and flesh or some existential threat?

He was in a philosophical mood today, he always was. She smiled to him disarming his irritation because she didn't verbally reply.

– You have such broad shoulders and dense muscles, he mumbled in her hair, rubbing her arms affectionately. – More than any girl I've seen.

– I always exercise and train myself from an early age, she shrugged.

He frowned, but didn't quite get it, didn't realize the hidden truth in her words.

They sat down by the table, both feeding like wolves, both enjoying the meal to the fullest.

– So, why are you calling yourself Wolf? That isn't your name, is it?

– That is my name, she stated.

– That isn't the name in your passport. That says your name is Anya, Anya Kerien.

– My, oh, my, what a precious little boy you are.

He blushed. That cute young fucker.

She closed her eyes briefly, eliciting all kinds of additional sensations.

– That is the name others have given me. Carla and Wolf is what I've given myself.

– I… understand, he said startled.

– I know you do, she said. – I know you do.

He faded away in front of her, never quite fading. She was alone again, together with all the other people crossing her path on the street.

The ring of fire and shadow burned around her, moved when she moved, an age-old ghoul haunting her every waken moment.

When the street musician played his tune, when his fingers touched the guitar strings she could see the vibrations it created in the air.

She comes through the night

He sang, he ended the song.

Encircled in a ring of fire

The song, the strings, the music awakened her further, doing so without any conscious effort on her part.

She walked to him, walked past the halfmoon of people he had gathered, had drawn to himself and stopped in front of him.

– Hello, she greeted him, just as he played the final chord.

Eyes met. She made sure they did. He shivered imperceptibly.
– Do I know you? He wondered.
– I don't know, she said. – Do you?
– I feel like I've seen you somewhere before, but I can't say I recognize you.
– My mistake, she said, pulling back and out of the half circle of his gathering.
– Hey, he called after her, – what's your name?
She told him. There was no sense of distinct, powerful recognition this time either.
– My name is Linsey Kendall, he said, as if it was supposed to mean something, with the boasting she so easily recognized. – I'm with a group called Mystic. We're gonna set the Big Apple on fire.
– I'm looking forward to that, she called back.
She kept walking. He didn't follow.
The solitary figure of Carla Wolf moved through streets of ash and fire. Both grew notable to her, in various stages of awareness. Open eyes saw something. Half-closed eyes saw more.
– Anya? Hey, ANYA!
A girl called out to her a while later. Carla stopped, waiting for the other to catch up.
– Anya? Is that really you?
Another girl in her late teens stopped before her, catching her breath.
– Anya is gone. Only Carla and Wolf remain.
The other girl first stared dumbfounded on her. Then she giggled.
– Oh, you've changed your name. Many people do that these days.
Carla recognized Maeve Donovan from the mist of the ages, even though it was hardly more than a month since they had last seen each other.
– I'm here with the gang, Maeve said excitedly. – We did it, just as you did. We *left!*
Images and sensations of the small town, or rather village of Sligo passed through Carla's consciousness.
Maeve dragged her with her, across the street, into a coffee bar, where Isolde Harris, Tess O'Hara and Fiona Mc Swain waited for them with wide eyes.
Music flowed from speakers, chords filled with potency and fate. She enjoyed it, as she enjoyed the red wine they all drank, and the presence of young, excited souls.
– We all wondered what happened to you, Tess said. – You practically disappeared without leaving any trace, without saying goodbye.
There was a sore subtext to her voice.

I did say goodbye.

– I didn't really disappear. I just left, that's all.

– I guess you were fed up with waiting for the rest of us to get going, Tess nodded.

Her features and those of the others softened, and they grabbed Carla's hands, and Carla Wolf enjoyed that, too, enjoyed the company of brave young hearts breaking away from the confines of their upbringing.

There had been more, many more potential companions in Sligo and surrounding area, but only these had followed her, followed her here, to this center of the world.

– They didn't understand, Maeve said sadly.

– They were afraid, Fiona said. – And they let their fear rule them, until they were nothing but the timid girls others told them they were.

Carla remained mostly silent, content with listening to their voices, enjoying the fleeting moment of their passion and unflinching dedication.

– But you are here, now, she finally said. – Scrounging money for your plane tickets, you broke away from your roots, from your mother, father and condemning family to join me, here, in this city of cities.

And their passion and unflinching dedication grew to something more and lasting.

The swords cut the air in the dusty storage room. The sound of the metal cleaving the misty space brought back more memories, more sensations that weren't there.

– I remember, she said. – I've remembered from an early age, but it turns clearer and more detailed for each new day, now. I knew it would.

But I wasn't certain. I feared I was mad, that I was born insane.

They were all sweating hard, staring at each other with wonder in their eyes.

The morning passed like that, in a sort of dream they knew to be true.

I can see a woman in prehistoric times, the woman at the center of the small circle said with dreaming eyes. – She sits on her heels on a rock on Africa's Great Eastern plains, under the ice-capped mountain of Kilimanjaro, where it is theorized human life began.

She imagined there was a campfire between them, one spreading, to consume them all, but there wasn't, not yet.

– I can't remember, Maeve said. – I know I'm supposed to, but I can't.

– Don't fret, the young girl from Old York and far older places besides said. – You will!

She watched how the awakening changed the others, as she had so many times before.

The five of them rose.

It was the same here, as outside and everywhere else. He watched the world and all people in it with new and different eyes. His friends didn't look the same as they had only a week earlier.

The place gave off a very bland impression, with an even light creating very few shadows. He walked to the table by the wall, where Eloise Sargeant, Immogen Walls, Lester Foley, Gavin Franklin and Thomas Gentry waited for him.

– You're late, Lester said, – but I guess that was only to be expected?

– Lee is beyond mortal consideration these days, Immogen grinned.

The teasing was obvious, heavy handed, but not cruel. He saw something in their eyes, however, that hadn't been there before. Even Eloise looked at him with a sense of hurt beneath her mask.

He sat down on the only available spot and writhed in discomfort almost from the first second. The seat was too small for him, like most seats were.

They kept looking at him. He read reluctant admiration and envy in the boys' eyes, and scorn in the girls'.

– Carla isn't very fashion-minded, is she, now? Immogen said, after a prolonged break.

Most people here, Immogen and bunch included were clearly quite fashion-minded, wearing the latest fad from the seventies' disco scene.

– Another of her great points, he shrugged.

They laughed together.

There was a confidence, a quality to him, now, that hadn't been there only a week ago. Even the most insensitive person would notice the change. Immogen turned moody and withdrawn.

Lee had his soda with them, toasting with them, laughing with them.

He went to the john and relieved himself. The hot stream hit the bowl in front of him, briefly changing white marble to yellow.

– They don't understand you, how can they?

He turned startled. There was no one there. He looked at the man three steps away, one of the maintenance crew also taking a leak, one looking just as startled.

– It was a woman's voice… wasn't it?

Lee heard anxiety in his voice.

– A woman's voice, he replied, both confirming and soothing the other man's fears.

He went through the previous moments in his head, something he had always been good at. Someone, a man leaving the restroom had opened the door, of course, and then the woman had spoken. A sense of relief grabbed him. The other man opened the doors to the toilet bowls. Lee wanted to tell him not to bother, but couldn't find a voice to do so.

The boy stepped into the hallway, but saw no woman there, saw almost nobody. Most of the guests had pulled into the darker inner hall in anticipation of the afternoon dance to begin.

Hot Stuff by Donna Summer began roaring from the speakers the moment he crossed the threshold. The coincidence, the good timing on his part created a well of sudden, unexpected expectation within. He joined his friends there on the dance floor, submerging himself in the flashing lights, among the bits and pieces faces.

A poster on the wall said with huge, capital letters:

DISCO IS DEAD

Hot Stuff was really more rock than the disco rapture Summer had released earlier and even sold better than the typical disco songs on the Bad Girls album. Disco was dead.

Lee shouted in enjoyment. Nobody, nobody he was aware of heard him in the loud music shaking the floor and the people on it, but he did, felt the shout rock the room far more than the electronically enhanced sound.

Eloise glanced at him, briefly, before looking away. He noticed, and saw that she noticed, saw her redden in the shifting radiance.

Between the lights and the shadows, he glimpsed Carla. He knew she wasn't there, but her presence permeated his body and his every thought.

She was there.

– My knight, she moaned while rocking up and down in his lap. – My brave, brave knight.

Suddenly he feared he didn't get enough oxygen. Before he realized it, he stood outside, gasping for air, the pervasive stench of blood overwhelming him wherever he turned.

Eloise approached him from behind. He was amazed by the fact that he knew that it was her, without turning his head and look. She caught his attention before she exited the building.

He smelled her perfume in the soft wind, but it was more than that.

– Are you alright? She asked softly, her voice devoid of the disguised but evident malice Immogen had displayed.

– I'm more than all right, he said, as he turned and faced her. – I feel great!

His eyes met hers, in a frank manner clearly displaying interest that wouldn't have been possible just a few days ago.

She was blushing.

– You've changed so much, she whispered. – I hardly recognize you.

– I haven't. He shook his head. – Not really. I've just opened up a bit, that's all.

A tiny bit, compared to everything still resting and hiding within. Confusion and clarity riddled him.

– There's a lot more where that comes from, he told her, touching her jaw, holding her eyes.

She shivered, but made no attempt at moving, at pulling away. He bent forward, as if to kiss her, but stopped and stepped back, avoiding her eyes.

– You're thinking about *her* again, aren't you? She cried angrily.

He didn't reply, or at least he didn't voice any, hesitating.

She stepped close to him, grabbed his head and kissed him fiercely on the lips. He found himself responding, the sound of their hammering hearts echoing in his ears and mind.

The girl pulled back, stricken, gasping for air and space.

– What was that? She cried. – *What was that?*

I don't know, he wanted to say, but words failed him. He wanted to shake his head, but nothing happened.

She walked off, leaving him alone.

He stood there frozen, feeling like his surroundings were shaking him apart.

Only slowly, painfully slow he began moving again. It seemed like he had been standing still forever.

The first thing he did after he left his friends was to buy a new tri-pack of underwear. The girl behind the counter studied him with a patronizing grin, or so he imagined and strongly suspected. Everyone, everywhere stared at him.

In what seemed like hours later he was still walking aimlessly through the streets. He was walking alone, but it didn't feel like he did, as the people around him felt much closer than they appeared, and those close like they… touched him, or he touched them. With every move he made, he felt something, a charge, a sensation. He almost panicked, but focused on calming down. When he finally managed to do that, and it, whatever it was stopped, he sighed in stark relief.

He looked down at his hands. They were just hands, with no peculiar attributes.

But wherever he looked he saw her face.

He had met Carla a week ago. It had been in the afternoon. He and the gang had visited a burger joint nearby. She had entered it through the main entrance, while they sat there and devoured their burgers. He remembered that moment, remembered it vividly. There was something about her. He had noticed her at first glance. She looked quite striking with her athletic body and the exotic face added to it. It was clearly Caucasian, but yet different. Several of the present males had looked at her with hungry eyes, as she made her way to the counter. She had ordered salad and nothing more. It had struck him as odd that she had come to a burger joint to have only salad.

She sat down by a table and started devouring her salad. He imagined she was devouring a giant piece of steak. Everybody stared at her, but she ignored everybody. The way she behaved. it seemed like she was the only person in the room.

– What a bitch, he heard a girl say to her boyfriend. – She has worked hard for that body.

Some of the grown men spoke to the girl munching salad, made a pass at her, but she rejected them with a shrug. She remained sweet and all, but still conveyed her lack of interest, somehow. All the panting dogs pulled back, not really sure what had happened and how it had happened.

Lee exchanged words with his friends, but didn't really speak with them. He spotted the first twinges of annoyance and hurt in Eloise's eyes.

Lee drank his soda. Then he had another, shifting uneasily in his chair. Everything sounded loud in his ears. Every time he moved his eyes, they seemed to be locked on the target, freezing the image solid, overwhelming his mind with the details.

The need to pee turned unbearable and he rushed to the restroom. The quietness and emptiness in there… unnerved him, somehow. Daylight through the open windows shadowed the room. The doors to the cubicles were all open. He hesitated a bit, before opening his fly and relieving himself. The piss flowed into the bowl. He looked behind him now and then, but there was no one there.

He stepped back into the corridor and she stood there, leaning casually against the opposite wall.

– Hi, she greeted him, with the tiny smile playing on her lips and radiant face.

Her eyes looked at him, filled with all the promise in the world.

– Why… me? He asked, he wondered, in a glimpse of understanding.

– I could say that it was because you were the only one not staring at me, and that would be true, too…

He noticed the weird accent, but discarded that, that, too as unimportant.

She walked to him. Her eyes stopped right in front of his.

– I've missed you so much, she cried.

Her shivering lips touched his. She grabbed him. He grabbed her. They stood there, clutching each other in a fierce embrace.

The memory of that first, memorable encounter faded, staying with him, lingering at the forefront of his mind.

He looked across the water, at the Twin Towers, not really certain if he was here or somewhere else.

She mumbled in her sleep, writhing on her back in what was obviously a nightmare.

He heard a dog bark. At least it started as a bark, but then it changed… into a howl.

– Sometimes, there are riders, she mumbled.

And she sounded sore afraid. And that was so unlike her that he couldn't help but feel it, feel it deep down.

Something scratched his back, his neck, his earlobe, touched the tip of his longest hairs.

When he turned and cast his sight across the street he spotted a tall, giant woman. She returned his stare, he knew she did.

A sound distracted him. He looked away for a moment.

When he turned his attention back at the opposite sidewalk the woman had vanished. He looked up and down the street several times. Quite a few people walked back and forth. He had an excellent view of it all.

The woman was gone.

Chapter 2

Patrick Warren looked down at Manhattan from his office in the South Twin Tower.

He looked west, at the vast scenario below.

And then his eyes traced Broadway north.

It stopped at a certain point, before he turned away.

He pushed the button on the intercom on the desk.

– Cancel my appointments for the rest of the day, he said casually.

– Will do, boss, Caitlin Rowe replied. – Shall I call Robert?

Robert was his private chauffeur.

– That won't be necessary, thank you. I won't need him today.

A few more moments of hesitation followed before he left the space behind his desk. An eternity passed, or seemed to be passing before he reached the door and could open it, and reach the outer office, where Caitlin waited for him with her usual glowing smile.

– You look ravaging today, my dear, he said.

She blushed hard, turning soft and ready for whatever he wanted of her. He walked on. Other employees, men and women glanced at him, too, he was keenly aware of that, like a second nature. So was ignoring them, an easy beyond easy task.

Sliding doors opened for him. He left the offices of BURNTRAP & SON, and entered the general area where the elevators were.

Activity from all sides echoed in his ear, in his consciousness. He saw right through them with a glance not a glance. They looked at him with uneasiness playing in their shifting eyes. Reality shifted around him like a vice.

When he stepped into the elevator several people on their way there had done their utmost to not reach it in time. He kept the door open, held the elevator deliberately longer than he normally would have, smiling at them, as he kept ignoring them, and they shrunk in his presence.

A slight pull and the tiny cage set out on its way down. He emerged into the subway station, the buzz suddenly sounding like a waterfall around him. It wasn't really a bother. He had learned at an early age to control it.

This wasn't during peak hours, not in the morning or the afternoon or lunch break, but there were still lots of people around. They brushed off him like cotton.

He took the subway to West 4 Street. The time between the two points didn't truly register in his consciousness. It was done in a whiff, or so it felt in his distracted mind.

Flashes in color and gray passed before his eyes and nothing more.

Quite a few people had gathered at Washington Square, as was usually the case, as he approached it from the south. He spotted the sweat, the pearls of sweat on their naked skin. The stench tore at his nostrils. Today was a red-hot day, today, too.

He crouched imperceptibly, couldn't help it, as flashes of memory assaulted him, as he saw the place like it had been. The place had been filled with people that day, with loud and angry and passionate voices.

A girl looked up at her boyfriend with laughter in her eyes.

Patrick Warren passed under the arch and stopped in its shadow. Its chill hit him, like none of the seething hot air had done.

The girl's laughter echoed in his ears, only slowly fading.

He turned, in the direction where the school, the University was, and there he was, the other man. The two stared at each other in what were both intensively and casually, familiar and not.

– Hello, Eric, Warren said, striving to make his voice loud enough, unnecessary, since the other would have been able to hear a whisper in the loudest noise.

– I'm fine, thank you, Eric Carr said.

– Hell, Eric, how long has it been?

– Only five years, Carr replied, – just before I went to Florida.

They stared at each other across that abyss.

– It feels longer, Warren said, no longer able to hold back the hoarse whisper in his voice.

– It feels like yesterday to me, Carr shrugged.

He seemed to be covered in shadow, one a far cry from the intense sunlight bathing him.

– Wanna grab something to eat? Warren heard himself say.

Carr didn't reply vocally, but he followed Warren when he sat course towards University Place and the luncheonette there. The pain chopped Warren almost instantly, as he walked in the tracks of himself almost ten years ago, at the height of the Vietnam controversy. The two names of the place on the corner of University Place and Waverly Place then and now blurred in his mind.

They sat inside and had their sandwiches, with a straight view of the University Place area. Carr wolfed down his food and ordered more. Warren sat there, not really eating at all.

He stood there, outside, with Eric and lots of others, the place, fairly empty now, so filled with people then.

Everybody held up their draft notices, for all to see.

– We REFUSE, Patrick Warren cried for all to hear.
– We refuse! Eric Carr and many others echoed.
– We refuse, Patrick shouted, – to fight an unjust and illegal war. We are not murderers killing on command, but human beings with emotions and a conscience, one refusing us to partake in this ruse, this cruel joke staged by the industrial/military complex and their puppet in the White House.
The cheers, the wall of sound rose from everybody's throat and hit him like a wave, and strengthened him, strengthened him beyond belief.
He tore into his draft notice with both hands, and ripped it to pieces.
All the other males at the center of everybody's attention did the same. The shouts of triumph and joy shook the very foundation beneath their feet. Patrick threw the pieces on the ground, and the others did, too, and when everybody had done that and created quite a pile… they sat fire to it all.
The crowd went wild.
– My Goddess, Eric said in a muted voice, – I see those young faces everywhere. Do you see them?
– I see them, Patrick acknowledged.
– You haven't really changed much, of course, not in appearance…
There was something there, in his voice and wording, making Patrick frown and pay attention.
The faces and bodies shifted. The males turned dirtier and clothed in green and brown. Ashes fell like snow and the thunder of munitions surrounding them turned them slowly deaf.
They walked through another burned-out trail in the jungle, their fingers whitening around the trigger, horror beyond horror stuck in their throats.
The female faces changed into Asian features, women dancing nude on a stage or gasping in need and helpless fascination beneath them, an endless row of them.
Patrick closed off the visions, slammed the door shut.
– How many of us are left? Patrick asked rhetorically, as if from far away.
– Of our platoon? Only the two of us, really. You probably didn't hear, but Miles jumped off everybody's favorite suicide spot, the Golden Gate Bridge in '77.
«You probably didn't hear…»
Patrick nodded in a burst of anger and acknowledgement.
– And…
– Yes, Eric choked, finally showing some emotion.
They both saw the man in a wheelchair and the other without a leg, and it made them feel even worse. The memories of the worn, way too early wrinkled faces diminished them further.

– You could probably have been discharged from the service without much effort, you're aware of that, right? Eric said. – All sons of wealthy people could.

He finally said it.

Warren did not physically respond to the charge, but it did give him that irrational sense of guilt.

– Perhaps not after you burned your draft notice, though.

Eric let out a barf of laughter.

Silence reigned for a while. The two searched for something, anything to say.

They turned simultaneously, as one towards the woman approaching them.

– Patrick? She said. – Patrick Warren?

He looked at Sylvia Bertrand across yet another abyss.

– It is you, isn't it?

She saw it in his eyes, his twinkling brown eyes and uttered a squeal of happiness, and practically jumped him and embraced him standing.

– I wasn't sure, she giggled. – You haven't changed at all.

She had, no longer looking like the teenager he remembered.

He watched how she pulled back a little, catching herself, before she sat down in the available chair between them.

– And that *is* you, isn't it, Eric?

– It's me, he acknowledged hoarsely.

– Wow! She cried. – I can't believe I encountered the both of you together after all these years, and here of all places.

Then she caught herself and pondered her words, shaking her head.

– I guess the place isn't very surprising.

She turned to Patrick and then to Eric, and then back to Patrick.

– Several of the old gang is here, she said. – It's a sort of anniversary. That's why I'm here, back in New York. We're supposed to meet at Wexler's, at five o'clock.

Wexler's was one of the few places in Greenwich Village still holding on to the old counterculture ways, what had made the area famous or infamous in the sixties and early seventies. The entire area had been one single alternative venue of drugs and rebellion then. Patrick and Eric nodded to each other, acknowledging that they would probably have ended up there by themselves later today, and marveled at the synchronicity of it all.

– Christine sent invitations to everybody, she said. – But she sent letters to the old addresses of those she was unable to track. I guess you didn't receive them.

Eric shook his head, but he didn't do so in denial. An expression of amazement lit his face. He mumbled something. Patrick didn't understand what at first. Then, during the following seconds, as the moment replayed itself in his mind… he did.

It was «tapestry» or «the tapestry».

The sound echoed in his mind.

– It's so strange being back here, Sylvia said. – I never thought I would be.

– Neither did I, Patrick said abruptly. – And I never left.

Suddenly his voice was choke-full of emotion. He had hidden himself, hidden from the world. Sylvia grabbed his hand and held on. Stunned, he let her.

Shuen Parker's face flashed before his closed eyes.

«I can break all those others easily», she told him. «They're mere clay to me. I can mold them into anything I want. But how can I do that to you, one of the gods that will ravage the world».

A girl then, a woman, now, he presumed, out there somewhere, lurking in the shadows.

He glimpsed her, now and then, mixing with that of another, older woman.

Patrick threw some bills on the table without counting them and they left it, left the place and set out further into Greenwich Village, into the depths of memory.

He looked casually at Sylvia, at the tall and big black woman. She noticed and she blushed. He knew she did. She put her hand into his, and he squeezed it lightly. It was sufficient. She looked at him with expectation and longing.

– Patrick is working for his mother these days…

There was that hint of venom in Eric's voice that Patrick had sensed all day.

– I know, Sylvia said brightly. – I saw a picture of him in New York Times some years ago. I assumed that Christine had seen the picture and knew his whereabouts, too, but she didn't.

The devotion in her eyes wasn't diminished. That pleased him, somewhat.

Wexler's at first glance looked like a very conservative place, a gathering for soldiers, a celebration of militarism, but those taking a closer look and being somewhat observant would easily notice discrepancies to that impression. There were pictures of what were clearly soldiers on the walls, but they didn't wear uniform and other pictures showcased late teens burning draft notices. Then there were pictures of some soldiers in uniform, but they were wearing the antiwar sign and speaking at antiwar rallies and had clearly been discharged.

The gang sat around the long table in the deep part of the place. Patrick recognized David Weston, Chuck Palmer and some of the females.

He recognized all the males, really, even those he had never met. They had the same twitch in their fingers, the same wavering eyes.

– Well met, Weston cried, brightening like Palmer and the others.

They clasped hands, and the newly arrived tasted the first gulps of beer, made the first toasts, meeting and parting of big glasses. He remembered Christine's lips against his then and now. They felt the same.

Weston had married a Vietnamese woman and brought her back with him. When Warren looked at her face he saw Shuen Parker. He fought to keep his expression even.

The table had a deep gash a bit to his left. It seemed to expand as he watched and swallow him whole.

– We're the few, the proud, Palmer cried. – Cheers!

There were more toasts, more beer wetting their lips and tongue and throat. Warren noticed a sharper taste than the others, he knew he did.

He looked at the stage. There was no band playing tonight, but there had been ten years ago. He heard the music, and he knew the others did, too, though not with his magnified clarity.

Everybody wanted to say something, to comment on Palmer's words, but no one did.

No one found the words.

– There are so few of us left, Palmer finally choked.

They nodded, blessed him with their silence.

– There are times when I wonder, I mean really wonder about it all, why we didn't end up like a heap of bones and flesh like the others. We walked out of it virtually without scars on a battlefield where people died left and right around us. Some of us even escaped from a hellish captivity. What makes us special? Is it fate or a chain of coincidences or just plain luck, or a God fucking miracle?

He emptied the glass and it was clear to the newly arrived that it wasn't his first.

– Survivors have asked themselves that question forever, Christine said gently, and put a hand on his shoulder.

As if on cue, the live version of Shelter from the Storm by Bob Dylan began flowing from the speakers, bringing even more poignancy to the party.

– Dance with me, Patrick, Sylvia offered.

He accepted her invitation, to the dance, now and later, knowing beyond knowing what would happen without straining himself.

– What is it? She asked while slipping her arms around his neck.

– You don't need a crystal ball to know the obvious, he said.

Her eyes widened and then turned misty. She kissed him hard on his lips.

They danced tight and she turned sweaty after less than a minute. Her shiny dark chocolate skin blinded him momentarily.

During that single second several heartbeats passed by, stretching time, and he saw her in a moment he knew to be minutes from now.

– I'll give you shelter from the storm, she whispered, the mist in her eyes transforming into a tear.

They danced tight, there, on the limited floor space. He imagined the floor grew to become vast and deep.

He glimpsed the slimmer, devil-may-care younger version of her, blinking images finally settling in the clearly more mature woman striving to recapture what she saw as a glorious past. His touch made her breathe even faster. They were not alone out there on the vast and deep floor, but he imagined they were, and he suspected she did as well. The song ended, but they kept staying for the next, and the next. They imagined they spent an entire evening out there.

Nothing seemed to have changed by the table when they returned. The others sat on the same spot, drinking their beer.

She moved her chair close to his with twinkles in her eyes.

Those gathered around the scarred table bought yet another round of beer.

– I had to leave, she whispered in his ear. – It was too painful to look at you all, at the ruins of our dreams.

He turned and looked at her. She seemed to grow and beam under his direct stare.

– But dreams never die, she said. – They may shrink to embers, waiting for the heap of dry paper to explode.

She noticed the shiver passing through him and rubbed his cheek.

– To dreams, he said, raising his glass. – They may not die, but they belong to the night.

And she raised hers, and not long after that, the others did, too.

– TO DREAMS! Palmer shouted.

Lots of glasses met and parted with a tender sound, easily heard through the loud music.

A lone woman danced at the other side of the room. She appeared to be dancing alone, but it didn't really look like that to Warren when he studied her. To him she seemed surrounded by shadows.

Weston looked deep into his glass, very somber, very sober.

– What happened? How could we back out like that? How could we… fail?

Carr shrugged, not really fooling anyone.

– Many draft «dodgers» eventually buckled under the pressure. I guess we were young and full of bluster, like so many others.

– But not anymore, right? Christine said.

– NOT ANYMORE, Weston cried.

The laughter shook them, like the hardest wind.

– To the bestselling author, Christine cried.

Everybody turned towards Eric and raised their glass in salute. He took a bow, clearly uncomfortable.

Christine took his hands and pulled close to him.

The beer-consume and their speed of consuming it increased steadily, as the day first turned to night inside and then outside. Weston didn't seem to become drunk, no matter how much he consumed, no matter how much he or the others shouted and cheered. Eric let himself be distracted by Christine's advances.

– Yeah, congrats with yet another bestseller, Patrick said.

He looked at the watch. It had taken five hours after they had met before any of the two had mentioned it.

Christine remembered. Patrick noticed how she made no attempt at kissing Eric. She knew how he disliked overt signs of affection.

Aside from that she did everything to attract his interest.

Patrick drank, too, drank a lot, but it worked even less on him than on Weston.

They all drank a lot, by an unspoken agreement. Chen Ya ran off to the toilet at some point, with a hand pushed at her lips. She returned, stinking of vomit and excessive use of perfume. Patrick almost threw up on the spot.

– Your great sense of smell is still great, I gather? Sylvia slurred, very tipsy, but with amazingly clear eyes. – Or has it grown even more astute these years? It probably has.

She nodded, more to herself than to him. They danced some more. He found himself back on the floor and couldn't recall that they had moved from there to here, and he wondered if he was finally getting drunk. The music, Jefferson Airplane, with Grace Slick's growls played in his ears. He recognized that as well, far beyond ordinary recall. Sylvia had unbuttoned her blouse almost all the way down. She changed her approach from swaying before him, displaying herself and pushing the large, practically free-ranging breasts at his chest, rubbing them back and forth on him. The nipples hardened as he watched. She had always been big, with generous curves, but had become even more so, and he found himself turned on beyond casual interest, like he had known he would be.

He noticed the birth scars on her belly.

– They don't matter, she said, she whispered huskily. – I'm yours. I was always yours.

They noticed the people at the table in glimpses now and then. Except for Eric and Christine doing their thing, it was pretty much uneventful.

– Some parties with lots of drinking go wild, Sylvia said, her head on his shoulder during a slow dance, – but this never really… took off. I guess it was very similar to whipping a dead horse in the first place.

Sad and hungry eyes focused even harder on him. Swollen lips pushed that much more desperate at his. He felt himself awaken from a long sleep. His cock pushed at his pants. Pain, or something very similar, made him bite his lip.

He grabbed her, grabbed her hard and kissed her, a fire-spitting dragon on the prowl, a devourer. She gasped, stared at him in sudden twin apprehension and expectation. He held her in a hard grip and began touching her there and then in ever more invasive ways. She didn't resist but turned limp in his grip. If she had ever resisted his advances she had stopped doing that long ago. Two pairs of feet practically rushed to the staircase across the room,

They moved upstairs or downstairs, he couldn't tell, even though he knew he should have known which way the bedrooms were.

– It isn't of any consequence, is it? He said to her, apparently very cryptic, without any previous conversation about whatever subject he spoke about.

– No, she assured him, – it isn't.

They finally reached their destination after a walk with several interruptions, where they were sorely tempted to stop and start doing it more than once. He knew she wouldn't mind. She signaled that with every tiny movement she made.

He undressed her, undressed himself, in a room filled with shadows. Somehow, he had known that it would be. She giggled in his strong grip, grabbed by desire and need. He bit her on the shoulder. She cried out, but it was muted, hardly audible. It was her moans and begging chant that reached his ears.

They crawled onto the bed without letting go of each other. She displayed herself, offered herself to him without thought, without hesitation. They clinched, and just like that, he had pushed himself deep into the wet and warm hole. She moaned happily. He rocked up and down, sliding back and forth on top of her, in the big rocking bed reminding him of a boat at sea, of tall waves and stormy seas.

– Everything is *open,* now, he grunted, – like a wound not closing.

She gasped in pain and joy and growing need beneath him.

His dark hair fell down and covered his face, but he was still completely capable of seeing, seeing the dissolved, sweaty face below. She screamed again, just as muted, just as inaudible. In the end, it was her happy giggle, as she collapsed beneath him, in the seconds after her warm water had flooded his groin and thighs he remembered, as he turned her around and took her from behind and grabbed her hair and pulled her head back, long enough for him to taste her sweet and bloody lips, remembered long afterwards when he let go of her and finally fell asleep, fell into an uncommonly deep and relaxing sleep.

2

The dream, the restless dream came to him still. That stunned him, and he groaned in protest.

Captain Patrick Warren led his platoon through the tight and wet jungle. His men and himself were sturdy survivors, a jigsaw puzzle pulled together from a dozen insane battles, from a dozen disintegrated platoons.

– I always wonder where the water comes from, Andrew Benedict complained, very loud and annoying. – I mean, it's fucking water in the air we breathe, okay, not moisture. *Water!*

– Shut the fuck up, Benedict, Miles grumbled, – or I will spend my hard-preserved energy on spanking you.

– Just you try you overgrown fuck, Benedict replied, suddenly very assertive and controlled.

Miles was a huge man, strong as an ox in body and mind.

Laughter, or some kind of facsimile thereof.

It was laughter cruel and rough. In Warren's ears all those years later, the sound resembled sobbing.

They moved through a valley, along a quiet river. Warren sensed the location of the scouts ahead. The sound of distant battle hammered like light machinegun fire everyone's eardrums.

– It makes me crazy, it does, Meldahl-Johnson mumbled. – It never lets up, never in a million years.

Warren heard much more than Meldahl-Johnson and the others.

He always had.

The soldiers often spoke of hearing the jungle breathing around them, making light of it, because it didn't, really, not to them.

To him it did. The very air moved, in a constant draft, as the invisible mouth pushed and pulled the more than moist surroundings between its lips.

He heard every time Cochran and Stephens put one foot in front of the other and sensed how their boots turned a bit wetter as one step became many. Sounds mixed with the breathing jungle, and he heard his mother's words.

– Sending a Janus Clan member to war is like inviting hell on Earth, she grinned viciously, affectionately, as affectionate as she could be.

Mother didn't seem worried, no matter how many times he relived it in his mind. Thoughts resurfacing several times during his adolescence did so again.

He noticed the looks his men, even Eric and Andrew sent him. Memories of boot camp flashed through his mind, as it yet again struck him how easy it had been, how he had excelled in it all.

What had been rough for others had been smooth for him. What had been somewhat smooth for them had made him feel like a dog pulling its restraints. The brutal, sadistic sergeant had only made his prowess all the sweeter and exhilarating. He had left the bitter, cruel man in the ditch without touching him, beaten him without fighting.

– I need to be excused, Captain, SIR! Carr declared, with his usual flair.

More hearty laughter accompanied his statement.

– You're excused, Captain Warren granted good humored.

– Goddamn, Carr, Goddard shook his head, – when does that stomach of yours not act up?

Eric was a little green in the face. His system had never truly adapted to the local cuisine.

He headed for the bushes accompanied by a lot of whistling and rowdy comments. They saw him head for the bushes and pull down his pants and underwear.

– Hey, Carr, Stoltz belched, – I can see your fat white ass.

Your faaat white aaas

The drawl became very pronounced.

Warren saw it, too, the pink surface almost blinding him as it, in an eerie way reflected the hot sun.

The buzz of insects rose loud in his ears, almost like a banshee shriek.

The painting began moving around him. He heard the splash in the water, but there was no splash. Something resembling bullets rippled the surface. Cold sweat shook him.

– Seek cover, he mumbled, and then, aloud: – SEEK COVER!

Carr threw himself on the ground, without taking the time to pull up his pants. Something with a sound like an angry wasp passed right over him. They heard the sound of a rifle being fired, as the bullet hit the tree not far away.

Everybody ran for the trees, towards Carr's fairly high-rated cover, throwing themselves down behind logs and the rise in the terrain.

Stoltz chuckled, his amazement clearly revealed in his coarse voice.

– Damn, man, they aimed for your ass, but *missed*. The gooks can't shoot.

A grenade hit the water right by what had been their position not many seconds earlier. Thunder rocked the ground. A huge cone of water rose from the river, hitting Benedict just before he managed to jump into the jungle. Blood flowed from his left arm. The radio buzzed with Cochran's excited, way too late warning.

– Hostiles approaching. I repeat: HOSTILES APPROACHING!

Warren noticed that they were all looking at him again, even as they returned fire and positioned themselves in the terrain, bracing against the enemy.

The valley spread out far below him as he flew across it like lightning, and easily noted everything in his sight. He saw the hostiles' move, saw them move in on them on all sides, and saw the flaws in their tactic.

– Follow me, he cried.

And they did, like they had done three times before this during the last month.

He ran, with his platoon on his heels. There was a narrow passage no enemy soldiers covered. They ran through there, towards relative safety.

Benedict signaled to him, unnecessary that Cochran and Stephens, having started out far behind were caught with the North Vietnamese force ahead of them.

Warren had already given the turn around signal. Benedict shook his head in awe and an attempted apology.

The enemy was right in front of them, with their backs turned, expecting Warren's men to come into view.

Fire, Warren signaled.

Sudden thunder roared in the jungle and the North Vietnamese soldiers fell like dominoes or dolls on a firing range. A few of them managed to return fire, but there was really nothing to shoot at. They all died clueless. Patrick watched his vision turn blood red, as the enemy soldiers in the other positions around them reacted to the shooting. He knew they would, of course, and led on to where the massive number of opponents wasn't headed. Cochran and Stephens caught up with them, gratitude and an even stronger incredulity painted on their faces.

Crossfire! Warren signaled. We fire and keep firing until every single one of them is down and out.

They spread out, but key members of the platoon kept eye-contact with the captain and could convey it to the others out of sight.

Once again, the trap closed almost to perfection. The firefight began. This time the Vietcong was way too many to easily vanquish. They went down in droves, but there were so many. Stephens was hit. Howard was dead before he hit the ground. Time moved like heartbeats sounding like sledgehammers. There was a brief respite. The last of the human beings below them had been killed. The river really turned red with blood, or so Warren imagined.

– We are made, the Captain shouted. – We move out and pull back, flee like rabbits.

Stephens could still stand and run. He giggled in a mix between hysteria and euphoria.

– We walk away from impossible odds *again.* This is amazing, so amazing.

– You'll be a major soon, Captain, Stoltz said, his eyes filled with the same admiration and wonder.

People died under Captain Warren's command, they knew that, had seen that both just now and earlier, but also knew that that was the exception, not the rule. They ran, knowing they were compromised, that Vietcong was very much aware of their approximate whereabouts.

Patrick heard the whistle of the grenades, heard the thunder well before it actually struck the ground. The explosions made them deaf, blind and senseless. He knew where to go to avoid the worst of the damage. Only moss and remains of the forest rained down on them.

Something happened. He ran left when he knew that the grenade would hit to the right, but not long afterwards another was on its way to a spot ahead of them. He realized that… that there was a distinct pattern to it.

– DOWN! He shouted.

It was as if they were being herded in a specific direction.

The grenade blew. They managed yet again to avoid the brunt of the explosion. There were more men charging them. Warren saw it in his mind's eye. Even now, as movement speeded up to an insane level, everything kept playing slow in his head.

But they still had to act on the slow flashes in real time.

An inspiration struck him. Realization hit him like the coldest wave.

– SPREAD OUT, he shouted. – SPREAD

And then the explosion in his mind and the one out there happened simultaneously.

They came and fetched him as the stench of blood and rot in his nostrils woke him up. Confusing imagery and sensations rocked his being. He glimpsed people on horseback and he was one of them.

– Sometimes there are riders, the girl spat at him. – They come in the early morning light and death and destruction follow their hooves.

The Vietcong soldiers grabbed him and when he made a feeble attempt at resisting, they began beating him up, and kept doing so until he had become compliant. They tied him hard, tied a noose around his neck and walked away with him, while they kept striking him with branches and sticks. He was amazed by how much that hurt. The initial confusion gave way to an enormous clarity of the senses. It was as if he could actually feel the sticks and branches before it hit his skin. He wanted to hit back at them, snarled at them with a fierceness he could hardly recall about himself at all, but his hands were tied behind his back and a short rope tied between his ankles and he was helpless. They laughed hard and spat at him.

And then, suddenly, he realized that he was the only prisoner, the only white man in the line, and then, later, when he walked with his platoon, his fellow soldiers, those few still alive he wondered if he had imagined the pale and bloody bodies in the field.

He remembered a girl, a young, preteen Irish girl on television during one of the many demonstrations in Europe against the war. It was right after the first news of the countless massacres had broken in Western media.

– Sometimes there are riders, she said subdued and almost hateful. – They come in the early morning light and death and destruction follow their hooves.

The memory made a deep chill touch him. It lingered, to a point where he feared he wouldn't be able to shake it off.

His remaining men looked at him, and he wondered if he still saw awe in their eyes.

– It is the Captain, I know it is. I saw him, saw his *eyes*.

It was just a whisper, a stunned shaking of the head. The whirling imagery in Warren's mind intensified further.

Then they all saw him, and he saw them.

They were all a part of the long line of prisoners making their way far, far north.

The noose around their neck was tightened to the point of choking them, but they kept moving, kept stumbling further, Vietcong's prisoners of war.

They heaved in an attempt to get air to their straining lungs, striving to keep putting a foot in front of the other, and after a while on their endless twilight path that was all they were capable of.

All of the prisoners were undressed and thrown into a cell that was basically a hole in the ground filled with dirty water. The door of bamboo bars was above them, their heads just about fitting between the water and the bars. They had to look up, push their face against the bars to keep their mouth above the surface. The water level kept rising and sinking and they had to adjust constantly.

Benedict's wound had been bandaged, but was still leaking, especially after a period of hard exertion.

– We will make it, Warren said. – We will get away from this hellhole.

And he imagined he saw a glimmer of hope in their dull eyes.

He saw it fade as time went by, as the rabbit hole became their home, the only home they had ever known.

Benedict's eyes began showing sign of the fever raging through him. Warren literally watched how strength left him and he became a victim of the increasingly stronger currents. The captain moved towards him, managed to reach his side and push him against a wall, giving him a break.

– This is just the start, he snarled. – They're softening us up before starting on us in earnest.

And he imagined he saw a glimmer of anger in Benedict's eyes.

– You're so funny captain, he giggled.

But endless hours passed down there in the hole, and their brief sense of defiance felt like a distant mirage.

It just went on and on. The relentless currents created by a deliberate setup hammered them, their bodies and especially their souls.

– Why did they put us together? Carr wondered. – Wouldn't it be more effective to separate us, to isolate us by mixing us with the Vietnamese prisoners?

They want us to see each others' suffering, Warren thought.

It went on and on, even though he imagined it was no more than a few hours, even though he couldn't swear there hadn't been a night there in the horrible made up river, in the rabbit-hole without exit.

The water finally receded, and they fell to the floor, completely exhausted, totally drained of energy, of willpower.

The sun boiled their blood and cracked their skin. Their tied arms had long since turned numb. It was if they weren't there at all, as if they no longer had any arms.

He remembered Miles' hard, accentuated laughter and it kind of comforted him.

Everything else just faded away in the numbness and endless pain their existence had become.

The sun entered their cage again and boiled their blood away, drying their veins until they cracked like brittle eggshells. They realized stunned that an entire night had passed without them noticing. Open mouths attempted to draw breath, but failed at every turn. Warren wondered in his fever if everyone around him had died and if he was, in truth surrounded by dead bodies and had just failed to realize the horrible fact. His head fell between his knees and he remained thus, unmoving, until moving and time once again was.

The Americans were pulled up from their grave and groaned in protest and ongoing suffering. There was no sense of relief. Their bonds were removed. Only the noose around the neck remained. They were whipped and beaten with sticks and branches until they managed to stand on beyond shaky legs, and then they were brought across the camp, brought before a tall oriental female standing in front of a building and made to kneel before her.

Warren felt strange vibrations only by looking at her. She seemed like little more than a teenage girl and was clearly not Vietnamese, but the soldiers treated her with a grueling respect.

– I am Shuen Parker, she shouted at them, speaking very calmly and measured. – I am your Goddess, the cruel entity defining your very reality. From this moment on you will never have anything even resembling free will, but be my servant in all things.

She spoke flawless English, clearly born to it, but there was an… an eerie intonation in her voice Warren didn't quite get. Had he…. had he heard it before somewhere?

– You're not prisoners of war, but war criminals waging terror against children and what is basically a helpless population. You don't deserve to be treated as human beings and you won't be.

Miles opened his mouth to speak. Warren saw it without seeing it. Miles never released a single syllable, only grunts of pain as they resumed the brutal beating. They were very clever, so clever that they knew exactly where to strike and make the tough soldier scream in pain and roll on the ground in a useless effort to escape the brutality.

Parker walked to him. They placed him back on his knees. The pain clouded his eyes. She grabbed his jaw and squeezed. He whimpered. It looked like the touch actually hurt him.

– You weren't given permission to speak.

The big man looked like putty in her hands. His comrades in arms feared they spotted tears in his eyes.

She pulled back, and walked away.

– Take him. He has earned the right to be first.

She turned briefly to his fellow soldiers.

– Before we're done with you, you'll know true terror, know many things and be very, very cooperative.

They brought him into the building. Parker walked in last. She left the door open. They wondered why in their dim minds.

The sun kept burning them. They imagined they heard Parker's voice from the inside, but couldn't tell if it was real or imaginary. The guards gave them water, but it tasted more like acid than anything like a life-giving fluid.

And then, a timeless time later, when Aldo Miles' horrible scream filled their ears, they wondered no more.

3

Insane images and sensations filled Patrick Warren's entire perception, once again becoming his very reality.

He sat up abruptly in the bed, covered by sweat and horror.

Soft hands touched his shoulder. He turned around and stared into Sylvia's big eyes.

– I'm here, baby, I'm here. It's all right, I'm here.

He stared at the wall across the room, still breathing hard.

– I was sleeping, he said. – I know I was. Then I wasn't anymore. Or… so it felt… feels…

She kept touching him, rubbing him, calming him somewhat.

– It isn't strange that tonight would remind you of everything… everything bad, she whispered.

He stared at the wall across the room and it was as if three-dimensional images played themselves for him, as if he was in the story, the sensations that kept playing themselves through all his senses.

They faded only slowly, their relative vanishing giving him little rest.

Her warm body stayed close to his, or it tried to. She seemed to just slip off him, like she wasn't there at all.

It rubbed itself against his. Soft, big lips caressed his skin.

– I really enjoyed it, she glowed at him. – Enjoyed the fucking. It was like a storm, like being… devoured. I've never felt anything like it before. You were always intense, but nothing compared to this…

She kissed his lips, kissed them again and again. He listened to her breathing, how it picked up speed, how she became ready for him again.

His already sharp hearing picked up the buzz of first one, then two flies in the room. The warm and willing female kept advancing on his fence of indifference.

And then she stopped, then the flies stopped buzzing.

Everything in the room just… stopped. A brown arm seeking his cheek froze in midair. There was no sound or movement anywhere within these four walls, no expression in the face surrounding the unmoving, staring eyes.

– Reveal yourself, he snapped, turning away from the statue by his side.

He noticed the shimmering in the air before the tall, imposing woman appeared.

– You sound vexed, my son.

He kept staring at Ethel Warren with all the annoyance he was able to muster.

– I just wanted to visit you, she said softly, – see how you were faring.

She sounded obviously insincere. To him she did. He stayed silent.

The fireeyes turned briefly to Sylvia before once again fixing on him.

– A big, muscular girl that one, an excellent breeder, broodmare for our blood.

He shrugged, very deliberately.

– I've left «our blood» left and right all over the town and the Earth.

– Which is a very good thing, she acknowledged, – which is what any Janus Clan male should do, but you might want to think about choosing a more permanent mate or set of mates with brood growing up in our care. One shouldn't underestimate that advantage.

– What do you want, mother? He asked with practiced ease.

She grinned, she actually grinned, though it was nothing like any other grin he had ever seen in others.

She turned solemn, intense, even more intense. It sent a shiver through him, and as usual he couldn't tell exactly why.

– I've observed something in you lately, she stated, – seen progression, seen you take new steps on your path. You've become an adult, my son, or you're about to, a man, doing a man's work.

The thirty-one-year-old man frowned. The burning irritation within grew.

– This isn't one more of your mind games, is it Ethel?

He spat the name out, no matter how he strived to remain calm.

– What are talking about, my dear Patrick?

She asked.

He stayed quiet. By a force of will he stayed quiet.

– The metal construct has fallen from the sky, she said. – You promised you would be mine until I released you from your vow.

He recalled the images of Skylab, the American space station falling through the atmosphere, and his own, strange reaction to it.

– That time has now come.

He looked startled at her. The stunned expression seemed to emulate that of the frozen woman by his side.

– Patrick of the Janus Clan, she said, very formal, – I release you from any vow, any duty you may have sworn to me. From this moment on you are, as far as I'm concerned free to do as you please.

She once again teased him with her girlish, sinister grin, as she turned and walked away. He watched as she faded, seemingly into the air itself, as she let go of her influence of this space.

The stunned expression didn't leave him. He found himself unable to look at Sylvia, to look for signs of her being unfrozen, being unstuck in time. She would be, eventually, he knew that, but it failed to concern or to engage him.

He knew, now, finally, after ten years, beyond doubt, after listening to this new side of his mother where he had heard the eerie intonation in Shuen Parker's voice.

4

He had the dreams again, those he had practically every night. Eric Carr opened his eyes like he did every morning, with them burning with the sweat filling them both, with his body soaked in the same hot and cold fluid.

There was no shaking, though, no sudden movements or outcry, nothing resembling a scream. He had learned to master the outward signs of his anxieties long ago.

Christine didn't wake up. She slept on with the same content smile on her face. He cautiously removed her arm from his chest and rose from the bed. His feet hardly made any sound, any sound at all as they touched the floor. He dressed quickly, without haste, put on the shoes and grabbed his jacket and made his way out of the apartment. The door closed soft and silent, as if it and the frame was flesh against flesh and not hard wood.

The sun hadn't shown itself yet, wasn't even hinting of its presence behind the tall buildings. He made his way back to the West Side through practically empty streets. It took the time it took, but he wasn't in a hurry and allowed the impressions to gather and gestalt inside. When he listened, with half his ear he heard both people and cars, but he didn't see any of them.

There was the occasional loud noise. They didn't startle him, but made him even more battle ready and edgy.

When he turned a corner, and spotted the entrance to the fashionable Chelsea Hotel he finally encountered the first human being, a drunken man stumbling from the taxi, yet another late straggler in the New York summer twilight.

Carr went to the reception. He waited patiently in line while the drunk strived to remember his room number. Carr said his room number, received his key and walked to his room. He walked up the staircase filled with various forms of art, but hardly glanced at it. The hotel breathed silently around him, not exactly like the jungle, but close enough.

The door closed behind him with a loud bang. He hardly heard it.

Everything turned silent. The breathing stopped. His eyes were drawn to the typewriter on the table. The white sheet flickered in the morning light, casting shadows across the room. He sat down without delay and began typing.

The sound echoed through the hallways and rooms through the morning and throughout the day. Everybody heard it or imagined they did so. They couldn't avoid hearing it, no matter where they found themselves within the building. It continued throughout the night and the next day with no end in sight.

Chapter 3

Ted and Liz Warren returned to the United States after years abroad, returned to New York City, a metropolis they had never before visited, walking through dimly familiar streets.

They recognized the buildings, even though their impression of them seemed skewed, strange.

– It's like a scene from all those movies, Liz marveled.

She frowned, as if something in her statement didn't feel quite right.

Everything was loud. It seemed to them that the tiniest sound was amplified to noise of an insane degree.

They walked on Broadway during a sweltering afternoon. The heat itself didn't really bother them. People around them were sweating and suffering, but they weren't. But it was an unfamiliar heat, both dry and wet. The concrete jungle imposed itself on them and unnerved them.

James Bond: Moonraker played at the Rivoli Theater. Rocky II played at the Cinerama Duplex. Other films included Bruce Lee: Game of Death and a new Dracula movie.

There were also lap dancing, burlesque joints and X-rated theaters everywhere, different compared to New Orleans, perhaps, but just as visible.

A heroin addict sat on the sidewalk, with his back to the wall, staring at the world with empty eyes. The sight made them feel unbelievably bad, made them feel a horror invading them, strengthening the one already there.

Homeless people rested in port-rooms, or straight on the sidewalk. Some pedestrians kicked them as they passed by.

Their surroundings battered them. This was different from every city they had ever visited, like London, New Orleans, Caracas and Las Vegas. And they were wide open and their defenses were down, and everything seemed to cut them and bleed them.

A drill, beyond loud was being managed by a human worker drone across the street. It felt like it drilled into their flesh and very self.

They were dressed pretty much like they usually had been in public, fairly revealing, showing lots of skin, but when they looked at each other, they hardly recognized themselves, saw very little of the old devil-may-care attitude.

The long hair felt unpleasant. The heat bothered them more than it should. They felt like all the eyes on the street were fixed on them.

And it bothered them.

They passed a bunch of youths hanging out under the giant Moonraker poster.

– Look at them, she said, her voice a strange mix of contempt and envy. – They seem so… at ease. It's a daunting thought that we could shake them out of their illusions, and pull every single one from their tiny world merely by snapping our fingers.

Both of them, alone and together had done that in all the places they had passed by.

– I miss Laurie, she said. – When she was there, there was nothing between us.

She snuggled close to him. He put an arm around her, attempting to comfort her.

Even here, where their partial nudity wasn't exactly a rare sight, they stood out very much like a sore thumb. And… they felt like one.

She rubbed his cheek, whispering comforting words in his ear.

– Big Mama, a man that was most certainly a pimp, cried at her.

– Such a cute boy, she deliberately shrugged. – I don't know if I want to kiss him or slit his throat.

She didn't really speak up, but he heard her, she knew he did.

He watched how she moved, the lethal economy of her movement, how she clearly just waited for him to make his move, and he didn't act on the anger swelling inside, but crouched in a corner like a little boy.

They turned right and walked west, on 42nd street. What had been pronounced before turned even more evident.

– Colorful, she remarked. – A nun would be very lost here. Even I don't understand all the references…

They saw in the dark, even in the middle of the hottest sun.

– «Hell's Kitchen», she mused. – It doesn't quite live up at its name, does it?

– It doesn't, Ted agreed.

– It's still daylight, though, she said. – There might be hope yet.

There were no tall buildings here, at least no one above six stories. There was no shade to speak of during the day in the summer. They felt how the sun burned their skin and that kind of sat well with them.

– It is amazing, isn't it? She said brightly. – How entire subcultures can exist in the open like this, how they can dominate with impunity much of the showcase of one of the major cities in the world.

She rubbed his arm, looking haunted and subdued at him.

– I'm not talking too much, am I?

– No! He shook his head, shocked that she would even ask such a question. – No!

Port Authority showed up on their right. It operated buses, trains, boats and airports in both New York and New Jersey and was a downright busy place. They stepped inside. Their eyes adapted instantly to the darker surroundings and that pleased and amazed them.

It was the busiest time in the afternoon. People arrived and left in an endless stream. There was a trite and repetitive pattern to it that everybody easily recognized, with very few people departing from the pattern. The two new arrivals sat down in a cafeteria and had their late breakfast. They looked for breaks in the pattern and still had a hard time gauging any.

A young black woman, about Liz's age appeared from the trains. She was dressed in expensive clothing, but had a nervous, haunted look in her eyes.

That look didn't go away, not when she bought her lunch by the counter, not when she sat down a few tables from where Liz and Ted sat.

– Ten bucks that she has run away from home, Liz commented lightly.

That made him look at her, at Liz, not the girl and shake his head.

– No bet.

– She's such a tasty snack. All the two-legged wolves of the big city are lining up to devour her.

This time he didn't voice a reply. He grabbed her hand and comforted her, and she let him.

They sat there, all three of them, during the peak hours, while the flow of commuters slowly dwindled, while daylight slowly faded within and without and dusk asserted itself.

You're mine! David Gidman hissed in Liz's thoughts, and the pain in her arms felt so real. She visualized his head, removed from his body, stuck on her sword and it comforted her.

Ted shifted uncomfortably on his chair, rubbing his back, and she didn't have to ask what was on his mind.

They didn't speak much, but was content, somewhat to just sit there, watching the world pass by.

Music flowed from a portable player somewhere. They didn't recognize the melody and didn't care to.

– The world has truly denigrated further in our absence, she commented dryly, with some of her old wit intact. – With «music» like that, it's no wonder everything is going to the dogs. It's a good thing we have returned to live it up.

He remained silent. She saw how he sat there, lost in the mire of his thoughts and memories.

The well-dressed girl rose, putting down her glass with fidgeting fingers. Liz watched her leave, crossing the hall towards the entrance. She saw a man, a white male dressed in outlandish clothes approach her, saw how he set out to cross her path. No one else might realize what was happening, but Liz easily did.

A battery of drums rose in her mind, rose to a far higher level than in her ears, and she rose abruptly and charged towards the entrance, towards the spot where the well-dressed girl and the man in outlandish clothes had now met. She listened in easily, across the vast distance.

– You got style, girl, he told her. – That, no one can take away from you.

She was blushing, *blushing*. Liz welcomed the red hot, cold rage and determination erupting from her comatose insides.

– I can handle myself, the girl assured the young man.

– Of course, the young man said, – a girl like you won't have any such trouble, but it's still nice to have a place to crash, a place where friends can support you and help you towards a deserved higher position in society. I won't lie to you. There are many girls who want to be models, to have a Fifth Avenue apartment and stuff, and the competition is stiff, but I know a few people that can make it a little easier and the road shorter for a beautiful girl.

She was crumbling. Liz could practically see it. She was giving in, because she wanted to, because she allowed herself to believe his slick talk.

– You won't fall prey to that nice, smooth-talking man, will you, honey?

Both turned towards her. She sensed his black rage and the girl's confusion and boundless anxiety.

– Don't butt in, he hissed at her.

– He will be nice at first. He's good at that, good at catching and keeping the fish. But after a while he will introduce you to older men «with connections» and he will be so good at it that you will be convinced that this is what you want.

It was very subtle the first second or so, how the girl moved away from the big white man and stepped close to Liz, but then it was obvious. Liz watched him, ready if he should try anything, but he didn't. He laughed short and sharp and walked away.

The girl choked, as the severity of what she had almost consented to dawned on her.

– Thank you, she whispered.

She tried to say more, but everything just stopped inside her.

– What's your name, honey? Liz asked, as kindly as she managed.

– Lynn, Lynn Fredericks. I…

Liz reached out a hand.

– I am Liz…

– Liz Warren, Lynn nodded stunned.

She grabbed the big girl's hand with both hers.

– Thank you. *Thank you!*

Liz felt a warm, warm trickle somewhere inside.

– It's a good thing that you do recognize me. That way I don't need to convince you that I'm not part of the setup. I could have been, you know. Pimps and their plots are getting increasingly sophisticated these days.

A burst of laughter erupted from Lynn's mouth. Then after a moment's silence they both started laughing… and then they embraced each other.

A blonde woman approached them. She wore expensive clothes, but there was something about her, an edginess Liz easily recognized. Lynn tensed. Liz didn't.

– That was a very brave thing you did there, the woman said.

Liz looked good humored at a woman almost as tall and big as herself, one who had the moves of one with major defense capabilities. She studied her carefully, but wasn't really worried.

– I tried to reach her, but I can't be everywhere.

Liz noticed two big bruisers behind her, forming a protective sphere around another young, vulnerable girl.

– My name is Frances Stern. She handed one card to each of the two young girls. – You should check me out to make sure. I run a place for runaway girls in… trouble. Justin Bieber, bad as he is, is merely one of many wolves preying on the innocent and the lost in this city.

– Thank you, Liz said. – Not really that brave, though.

– No? Frances said. – You've just made a very dangerous enemy. I have bodyguards, but you…

– Liz can handle herself, Lynn stated proudly on Liz's behalf.

And Frances' eyes turned big and wide.

– Yes, Frances said slowly, – I imagine she can.

There was both pity and admiration in her eyes. Liz had quickly learned to recognize that look.

She put the card in her pocket.

– Let's look each other up, she said casually.

And turned and walked away.

– Wait, Lynn cried and rushed to her side, - let me come with you.

– I'm with someone, Liz said.

– I know, Lynn said enthusiastically and needy.

Liz didn't say no, didn't say yes. Lynn followed her.

– Can you feel it? Liz said, as they crossed the hall, her voice shivering in contempt and despair. – How dreams are broken down, distilled into dull nightmares and claws?

– I can, the girl replied promptly. – That's why I left home. They told me

I was an ungrateful… brat, but I discarded their automated responses. I no longer want to walk among the wounded.

Liz lowered her head briefly, unable to keep it high.

– I'm afraid that is difficult, bordering on the impossible, she choked.

– I know, Lynn said softly, rubbing the big girl's back. – But you still saved me. I will follow you *anywhere.*

She felt a feather-light, invisible touch on the cheek. Her fingers touched the skin right afterwards and it felt exactly the same.

– That just shows how young and foolish you are…

There was a shadow of a smile hidden on the full lips.

Liz slipped onto Ted's lap and kissed him.

– I bring another stray dog, she sighed.

Ted brought his full attention on Lynn. She had imagined he had already done that, but that had only been a pale reflection of the real thing.

– Hello, he greeted her.

– Hello, she returned his greeting, and managed, somehow to remain coherent and solemn.

She boldly put her hands on his shoulders and kissed him on the lips. He grabbed her and returned her sign of affection tenfold, and she instantly softened in his grip. She finally pulled back, unable to look at him, unable to pull her hazy eyes away.

The two fireeyes rose and overwhelmed her further with their presence. They noticed her quickened pulse and wet eyes.

– Why did you wait here until dark? He asked her.

– I was supposed to meet a friend here, she replied, – but she never showed up. Uh, why did you?

– We love getting to know new neighborhoods in the evening, Liz grinned.

And an excited smile lit up Lynn's face.

They started moving, leaving Port Authority, pushing into the deep New York night, the two bigger more or less in tandem, in an even flow, the smaller form tailing them somewhat awkward, hesitant.

The teeming life outside pushed back at them from all sides. The two Warrens kept forcing themselves forward in the quicksand of the concrete jungle surrounding them.

Liz chuckled. She did so at exactly the moment they passed a big bruiser and his court. Everybody easily saw how he was fuming, but he made no move.

She turned towards Lynn with a slight smile on her lips.

– Let me guess, she said, – you're worried, aren't you, little one?

– A little, Lynn agreed with frozen lips. – Is it wise provoking them all like this?

– I decided long ago to live a confrontational life, Liz said.

She shrugged.

– Besides, this isn't much in the manner of risk-taking. There are people out there it would be wise to fear. The mere presence of David Gidman would make all of these tough guys wet their pants, and we put his head on a stake and roasted it and his body over open fire.

– This is just to discourage these fine gentlemen from marking their territory in our presence, Ted said. – Some people are just dumb. They need to be told the obvious.

Lynn felt both fear and prolonged excitement stir further within her.

People heard them, either the voice or the voice of the wild body moving through the concrete jungle.

Hell's Kitchen exploded that night, like a slow burning fire, from the sewers to the rooftops. The two Warrens easily sensed it. It was as if every piece of the air was charged and sizzling, with something far more powerful than mere heat, and that was just after the first few minutes of the relaxed walk.

The seedy apartment hotel in the seedy area pointed to itself, somehow. It had no name, at least none painted above the entrance. The entire «lobby» and the people present seemed to freeze when the trio entered. Everybody stared without staring.

The clerk had the keys ready before they reached the counter. Ted took it and they ascended the moldy steps. The walls seemed to be closing in on them, even when they closed their eyes, thus also making it real to their deeper senses.

Loud shouts reached them from outside. Shots were fired close to the hotel. Response was swift, immediate, catching on like thunder, spreading like tall waves from a central point.

A solid door appeared in front of them. It had five keyholes and was clearly built to last, beyond casual punishment. The grin continued to feel strange on Ted's face.

A fairly spacey apartment revealed itself to them. It had two bedrooms and a pretty large living room.

– It isn't… bad, Lynn said hesitatingly. – I kinda like it. But I could afford better and so could you, I would venture. Why don't we?

– We can, now, Liz acknowledged, – but what about in a two months' time? I'm certain you've spent virtually every waken hour since you fled from your parents' lush house worrying about the future and your dismal economic prospects.

Lynn bowed her head, nodding in acknowledgement.

– And luxuries are a trap, anyway, Ted stated firmly. – I don't need to tell you that.

– No, Ted, she replied, both subdued and blushing.

She put down her small suitcase and glanced around the room, her new home. The interior, while clearly worn was fairly clean. In fact, she would venture that it had been cleaned less than a week ago. She sighed in relief.

Liz walked into the left bedroom, what had clearly been in use last night. Ted followed her.

She dropped her clothes on her way to the bed, the large bed. He did, too. She climbed onto the bed on all fours, never taking her eyes off him. Her groin and thighs turned wet. His cock twitched and rose.

– I know why you sat there all day.

Lynn stood in the doorway, undressing, dropping her fine jacket and the rest of her clothes on the floor. They fixed their burning eyes on her and she turned even more excited.

– I'm well read. It's an old tactic used by rival gangs before moving into a new area, in order to make the current residents go bananas with worry and speculation. You sat there, on your spot at Port Authority and did nothing, and while you did the rumors flew like chickens and tension grew everywhere.

She stood there, nude, displaying herself.

– It's so funny. You destroyed meticulously erected social constructs in less than a day by sitting on your ass. The fact that the various gangs are familiar with the tactics didn't stop them

The shooting picked up outside. Several windows were broken. Screams shattered the silence, the city's silent noise further.

She joined Liz on the bed, kissing her on the lips, before both returned their attention to the male casually approaching them.

They were all in bed, moving against each other.

– I see something, Lynn gasped, – something that has always been… hidden.

– You're waking up, Ted told her and touched her jaw. – Enjoy it.

And she stared in awe at him.

– Poor girl, Liz mused.

– I didn't know what I was looking for when I started looking, the girl said, – but now I know. Thank you. THANK YOU!

She infused them both in grateful kisses, slowly turning hungry, demanding. Some played music in the neighborhood apartment, one, two, three apartments to the left, mixing with the sounds of the ongoing war in the streets. All those sounds and more seemed to be present in their midst, in the very air between them. Lynn rubbed her body against theirs. Liz closed her eyes briefly and when she opened them again they were twinkling in dark fire.

– You like this, don't you? In fact, you *love* this.

– You have no idea, Liz said hoarsely and darkly.

Lynn felt a momentary spell of dizziness, but the growing fervor quickly overwhelmed that, as it overwhelmed all things, all other considerations. Eyes twinkled, then glowed and then burned. The dark fire rose between them, surrounded them and consumed them. Lynn's scream of ecstasy drowned in the roar of the tall flames.

2

Lynn slumped on the bed, dead to the world. Liz slapped her on the butt, slapped her hard. There was no visible reaction.

– Pretty girl, Liz shrugged. – A tasty snack.

The tinder in her eyes brightened slightly. She twisted her body a bit, to display herself better to him.

He stood by the window, not turning his head. She slipped out of the bed and walked to him, snuggled close to him, as close as she could possibly come.

– We will teach the defenseless chick to be a raving hungry wolf, of course.

She kissed his lips, his hand, playful and dark in her tinder eyes.

He looked at her. It was sufficient. He didn't have to say a word. She knew he had seen right through her and crouched in his shadow.

– I didn't… come, she said.

He didn't move, not an inch.

– It's a first for me, she added subdued and down. – I've heard the poor chicks complain about it all my life, but never understood their whining before. It was almost as if we didn't fuck at all and it leaves a *sour* taste in my mouth.

– Sorry, he said.

She raised a brow.

– Sorry? You have nothing to be sorry about, have you?

There was no moment of clarity in her fire, but the same wet wood.

– You're so preoccupied, she said, she stated slowly, – even during the fucking. You attempt to hide it, but I know you so well.

He still didn't look at her.

– My power is gone, he said. – It has been gone for some time.

She looked at him and bowed her head further.

– I didn't notice, she sniffed, – and I should have. We're… off with everything these days, aren't we?
– I guess we are.
His voice sounded like it was a thousand miles away.
– People remember everything, she said, – but they don't recall most of it. We, however recall so much more than most people. Why can't we be more like other people in this one thing, learning to forget?
They stood very exposed in the window, easily visible down on the street. They didn't move.
– It's almost funny, she choked. – Considering the state of the world, it's absolutely hilarious how I complain about a momentary glitch in my otherwise beyond excellent sex life.
The words he wanted to say didn't come out.
– Don't worry about your power, she said softly and touched his shoulder with a feather-light hand. – It will return when you're ready, stronger and better than before, making you even more a god among men.
The police finally showed up, or finally showed up in force outside. The sound of sirens and big males shouting into bullhorns were added to the ruckus.
– But this isn't good, of course, she said. – We should have been at our best for what's coming.
She shrugged.
– We just have to make do with what we have. It's quite considerable, don't you agree?
– It is, he replied hoarsely.
A giant explosion rocked the neighborhood.
She smiled, as she began touching herself, as her breasts and nipples hardened, as she turned wetter between her thighs again.
– My cunt is glowing, she whispered. – Make it burn.
His cock began twitching. He grabbed her and pulled her close. She gasped in unbridled expectation.
– It feels so good being in your strong arms…
He slapped her on the butt, slapped her hard. She let out a loud, sensual bark of laughter.
– Take what's yours, she said curtly. – Don't be weak.
He slapped her again. She gasped. He slapped her again, so hard that she yelped in pain. She tensed for a moment, before turning slack in his grip. He didn't have to hold her, but he did anyway, squeezed her wrists in his strong hand, fondling the breasts with another. They swelled in his palm and between his fingers.

– Scratch me. Scratch me hard. You know where, know where, know where…

He pushed her at the wall and tore down the thick wire holding up a curtain and tied her wrists behind her back.

– Please, she begged him, writhing in his grip. – I'll be a good girl, a very good girl.

– You *talk* too much.

She drew breath. He tore pieces off the curtain and put it into her open mouth, and then he tied the other wire around her head, used it to keep the gag in place. Her big, wide open eyes looked at him with a touch of fear and he grunted pleased. She tried to say something, but it just came out as mumbling, of course.

– I know you can break free easily if you choose to, don't think I do, but you're not gonna do that. You're just yet another bitch kneeling before the strongest.

She sniffed, but made no attempt at freeing herself.

– I hurt you, don't I? Every word I speak hurt you, just like you want them to do. You weak, worthless cunt!

There was a choke, then a loud, prolonged, muffled moan.

He pushed her at the wall. A board cracked. A collarbone snapped. He grabbed her hips and pushed himself into her. This time her gasp and moan was the same, the same savage, muffled howl. He shouted in rage. The room shook. Those hearing the beastly sounds imagined that the entire building shook.

They were in bed. He held on to her hips. She stood on her knees before him, her face being pushed forward and pulled backwards across the bed, the big bed. Her body hit Lynn's sleeping unconscious form and pushed it off the bed. It hit the floor hard. There was no sound of anything breaking. Ted didn't hear any.

Liz strived to breathe, but couldn't get enough air. Heat and pleasure hit her hard. She tried to free herself, but was unable to do so, as joy flooded her, every single piece of her body and mind and what was behind. He pushed his load into her and joy kept flooding her.

A few seconds passed. He pushed her away and left the bed, returning to his spot by the window. Black filled her vision amidst spots of flashing colors and shadows and endless mist.

The bonds were so strong and she couldn't focus. They were like chains canceling her powers. She gasped in panic, in despair and horror.

Then she turned calm, calmed herself. She couldn't break the wires, but she could stretch them, making them malleable, until she could remove them from her wrists, and then she used hands stinging in pain to remove the wire around her face and pull out the gag.

She didn't move, didn't look at him. Time passed, as she fell and kept falling.

Elizabeth Warren crumbled there on the bed, wishing she could cry herself to sleep.

– I *pushed* myself at you, she said thunderstruck. – I'm a shameless tramp.

She crouched there, in fetal position, half into sleep and dormancy.

He stood by the window, yearning to go to her, but staying put.

– I can see us, she mumbled, – we're together.

She sniffed and choked, until sleep did catch her, did make her crumble and fall further into the pitch-black hole her consciousness had become.

3

Lynn awoke on the floor. She stretched her body and grinned to the two standing by the door fully dressed.

– Good morning, she greeted the dark man and woman.

She rose and ran to them, kissing them on the lips. Being close to them felt so good, so beyond great.

– It was quite… wild… wasn't it?

They didn't say anything, only looked at her with their beyond penetrating stare. She reddened.

Liz grabbed her and kissed her on the lips.

– Your lips burn, Lynn whimpered.

Ted grabbed her and kissed her on the lips.

– Yours don't, she whispered.

She drowned in his embrace, slipping effortlessly into it when he pulled her closer. He began touching her, increasingly invasive.

– Oh, she exclaimed.

He let go of her and began undressing.

– Oh, she breathed.

He led her back to the bed. She speeded up her pace to keep up with his. He kissed her again, a powerful, demanding caress. She glanced at his fully erect cock and her eyes turned hazy and wet.

They moved on the bed. She screamed in joy-filled lust. He spent the first few seconds to measure the effect on himself, but felt no rush, no transfer of energy and then he let go.

– Yes, Ted, she shouted. – YES!

She pushed herself at him in her wild abandon and he did the same.

– YESSSSS

They took a shower together afterwards, cleaning each other. She rubbed in awe his hard, very functional natural muscles. He witnessed how she once again turned excited and knew he would be, too. It was pleasant to wait for it. He enjoyed the lingering, growing expectation. She bit her lip.

– It's amazing, she said. – I've never felt it anything even remotely like this before… so powerful.

– You're just putty in our hands, Liz said from the door, – clay we warm and form any way we desire.

There was the cold trickle down the spine, but it didn't decrease Lynn's need, but on the contrary increased it further. She began gasping, a virtually constant hard breathing.

The fast breathing made her dizzy, but awareness still soared, still made her aware of herself in a manner she had hardly glimpsed before.

He saw her, saw himself. His push lifted her up and glued her back to the wall. He fucked her with a strange and different abandon, holding her in place without effort. She embraced him with her legs and pushed at his back, mindlessly clinging to his body, to the wolfish grin snarling in her feverish mind.

They released each other. He put her back on the floor. She slipped out of his grip, staying in contact with him with her sensitive hands, her still hungry lips, marveling at the prevailing sensation pleasantly assaulting her. Her dreamy smile kept focusing on him, at his beastly, so very human face.

– I feel so good, she mumbled, – so beyond good. That was so amazing. Thank you, thank you…

They cleaned each other and afterwards dried each other. Liz helped out, too. It was all so pleasant, such a lack of consciousness, even as consciousness soared.

Ted sensed the girl's insides and enjoyed it, enjoyed the blast of growing awareness he sensed in her, like he so often had in himself. The room faded away and as he so often experienced, the walk down the stairs excluded itself from memory and they strolled through the hot summer streets.

He walked between the two women and felt a great, brief swell of joy.

– We shared you, Lynn whispered to him. – I love that, just love that.

She was radiant, bursting with excitement. They couldn't help but noticing similar emotions in themselves when she ran ahead, dancing through the practically bombed-out streets of Hell's Kitchen.

– This is different, Liz said. – She brings a kind of fresh perspective, don't you think?

– I do, he replied with a catching in his voice he didn't attempt to hide, –

and it's so very valuable.

And Liz grabbed and squeezed his hand.

The result of last night's warfare was very much visible everywhere. There was hardly an undamaged window anywhere. Car wrecks, burned-out and perforated with bullets dominated several streets.

– This is amazing, Lynn breathed. – This is just amazing.

They easily saw and sensed that she wasn't put off, but was, on the contrary excited, and it both comforted and worried them.

The three of them had breakfast at a cafeteria somewhere on the outskirts of Hell's Kitchen, one of the few places unscathed by the night's loud activities. Lynn wolfed down the food and needed a second helping.

– Are you okay, honey? Liz asked her, touching her forehead, as if checking for a fever.

– I feel a little weird, the girl grinned, – but I'm okay. I'm hungry, so very, very hungry. My aunt says I eat like a bird. She should see me now.

People glared at them. Lynn didn't notice, but Liz and Ted easily did, of course.

– I just love those rings of yours, she said in awe. – The stone looks like blood.

They let her prattle on, while listening to their surroundings, while the familiar warm trickle strolled down their spine.

Both watched people, looking for the potentially dangerous among them, for those with twitching fingers eager to use their concealed guns. There was a man with shades across the street, another on the sidewalk right outside the cafeteria.

– Your eyes, Lynn eventually said with a chill in her voice. – They never rest.

– Can you see them? Liz asked abruptly. – See the potential threats to us?

Ted watched her, watched Liz. Lynn shook her head subdued.

– Before we're done with you, you will, he said.

Liz spoke, but not much, not like she usually did, not like the usual unending, excited motormouth he had learned to know. He strived to keep his mask an even expression and knew he failed miserably.

They waited. Nothing happened. They waited a bit longer. Nothing happened.

– Time to leave, wouldn't you say? She said casually.

– Time to leave, he shrugged.

They walked, took the stroll east, with casual detours, slowly circling in on their goal. Their surroundings changed, subtle at first, then clearly becoming a more affluent area. They passed Grand Central Terminal. Lynn brightened a bit, darkened some more, a victim of conflicting emotions. They walked on Fifth Avenue.

– I can't help feeling a little ambiguity here, Lynn mused. – Shopping has always been fun to me. Most empty-headed rich kids have no other occupation…

They passed one expensive store after another.

– Unimpressive, Liz shrugged.

Lynn giggled, looking at the other young woman with worship in her eyes. They walked up and down a few times, as if to drive the point home.

St Patrick's Cathedral loomed above them.

– My contempt is approaching boundless, Ted snarled.

The girls nodded in unison.

The dreams began, effortlessly, almost uncontrollable. The city, the rot surrounding them briefly went away. The forest, the ancient forest embraced them. When they looked around them, they saw trees, not giant concrete tombstones. The cathedral was nothing but ruins in a transformed world.

– You notice, too, don't you? Liz told him softly.

He nodded, hardly able to, a happy catching in his throat almost overwhelming him.

– It was the same with me, when I was depowered, she said. – Only my active powers went away, not those involuntary and empathic.

Lynn looked at them with her constantly curious eyes.

– I wish we could show you, Ted said. – Show *all of you.*

– I want you to show me, she insisted, – want you to show me everything.

– One day we will, he stated empathically, and a thrill charged her to the brim.

Their destination wasn't hard to find. They sort of dumped into it without looking, recognized it from the descriptions.

– It is… different, Liz said. – Perhaps not so much in outward appearance, but to people who can see… see…

– … beneath the surface, Ted completed her sentence.

And they had seen it before, in their visions. Reality deviated very little from that. Anxiety and anticipation riled them.

– Ethel Warren is related to you? Lynn gasped.

Then catching herself, shaking her head in bewilderment.

– Of course, she is.

Evening descended on New York City as they made their way to the entrance, as several yellow taxis and luxury cars queued up in front of it and many well-dressed people stepped out on the sidewalk.

There was no guest list, no guards standing there crossing off names as the various people entered the building and ventured deeper into its cave, as they stepped into the elevator and climbed the mountain, but Ted and Liz watched the doorman and other sentries invisible to most people and noticed the tiny twitches around their eyes.

Everybody, even the most unaware entity noticed the eerie, pervasive mood. Lynn sought closer to Ted, attempting in vain to hide her growing anxiety. The sliding door of the elevator opened, and they stepped into a hall that seemed infinite. It looked so much bigger than it appeared to be from the outside, as if its space had been expanded, somehow, and they realized startled that it had been.

The other guests stared at them, of course. Some of them didn't even attempt to conceal it. Gossip and rumors and selected newspaper columns told people that an evening with Ethel Warren always was quite… special. Tonight, the visitors realized startled that it would be even more so, that they were in for a rare treat.

– I feel the tingle, Liz said excited, anxious. – I can sense her, sense them. Can you?

– I can, Ted said hoarsely

In the space ahead of them, they noticed the shadows standing out from the rest. At the end of the long tunnel they faced the young man and youthful woman.

Eyes with a dark fire matching their own greeted them, Patrick's twinkling more than burning, more brown than red.

She rose from a chair at the other end of the exotic living room. They met at the middle. She was half a head taller than Ted.

– Ted and Liz, this is such an exciting moment, isn't it.

Hands grabbed hands. There was a tug of war of sorts, but no one gained any advantage.

– You don't look so fearsome close up, Liz joked.

– Of course, Ethel said, – you've dreamed about me, like I've dreamed about you.

– We did dream about you, Liz stated slowly.

You weren't worth much then, you snotty bitch.

Ted remembered her in exquisite detail, a flaring memory from a timeline that never was.

Patrick reached out a hand, too. It dawned on them that they had almost forgotten he was there. This was how they would always think of him, like a shadow in the vast shadow covering him.

– This is Lynn. Ted presented her before Ethel said anything. – She travels with us.

– She is cute, Ethel said, playing the vamp, fooling no one.
I remember you, Ethel's eyes told him. Do you remember me?
He shook with the flashes of memories he had never lived.
– I knew you would come to me, but not before you had become infamous, when you had become savage beasts taking shit from no one…
The other guests heard the exchange, but it didn't seem like they did. They made every effort to pretend they didn't, but they were transparent like glass.
– Come, she cried, waving her arms, including the entire room and everybody in it. – Let tonight's feast begin.
She led them to a long table. Ted and Liz were placed at her side, at the head. Lynn was given a place further down.
– By the way, I knew you would come today, Ethel practically apologized, – but not whether or not anyone would accompany you. The details in the mists of time are often obscure and reveal themselves reluctantly.
– She sounds completely casual, doesn't she? Liz spoke just as casual to Ted. – As if she was speaking about the weather.
People kept staring at all the four fireeyes, or looking at them with cautious and beyond curious glances.
The room… settled. Food was served. Wine was served. Everybody, even the most mindless and unaware guest noticed the special quality of the present mood.
Light faded away and shadows entered the room, recreating it, and very few noticed.
– You're so very perceptive, my dear, Ethel bowed. – I knew you would be.
Candles lit the room. Dark curtains covered all the windows. What had been daylight and electrical lights only minutes ago had been transformed into something eerie and different.
Liz and Ted noted the space and its people. They caught each other in communicating without words and thoughts and even emotions, as if they were born to do so, and the hard catching in their throats grew.
They listened to the chatter noise, like they always did, with all their senses.
The loud woman fairly high on the table became even louder for a while, before fading back into the general background. The tall man further down engaged himself in a conversation with the woman by his side.
Ethel rose with the glass of wine in her hands.
– Join me in welcoming my dear relatives to the rotten apple, she cried. – Welcome to the rotten apple, Ted and Liz. May thunder stay with you during your stay.
There was something about the different ways she pronounced «stay» that rattled Ted. He shrugged deliberately.

She waved her free hand, directing her troops like they were an orchestra.
– WELCOME TO THE ROTTEN APPLE, TED AND LIZ. MAY THUNDER STAY WITH YOU DURING YOUR STAY.
Ted bowed sitting.
– Thank you, Aunt Ethel, he replied. – That's so generous of you.
– «Aunt Ethel», a man snickered, quickly falling silent in s mire of anxiety.
The smile twinkled on her sensuous lips.
– It resembles Mark's welcome in New Orleans, doesn't it? Liz spoke with a loud voice, but one very pleasant. – He, too, enjoyed blustering.
Ethel ignored her words. It looked like she hadn't heard them at all.
The talk went around the table hushed and not. Stolen glances kept returning to the dark couple. The mundane guests spoke mostly about mundane matters, desperately attempting to pretend that life was completely different from what it in truth was and failing miserably.
– The President is quite fond of visiting downtrodden New York City, isn't he?
– He is quite fond of blustering about all the good things that will happen because of him.
– Has anything happened in Bronx or on the Subway since his visits?
– Carter is the last hobby-politician, Ethel shrugged. – He rode into the White House on a giant anti-Washington DC wave, but don't know how to stay there.
She had put everything in perspective and everybody shut up about it.
– Cheers, a very anxious man shouted, totally out of the blue.
The sensations around the table grew distinct and deep. Ted and Liz visibly excelled in it, in the conversation and the prevalent mood. They overdid it in the presence of their older, imposing relative.
– So, how was the jungle? A woman asked casually, very casually.
Liz forced herself to project the brazen confidence she dimly recalled from her younger days, ignoring the prevalent painful catching in the throat.
– It was sweaty, Olivia, she grinned. – We walked around nude all day and mated like savages whenever we felt like it. You should try it sometimes.
Do they see through me? She wondered. Do they call my bluff, penetrate the wall I've erected around myself?
She drank, drank too much, like she always did. The voices faded and softened in her ears and in her mind. She spilled wine. It looked like blood on the white cloth and on her skin.
The party eventually left the table and started circulating around the room, the both confining and boundless space, breaking into smaller groups, the way any gathering tended to do. Ted and Liz and their host circled around

each other like predators, until finally approaching common ground at the center of the room.

The two travelers sensed it, how the room and the people around them seemed to grind to a halt. Everybody froze in mid-movement, except the four of them.

Patrick shrugged and didn't seem that interested, though. He walked to the punchbowl, leaving the scene to his mother and the two dark creatures.

– That's a nice trick, Ted said with obvious insincerity in his voice and stance.

He was being deliberately patronizing and sarcastic and didn't quite know why. It gave him a strange feeling, one he had never quite experienced quite like this before.

She waved a hand and the air thickened even more around them.

– There are things I can tell you about the future, she said, – but also many things about it you don't need to know. You're quite powerful Seers in your own right.

– Right now, we are more interested in the past, Liz said pleasantly. – You are one of the closest existing links to our unknown lineage we've met.

– And Trudy won't tell? She chided them.

– You know what happened, Ted said angrily, deliberately. – Tell us!

It was an order, a command.

– I know some of what happened, Ethel conceded, seemingly totally unaffected by his outburst. – But the big picture keeps eluding me, no matter how hard I try to catch it, catch its breath. I know the others chose to leave New York, leave the world. Only I and my brood remained.

Her smile hardly looked like a smile at all. An unfamiliar shiver passed through Liz when her relative turned and fixed her stare at her.

– I can tell you your fate, she said to them, – but not in much more detail than you can yourself.

She fixed her attention solely on Liz.

– I can tell you three possible outcomes of your life, though.

She gestured and something incredible, even to the two dark Warrens happened.

They sensed something that felt like a rush of air, a shift in their surroundings.

Something seemed to be… pulled out of Liz, an exact copy. She felt nothing, but there it was, a mirror image existing at an odd angle of them all, one changing before their eyes.

– This is you, not really that long, not that many days after you leave this building tonight.

Liz looked at herself, at the pretty girl standing there, a model dressed up and with a painted face.

– You will be quite desired, an idol of millions of young girls. Your runners will take good care of you. You'll want for nothing.

The image faded and another replaced it. It was similar, but clearly different. Liz looked at the heavily painted face and the girl standing there in revealing clothes, in a type of revealing clothes she would never have chosen. She saw the empty eyes, the sick, inviting smile and drawn face. It chilled her to the bone.

– This one will give pleasures to many and earn quite a lot of money for her pimp as an exclusive girl-for-rent, before ending up on the street with not a single independent thought behind her tired, old features.

The third appeared, a wild creature dancing nude on a stage, snarling to a stunned audience, a sight both shocking and enticing.

– You've shown me three possibilities that won't come to pass, I guess, Liz snorted before the other said anything more, striving to breathe evenly. – A nice touch that.

The other's beyond pointed stare penetrated her like the ice and fire it was, but she rode it out, and the stare she returned made Ethel Warren stagger and fade, and triumph swelled within Liz' shaking insides.

She noticed it, how the bubble ruptured and broke, and they returned to the room, to the space and time they had briefly left.

Ethel bled from her nose. Patrick looked astonished at her, at them all. Ethel spoke with her ghoulish voice, in what was still a whirlwind of air and time.

– I can see the future, like strands of night and fire coalescing into just a few possible outcomes. I know what you are, what you will eventually become. In one timeline, it will happen fairly quickly, in another it will take longer, but the end result will be the same.

She rubbed her left temple, using the other hand to wipe the blood from her upper lip.

– But you haven't really told us anything, have you? Ted said casually.

She looked at him, and there was another battle of wills before she once again bowed her head and bared her neck, and a little poison slipped out and exposed itself with her words.

– I can tell you one thing: you *will* find all your answers and know everything there is to know.

– Understanding will come, I promise you that, Betty told him in the cabin.

They separated, backed off from each other, denied what had never been.

The party… ended. It had run out of steam before it began. Ethel Warren said goodbye to her long-lost relatives at the door. She smiled brightly.

– New York City is a melting pot, one of the biggest and most potent on the planet. You will thrive here, like all Janus Clan children.

– Children? Liz queried. – Do you see us as children? We're not, you know, as you probably *know* by now.

– Did I say you were? Their host beamed, ambiguous like a sphinx, poisonous as a snake.

People stared, even more than they usually did.

They left the room, left the clammy cave, made their way down to street level. When they walked outside, it did feel like they could breathe again, could feel their lungs being filled with air again.

Photographers took everybody's photo the moment they stepped outside. The flashes startled them a bit, made stars fill their vision and they felt how their eyes contracted and expanded again in an effort to cope with the abrupt change in conditions.

– I could do a lot with you, baby, one of the men with cameras told her and handed her a card, one she without thinking about it put in her pocket.

The image Ethel had shown her revisited the forefront of her mind. She shook her head.

Several other women were also handed cards.

– They're here all the time, one of the departing women shrugged. – They're like leeches. Ethel's parties are considered top priority by photojournalists.

The card burned in Liz's pocket. It hurt her thigh. She crouched slightly, straightening, moving on.

They walked through the streets again, with Lynn in tow, realizing with a little shock they had actually forgotten she was there, forgotten about her altogether.

– She *didn't* say we were children, he said offhand. – She was…

– I know, she grinned, – I'm not stupid.

She walked a couple of stops more before adding to her statement.

– Or perhaps she did, anyway. She's a tricky and vicious witch.

– I do believe she sees everybody else as being beneath her. He nodded, walking a couple more steps before speaking again. – She's exactly like we envisioned. We can't expect any true help from her, at least not when it truly counts, not from her and not from her «brood». She has trained him well. We're alone, like we knew we would be.

The whirlwind of time and space she had revealed to them was still with them, here, on the streets, among its people. Shouts and whimpers and flashes and smells and the taste in their mouth coalesced into a single, vast impression.

– And to point out the obvious, she said, her grin hardly visible, – she showed us my possible fate, not yours. She didn't reveal anything about you.

This time she didn't pause, didn't wait a few steps.

– Perhaps she doesn't know for some reason… or perhaps it is because your fate is fixed, that it can't be changed?

The darkness, the Shadow flared between them. He grabbed her arm, light as feather. She whimpered.

– I swore I would never return to my stupor, step off the pathless path, and I won't, do you hear me?

– I hear you, she replied, visibly frightened and timid by his intensity, not encouraged by it.

She turned to Lynn, with a snarl hardly visible on her lips. Lynn froze, as if she was caught in the other's stare, in a vice squeezing her harder than anything physical.

– Remove your shoes, Liz said to the girl.

– Remove my…

– Discard them like yesterday's laundry. High heels won't do, won't do at all, not when we turn you into a lethal creature, and not afterwards when you've become one. Girls with high heels don't last long in true combat.

Lynn obeyed, in quick bursts of movement. When they moved on down the street, she left her shoes behind.

Their surroundings faded, faded until it was all gone, completely, with nothing left but a total, unending blackness. Ted slept, or at least he believed he did. He writhed on the bed, with Liz and Lynn in his arms. New York revealed itself to him, in all its colors and shades, but that was just the start. The rest of the world, of reality kept rushing in, like a storm, like *the* Storm.

Dreams chased him, deep into sleep, beyond sleep, into a shadowy world he could only glimpse.

Dennis Murdoch's hardly recognizable face burned his eyes, as he looked at him, as he looked at the boy dying in one of the pyramid's torture chambers.

– Heart-attack, the woman, the chief torturer shrugged. – Get a medic, a medic, now.

The mist shifted again and he found himself elsewhere.

He saw a woman standing on Times Square, greeting him with a wolfish grin, and he knew her, knew her every corner and twinkle.

Pain and fear and even terror squeezed him.

She stood on a battlefield, one filled with torn and bloody bodies from horizon to horizon.

She smiled to him, an open and caring and wicked and witty smile.

– When you remember me, you're not only remembering me, but yourself, and that will always hurt.

– Being born hurts, he whispered.

The young girl, the grown, mature woman stepped one step closer. One move was a mile.

– Forgetfulness is our nature. Our nature is remembrance. What we learned once we must learn over and over again throughout eternity. We must die and be reborn countless times to remember. Forever.

Every word, every nuance and inflexion stuck in his ears and echoed in the vast cave that was his mind. In a glimpse he sensed the world, sensed it a thousand times over.

And then, in a whirl of motion and water and wind and pain and joy and horror he could indeed see Forever.

Chapter 4

Sometimes there were riders, in the early morning light, in the twilight of early evening.

– WHY? Why are you doing this to me? I've done nothing.

A boy that sometimes was a girl was chained to a post in the wilderness.

– WHY? ARE YOU REALLY THAT STUPID, ASKING THAT QUESTION? The voice of the city people, the voice with no form, no substance behind it snarled viciously at him. – WHY NOT?

The scenery changed. He stood in a field filled with mangled bodies. He and several others faced She Who Dances in the Forest.

– This is just one more misstep, she told them, – one more blip in eternity. There will come many more battles, many more chances to get it right.

They looked strange those standing with him, their features shifting, as if they had more than one face.

Even the surroundings kept changing, as his rollercoaster emotions kept charging through him like a billion electrical currents, way too much for him to assimilate into his conscious mind.

It rose from there into the sound of a roaring waterfall threatening to push him off his feet and pull him down the mighty river.

They ran through stretch and stretch of sand, beyond fearful, beyond anxious. Carla ran by his side and so did other strange creatures with… with fireeyes. He was strangely unafraid. There was danger, even deadly danger, but he was more enraged than afraid.

The desert looked and appeared… odd to him. It didn't look like any desert he had ever seen, the landscape almost resembling that of another planet.

The sand rose into the sound of a roaring sandstorm threatening to push him off his feet and pull him down, pull him into the air and take him far away.

Lee woke up in his bed in his bedroom soaked in sweat and with a deep frown painted on his face. The strong sunlight through the window heated his skin. He sat up, still immersed in the dream. It wouldn't go away, its overpowering presence persisting in his conscious mind.

He stood by the window, looking at the skyline, at the cloudless sky.

The streets below seemed close, so very close. He heard the birds, saw ravens flap their wings, as if there was no glass between them and him.

His mother entered the room behind him.

– Breakfast is ready, she said. – School will start without you, you know. You're dreaming yourself away again, aren't you?

And then he realized that he had stood there for minutes, without noticing the passing of time.

– I can see the lightning in the horizon calling me home, he said, not quite aware of speaking.

He turned and studied the bland, middle-aged woman, gauging her reactions, realizing that she gave him a strange, anxious look.

– Mom, he said casually, – I had bad dreams when I was younger, didn't I?

– When you were very young, she said, sort of correcting him in a soft-speaking manner. – Thank God, they faded away with the bright morning of your childhood.

He realized startled that she had always spoken like that, a little formal and poetic.

That was it. Breakfast, a little less uneventful and dull hardly registered in his mind beyond those few sentences. He ran through the streets and reached school just as the bell called the pupils to the classroom.

It was the last days of summer school. Most of the regular students were in attendance. Parents zealous on behalf of their perceived gifted children made sure of that.

Eloise glanced strangely at him when he entered the classroom. He basically ignored her, as he sat down by his desk.

She kept glancing at him. He sat a few rows in front of her and practically sensed her stare in his back.

He went through the motions during the day and hardly anything else, hardly listening to what was being said, replying each time a teacher asked him anything, hardly aware of what he was saying.

Blades whistled as they cut through air filled with red mist on a wet and gray day. He felt the handle of the sword in his hand, felt the resistance as the soiled metal broke skin and drank more blood…

– Lewis.

He recognized the teacher's voice and strived hard to cast her a casual look.

– Yes?

– You need to keep your attention on the subject at hand, she cautioned him.

– Lewis' attention is far away, a girl snickered.

– If you only knew how far away, he told her calmly and centered.

And Lydia, the girl faltered and stared stunned at him.

– You look like you want to come with me, he drawled, something vast and dark opening up inside him. – You've always wanted to, but haven't had the courage or haven't been sufficiently encouraged before.

She blinked and kept staring at him.

– What are you doing, she asked incredulous, with a distinct touch of whimper in her voice, – doing to me?

The teacher cleared her throat, temporarily ending the exchange.

But Lewis didn't forget. The dangerous mood didn't leave him, not during the hour, not during the free time or the rest of the day.

He sought out Lydia during the free time, walked right up to her and her close-nit crowd.

– Hi, he greeted her.

– Hi, she replied, blushing hard.

There was no anger or even anything approaching that. He kept his cool and casual outer and inner frame of mind.

– You're very beautiful, he said.

Everybody stared open-mouthed at him.

– You were right about me, he said. – Am I right about you?

She replied, parted her lips and spoke, but there was no audible sound.

– Yes, she repeated.

And with that one word, she changed her entire life.

She stepped forward, stepped close to him, suddenly far more mature in manner and inclination.

When class resumed she moved to the empty desk close to his.

School eventually ended, like it did every day, and everybody breathed a sigh of relief and opened like flowers.

Lydia followed him on his path, and so did Eloise and even some of the boys.

He studied them with curious eyes. At least some of the boys were clearly embarrassed and didn't meet his eyes.

They visited their usual haunts. The Donna Summer poster caught his eyes at some point, and stayed at the back of his attention. He knew that, even as he delegated the memory to a distant part of himself.

– Bad dreams again?

It was Eloise. He looked closer at her.

– You're troubled. She shrugged deliberately. – I've always been able to tell, since we were children.

He nodded to himself, acknowledging the truth of her words.

– I don't know. He frowned. – There is a flow of chaotic images and sensations making me sweat.

He closed his eyes. He opened them again. The images and sensations they created were still there.

– Eventually everything is fading, except this: I'm walking on an indistinct desert path and I face the Dragon. But I'm not fighting it. I don't wear armor. There is no sword or shield in my hands. I'm willingly joining with it and it is devouring me, and I become more than I've ever been, and I feel happy, even exalted.

Everybody looked at him, and it didn't feel bad. He knew they wouldn't make fun of him, knew beyond certainty so many things, and it didn't feel strange at all.

He was dancing, first with Lydia, then with Eloise, and then the others were there as well, there on the dance floor. At first, it looked like they were alone, like everybody else faded away around them, and they were, but then they weren't, and the people gathering around them didn't even resemble those he remembered from only seconds, minutes ago.

The group gathered outside. He didn't have to look to see stars in their eyes.

– Wow! Stane cried. – That was really something, man!

He and Lewis clasped hands, and the others joined in.

– Fucking unreal, Terrence chimed in.

When they left their spot outside the disco, it didn't feel awkward or weird at all, but as natural as breathing.

They made their way through the streets, moving through them like one being, as if they didn't have many pairs of feet, but only one, as if they had become one being.

He, they stopped below the Brooklyn Bridge and all of it felt so very, very familiar.

Approaching steps echoed in the night. This time Lewis felt a strange foreboding, but still that distinct lack of fear.

He recognized Carla before he saw her face. She led a group of five girls. He noticed how they walked, how economical was their movements. The small act of watching them felt like an amazing experience in itself. The six stopped in front of the Brooklyn gang.

– Hello, Lewis, she said softly.

– Yeah, hello, Lewis, Terrence snickered.

– H'lo, he mumbled a bit.

– And these are your friends? They look quite capable and able to take care of themselves… most of them.

She sounded very patronizing just then. Lewis couldn't help but grinning.

He easily noted how taken they were by her, how she drew them to her, and he couldn't fault them for that.

– Come with me, she told them, just like that.

They followed her as she and her entourage retreated back into the dark alleys and hidden corners of the big city. Several of Lewis's friends looked around them wide-eyed, as if they saw Brooklyn and even New York City for the first time.

He blinked, imagining he saw streams of light, of golden light in the air around them. It resembled sunset, except it was more elaborate, filling the air more, shifting occasionally in gray and shadow. When Carla drew her sword, just after that they had arrived at the dusty, old warehouse, it was as if the blade cut through the air itself.

– You will all learn, she told them, – learn the way of the warrior and the blade, and you will wield all the weapons at your disposal with great skill and accuracy.

They looked strange those standing with him, their features shifting, as if they had more than one face.

– You will be great at it, she stated with conviction. – And when the riders charge you, when they charge you in the early morning light you will defend yourself with steel and a determination outmatching theirs.

Ice filled him, fire filled him. Every time he blinked, every time his blade cut the air and met those of his training partners it filled him more. One whirl of the blade became many.

And the golden light turned red.

2

They used electric needles on them, used any conceivable instrument of torture, some he hadn't imagined existed. He and his friends and fellow soldiers sat in a chair at the center of the room, suffering every possible known and unknown pain in existence.

The moisture and sound and stench of the room surrounded him. He couldn't escape it, no matter how hard he tried, and he tried hard.

It didn't matter if he kept his eyes closed or open. The insane dance continued. The horrible screams filled his mind, bloated every piece of his cells.

Sometimes it was as if he experienced a given event twice or ten times, never quite certain it was actually happening.

The scream came from him, from his raw as meat throat.

She stood there, the sweet demon, stood there in the dark studying him with her green eyes. He gasped, in yet another desperate attempt to climb up from the pit he had fallen into.

– We were testing you, you know…

«We»? He glanced at her.

She stepped closer to him, but was just as far away.

– We had heard great words about the fierce warrior that seemed to be able to anticipate his enemy's actions. So, we decided to test you and it was a glorious sight to behold. Even in your nascent state of might you held out against our carefully orchestrated onslaught for minutes. You're indeed your mother's son.

The words, not really coming from her, but from the depth of his mind told him something, something deep and profound and horrible.

– You don't believe I will torture you, do you, attempt to control or do harm to one of the future gods of the Earth?

He sat there, in his cage, with his buddies, his companions on this wretched Earth. They had stayed there forever, practically lived there. He could no longer even guess at how long. Moonlight shone at them and burned their skin.

– I walk in the desert, one of them said, or sang or hummed. – I've had that same dream forever, for as long as I can remember. We walk in the desert on a pathless path with the burning bird in our midst.

He never found out whom that voice belonged to. It became just as much a part of the fever dream as everything else, the unending torture pounding them.

They heard the scream all the time. Aldo Miles screamed the loudest and longest, they knew that, or at least Patrick imagined he did.

– The pain never goes away, Miles sobbed. – It's like a thousand burning hot needles are stuck in my body. I grab them and pull, but no matter how many I remove, there are still many more left. They are hidden. I try *finding* them, but I can't, no matter how long and hard I search.

The big man seemed so small, so very small.

Eric Carr just sat there, staring at nothing.

They worked, worked in the ditch surrounding the village with the other prisoners. Everybody worked until they dropped, and then the whipping and punishment began, and they worked some more, until they were only functions, not mind.

– These are the elite soldiers of imperialism? The girl spat in contempt. – These are the Empire's finest? What a pathetic sight!

Then there was more torture, and imprisonment in the current of the cage, a rest hardly even resembling rest at all. Their thoughts kept hammering their numb mind.

– You and I will share a secret.

He saw her whisper into other ears, wondering ceaselessly if she in truth spoke to him also when she seemingly didn't.

– I can't take this anymore, I can't take this anymore, I can't take this anymore.

That both sounded and didn't sound like Aldo Miles. Patrick's thoughts drifted away, reality shifting and burning around him.

A loud, metallic sound woke him up. His attention, for some reason was instantly on the lock of the cage. Suddenly, in the middle of the night, he was wide awake.

He pushed open the door. It was ridiculously easy. He crawled out and up, hardly exerting himself at all. His eyes moved constantly above the terrain. There was no one there, no guards in sight. He couldn't see any and there were no shouts or alarms going off anywhere.

Returning to the cage felt like descending into the worst kind of hell, and for untold days and nights it had been.

He shook the men.

– C'mon, soldiers, he growled, – let's go!

They opened weary eyes and looked astonished at the open door.

– You go without me, guys, one unknown voice, a defeated man said.

– We will all go, Warren swore. – We will carry those who can't walk on our backs, and when we can't walk anymore, they will carry us.

– Very funny, captain, Carr chuckled. – My sincere compliments…

And the horrible joke, more than anything made strength flow through their muscles.

They moved, one by one leaving the cage that had practically become their home, freezing in fear and potential horror, waiting for the other shoe to drop.

The gate to the camp was guarded. They moved elsewhere, through a hole in the fence. Warren felt such strength flow through his muscles that he feared he would glow in the dark. They ran and stumbled and ran. Each noise sounded loud enough to wake the dead.

And they felt like they were dead waking up, waking up from the nightmare that had seemed to be without end.

He turned, as they reached across the muddy river, and looked back.

She stood on a rise and saw them off, or at least he imagined she did.

He realized he spotted love in those green eyes.

3

Patrick Warren woke up in his apartment with the two warm bodies, two big smiles by his side. Caitlin Rowe and Sylvia Bertrand stretched and yawned happily, curled up close to his stronger and bigger body.

The vivid experience of the streets outside mixed with his equally vivid memories of the jungle.

They took a stroll through Chinatown's Columbus Park, walking past a big heap of black plastic garbage bags.

– It's such a beautiful day, he mused. – Isn't it such a beautiful day?

The two sensual creatures pulled even closer to him, if that was possible. He chuckled.

– This feels like the dream.

Ethel stood there again then.

– This is no dream, she stated firmly. – I explained this to you. Your dreams and your reality are closer compared to how most people experience it. That's why it feels like it's all blurring sometimes.

– I understand what you mean, Caitlin giggled. – It's often hard to tell, isn't it?

Caitlin, a tall redhead had been his secretary and part time lover for the last six months, but she suddenly seemed completely different, as if she had stumbled on a major truth.

And she had, of course.

He had shown her a life completely different from her previous experience. She had been shy and slightly upset at first, when she had joined him and Sylvia in bed, but then she had blossomed like a flower.

She still was.

– «A dream is real, for as long as it lasts», Sylvia quoted, – «can we say otherwise about life»?

That kind of hit him home, even though he couldn't say in what way.

The park, with all its sounds and visuals and sensations hit him from all sides, all angles. A boy rode his bike through the red gate or what Patrick perceived as a red gate.

– Dreams are doorways, he mused. – I remember dawn, even though I slept through it. There are many dawns.

They lapped up his words like chocolate, hardly ever taking their eyes off him, looking at him with devotion in their wide eyes. He hardly noticed.

There were quite a few people of Chinese ancestry in the park, more than it would be in most other parts of the city, but not excessively so. He studied their faces, and they didn't turn Vietnamese, and that was also something he took great comfort in.

This looked more like a multiracial area than a pure Chinese, and that sat well with him.

– Patrick of the Janus Clan, Ethel told him. – I release you from your vow. You are free.

Free! He breathed the word, whispered it unheard, and it tasted sweet and strange on his lips.

He observed people, as they walked back and forth, as they crossed each other's path, and was able to read that path so much better than before. Something had… turned in him. A door slammed somewhere. It opened wide and slammed the wall, staying open. A dark golden light flowed through it. He enjoyed the warm sunshine, the summer heat and the company of the two lovely creatures.

When he rose and offered them his hands they complied immediately, and he enjoyed that.

– Let's dance.

– D-dance? Caitlin stuttered happily.

– Sure, can't you hear the music?

He could. It was everywhere.

They giggled, like star-eyed teenagers.

He moved across the children's playground, and they moved with him. He giggled, astounding himself.

– It's like I've just learned to walk.

– You're just learning to walk again, Sylvia whispered with tears in her eyes. – It's a wonder to behold. You lost something in that horrible jungle and you have struggled all that time to get it back.

He kissed her, making her whimper of joy in his arms, not sure if she was correct or had the right idea at all, but it felt good to please her.

When he turned to Caitlin he was ready for her. She reddened, handing him a rather badly produced leaflet.

– You know, the relative you asked Synos to keep an eye on? He and his band are having a gig at Freshwater tonight.

Larry Synos was the company's «Can Do» man, quite an unpleasant, but useful character. Patrick had to stress it every time he just wanted information or Synos would get creative and way too eager in his vocation.

Caitlin, always the eager secretary smiled in exalted joy when he touched her cheek.

Freshwater was a dump, a combined Off-Broadway theater and concert hall.

– Sometimes there is fresh water to enjoy, even at Freshwater, right? He joked.

He actually joked.

– There has been the occasional miracle coming out of there, Caitlin nodded and grinned widely, eager like a girl in his presence.

He saw it, as their dreams mingled and he mingled their dreams with everybody around them, and then he practically experienced the scene in front of the derelict building later that night there and then.

4

Liz and Ted sat relaxed and tense in the chairs at the center of the room, surrounded by Frances and the girls gathered at Frances' center for abused women.

– It isn't easy talking about this, Liz said. – You know it isn't, but we must all confront our fears and shame.

The battered girls looked astonished at the tiny figure, the vulnerable young girl sitting there before them.

– I so craved my master's approval, Liz said. – My entire focus and life was directed at serving him. I had thought myself so strong, so independent and wicked, but he made all my confidence Go Away by a single snap of his fingers. He made me his, taught me his credo, his brutal doctrine, showing me that the strong rule and that the weak is hardly more than dust blowing in the wind. Once he had shown me, shown me beyond doubt what a weak, codependent creature I was, he started teaching me how to serve him, serve him better. And I was an eager student, a willing slave. I so craved my master's approval. There was nothing I wouldn't do for him. Nothing! I became a pleasing creature, longing for his approval in all things and each time he rewarded me I felt like heaven, and each time he punished me I knew I was willful and stupid and didn't know what was best for me and deserved every stroke or lash. I even became his extended arm, eagerly aiding in the enslavement of others, failing all my friends and loved ones, and I became more his with each passing moment.

Silence reigned in the room. They saw the dry tears on her cheeks.

– But you freed yourself from him, Tammy said with a thin voice. – He lost his hold on you and vengeance was yours.

– Yes, Liz acknowledged. – We all freed ourselves, aiding each other and together we showed all his rhetoric and false sense of superiority down his throat.

– And put his head on a *stake!* A girl shouted triumphant.

On a blade, Liz thought.

The brittle laughter shook them all.

– We did, Liz said. – But to me he isn't really dead. It would please him greatly, I think to know that he remains in my thoughts and nightmares, is very much present during my worst moments, where I second guess and doubt myself the most, and I hate that more than anything, but I just can't help myself.

Her voice cracked, and she choked and couldn't go on.
The silence lasted forever.
– Okay, girls, Frances said, – let's thank Liz for being brave and sharing her thoughts and bad experience with us. Let's make her feel welcome and loved.
– THANK YOU, LIZ. WE LOVE YOU, LIZ!
And the warm, warm feeling hit her and somewhat comforted her.
– We also have Ted her today, Frances said cautiously. – He will share his thoughts with us and need our grace and support.
They looked, somewhat curious at the other small figure at the girl's side and felt a strange, unfamiliar empathy.
– I have been raped and violated more than once. Ted began hesitatingly, haltingly, creating a stir in the gathering. – In fact, it has happened so many times that I've lost count over how many. Society's claim that men can't be raped doesn't hold water.
There was a pause, one that, to him felt endless.
– It began in my early teens. My «classmates» at school and my older brother hassled and hounded me to the point of me considering suicide more than once. Later, as almost an adult, when I believed I had put it all behind me, I and my classmates, at that point my friends were kidnapped and brutalized beyond belief. You've probably read a little about it in the newspapers and heard about it on the news, but I can assure you that that ridiculously unsatisfactory coverage hardly even touched the horrors we lived through before we were freed, before we freed ourselves.
– I thought I had problems, Wynette whispered, – but I had no idea.
More brittle laughter. Warren smiled.
– You freed yourself, she stated solemnly. – You did it time and time again. You must be harder than steel.
They looked at him with sympathy and pity.
– Perhaps I am, he acknowledged. – I know I can be, if I have to. Perhaps I am better prepared to deal with the world on its own terms because of what I've experienced. Perhaps what doesn't kill you does make you stronger…
The ambiguity in his voice didn't escape them. He knew it didn't, feeling everything they did. Liz leaned close to him, rubbing his back and his cheek, and he felt somewhat comforted.
– But no matter how strong you are, how invulnerable you believe yourself to be, there will be times where you will be battered and bruised by the circumstances and horrors of the world. Even if men, as a general rule are physically stronger, we're just as vulnerable, you know, just as defenseless. We're all just dust blowing in the wind.
They practically saw it, felt it like a poignant kick in the gut, how he picked

himself up from his mire, how his very form seemed to grow there in the chair and both anxiety and anticipation ravaged them.

– Well, let's embrace that, embrace the random qualities, cruel and great of life and fight tooth and nail against those who would diminish it. Let's keep empowering ourselves and each other.

They knew what he meant and didn't misunderstand, as he had feared they would.

– We will teach you to fight, Liz cried softly. – We will make you prepared, physically, mentally for what's to come.

The quiet applause embalmed somewhat their delicate confidence.

The… séance ended.

Marlene, red-haired and tall and hateful and needy, brittle and strong came to him afterwards. He looked at her across a gulf of time he could hardly bridge.

– Look at us. She kissed him on the cheek. – What are the chances of us ever meeting again, and here we are.

He didn't voice a comment. Her inner turmoil was hard to read.

– I don't hate you, she said. – Perhaps I should… a little, but I'm more grateful, in a backwards kind of way. You were a mean bastard and certainly didn't care about showing me the error of my ways, but you did nonetheless. I was a mean, codependent bitch and couldn't free myself from what Frances, sweet Frances calls «a vicious cycle of abuse», but you freed me, doing so by snapping your fingers. The fact that you didn't intend to do so shouldn't matter, right?

The venom and longing in her voice and her seething emotions haunted him.

Liz and Frances watched him from across the room, as he was being surrounded by the girls, as they coddled and admired him, and wanted to *comfort* him.

– Look at that, Liz said with disgust in her voice and eyes. – See them melt in the heat of his sore smile. There's nothing they won't do for the poor boy.

She closed and opened her eyes once, her features softening.

– He's… letting go, she said. – He can do that, now. I wish I could.

– He's a guy, Frances said. – It's easier for them.

– No. Liz shook her head. – It isn't that, isn't like that. You don't understand…

There was a slight break, followed by a wicked grin making Frances shiver.

– But you will!

5

The final rays of the sunny day faded to neon lights and shadows. Freshwater, the derelict and condemned building where raffle and artists gathered was lit up by distant lights. People arrived early. Some of them walked inside immediately, while others lingered outside, chatting and relaxing.

The buzz picked up as the strangers, the true strangers arrived. Glances and stares followed their every step. Patrick Warren and the two women in his company met Liz and Ted and the guys by the rusty fire hydrant between the north corner and the entrance.

– Hello again, Patrick said cheerfully.

– It is so nice to meet, isn't it? Liz said and nodded to herself.

From the opposite side Lee and Carla and bunch approached. Lee and most of the teenagers stared just as much as the others. Carla didn't. Lee noticed and noticed the eerie expression shifting on her face. She noticed that he noticed and uncharacteristically squeezed his hand.

– You will be there. Carla nodded, too, more to herself than to him. – There is no way around it. We will all be there.

– What do you mean? He asked, but didn't really expect an answer.

And that was a correct assumption. She downright ignored him or at least his query and kept walking.

They penetrated the deep darkness and shadows of the «establishment». Everybody moved through a long hallway with shifting light. There was a kind of art on the wall, sort of horizontal stripes illuminated by a glow coming from nowhere. Lee couldn't keep the dream visions from coming. He sort-of experienced them as fleeting glimpses in the haze surrounding them. They emerged into a window-less hall with glowing red window frames and eerie drawings on the walls. Everything turned even more surreal.

– I'm getting goose bumps all over, Lydia smiled sweetly at him, – and they don't let up.

A guy was snapping photographs. Lee, in a daze recognized Eric Carr, yet another infamous face from the papers and realized he was photographing everyone present. The guy looked downright... elated.

The eerie feeling of displacement only grew when the boy caught the sight of the giant woman that had been... stalking him at the edge of his vision.

Linsey Kendall and the band entered the stage. The first few chords sounded through the speakers.

– Welcome to tonight's performance at Freshwater, he greeted his audience with what seemed like the confidence of a seasoned performing veteran. –

We are so happy to be here tonight, at this palace of thoughts and music and art.

There was a light irony in his voice sitting well with the audience drawn to informal places such as these. There were a few clapping their hands and cheering, all of it sounding flat and unconvincing and unappealing. The first roar of a riff drowned that and everything else.

– The christians are coming, sire, the man by his side said. – They're coming fast, faster than the horses they ride.

Lewis blinked. There was no man by his side, at least not anyone resembling the one he had seen in his blink.

The music… touched him, evoking sensations he couldn't quite identify. He observed the others, noticing how it penetrated them.

Linsey began singing. Lee's companions and most people present began swaying and clapping their hands. Sudden hard guitar riffs slashed everyone present.

Or so it felt, like actual waves hitting flesh.

Ted Warren walked around taking photos as well, using a fairly expensive SLR-camera, but not of the same class as the one Carr used. He worked fast, so fast that the camera seemed to be alive in his hands. He didn't use flash. Lewis imagined that he perceived the world as brief, frozen images. The boy frowned.

Carla studied him, and the giant amazon across the room did as well. He frowned again.

Ted took her picture. She looked at him with her steady and intense stare. Suddenly Lewis was so dizzy that he could hardly stand.

The well-muscled man hammered his drums. He missed a beat. The pause seemed to linger forever. Linsey hammered his guitar. The bass player did as well. The drummer joined in again. Time started anew.

What little light there was seemed to take on a different quality, slitting into colors. There was something there, too, jolting many of those present.

Lewis found himself on a dark field lit by a few candles, a field filled with people. The candles didn't really breach the darkness at all. Everyone seemed cast in Shadow.

There was a group performing on a low, makeshift stage. Their music sent wild, heathen moods into everyone's elated minds.

The first song ended. Relative silence reentered the hall. There was applause of a kind. There was excitement, even though it was muted.

– We are *Mystic*. Jesse Coleman plays drums. Alvin Draper plays bass.

– And Linsey Kendall plays guitar and screams, Draper added, ending the presentation.

Linsey smiled, very pleasant.

– This place will be famous in a couple of decades, I guess, he said, – the place where it all began, or one of 'em. We *know* when we play this that it is forever.

That statement *would* gain immense notoriety…

– Disco is dead and we celebrate, Draper shouted.

Beginning his deep rumble, the start of the new song. Coleman joined in, and then, after ten, fifteen seconds, when it seemed that he wouldn't Kendall did.

Lydia swayed in Lewis' arms during the calmer parts of the music, and rocked in his vision during the hard and wild. Mystic shifting between this and that seemed like a rollercoaster ride and the majority of those present began participating in earnest. Except for Patrick and Eric and the women standing with them, and the giant woman towering above everyone, everybody was young, in their middle twenties or younger. There was dance, but not only the dance apparent. The floor was hardly more than half full. There was plenty of room. Everybody swayed. Almost everybody in the hall swayed in one dance, superimposing that of each individual.

They were dancing, alone together, or so it seemed, but only seemed.

Lewis saw swords raised and swords falling, cutting warm, warm flesh, saw heads roll and limbs severed. The child, the girl stood among countless dead bodies, unharmed. He knelt in front of her, a thousand tiny wounds leaking his blood, the heart hammering in his chest.

It beat so loud, overwhelming the sound of swords and screams and whining guitars and drums.

Lewis ran off, fled from the overwhelming noise and his own, hammering heart.

He stood outside, sick to the bone, hardly able to hold on to the rail at the nearby corner, his gasps loud enough to wake the dead. He felt them, felt them wake up, all around him.

– Are you alright?

The giant woman towered above him. He stared incredulous at her.

– I'm fine, thank you, he replied without thinking.

– You don't look so good…

– What is it to you? He wondered sullenly.

In spite of the typically teenage male bravado response he was unable to keep his curiosity from manifesting itself.

She was smiling, he knew she was, behind that immovable mask of hers.

– Come she said, – let's go back inside.

And he followed the broad and tall figure, the sexy, well-curved woman back into the mist and shadow. He realized that the hall was strangely silent and no more loud noise was forthcoming.

Sparks seemed to fly everywhere and smoke flowed from much of the machinery. The stench of burned rubber and heated metal ripped into his nostrils. Strangely enough, it hardly bothered him and certainly not in any way he could easily identify.

– Sorry, guys, Linsey shrugged from behind the microphone, one not amplifying his voice at all, – looks like the setup is permanently fried, at least for this particular night.

He left the ruined stage. Liz met him and embraced him and kissed him.

– Too bad, she shrugged, too. – You guys have become pretty good, especially considering the low point you started out…

– Thanks, I think, he said.

Ted was there, and Patrick and Eric and several others.

Lydia rushed into Lewis' arms, kissing him passionately, very passionately on the lips. Lewis followed the giant to that place in front of the stage and his friends followed him.

– Lewis, she said, – these people, Liz, Ted, Patrick and Linsey are your kin.

He blinked. The others smiled, smiles tinged with a sadness he suddenly understood remarkably well. He turned towards the tall, towering woman.

– Who are you? He blurted out.

– I? I'm your mother, Lewis.

And it was at that point his smile grew and that warm, warm feeling inside grew as well, until he imagined that it drowned him, like the warmest and tallest of waves.

Chapter 5

More than anything it was the smell that got to him.

The rows of beds seemed to go on forever. The drab colors on the walls augmented the sense of despair.

He looked at all or most of the Abraxas Omega slaves that hadn't enjoyed Mark Stewart's special touch. He sensed their dull minds, even though he knew he, logically speaking shouldn't.

– Ted is here, Jane Morris, the nurse said to Diana McKenzie. – Do you remember, Ted?

– Ted, Diana repeated dully.

There were no signs of recognition in those empty eyes.

She was wearing a straightjacket, like all the patients in this room, at this hospital north of Washington DC. They were considered dangerous. There had been incidents where they had injured and even killed, practically slaughtered hospital personnel.

The violent, engraved lessons rested within the dull minds and seemingly weakened bodies.

– Ted is here, Jane said to Helen Cumbes. – Do you remember Ted?

There was no discernible reaction.

They repeated the procedure in what they both felt was an endless line, with the same, dreadful result.

The most boring classical tune attacked them like sleep from all sides.

– I can't stand that music, he snarled dully. – It's lulling them to sleep and making them stay that way.

– It's supposed to be soothing, she said promptly.

Then she giggled hysterically, on the verge of tears.

He actually felt physically tired, his feet sore when he and Jane finally retreated to the room beyond the fortified walls and iron bars.

She pushed herself at him, sobbing against his chest.

– It's so good to finally meet you again, she sniffed. – It was never the same after you and the guys left.

Images and sensation of his time in the squatted building in London flashed through his mind. He remembered mostly rage and loss.

– Look at me. She pulled back a little and smiled through her tears. – I'm sipping like a baby.

She started pacing the floor.

– I remember, she cried out, – remember everything, our discussions, our passion, the dream of a better world, everything we shared. I will never

forget.
She looked at him with a familiar hope and despair in her eyes. He knew well how that was.
– I haven't forgotten my… pledge, she said. – I will just stay here a while and help out.
Her words brought even more powerful sensations and associations to his conscious mind.
And all of it kept haunting him.
– You're so different, she mused, – so… mature, but still the same, perhaps even more than ever a walking fighting machine in human form. Everything I've heard about you in recent years confirms that you are. I love that, I just love that!
Her spirit and passion rocked him. She had not truly changed from the spirited and radical young girl he had known either, even if despair had entered her eyes, had diluted her spark.
Eric waited outside. He hadn't been allowed inside.
– Anything? He asked.
– Nothing.
Ted shook his head, shook it again.
He struck his right hand through the window. The guard watched while he did it, but didn't move from his position and his newspaper. Ted pulled the hand back out. Blood flowed for a brief moment and splinters of glass seemed to cover his hands. The splinters were pushed out as Eric watched. The hand healed in a matter of seconds and completely, without any remaining marks in less than a minute.
They walked back out, to the parking lot and the queue of taxis.
Both caught the sight of the woman, of Carla just as they turned the corner. Ted didn't have to look at Eric to know that the older man reacted very similar to Ted himself. They froze, even as they kept moving forward. They blinked, even as the blink didn't bring darkness, but a confusing array of images and sensations, of illumination inverted.
– It was a nice concert, wasn't it? She grinned.
And the two young men saw a rainbow of somber colors in her eyes.
– How did you know we were here? Eric demanded.
Carla didn't reply. Ted didn't speak.
– The world just doesn't make sense. She shook her head in sadness. – It doesn't make sense even if we take a step back and enjoy the painting, but it makes slightly more sense.
Ted looked at her, studied her, recalling her from every angle he had observed her during and after the brief concert, when they had all gathered

around the long table and celebrated like old friends.

– But this veil of tears… is just that.

She indicated their surroundings. He understood, without further considerations that she didn't mean merely what was right around them.

– You're right, he acknowledged. – It shouldn't have any significance beyond itself, but it has.

– It sticks to you, she said softly. – The horror of the modern world never truly let you go. It gets to you, inevitably.

He recalled the moment when she had raised her huge glass of mead and tipped it over and the content had flowed into her mouth and down her throat. Her laughter still echoed in his ears.

– You have traveled the world? Eric said incredulous. – You must have started early, in diapers to be exact.

– I always start early, Eric, she said.

The first in the long line of taxis stopped in front of them. Ted could easily note the impatience, the high stress factor in the man behind the wheel. It didn't impress him, and he didn't move, or make any move to sign that he was ready to move.

Lee had presented her to his new kin with a strange look in his eyes, one that the others had no difficulties understanding after they had been properly introduced.

– Ted, she had said and repeated softly, as if tasting the name. – Ted.

And then:

– Liz… Liz.

She hadn't said Linsey or Patrick's name.

– Hello again, she had said and taken his hand.

Ted joined Eric in the backseat.

– She adds another layer to the word enigmatic, doesn't she…

Ted nodded with a remote expression in his very expressive face, as the car started moving and drove away.

In his eyes reflected in the window he saw hers, saw more glimpses from the night after the concert, heard her laughter, the music when she spoke.

– Yes, I would say you're more than…

He stopped, as if catching himself.

It was then they both realized that Carla hadn't joined them in the taxi.

2

Liz met Frances at a fancy restaurant on the East Side. The entire scene rubbed her off the wrong way from the start, even before she had actually entered the premises. She stopped outside for a moment, two, a look of disgust on her face, before shaking her head and moving inside.

The smile that broke on her face would have scared people to death if anyone had seen it.

The low growl of a chuckle made people turn their heads as she walked up the stairs to the restaurant on the second floor.

Liz Warren, a young girl of twenty with a sweet smile wore a dark violet dress. Her waterfall of hair reached to her hips. It flowed and danced around her like fire, like shadow.

– Good evening, Miss Warren, a waiter coughed. – Miss Stern is waiting by the window table. If you will follow me, please?

– By all means, she grinned. – Lead on…

The way she moved reminded all watching her of a wild beast, she knew that, even though they didn't.

Frances brightened when she spotted Liz and waved enthusiastically. She rose and greeted the newcomer with a kiss on the cheek. Liz returned it. They sat down.

– They stare at you, Frances said conspiratorially.

– They always stare at me, Liz shrugged.

– I'm so glad you agreed to meet me, Frances said. – We have so much to talk about.

– As I said, Liz grinned darkly, – as long as you were willing to take the risk of inviting me here, I'm more than willing to oblige you…

The two laughed together.

They looked through the menu. Liz hardly saw the golden letters.

– I can recommend the veal, Frances said. – It's quite good.

Liz mumbled something, replying to the voice mumbling within. She didn't really pay attention. The pair of glowing embers penetrated Frances and revealed her insides like a flaying knife. The blonde woman shuddered.

They both ordered the veal.

– Raw, please, Liz flashed her fangs to the poor waiter.

The two young women sat there, facing each other. Liz looked at Frances. In one glimpse, three, she saw three different faces. Memory assaulted her. She heard the sounds and noises from a battlefield. Her lips moved. She mumbled something.

– What language is that? She heard the other speak from far away.

– Huh? She replied before she could stop herself.

– You were distracted, Frances grinned. – Don't worry about it. I get that a lot myself.

She raised her glass. Liz raised hers. They had a toast.

– To freedom, Frances said.
Liz echoed her sentiment.
They drank.
– Do you like it? Frances asked anxiously. – I took the liberty of picking it. I hope you don't mind.
– I like it.
Liz looked around her without moving. Her eyes, often constantly moving were fixed on her companion.
– It was Old English, she said distracted, not distracted.
– Pardon? Frances said nonplussed.
– The words I spoke. They are Old English, «the tongue of the enemy». They are from Eboracum, Jórvík, Old York, first heard in the city by the Celts and the few remaining Roman citizens when the Anglo-Saxons invaded the country in the fifth century.
Frances frowned a bit, but then her face cracked in a smile.
– You know so much, she marveled. – It is as I thought: I can learn so much from you.
Liz felt herself opening. Unable to put a stop to it, she let it happen, let it flow freely.
– Have you heard about Michel de Nostredame? She asked.
– You mean Nostradamus? Frances giggled. – Yes, definitely!
– Many get him wrong on at least a couple of points. Liz closed and opened her eyes. – They say he could predict the future, but that isn't entirely accurate. He remembered, remembered the past and the future equally. He said that we had forgotten our most crucial tenet and that we all must learn to remember to become fully human. They said he suffered through his visions, but he didn't. He suffered because he was never able to recall enough, to make them powerful enough to see everything he wanted to see.
– You sound like you knew him, Frances joked.
Liz held her eyes closed a moment longer.
– They said he was falling, not through space, but through time, that he repeated his life in an endless loop he was unable to escape from, and that no matter what he did he could never make things right. Some say he died screaming, that he is screaming still, living his endless loop in some history different from our own.
She shook visibly and Frances did, too.
– Eboracum was a fairly important Roman conclave, Liz mused. – Constantine was proclaimed emperor there. His father died there. But the Celts kept fighting the Romans - and the Christians until they left. It was the Anglo-Saxons that brought the final end to the old ways of life on what

is now known as the British Isles. The Anglo-Saxon riders arrived at dawn, forever casting the night in darkness.

She knew that Frances cast her eyes at the rest of the room, not really seeing anything but Liz and her immediate surroundings.

– I've always dreamed about riders, Frances whispered, – suffered nightmares of soldiers riding in the early dawn.

– I know you have, Liz nodded.

And from that moment on, Frances never took her eyes off her.

Frances sat with a man with fireeyes in a dining room in a castle with only natural lights. She stared deep into Liz's eyes. The brief vision seemed to last forever, and lingered long after it had ended.

The food arrived with the usual politeness and splendor. A few common phrases of good wishes were uttered.

«Hope you will enjoy the meal».

Liz began devouring the food. She grabbed it with her hands and began feeding, never even considering the knife and fork as tools.

Frances giggled, chuckled again, striving to contain herself. Liz kept talking between the bites.

– To remember is to know pain, to embrace all parts of life and sadly we're all reluctant to do that.

– I try to figure out how you can be such an expert in languages, Frances mused, a catching audible in her voice. – Nothing I've heard about you even suggest the how concerning that.

– I guess there will be great confusion and controversy when future historians look back at my life and try to look beyond the juicy bits, Liz grinned.

Frances, with a determined look on her face began eating with her hands as well, creating shockwaves throughout the room.

– It is said that Satan speaks all languages, Liz said lightly.

A deep chill entered the room, or so many imagined.

– That is also said about three of his servants or *aspects*.

She shrugged.

– It's all bullshit, of course. There is no Satan, no God.

And the stench of sweat in the room grew even more pronounced. She knew it would linger, long after they had left.

They walked through a tiny part of Central Park afterwards.

Frances laughed heartily.

– I can never show my mug in that restaurant again.

Their walk seemed peaceful, slow-moving and casual, two young women on a pleasant, daytime stroll.

They sat on a bench by Bow Bridge, looking at people passing by. The flock of birds rose from the Lake. Liz rose with them and fell with them, fell from the tall, tall sky. She heard the sounds from The Ramble, the domesticated forest nearby.

– We walked through the jungle, Liz related. – We encountered a tribe and spoke its language. It was ancient. There was no way we could have learned it, and we didn't. We knew it, knew its heart and by heart. It is so easy remembering in the jungle. We forgot everything not important.

– It is so great hearing you speak about it, Frances said. – I feel like I am actually there, with you.

– It feels so long ago, and still so close in space and time, Liz mused passionately. – I can reach out and touch all the bad and the good and great.

Frances jumped on her feet.

– C'mon, she called, eager like a girl, – let's take a walk through the forest.

Liz rose and joined her on the trail through the city forest. Frances grabbed her hand and they held hands. Liz easily felt the other's churning emotions.

– What do you think? Frances wondered.

– I like it in here, in spite of it being a fake forest, Liz replied. – There are lots of spirits in the city, both living and dead, angry and clingy, but not so many here. I can be alone in my mind.

And the puppy-look in the other woman's eyes grew even more pronounced.

The fake forest of asphalt, shingle and fences imposed itself on Liz. She kept holding the other woman's hand.

Impressions, small and big events in Frances' life assaulted her.

– I'm a psychic vampire, she said flatly. – I can't hold on to you for long without seriously draining you. After a while you won't be able to stand, and then, a while after that you will die.

Two hands let go. The pleasant flow of life was cut off.

– I'm sorry, Frances said, both startled and sympathetic. – It must feel bad for you.

– You didn't know, Liz said. – Now, you do! Take comfort in the fact that you believe my outrageous claim, that there is no disbelief in your mind and stance.

They walked on. Liz felt the other's eyes on her, the constant glances of curiosity, fear and fascination.

And growing worship and affection.

– You are an open book to me, Liz stated, with a touch of a patronizing sneer she couldn't conceal. – I know you from your very first breath.

– I've never met anyone like you, Frances Stern whimpered.

They entered a particular spot in the forest. Liz noticed that, too, easily, the expectation in Francis, the passion and nervous energy surrounding them.

Two men sat on a bench, engaged in obvious, passionate kissing. She looked at Frances. The woman, suddenly as nervous as an inexperienced teenager, looked down. Finding the necessary courage, she grabbed Liz hand again and stepped close to her, and kissed her lips.

– They burn, she said, breathing faster. – Somehow, I knew they would.

She kissed harder and didn't back off. Liz found herself responding.

– Vampires have familiars, have they not? I offer myself…

Liz' eyes began glowing, glowing more than strong enough to dwarf any light in the shadow of the forest, in the suddenly so very dim light of the forest. Frances sighed content.

She looked in awe at the shadow towering before her.

– This is a secluded area, a free zone where we come to…

Liz stepped away. The glow in her eyes remained. The excitement in Frances' eyes faded.

– But you're not interested, are you?

– I'm not, Liz said, not unkindly.

– But I saw you on the photographs from the jungle. You kissed and fondled several women.

– That was different, in the heat of the group fucking. We shared ourselves generously with our tribe.

– And they came to you, giving of themselves, paying homage to their Goddess, didn't they?

Liz didn't say anything.

– I can do that, Frances choked. – Please, I want to.

Liz was about to respond, but got distracted.

She turned around. A group of well-dressed and well-groomed men and women had entered the tiny spot of the world, already disrupting whatever peace existed here.

– They…

– I know, Liz said.

The despair in the other had become even more pronounced.

– Look what we have here, the leader cried. – Such sweet people, but people being sweet to others of the same sex. What's *wrong* with this picture?

The male couple had frozen, looking sullenly at the new arrivals. Several other approaching people stopped and was about to turn and leave.

Liz stepped forward. Everybody noticed it when she did.

– Everybody stay, she said. – Do not let yourself be intimidated by these… intruders.

Everybody recognized her. Those she called intruders did, too.
She turned towards them.
– I had you figured out by a glance, she told them. – It isn't difficult for a human being to recognize people behaving like inhuman scum.
– Now, listen… the leader began.
He faltered. Everybody easily saw that.
– No, you listen! She snapped, eerily calm.
She moved fast, so fast that they could hardly see her move. She walked slowly, casually to the big man and stopped in front of him. She was slightly taller than he was.
– You and your entourage will leave and you will never return here. Have I made myself clear?
– Are you threatening us? He yelped, unable to meet her burning eyes.
– You will never return. If you do, and if you bully and harass and use mental or physical violence against anyone ever again, I will come for you. Do you *understand?*
– Y-yes!
She turned to the rest of them.
– YES! They choired.
Suddenly, during the course of just a few seconds they had been reduced to simpering cowards, revealing their true nature.
– You're not so brave when you cannot beat up on defenseless people, are you now? She asked softly.
Her burning stare focused on a rather large woman behind the leader.
– N-no.
– You are Hugo Manning's pathetic brethren, are you not?
– Yes, the other woman nodded eagerly.
– Well, take this to your leader then. Impart the importance of my message to him, tell him that if he or any of his flock beat up more people because you guys disagree with their sexual orientation or for any other reason what so ever, you will all pay. *Do you understand?*
– YES! Everybody choired in body and mind.
– Very good. Liz smiled. – Now, you assholes will remove yourself from my presence.
They ran, they stumbled, they ran and couldn't run fast enough.
Everyone remaining stared at her, the beast in their midst in awe and fear.
– America is a country where open racism, misogyny and homophobia are considered acceptable and desirable, she said. – Whatever we do in a smaller scale will not be sufficient to correct that, but know that from now on this place, this entire forest has become a sanctuary, one protected by the Janus

Clan. Seek me out when those with venom in their minds and mouths, and burning crosses in their hands breach that. I won't be hard to find.

Those remaining looked at her, they all looked at her.

– Thank you, one of them men said. – Thank you so much.

Liz nodded, once.

She left. Frances followed her, flowing in her slipstream.

– That was *amazing,* she breathed. – You stopped them, stopped them without lifting a finger. They believed, believed to their core every word you spoke to them.

She hurried to keep up with the younger woman, rushed to her side, glancing coyly and somber at her.

– As do I.

They crossed Bow Bridge again, and continued walking east, leaving the park. They emerged back on the Upper East Side. Liz instantly felt vomit gather in her throat and decided she wouldn't stand for it a second longer. They headed south.

Liz passed people on the street and in the subway. She spotted them, marked their faces and features, but didn't truly see them.

– Look at them, she said to Frances, indicating everybody around them. – They look like mannequins in display windows.

The surroundings raced slowly, but indistinct around her. She focused briefly on the occasional face, but it soon joined the others in her inner display window.

They had drinks in the bar at some seedy off-Broadway theater. Frances cast nervous glances at the dubious clientele, at practically everybody else in the room staring at the two girls, leaving no doubt what was on their mind.

– See what I mean? Liz said. – A fair-haired, tall and curvy female like you is worth a lot on the meat market. I can get fifty grand for you, perhaps twice that in a lucky moment.

Frances frowned. She had forgotten what the conversation had been about and could not grasp the context.

– You don't understand, Liz said softly. And then adding, grinning in spite. – But you will!

Low keyed music was playing in the background. They didn't have any trouble hearing each other speak. Liz could easily hear everybody else in the room without the gathering noise intruding on her acute audio sense.

– I would say almost half of the males in the room talk about fucking us right now. Most of the other half and also some of the women are thinking about it.

– They haven't spiked the drinks, Frances joked. – That's something, right?

– You're right, Liz acknowledged. – They haven't, but they could have, and we wouldn't have been able to detect it.
– You couldn't… either?
– I can detect more than most people, but there are poisons I wouldn't be able to taste in liquor, I know that.
– «Date rape drugs» are one of the most used «introductions» to prostitution, Frances said, a visible chill passing through her. – By the time a given victim comes out of it she may be well beyond the first stages. I have to admit I would never dared go here if I was not with you. Look at them. They know Liz Warren sits here and want you, want you badly, but they don't even dare approach us. You would make mincemeat of anybody threatening us.
She squeezed the other girl's arm.
– You know I will destroy you, you know that, right?
Liz Warren said, with such a dull voice that it made the other girl turn cold to the bone.
She drank the entire glass in a sweep. Frances knew she couldn't keep up with her and didn't try. She only looked glum at the dark girl across the table.
Liz went to the restroom, leaving Frances behind. She did her best to appear unaffected by the other's absence. A man crossed the floor. Suddenly she had trouble swallowing. He didn't approach her, but choose a completely different direction. Relief mixed with shame and determination in her mind, her dulled and burning mind.
Frances found her small tape recorder and spoke into it.
– I want to challenge myself. I've started documenting things, mostly in an attempt to get a grip on myself.
She put it away quickly, well before Liz returned from the restroom. Everyone glanced at her as she did. She was humming a dark, dark melody, one sending chills down everyone's spine. They got a sense that they weren't in this room at all, but somewhere completely different and sinister. Reality itself seemed to change around her form.
– Relieving myself always feels good, the dark girl said, flashing her fangs.
Frances downed another shot of Scotch…
They walked back towards the apartment in Hell's Kitchen, taking a detour. They sat on the bench inside Port Authority at night, pissed drunk.
– You show them, Frances mumbled happily, - show them what pathetic losers they are.
Beggars, homeless, scam artists, pimps and late travelers walked back and forth. Liz spotted Justin Bieber at the entrance, performing his snake oil salesman tricks on some young, innocent bird. Frances didn't notice or seem

to notice. Liz leaned her head on the other woman's shoulder, her forehead touching the skin on Frances's neck. She waited for her powers to kick in and purge the alcohol from her body, but it didn't happen, at least not in any noticeable way. The despair returned with a vengeance. She fought against it, but couldn't keep it from happening. Weary eyes closed. She drifted off, into the night, into the endless dark streets of her mind.

3

– I don't need to tell you, Ethel Warren told them. – I can do much better than that. I can show you.

They were gathered at Ethel's penthouse, not that many of them, Ted, Liz, Patrick, Lewis, Eric and Carla, and some in their circles. The room, lit by candles was cast in Shadow.

Lee studied Carla. She drew him to her, as always. She looked both interested and not, as if she was both present in this room and not. He noticed her strange smile, not only when she looked at him, but at almost all others in the room. She looked at Ted and Liz, and they studied her.

They all studied Ethel, as she prepared, as she made her kingdom. Walls rose around them, as their surroundings, as everything around them became the old Warren family crypt in London thirty-five years ago and ghosts of time seemed to recreate themselves before their eyes.

4
DISTANT BUTTERFLY WINGS
London 1944

Nick Warren stood there, wrecked with sadness, filled with burning passion and determination. He held the attention of Jonas Bergli, of his young kin Mark, Ethel, Jack, Joel and Trudy.

– We are so few, Nick said, – and so each we lose is precious to us, and these two were precious beyond life itself.

Nine-year-old Ethel could spot Dust in the air, in the heavy rain. It brightened the darkness to the point that she imagined she experienced slow flashes of daylight. She saw it dance around everybody present.

– We will stay together, Nick stated passionately, – and we will prevail against anyone threatening us. There is something special about us, something making us different from almost all others. We are special, and we will seek out everybody else that is special out there, both kin and not, because in a way they all are.

Ethel closed her eyes for a tiny moment, and the scenery changed, but didn't truly change at all. She witnessed other places like this, other funerals and sad partings, and she experienced all of them, all of it simultaneously. Carla was there, a different-looking Carla, but always the same. Everybody was there, even those currently in the coffins. None of them looked the same, but she still recognized them. In New York, in 1979 everybody gasped in true and sweet and sad shock and awe.

Nick stood there, before the children in a shimmering light, as if he wasn't really there, even if he was very much present. The children looked at him with sad eyes.

Everything not matter faded away. There were only Nick and the rain. He held around the children and Jonas did, too. They both did, held them in a protective embrace.

– It will be alright, Nick, Ethel stated serious-minded, very adult.

He ruffled her hair and looked at her with huge, sad eyes.

The children reached for the sound giving life to the air, any sound they could grasp, but there was none, except the steady downpour of the rain.

The gathering of family and friends pulled back to the house eventually, to the warm and pleasant mansion. The kids began playing again, after a few, uncertain glances at Nick. He nodded to them, not pleased with that, and nodded again, giving them a brittle smile.

He walked to the library and found Carla there. She stood by the window, looking out at the empty garden.

– You should have been there, he said.

– I don't care much for funerals, you know that.

– You should have been there, he repeated.

She turned to face him, smiling softly to him. He noticed more than before how her hair had turned gray and her face more wrinkled.

– I am fed up with sad partings, Carla said.

He perceived her as pale in the warm glow from the fireplace. Somewhere within him something scratched and burned. It always did.

– I don't know why exactly. It shouldn't be that much of deal. We're only burning ashes, after all.

He knew what she meant, even though he didn't quite understand it, not yet.

– We're burning ashes, waiting for the fire to rise again.

She smiled and turned, meeting him halfway. He felt her energy. Even now, fading, in its almost dormant state he burned in her glow.

They kissed and touched. She wanted him, desired him with a growing desperation that couldn't be denied.

– I hate growing old, she said abruptly. – I hate being old.
The vision and sensations of those that listened and watched from a vantage point far away in time and space turned soft and misty. Focus shifted to another part of the estate.
There was a tiny pond at the back, in the colder shadow of the building. Mark played there, in and out of the water. His eyes caught a frog swimming, swimming towards land. He studied it as it reached the shore, as it made its first jump on land.
The waves kept twirling in the water. The boy felt like he was immersed in it, in them, in the unending waves.
A foot stamped on the frog, crushing it to a pulp.
Mark frowned, as he looked up at Jack, as his eyes met his, and in that moment, that instant of time both their futures were mapped out like two railway tracks.

5

Lewis walked with Jean through busy streets. He felt more than a little awkward and silly walking side by side with a woman so much taller and bigger than himself. Countless confusing emotions raged through him.
– Your father and I grew... desperate. We decided that in order to protect you from beyond dangerous enemies we needed to give you away, hide you in obscurity.
– And now he is dead? The boy stated quietly, sullenly.
– Yes, both he and the man we hid you from. A feud started before you were born has been resolved. Another begun long before that remains unresolved.
She smiled to him, an affection smothering him.
– You're a part of the Janus Clan, she told him. – So am I, even though initially only through association and then affection and then horror. I married one of my brothers and helped kill the other. Already during childhood my fate became yours, but I didn't realize that until that day in the horrible ruin.
– Yours, not mine, he said, accusing her, – the «Janus Clan», Ted, Liz, Carla, Patrick, Ethel and god knows how many others.
– We have become many, she said. – I have been told that hasn't always been the case. Ethel has told me much about it, about centuries of violence and strife where your ancestors barely survived long enough to breed. We're finally coming into our own.
Flashes raged through his mind, sensations and images without attachment.

She looked at him with affection and worry.

– I'm strong, he stated. – I can handle this, all this.

– I know you can, she said sadly. – I still wished a different life for you.

She walked a few more steps towards the sea below the Brooklyn Bridge.

– But I was fooling myself. There was and is no escape from the vast forces tugging at us.

The big woman grabbed him and kissed him on the brow. He resisted, but it was like overcoming a tall bulldog. It took her no effort at all.

– I will be around, she told him softly, – but those posing as your parents during large parts of your life will manage fine a few more years, until they're no longer needed for anything.

One second, ten after that he stood alone by East River. Ten minutes, ten seconds later Carla snuck up on him.

– Come, young Warren, she joked, – I've been charged with your further training, both in the mysteries and in the arts.

He knew what she meant, or at least glimpsed the facts behind her words.

– My grandmother's surname was Warren, he pondered, – but you use that as if it is mine.

– There is truth behind my words, she said casually.

She snuggled close to him, kissed him on the neck.

The crossing of the bridge was lost in incalculable time. Sometime later, while the sun still hung high on the sky he joined Carla's other warriors at the warehouse on Manhattan. It was still dusty there and the dust split the light in the air like a haze.

– You have dreams, haven't you? She spoke to him softly by his ear, in the midst of the fighting and sweating and pain and increasing awareness. – You've had them since you were a child, haunting images and sensations of a group of people charging through a desert. You see me there, and Ted and Liz, and many others.

And on some level, even though it didn't quite seem real to him, he acknowledged the truth of her words.

They trained and fought with wands. It seemed like every thrust, every move was familiar to him, as if he didn't really have to learn anything, but only remember.

Loud, muffled sounds of thunder reached them from the basement, where one group trained with firearms.

The feeling of the gun in his hand still lingered on the skin. His wrist hurt.

Firing the gun had felt awkward at first, but he had quickly gained mastery over it. He could hardly believe how fast he had learned to fire with deadly accuracy. It was as if he had been born with the ability to do that.

Suddenly pain surged through him and he couldn't quite tell if it was his flesh or the vast emptiness within being filled that hurt the most.

Eric Carr had joined up as instructor some time ago. He seemed to be everywhere simultaneously with his nervous, excited energy.

She stood there, Carla stood there in their midst, in the mist of their vision, speaking softly, making everybody listen.

– Speak to me, shadow, speak about nothing at all, about all things and none in the long chain of our existence.

They repeated the words, as if they had spoken them and she hadn't. Voices hesitant at first, rose towards the ceiling, penetrated the mist and shadow brightening their awareness.

Terrence and Stane fought, clumsy at first, but then remarkably fast getting less clumsy somewhat.

Eloise, right there in front of Lewis, at the other side of the circle, met his eyes. He blinked, and in that moment, that blink he imagined he didn't see her face at all, but one startlingly different.

Lydia smiled to him with promise in the deep wells she used to study him.

She looked like an older woman he didn't know. Then she looked like the spunky, sensual teenager again.

He felt a scream inside, a pain tearing at him, a joy he could hardly contain.

– We need to learn to remember, Carla stated.

Then they did, briefly, in a slice of time lasting forever.

6

There were riders, in the early morning light, in the twilight of early evening. The tall and big man standing on the palisades surrounding the township stared into the night, seeing far more than his eyes could show him.

The woman stood behind him. He could always sense her, even smell her without wind. He turned and knelt before her, like he had done in a field of bloody and mangled bodies when she had been only a girl.

– My Lady.

– Please, Melville, she said, fingering with the wolf-head pendant hanging in a chain around her neck, – you know how I feel about those groveling at my feet.

He got up, a little awkward.

– That's better, she said pleased. – Isn't that so much better, my friend?

He didn't voice a reply, but bowed his head to her wisdom, as always. She sighed.

The big township of Jorekstad woke up around them, those not already awake after a restless and practically sleepless night of fear, of terror and rage shaking them to the bone.

People filed towards the two of them, paying their respect, an act always making both of them uneasy, and Melville understood a bit of what Wolf always attempted to convey to him. It took some time, but people, men, women and even older children found their spot on the wall, standing there with their spears, bows, and knives and any sharp object they could find.

Everybody looked into the mist. No matter where they looked there was nothing but mist.

Melville turned tense, as he sensed movement, inside and outside the wall. People were running. Panic, abject fear was picking up. One man approached the woman and man on the palisade.

– The christians are coming, sire, the man said to the man, not quite daring to look at the woman, at the somewhat serene figure to his right. – They are coming fast, faster than the horses they ride.

Melville saw them, Lewis sensed them, as they moved across the plains, approaching the fortified township ahead, as they moved through the ether, through the centuries.

– They are men, you know, he said quietly, – even despicable men, with no support except their brutality and numbers and beyond wicked ways.

The messenger nodded, and everybody else did as well, glancing at the two of them with reverence in their eyes.

They believe we are equal to them, he thought, equal to the riders, and they see that as a good thing.

He took a step forward. The sound of that step reverberated throughout the fortress.

– We will FIGHT! He cried. – We will fight as if the riders' version of hell is at our heels, because it is.

Shields, weapons and various forms of cutlery were raised to the heavens with the loud response, the battle cry sounding across the land.

– They will slaughter every single man, woman and child within these walls, he shouted. – Our only recourse is to fight and keep fighting for as long as we breathe and even beyond that. Kill them, kill them with every weapon and opportunity at your disposal. Never give up fighting, not even in the land beyond!

The warriors, everybody within the fortified structure repeated his words, mumbled, swore to themselves.

He saw the enemy beyond the mist, felt them on their horses, the dead men riding to spread their insane gospel. The sound of riders appeared before they became visible. Facing them, welcoming them was quickened heartbeats, the shaking of all available blades.

And the water in the rivers and the moisture in the air turned to blood, and Dust filled more of the shadowland beyond.

Chapter 6

Liz placed herself exactly at the entrance of the Port Authority. There was a breeze so very cold. She started shivering, and wanted to leave, but was unable to move.

– That's not thighs, Liz blurted out in contempt to a skin and bone woman passing by. – That's skinny sticks masquerading as thighs.

The woman speeded up, passing by as fast as she was able, without actually running. Liz grinned, but she felt no true triumph, only more of the same hollow within.

Justin Bieber was close, she knew he was. There were others of his kind here as well, there always were, but he would be the one approaching her. He waited several minutes, very patient. She stayed put. He crossed the street in a casual stroll, and eventually stopped in front of her. She lowered her eyes, unable to meet his wicked, mocking stare.

– Hello, Liz, he said sweetly.

– H'lo, she mumbled.

He grabbed her and kissed her. She responded without resistance. He grinned in triumph and began fondling her with a rough, inconsiderate handling. She made no attempt at stopping him.

– I've been expecting you, he spat. – I knew what kind you were.

He let go of her. She didn't move.

– Come with me, he bid her.

He turned and walked away. She followed him, tailed him, looking neither left nor right.

Frances Stern, clearly out of breath blocked their way on the other sidewalk. Bieber stopped and Liz did, too.

– What are you doing, Liz? Frances said with horror in her voice and an expression of terror in her face.

– Nothin', Liz mumbled, evading her eyes.

– Liz has agreed to, volunteered to come with me, Bieber boasted, – haven't you, Liz?

– Y-yes.

The hollow voice was hardly a sound at all.

Frances grabbed Liz and shook her.

– You can't possibly *mean* that?

Frances glanced around her with wild eyes, before once more looking at Liz.

– Go home, Frances, Liz said quietly.

– No, I won't! Frances said, a determined look growing in her wavering eyes. – You need me. You…

Bieber walked on and Liz kept trailing him. It was as if a curtain covered Frances' eyes and then she followed them both.

They crossed one street, two. Liz didn't look around her, but kept her eyes on Bieber's back. She sensed Frances' nervous energy behind her. A car, Bieber's limo pulled up in front of them. He opened the door for Liz and grinned at her. She climbed inside and sat down and he joined her. Frances hesitated briefly before jumping inside just before he slammed the door behind her. She shrunk in her seat. The car started moving.

He grabbed Liz's already sparse clothing. It didn't take much maneuvering to expose her breasts. He began fondling them, squeezing them, hurting her. She didn't offer any protest.

– I love your big and juicy tits, he marveled. – I love all about that curvy body or yours, but the tits are my favorite.

She tumbled over, putting her head in his lap. Her eyes retained the distant look. She breathed harder and began writhing as he began exploring her body in earnest.

– I knew you would be easily excited, he spat, – but you're turned on as easy as any animal bitch in heat, aren't you.

She didn't speak, hardly changing expression as he played with her. She pushed her body at his hand, as the first moan rose from her open mouth.

– Oh, no, he chuckled, removing his hand, – you will have to work a little harder for it. Rest assured that you will eventually get more than enough of what you're begging for.

He squeezed a nipple. She yelped in pain.

– Stop! Frances cried. – Leave her alone!

He slapped her. She looked at him with horror in her eyes. He slapped her again.

– Shut the fuck up, you whiny bitch. I will attend to you as well.

Her eyes turned wet and dull, as she crumbled and crouched in her seat.

The car turned into an abandoned street. A door, a large door opening revealed itself in a tall building resembling a warehouse. The car entered the building. The door closed itself behind it.

Bieber opened the door and the two women stepped outside. He grabbed them both around the jaw and looked at them with a strict expression in his cruel eyes.

– I used to take it slow, make a slow transition in the training of my bitches, but I get tired of all that shit, such infinite patience. You know the score, know why you're here.

Frances opened her mouth to speak, to protest. He slapped her again, and again. She choked and bowed her head.

There was no one else here. Liz had no trouble hearing moans and screams from elsewhere in the building. The two of them trailed Bieber to an elevator at the other side of the hall. The door slid aside and they stepped inside. The door closed. The tiny cube rose upwards.

They appeared in a luxurious living room. Males and females looked astonished at them. Bieber ignored them with practiced ease. He walked on with his new charges. They walked into another room where four armed men, his closest confidantes waited. Bieber nodded to them, keeping his cool with an effort. Liz sensed how his exuberant mood bubbled and grew under his surface, how he fought to keep it contained. She sensed how the admiration and respect and fear the four men felt for the boss rose several notches.

That room faded behind the pimp and his two recent acquisitions as well. They entered a mix between a lush bedroom and photo atelier. Two pairs of eyes were drawn to the giant bed.

He grabbed a camera, a very expensive SLR camera and began snapping photos of them, doing so from all angles. They looked at the walls, at space filled with pictures of timid and nude girls. The indirect flash lit up the various reflectors placed around the room.

– Yes, he nodded, – all of them were asking for it, just like you are, like all cunts are.

Frances wanted to say something, anything, but even though her mouth kept opening no sound came through. She stood there with a pained expression in her eyes. Liz smiled to the photographer, but the smile lacked conviction. She looked timid and apprehensive, exactly like Bieber desired.

– On the bed, he commanded casually.

They stumbled there, like sleepwalkers.

– They call me a pimp, but I'm not. I'm an artist, so dedicated and skilled at capturing women's submission, to expose them as what they all are, as bitches in serious need of readjustment.

They crawled into the bed.

– Half facing each other, half facing me, please. Show your fear, your timid eyes.

The camera clicked in quick succession. There was no more film. He found another camera and kept at it.

The girls swayed on their knees on the bed with half closed eyes, as if they had been drugged.

– Kiss her, Liz. Do it to her. The fucking dyke has waited with breathless anticipation for you to kiss her.

Liz turned to her and smiled. Frances looked anxious at her, pulling back a little. Liz quickly covered the distance between them. She grabbed the other girl's head and kissed her on the lips. Frances gave in quickly and helplessly returned the affection. They writhed in each other's grip, swaying, swaying before the camera.

He clapped his hands twice. They instantly stopped what they were doing and directed their entire attention at him.

– Who do you serve? He snapped.

– You, Justin, Liz replied promptly and sweetly.

– You, Justin, Frances mumbled an echo.

He began unbuttoning her blouse, tearing enough in her collar to expose her breasts. They were half exposed, like those of the other girl. He walked back and snapped more pictures.

– Start stripping, and you better stay attentive, or I'll flay your skin off your bones.

Liz giggled or choked, unable to tell which, as she worked her jacket down her arms, exposing more and more of her firm muscles and dark skin.

– Sorry, Justin, she mumbled.

He snapped a close up of her face just then, catching her twinkling eyes, immensely fascinated.

Frances was trailing a little behind at first, but soon caught up. Soon it looked like they were one being moving there on the big bed.

Bieber's throat was parched. Liz sensed that and hers became parched as well. She moved her body and displayed it in sensuous ways, and he began snapping pictures without having control of his finger.

The two girls knelt nude on the bed an incalculable time later. Bieber approached them with thick bracelets and chains. Liz shook imperceptible then and he grinned in glee.

– It's finally sinking in, isn't it? He asked pointedly. She nodded meekly. – That is good! That is excellent!

He stopped a bit and stood there, towering above them.

– These aren't really necessary. He held up the chains for them to see, to behold. – They are mostly for decorative purposes, merely confirming the long-established fact of your enslavement.

– You're so eloquent, sir, Liz said huskily, looking at him with admiration dancing in her dark fire.

– I like the sound of your voice when you call me sir, he mused. – I think I would like you to always call me that.

He grabbed her jaw, fondling her face with rough affection.

– Present your wrists to me, he commanded briskly.

She did, biting her lip. He grabbed them and slapped the bracelets around them. The cold metal made her shiver further. He put the collar around her neck and the bracelets around her ankles. Casting her an even deeper appreciative glance, he stepped back and took pictures.

– I note that you don't shave off your body hair. That is fucking disgusting, but rest assured that I will fix that, too, fix you good, in all things.

Frances didn't move when he turned his attention to her, and allowed him to do his thing. Both girls performed for him wearing the chains. It was hardly necessary for him to direct them. He took more pictures.

– The chains are much thicker than they need to be, in order to better show on film and photo.

He chuckled in dark triumph.

– Kiss them, he directed Liz.

She obeyed, looking at him and the camera with dark, twinkling eyes.

– That's my girl...

She began licking them, writhing her body in obvious excitement.

– Those lips and that tongue of yours are made to service cock, he chuckled. – You have lips like a nigger and a tongue like a snake.

His laughter turned even louder and more vicious. He grabbed the girl hard in the upper arm and squeezed, squeezed hard, making her cry out in pain, making her look at him with wide, unfocused eyes.

– You're such a great fuck.

Her eyes focused, but remained wet and dirty.

– Do you know why? Because you submit instantly to your master's touch. You may pretend to be independent in daily life, but that's just a front for what in truth is a docile cunt.

He turned to Frances. She didn't look at him. Her entire frame shook.

– You're even worse off, constantly signaling your eagerness to submit to an alpha male.

He slapped her, slapped her again and again. She fell on the bed.

– Down, bitch, he commanded Liz.

She obeyed, kneeling deeper, putting her head and palms on the silken sheets. He took more pictures.

Then, after a while he went to a drawer and pulled out two needles.

– You've been such good bitches, and you deserve a reward.

Understanding instantly lit Frances' eyes and she shook her head.

– No, please, sir, no.

– The White Tiger will aid in your teaching, in the process of making you better bitches.

He took his time getting there, taking it slow. She blinked once. He grabbed her arm and pushed the syringe into the skin, injecting its content. She blinked slowly. A haze covered her eyes.

Liz didn't move while he repeated the process on her. Both girls slumped on the bed. He grabbed them, pulled them on their feet and dragged them to another room with five empty cages.

– You will spend some time here, enjoying the gift from your kind sir.

He pushed them inside and slammed the door shut. Then he left them. He returned with a camera. His persistent chuckle thundered in their ears.

Both girls grabbed the bars and clutched them. His grin widened to an insane degree in their fever vision. Then weak hands let go and half-closed eyes turned completely unfocused and unresponsive. He kept snapping pictures. They collapsed on the tiny space they occupied.

He stepped behind them, knelt behind them, pushing hands into their holes, roaming them with impunity. Liz started moaning after just a few seconds. The echo that was Frances followed after just a few seconds more. There was no resistance in either of them anymore. His triumphant laughter hurt their eardrums. He just lost it and kept laughing for a long while. It felt like forever in their ears.

It ended, and Liz felt even more empty. He stood up. She heard him do so, and pictured him as a mighty giant in the empty eyes staring at nothing.

– That's my eager cunts. I will leave you for now, and you will be eagerly anticipating my return, craving it ever more with the increasing itch in your veins.

They responded instantly to his light prodding.

– YES, SIR!

Exuberance overwhelmed him once again. He crouched there and slapped his thigh.

– You're mine! He shouted. – You're my beyond eager *playthings*.

They found themselves nodding to themselves. He grew, and they shrunk with every new act of dominance on his part. His experience had made him so inventive, so skilled in his trade, and they felt further diminished with every new moment they spent as his captives.

Liz sat there, her expression frozen in a smile. She knew how heroin-users looked, had seen it often enough in her young life. They looked like they weren't there, weren't present at all.

He had left them again, like he had stated that he would. She hadn't really noticed the moment it had happened. The heroin worked on her, spread to all pieces of herself. The chains kept her healing power from working properly, disrupting her thoughts, her very being. She echoed the mirror image in the other cage. It was as if she saw multiple images of herself, as if being split apart countless times, and each time was heaven and hell doubled, tripled.

Sweat poured from her brow, from every piece of skin she possessed. She gasped and kept gasping. Dull pleasure charged through her in an unending flow.

The mirror image spoke. She didn't really catch the words, or at least not their meaning, if any meaning there was.

– Please, Liz, I can't take this anymore. It's so awful, so… pleasant. Please, Liz!

She moaned under the onslaught of the rising euphoria.

The incessant whining made Liz frown briefly, but then she was once again lost in the maelstrom overwhelming her.

The dark sun rose above the horizon. It had wings and a face. In her mirror Liz saw herself. She whimpered in terror and joy. She imagined she heard herself screaming, or perhaps there were only tiny, weak whimpers hardly heard by the world at all. She writhed in the cage. She never stopped writhing.

– So hot, Frances mumbled. – SO HOT!

A timeless time later Liz knelt there, falling into a hole even deeper, with even paler shadows, the poison leaving her system. She choked and wanted to cry, but no tears came. She glimpsed the other girl, the one still high, her system still in the throb of the poison, still riding the white tiger.

Time didn't exist in the hole. Existence itself seemed distant, unreal. Flesh felt like wood.

It was later, much later, or so it felt. All kinds of unpleasant thoughts rode them both. Tears flooded Frances's cheeks. They just flowed from her eyes like a waterfall, and despair shook her in its beyond vicious grip. Liz felt pretty much like the other girl looked, but she didn't cry. She desperately wanted to. The hollow within expanded to a vast abyss, and it shook her apart, and she could do nothing to fight it. Her wound stayed open, and she did as well. A loud wail rose from her sore throat.

The man returned, and their dull eyes turned a little brighter. He stood there, holding his hands behind his back, towering over them for a long, long while without saying anything.

Or so it felt.

– … thirsty, Frances gasped with a coarse voice.

– Thirsty, Liz agreed somberly.

– Push your heads between the bars then.

They obeyed, doing so before he had finished speaking.

He produced bottles with teats from behind his back, and held them in front of their lips. They strived to reach them, but could not do so, panting in frustration.
– Not so fast. You will lick and suck them, like you would a cock. You need the training, and when all your training is complete, you will be so good at it.
He pushed the teat at their lips. They began licking it, sucking it, while moving their heads back and forth.
– It's so easy teaching you, he snorted in contempt.
They sucked the bottle empty. At his light prompting they let go of the teat. He opened the door to their cages, letting them out.
– You will stay on all fours, he bid them.
They did, looking attentive at him. He carried two chains. Each had a collar at one end. He put Frances' collar on first. It fit snuggly on the one she already wore. She made no attempt at keeping him from doing anything.
Then he put the other around Liz's neck, a little faster. She didn't move.
– I will keep my bitches on a tight leash.
He walked off and pulled the chains. They followed him on all fours, on his return to the bedroom. It made him chuckle. His good mood just kept improving.
– Oh, this is rich. This is beyond rich!
They reached the bedroom. It looked even more hellish in Liz's bloated eyes. He sat down on the bed. They knelt on the carpet with their eyes on him.
– So, how did you like my gift?
– It was a new experience, sir, Liz mused, frowning ever so slightly.
He studied her closer with a deeper and unmistakable frown.
She noticed his unease without trying. It was just as evident to her as the savage scream working its way up from her muddled depths.
– You're such a doll, he chuckled. – That giant nigger trained you well, taught you to behave.
– Dave taught me nuances of cruelty I couldn't imagine. In more ways than one he completed my education.
The scream hurt her ears.
He looked puzzled at her. She spotted the first glimpse of anxiety beneath the confident exterior he presented to the world.
– You know something is wrong, don't you? She asked softly.
The glimmer of triumph, of savage joy was lit in her eyes.
He grabbed her and pulled her on her feet.
– Now would be a good time to explain yourself, he snarled.
– Stairway to Heaven by Led Zeppelin. Which part do you like the most?

– Huh? He looked totally confused at her.

– You don't understand at all, do you? You're such a stupid fuck.

Clarity, a tangled web presented itself to her, momentarily at least fixing her confusion. She liberated herself from his cruel grip. It wasn't hard, wasn't hard at all. She struck him in the gut. He doubled over. She struck him on the side of the head, hitting him with the right bracelet. He fell like a tree.

Cruel eyes looked down on him.

– You don't believe your own hype, do you? You're not that stupid? How one person can spout so much bullshit in such a short time is *beyond* me.

She knew the first parts of her demonic visage revealed itself in her features, and her heart jumped with joy.

He didn't lose consciousness. His head moved back and forth. He was unable to clear his vision or his mind, no matter how hard he tried.

His confusion pounded her, and cleared her sky. Dust surrounded her and cleared her ground, the very air surrounding her. She grabbed him and pulled him on his feet. With a single move, she put the chain connecting her bracelets around his neck and tightened it.

– It's so fucking simple, she chuckled. – I can just squeeze at little bit more, and your head will pop like a cork. You know, now, don't you, what a major mistake you made, grabbing the tiger by the tail?

She turned towards Frances, the Frances brightening by the second in hope and disbelief.

– We're just gonna take a short walk into the other room, and do a little show and tell benefitting those nice gentlemen waiting out there.

He struggled, or attempted a struggle briefly, very briefly. She squeezed just a little and he turned red, gasping like a fish on land, and he turned very, very compliant.

– That's my boy, she whispered in his ear. – You understand.

Fear filled him, filled his balloon, and he choked hard. Small tears popped from his eyes.

– Hush, little boy, she whispered. – Everything will be alright. You'll see. Just wait and see, and great wisdom will be yours.

The fearsome, so very changed creature holding him in its unyielding grip made him shake violently. Suddenly, all his good feelings and expectations had been taken away, sucked down a deep, deep rabbit hole of abject terror.

She opened the door, pushed down the knob with her knee and pushed him through, releasing the chain around his neck, pushing him in front of her like a trophy.

Four guys, his loyal lieutenants sat around a table. They jumped to their feet, drawing their guns.

– You don't want to do that, she cautioned them. – Don't fear what I'm gonna do to him. Fear what I'm gonna do to you, if you boys don't behave, if you don't start behaving *right now.*

She kicked his foot with hers, felling him. He hit the floor hard. She kicked him in the belly. He gasped. She kicked him again. He crouched by her feet.

She felt it, felt the power rising. It hurt, as it pushed against what attempted to contain it. The metal practically sparked where it touched her skin. Exquisite pain charged through her. She smiled and the shadow embraced her. Sweat poured on her brow, as she fought to control it, as it fought to break free of its confines, as it constantly reached for the piece of meat, of food just outside its reach, as the last remains of the heroin was purged from her system.

– What are you? One of the guys gasped. – What the fuck are you?

He, more than any of them wanted to pull the trigger. She kept him from doing so, blocking the trigger from being pulled back.

Fingers twitching around triggers let go. She practically saw it, how they bared their neck to her, how they perceived her as bigger than life and death and all dark corners of existence. The malignant terror didn't just touch them, but burrowed into them like a warm drill.

– Good boys. Now, put your toys on the floor. They fucking *annoy* me!

Their hands hurt as they let go of the guns. One beyond twitchy guy dropped it before he could put it down on the floor. It released a loud, penetrating sound. Liz didn't react at all. The men shook hard.

– Go and fetch those pesky guns, dear, she told Frances.

– Right away, Frances said with numb lips, – at once, My Goddess.

The word… worked on the males, made them shrink further in the growing fright gripping them, gripping them hard.

She walked forward casually, her excited eyes on Liz and not on the four men.

One of them, the one closest to her glanced at her. She attacked him viciously, struck him down in a savage rush of blows, seemingly not slowed down by the chains at all.

– Don't look at me! She hissed. – DON'T EVER LOOK AT ME!

She picked up the four guns and returned attentive and eager to Liz's side.

– Okay, the dark creature in their midst shrugged, – now, with that out of the way I would appreciate if someone would bring me the keys to these manacles.

They reacted to her formal language, her strange speech, her hollow voice. It made her grin grow even wider.

– W-we d-don't know where they are, one of the men stuttered. – Only he does.

He pointed accusingly at the sack of bones at Liz's feet.

Liz directed her attention back at Bieber, hissing at him, not speaking.

– The lowest drawer, a hidden compartment, he whimpered.

A glance was enough.

– I'll get right on it, Frances grinned, an expression of wild glee painted on her face.

She rushed into the bedroom, tripping on the chained feet. Liz saw and heard her as she practically attacked the drawer. Frances returned. Liz timed it perfectly, just as her friend rushed through the door.

The bracelets unlocked and the chains fell off her. The feedback was instantaneous. With nothing to hold it back her power flared uncontrollably. The Shadow seemed to fill the room. The very air whistled as she moved it, as it created small wounds on everyone surrounding her. Cries of horrors rose from the males' throats. An expression of ecstasy crossed Frances' face, as the bracelets and chains just fell off her limbs.

– Come to think of it, we don't need those keys after all…

Bieber and his four henchmen rose into the air. They screamed in their terror. The commotion created the expected, inevitable reaction in the bigger, outer hall. Liz pulled the door off its hinges and parts of the wall followed. The fury flooded her and she couldn't quite contain it.

The males out there rose into the air and were pushed, pushed hard at the ceiling. Guns were wrested from their hands. Wrists snapped like dry twigs. The light clad females stared astonished at the sight, an astonishment only growing when Liz and Frances appeared with the five bundles floating around them.

Liz left Bieber hanging and let go of the rest of her bundles and of the guys pushed at the ceiling. Everybody fell and hit the floor, hit it hard. Two of them laid still, blood flowing from head wounds.

– There will be some profound changes around here, the dark creature solemnly declared.

She walked to Bieber, shifting his position a little, making him hang upside down. She grabbed his jaw and squeezed. Tears flooded his brow and wet his hair.

– How does it feel, she wondered softly, – to be at the mercy of a crueler and stronger being?

He attempted to reply to her, to speak, in vain. She squeezed him from top to bottom, making him hurt all over, not allowing him to articulate his pain.

– It was a rhetorical question, she shrugged.

A number of whips had been left on the floor and tables across the room.

She chose one of them. It rose into the air and into her hand, her left hand. She shredded his clothes. They fell off him. Everyone previously of the Bieber household gasped in further astonishment and horror. Frances kept giggling, her dark, triumphant mood growing by the second. Liz began whipping Bieber's back. And then he could scream and he did so, quickly turning hoarse, as she slowly turned him round and round, and punished him on all sides.

Blood started flowing from ripped skin, spreading all over the room, staining walls, ceiling, floor and all present skin.

He hung there afterwards, a haze not fading from his eyes, not seriously harmed physically. She heard his heart. It beat like a sledgehammer in his chest. He was healthy. A silent snarl curled her lips.

All the males rose in the air again, hanging there like the slabs of meat they had become. The loud laughter shook everyone present.

She turned towards the girls.

– Who wants to play «punish the pimps» with me?

Frances were in front of her in an instant, a dark shine clouding her eyes.

– Very much so, My Goddess, she breathed.

Most of the others joined her fast, the rest hesitating, but not for long.

Liz ripped the clothes off all the men, taking her time doing so, making sure it hurt.

– Prostitution in any form offends me. Slavery offends me!

She gave Frances her whip. The most eager girls picked up the remaining available whips.

The onslaught of savage rage began, and more howls of pain filled the space and all minds within it.

Liz returned to the bedroom, noting pleased, like she had more than suspected that she had no trouble keeping the heavyset bodies afloat even when she didn't have them in her direct line of sight. She found all the cameras and film rolls Bieber had utilized. There were more rolls there than he could possibly have used on the two new arrivals. She crushed them all. Choosing two of the cameras she put in two new rolls of film and returned to the torture progressing in the bigger room.

The men hung there, whimpering, moaning in distress, in horror. Even the obvious true tough guys among them looked haggard, terror-struck.

Frances and the other girls with whips in their hands turned to her with a triumphant expression painted on their sweaty and bloody faces.

– My cousin should have been here, now, Liz said with fake reluctance. – He's the photographer and would surely have appreciated an opportunity like this.

She shrugged.

– The good thing is that I can use this excellent opportunity to learn, learn the craft.

Her very voice scared the men and also at least some of the women. It cut into them like a dull blade.

She walked in among the butchered meat and started documenting the event. A big bruiser attempted to speak, to throw curses at her.

– SILENCE! She snapped.

Leaving both cameras hanging around her neck, she grabbed him with both hands, buried her claws deep within him as she drained and hurt him in a slow and deliberate punishment. He turned gray. His fire filled her and the cruel smile turned ecstatic. This was a new experience for her. She had never done it quite like this, and her control slipped and slipped. The dark fire expanded from her eyes and to the skin around them. It was like diving into a deep, deep sea of pleasure, and she didn't want to let go.

But in the end, it wasn't hard, wasn't hard at all. She smiled as she stopped, as she loosened her grip on him and pulled back ever so little.

He hung there, in her ruthless grip, shaking, unable to stop shaking. And the boundless fear shook his insides that much harder. He whimpered in all-consuming terror as she leaned closer to him again. Much of his reason and all his courage and arrogance had left him.

– I think you have learned your lesson, now, she said, kindly rubbing his shaking cheek.

He nodded and nodded and nodded, until she slapped him lightly, without effort on the cheek.

– I do want to extend your punishment, though. You were disrespectful. I want to rip your balls off…

Panic that never reached the surface briefly flooded his eyes. He never acted on it, in any way.

– … but I don't want to damage you. I could rip out your tongue, but a man without a tongue is unable to give full pleasure to a woman. I'll tell you what: I will let you get away with it, this one time.

She felt calm, almost tranquil when she turned towards the women again.

– The rest of you may commence your catharsis, now. Don't look at this as punishment of the dogs, but more of an exercise, an initial training. Punishment, when it is administered will be far harsher.

One girl clearly hesitated when she received the whip.

– So, what's wrong? Liz asked her casually.

– My Goddess?

She stepped forward and curtseyed.

– Who is the slick bastard making you love him? Liz asked, more than hinting that she already knew.

The girl cast a glance at one of the men hanging upside down.

– You dumb bitch! The man spat at her.

Her eyes hardened. Her lips tightened.

– I'm sorry, My Goddess, she cried. – I will atone. I will do anything to make up for my sin.

She was clearly serious, honest. Like most of them she looked at Liz with equal amounts of awe and fear.

– Get on with it then, little Christy, Liz shrugged. – The Goddess forgives you.

The girl's eyes widened when the Goddess called her by name, but it only made her more determined and eager. She delivered the first lashing. The man released another shout of pain. He looked aghast, as if he felt wronged.

The new round of punishment continued. It was a cacophony of noise, one sounding so pleasant in Liz's ears. She snapped more pictures. The calm hardness within her solidified.

Sweat and rage covered all the girls' faces, but most of all she who had initially been reluctant. She clearly gave her all. The men stopped screaming. They quite simply had no voice left. The lashing continued well beyond that point.

It ended. The girls, totally exhausted were hardly able to raise their arms anymore.

Liz let go and the men fell and hit the floor, hit it hard. The nude bodies crumbled there. They hardly moved, occasionally writhing in agony. Their skin looked more like raw, mangled meat than skin. Liz snapped more photos.

She commanded the girls' attention, snarling in contempt.

– You've been dependent on these guys, these *wretches?* Shame on you!

Frances stood by her side. The girls lowered their eyes in shame.

– You have a choice again, now. You can join up with us, strike out on your own, or, if you for some reason wish to continue a life of dependence I'm certain you can find another pimp or set of pimps to serve. For the latter choice, you will be wise to leave New York City and state, though, as the local working conditions for said pimps will be extremely difficult for the foreseeable future.

She gave them the lowdown in a relaxed, confident manner. It didn't make her any less intense or dominant or scary. They bowed down to her in reverence.

She picked one more body from the floor and started draining him.

Emotions and thoughts sifted through as well. This way of doing it still felt new to her. It was more brutal, uncaring, unemotional, thorough and deliberate. And with her practically sated from her previous, recent feeding she quickly felt bloated. The power rose further, charging through her like the dark fire it was. His squealing pleased her. Images, sensations filled her, of Ted and Carla and Lewis and many others, threatening to overwhelm her. She had to stop halfway. It was no big deal. She shrugged and let go again.

They stared at her. She laughed giddily, swaying and dancing to the silent humming in what to her seemed to last for hours, but to them was only a few seconds.

– The Goddess will train you, she mused. – Under her tutelage, after the trial of fire she will submit you to, you will become truly aware and independent creatures able to take on the world on your own merit. You will die or you will live. There's no middle ground.

Her words penetrated them like shards.

All kinds of emotions surged through them under the frozen features.

– Yes, you're open, now. Be thankful for that.

She bent down and grabbed Bieber's hair, doing so with her left hand, lifting up his head, in a brutal pull.

– And you? You never imagined that a creature such as I existed, did you? You believed you were safe in your little kingdom in an uncaring society? That will cost you, cost you everything. A loud, terrifying choir has descended on you all, and it will always be there.

She opened up her hand. His head hit the floor with a dump sound. She rose. The smile, the snarl included them all.

One of the girls stepped forward, curtsying.

Liz acknowledged her, gave her permission to address the exalted being in her presence.

– Witchcraft, magick is… real?

– Sure, it is, Abby, the Goddess shrugged. – But you know that by now. And know that what I have revealed so far is nothing compared to what the Power truly is.

– She knows everybody's name, another girl whispered, ever more impressed, in awe.

Not everybody's, Liz grinned to herself. She had caught some of the names when she touched and drained the males.

I'm both the Trickster and the Goddess, she thought.

– There is a history of… witches in our family, Abby said eagerly, – rumors of insanity and orgies and Goddess knows what. I've always wondered if I'm one. At least I used to… before… before…

Liz confirmed with one more casual glance that she was. There wasn't even any doubt. Her aura, her shadow had a very distinct and undeniable expression.

– You are, she nodded.

Abby gasped stunned.

Then she persisted in her intention and looked stubbornly at the much taller woman.

– Will you t-teach me?

– I will teach you, Liz stated, – teach you even more than I teach the rest. Your life, the life of all of you will take a completely different turn compared to what you once imagined.

All the females nodded somberly, eagerly and passionately. The Goddess experienced it like they were all growling like cats let of out of their cage and that pleased her immensely.

Another discharge of power within brought her sounds and impressions from the streets outside. She had a little trouble reining herself in, adjusting, and had to focus to stay within the room and mostly in her own flesh.

The rage, even in its less potent form helped her focus. It always did.

– Know that true freedom can never be given, but must be taken, she enlightened them. – Whatever push I or others give you can never be sufficient, if you don't follow up on it at your very core.

– We will, Liz, Abby stated firmly, with both hands rolled into fists. – I swear I will!

And then she looked stunned and anxious at the imposing figure.

– There was one major step right there, the Goddess grinned.

Relief hit Abby hard. Understanding cleared all the girls' eyes. And the rollercoaster ride their life had become took yet another wicked loop.

Liz turned her attention to Bieber again.

– You will sell all your holdings to me, she instructed him. – On paper, the amount will be substantial. In reality, it will amount to nothing.

He didn't visibly react to her words, but in his mind, she knew he was nodding, nodding, nodding.

– Put these wrecks in the cages, she told her subjects. – We will keep them in our care for a while, until discarding them like yesterday's laundry. They will have learned their lifelong lesson long before that happens.

The men looked at her with the same, dull stare.

– That's right, she confirmed. – You will pray for death, and eventually, the fact that I probably will not kill you will not be a benefit, but yet another curse.

She signed for Frances to follow her and returned to the bedroom. Behind her the pleasant sound of lashes hitting flesh rose to fill her ears.

– ON YOUR FEET, WRETCHES, Christy snapped.

Liz closed the door behind the two of them. Frances kept her eyes on her, attentive and eager.

– Everything that was his is ours, now. You are not dependent on your parents anymore.

– I know, Frances said. – It feels so good. Thank you.

Liz walked right to Frances' purse. Frances froze. Liz found the recorder there and rewound it. She played the tape and Frances heard her own voice and choked.

– *I wanted to challenge myself.*

Much more words were repeated by the machine, like the worst of torture.

Frances shrunk with the shame shaking her.

Liz finally turned it off.

– You shouldn't feel bad about your past self, Kwaiala, but use the certainty of your previous sleep of awareness to propel you into your far better future. You did not truly wish to challenge yourself then, but now you *do.*

– Yes, Liz, Frances said meekly.

Liz stepped closer to her, filling the remaining empty spaces of her perception.

– I needed to know without doubt what I am… and now I do. And you do, too, and are finally qualified to help your charges.

She walked outside, stepped onto the balcony. Loud cries reached her from the dark below.

– There's a nice view from up here, but aside from a few exceptions we will be down there, in the thick of it.

– What will happen? Frances implored her, following two steps behind her, the way she always would.

– Images and sensations of future blood, death and fire flow through my head, and I know my visions to be accurate.

She shrugged.

– It doesn't take a crystal ball to predict the obvious.

Her energies discharged themselves involuntary from her body again. The sensation felt very similar to burping.

She giggled, noticing without effort how the other woman hardly took her doe-eyes off her.

– Bloated, she mumbled. – *Bloated!*

– You've fed well, Frances noted eagerly.

– That I have, Liz Warren chuckled darkly and triumphant. – That I have! And it's so damn useful.

They returned to the bedroom. The other women still stayed away from there. The two of them once more entered the living room, what had been the whorehouse antechamber, where the girls had been on display for the customers. All the women, sweaty and bloody awaited the Goddess' word.

Liz placed herself in front of them, at the center of their attention, feeling how wind and time blew through her. She had felt that before, but hardly this pronounced.

– I know we can't put a stop to prostitution in New York City, but we will make one hell of an attempt.

They stared at her in awe.

– And it will be a great exercise for future delights.

She added, as an afterthought.

– We have already stirred up a lot of shit, but that's nothing compared to what we will do.

They listened to her and believed her, she knew they did. Her eyes burned so hard that it hurt. It pleased her. She saw without trying the nosedive admiration in the sea of eyes in front of her.

It pleased her.

– You will all come out ahead, as something far more and better than you were.

She watched them as they moved, studied them as weak and more or less untrained muscles and minds grew from their current low starting point to something fierce and powerful.

The cruel smile sent shivers of anticipation through the young women.

2

She was dressed in jeans, both jacket and pants, looking a bit boyish with short hair, but he would never mistake her for a boy. Her hardened nipples pushing at the t-shirt tightening around her luscious body was merely one of many signs of her heightened state of arousal.

She looked curious at him.

– What's with you today? She wondered. – You're preoccupied, not only occasionally detached.

– I just have a lot on my mind, he shrugged, not fooling her.

– After you met up with Patrick's extended family again?

He didn't really reply at all to that, and she didn't expect him to.

Eric and Christine had a number of beers at Wexler's. She leaned forward and looked at him with desire and infinite interest in her eyes and that pleased him somewhat.

– You keep such an interesting company, she declared solemnly. – That hasn't changed, hasn't changed at all.

They toasted and drank.

– You think so?

– I do indeed, she stated excited. – If anything, it's more interesting than ever.

– I do believe you're correct, he acknowledged.

– You've been a part of it all for years, haven't you?

– At least from the very moment I and Patrick met.

– And I am, too, by the same token, she mused. – What do you think it all means?

– I don't know for sure, he said slowly, – but I believe firmly that I have more than a good idea, and I know what we've seen so far is only the modest beginning.

She grabbed his hands, looking into his eyes.

– Carla wants you to keep training the kids, right?

He shrugged deliberately.

– I guess so.

– I want to join up, she stated. – I want to be a part of it. You will teach me, won't you, Eric?

– I have no qualms about it, he grinned.

The grin did feel a bit wooden.

They were dancing again, swinging slowly on the floor, staying close to each other. The music entered his ears as easily as her scent flowed into his nostrils. She pushed herself at him, like she had done constantly since they had renewed their relationship.

He grabbed her hair, holding her head steady, keeping her from kissing him. She made no protest, but easily gave in to his preferences.

– It would be great if we could do it at your place for once, you know, she chided him. – For the variation, if nothing else.

He didn't reply. She didn't really expect it this time either. Her expression didn't change.

– I've been training self defense and stuff like that, of course, she mused beyond excited. – Any sensible girl growing up in New York City has, to a point, but this is way beyond that. I'm looking so much forward to it.

They took a stroll through the streets. Both were clearly content with the slow progress, not really in a hurry to consummate their desire. They headed for her place again. In his mind they were already there, on the bed.

She frowned.

– It's like I've been waiting for this, she mused with astonishment, – like my entire life up to this point has been nothing but a standing in line for this moment to arrive.

She walked a little bit in front of him, with her hands resting on her back, both teasing and serious, both an experienced woman and the fairly innocent girl he remembered.

They walked past a window with a blue lamp displayed. He hesitated a bit before passing it. The lamp didn't glow.

Information flooded his brain. He couldn't stop it even if he wanted to and he didn't. The entire street painted itself in his astute mind.

He grabbed the woman and pushed her at the wall. She giggled pleased. He began rubbing her, caressing her. She rubbed herself at him, not trying to kiss him on the lips, but skillfully and eagerly caressing him with her entire body. He saw it, even as he kept his attention on the street and what happened there.

A car, a six-wheeler, a limo turned the corner. Another followed not long after that. The two cars stopped in front of the building with the special display window. A man and a woman with shaved heads stepped out through the front doors and opened the door to those in the back of the limo.

Eric kissed Christine on the lips. Her eyes opened wide and she looked stunned at him. Then she got it and glanced in the same direction he did.

– We are… undercover? She asked with a wimpy voice.

He didn't reply. There was no need.

She started shaking, sensing his concealed but evident anxiety, fighting to stay somewhat calm.

A man and a woman dressed in lavish clothes stepped outside. Other men and women with shaved heads and bland uniforms accompanied them, served them with every single gesture they made. Eric easily recognized them both.

Martine Rubleaux and Morgan Lombard and those accompanying them had returned to New York City.

Chapter 7

There is a smell of burning, of smoke. That's the very first sensation you notice. The fire was first. We were born in the Fire. And we are its Shadow.

You see a foreign place on television, a place you have never visited, feeling a catching in your throat, of longing and pain. You have never been to that place, but you know it still.

You experience a foreign smell. You sit in your own kitchen and know this scent doesn't belong here. It is coming from you. It isn't physically there, but has arisen from a prodding of your memory.

To many that's how it begins, one of many ways it might begin. And for most present day, narrow-minded people that's how it ends. Life is filled with reincarnation dreams, but we learn to discard them as insignificant from an early age, by parents, and by a society discarding everything deep, everything truly valuable, discarding Life.

2

A raven flew across the divide between the tall buildings. Carla heard it as much as she saw it, heard the bird as it slid through the air. When it flapped its wings in order to gain altitude, she heard it loud as thunder.

She stood at the inner balcony, looking down on the hall below, at the whirling mass of flesh and wands, in the no longer dusty building. She found herself down there, among them, being one of them, forever.

They had scrubbed the place clean, taking their time, deliberately, passionately, making the place theirs.

He approached her. She felt him from far away. She always did.

– I wanted to remember, he said, – but I didn't.

She didn't reply. He grabbed her from behind, nuzzling her neck with his lips.

– To forget is to die, not only like dying.

She turned in his strong grip, touching his cheek.

– But you do remember, now, or you are beginning to do so. Surely that is like birth then?

He kissed her, kissed her hard on the lips. She grinned self-consciously and returned his affection.

– You remember everything? He asked her, clearly expecting an answer.

– Not everything, she mused. – At least not all the time. I pick and choose like everyone else, but to a lesser degree.

She slipped out of his grip and walked down the stairs, immersing herself in the whirling and heated air, knowing beyond knowing that he tailed her. A hand reached out and grabbed a wand and she walked straight into the mass of excited flesh and mind. They stopped their exercise and looked at her, followed and noticed every little move she made, very eager and attentive, their young and innocent faces glowing in her presence.

Their faces and frames flickered and shifted in her vision. Some of them she saw dressed in helmets and armor, some in other clothes, and some were new, with only one, non-changing set of features, but everybody faced her with respect and admiration in their eyes and entire stance.

– I see so much progress here, she mused, not really speaking loud, but easily audible to them all. – You're off to a good start at least. You have much to learn, many miles to go before you sleep, but remember that most of it is about relearning what you already know.

She spoke in a light, but still solemn tone. They listened carefully. When they watched her, when they studied her more closely, her features and appearance began flickering and shifting in their vision.

But behind all the faces, all the different masks…

She remained the same.

– We will prepare ourselves, she stated calmly. – We will keep preparing ourselves for what's to come, what's finally coming. We've waited for so long, failed so many times. But now, I have it from a trustworthy source that everything is headed for that final, finite confrontation. My friends and warriors of the ages: the final days are finally close.

Not everyone present got it. Some of them shook their heads in bewilderment, but even as they did, she spotted understanding in their eyes.

And just as she did, there was a draft from the entrance, from the door that had just been slammed open.

The door opened. Light and shadow entered the hall and all hallways and corners within the building. Elizabeth Warren approached them accompanied by a score of young women.

Carla felt her in her gut. There was an instant connection, a chill, a fire below her heart. She rejoiced. She felt fear. Tears of joy threatened to fill her eyes.

3

Sounds of guns fired echoed through the building. The basement hall had been transformed into a shooting range, and the entire floor into an urban guerilla exercise field.

It felt like a forest in their mind and to their senses occasionally, with trees, scents and sounds.

The sword and wand training continued, becoming a part of a wider scope. They used everything from handguns to assault rifles. Liz oversaw everything, every little detail.

– Short bursts, she said. – Only short bursts of fire. It will save ammunition and keep the tool from jamming.

She looked like she had never done anything but firing any given weapon when she demonstrated it.

– Move through the battlefield like ghosts, she told them, – as if you aren't there, and the enemy will have no one to aim at. It won't keep you completely safe, since nothing can do that, but it will reduce your changes of getting hit to a stray bullet or bad luck.

They saw her or Eric demonstrate their abilities, and it was like watching a flash of shadow move across the floor, and that shadow seemed to surround the bullets when they left the barrel and reduced the targets, the bulls-eyes and a seemingly endless supply of mannequins to shreds.

– There will be very little real blood here, of course, Eric shrugged. – You won't truly learn until you have practiced your abilities in the field and survived.

The two of them complemented each other in strange ways, she a mountain of passion, he dry like a rock. His emotion was buried below the surface. She carried hers totally in the open.

– Marlene, Christine, Liz called, – step forward.

They did, facing each other. Marlene was calm, with a snarl on her lips. Christine's lower lip trembled.

– Fight!

Marlene struck out first. She missed by a mile. Christine ducked and struck back, hitting the other on the jaw.

– A love tap, Marlene snarled, shaking her head in contempt.

Christine, visibly angry struck her again, considerably harder. Blood flowed from Marlene's mouth.

– Better! The redhead grinned and struck back, hitting the other girl in the side, almost ending the fight right there.

Christine gasped as she pulled back, as she narrowly avoided another brutal strike.

She danced around the taller, bigger woman on light feet, doing so clearly beyond the skill of a newbie. She kicked and the foot contacted with Marlene's body with a loud thump. Marlene managed to twist herself enough to avoid the worst of its well-directed force. She still released a cry of pain.

This snarl was louder, more uncontrollable, beastly. She grabbed Christine's wrist and pulled her close, striking her hard in the belly. Christine gasped and crouched. Marlene struck her in the face. Blood flowed from her mouth. Marlene smiled. The third strike missed. Christine grabbed Marlene's arm and used the momentum of her movement to throw her on the floor.

She rotated and kicked out with her foot. It grazed Marlene's head, as she desperately attempted to avoid being hit. Christine kept rotating. One foot landed on the floor. The other hit Marlene in the back. Marlene moaned, but kicked upwards and hit Christine on the side of the head.

Both managed to stand up, but both were swaying, downright unsteady on their feet. Christine struck Marlene. Marlene staggered. Christine hesitated. Marlene struck her, struck her twice. Christine struck out blindly and hit her opponent on the jaw. Marlene threw herself at the other. Christine sidestepped. Marlene lost her balance and fell. Christine took one step forward, two, but couldn't make the third. Marlene had to really strive to get back at her feet.

– Stop! Liz told them.

They did, they practically stopped, her quiet, intense voice freezing them on the spot. Both fell on the concrete and remained there, more than half unconscious, hardly able to move.

Carla sat down between them and began treating their wounds. They both bit their lips, keeping sounds of pain contained.

– You did good, both of you, Liz stated. – You would have kept fighting until one of you was bested, possibly even killed.

A both hot and icy wind blew through the hall.

– You are fairly skilled, she told Christine. – Your moves show that you've trained for years, but you lack the necessary brutality, the willingness to finish a fight. With your level of expertise, you should have won easily.

She turned to Marlene.

– Yours is the opposite problem. You're well versed in brutality, but not in tactics and skill.

– When we're done with you, you will both be lethal fighting machines, Eric stated calmly.

They, he and Liz were a strange pair, and Carla, often standing back and watching made them a strange trio. Eric often seemed distracted. Those watching him wondered if he had his attention more on Liz than on those he was supposed to train.

– On your feet! Liz ordered casually.

Marlene and Christine obeyed, and found that they didn't were as bad off as they had feared they were.

The trio moved and everyone present emulated their moves, attempting to match their speed and versatility. The training continued for days and nights without number.

Jean was there as well, but she was more like helping out the other three, as a pure instructor between the moments of joint practice. Everyone knew instantly that she had professional experience as well. The quiet sadness was locked in her features.

Ted arrived eventually. He had been there in spirit, haunting them. His intense physical presence haunted them more.

Everyone sat in a circle around him and Liz and Carla, the true trio emerging. He spoke with a quiet conviction not making it or him any less intense.

– Our mental attitude is the most important part of our liberation. Those in charge have physical power at their disposal, and that shouldn't be underestimated, but what they, more than anything, have going for them is the power over our minds. Stephen Biko said that the most potent weapon in the hands of the oppressor is the mind of the oppressed, and that is such a great and correct observation. Move beyond that and you have taken a major step towards true freedom.

His words and wording made them wonder and ponder the further implications of what he was saying, what he was actually saying. They nodded to themselves.

Everyone, at least the trainees mostly stayed in the building all the time, now. They slept, trained and fed there and went outside only to fetch supplies. It became their world.

Jane arrived one day, equal to the nervous energy, intensity and desperation riding them all.

She walked straight to Ted, placing herself in front of him.

– I'm ready, now, she stated. – I'm so beyond ready!

At the hospital she had been brooding, withdrawn. Now, she wasn't. Seeing her up close, like this, with eyes lit up like stars, she reminded him once again about the girl he had known in London and before, and he was once again cast back there. Memories of pain and joy flooded him. This hall of concrete and decay mixed with that other so long ago.

– I've kept myself in shape, she stated, – waiting for this day to come.

She was rusty, but not that much. They could practically observe, when she joined the exercise and training, how she abandoned rusty, like an old coat.

– Look at her go.

He had noticed Marlene's approach, noticed her stopping by his right side.

– I feel good, she stated, continued without much delay. – In fact, I feel great! I thought I was in fairly good shape before, but I was completely deluding myself.

He turned his head and looked at her. She was blushing instantly. He knew she wasn't faking it.

She struck out with a hand, including the room and its people in her gesture.

– *This* is what I missed when I didn't join you in that clubhouse in London? She said excited. – I fucked up, fucked up royally in that as well.

There was honesty there, and remorse and burgeoning intensity, all of it rolled into one, singular expression of dedication. She had changed. Years of hardship and rows of mistakes had mellowed her arrogance.

– I know you're not «worried» concerning me, that you're not concerned about anything, but allow me to put your mind to rest anyway: You taught me a lesson and I took it to heart. I'm a good bad girl, now, finally a true mean and lean bitch at your service.

The smell of warm food filled the place. Everybody was drawn towards and gathered around a circle of tables and chairs in the inner, far cozier hall. It struck them again how intimate all of this was. Everyone could easily see all the others, never truly losing sight of them. They sat there, hugging in, drinking and eating to their heart's content.

– This is great, Lynn said. – All this is. It's the reason I started searching for something… and left home.

The others, all the others, from the teenagers to those from their twenties to early thirties nodded, understanding pretty much what she was talking about. Eloise nodded at Lewis' side, looking earnestly at him, conveying in every way her understanding to him. He reddened, suddenly understanding something himself.

Ted watched Jane, hardly taking his attention off her. He knew she didn't notice, that only a few others noticed whatever visible focus there was. Names echoed in his mind, names that to him were synonymous with strife and death, an awareness he had hidden deep within himself for years, and that now rose painfully to the surface.

«There is no way I'm allowing that to happen, no way».

His words to Tilla.

As he remembered them, anyway.

The familiar smoldering rage rose within him. It existed side by side with his joy, his enjoyment of the moment.

– Let's take to the streets, he told them.

The small talk faded into virtual silence from one moment to the next. They turned to him, noticing the special undertow in his voice, intrigued beyond words.

– Let's take a stroll through the concrete jungle and snarl at all the civilized

beings frequenting it.
Anticipation, just like that ruled them all.

4

The scene transformed almost imperceptibly, and they found themselves out there, crossing a constantly shifting environment, a whirl of motion and breathing and loud noise.

They drew attention to themselves, inevitably. A big mass of people with a majority of women moved with a singular purpose through the streets of Manhattan. The mere fact that Ted and Liz Warren walked in front served to draw the initial interest, but there was more to it than that.

– We do not walk or ride in a storm, she stated, she cried with a quiet, so very convincing confidence. – We *are* the storm or at the very least its proponents. It follows in our wake.

Her words and demeanor sizzled and burned within them.

She and Ted took lots of photographs, both of those in their group and of the others. They changed film rolls several times.

– Ignore the photographer. Ted implored them, a little frustrated. – Act as if he or she isn't there.

He took more photos, remained frustrated, but kept working, somewhat patient with his subjects. Slowly, slowly, they started ignoring him, moving as if he wasn't there, they and their features loosening up, and the photos improved.

The group appeared on Times Square, on a late, busy afternoon. Lewis's school buddies and Liz's «girls» were hardly recognizable to those who might have known them weeks ago. They were dressed differently, and wore their hair differently, but most of all the change was visible in their behavior, the way they revealed themselves to their surroundings, to the world. Lewis and his old friends did not really look like children at all, or at least could easily be mistaken for adults.

They relished what was happening just as much, if not more than those that had put their teenage years behind them.

Ted moved among them, whispering constantly in their ears, or so it seemed and felt.

– Listen, he told them, looking downright spooky, even more spooky than usual. – Listen to your surroundings. Look beyond the distractions, for what is truly there.

The traffic thundered in their ears, seemingly overwhelming almost all other sounds.

– Listen to the steps, he whispered in their ears. – Each human being has a distinct signature, big and small ways they can be identified, one just as obvious as looks.
– You can hear so much more than us, Lynn said good-humored. – You know that!
– But you can still hear *more,* he insisted. – Don't allow yourself to be overwhelmed by the noise of the machine. Discard it and dive into the true sound of the Earth.
They did, both because he told them so, because he had trained them to do so, and suddenly - because they wanted to.
The sound of the traffic faded in their ears. All the flashy visuals faded into the background. What remained hit them like a soft glove. Nuances of a thousand different steps were identified by their astute minds. Smiles and wonder lit up their faces.
When they moved on to Port Authority all that stayed with them.
It was just a short walk down 42nd street, and they were there, in an even busier place. They walked inside, in a hall where people's path constantly crossed and kept crossing each other. One creature of flesh and bones and seething thoughts passed them on the right. There was a *whoosh,* as if the wind moved close to them and not something soft and solid.
– It is true, Marlene marveled. – We can all be so much more than what we are.
Many of them nodded in solemn agreement.
– Now, *focus!* Liz told them.
Details instantly revealed themselves to their eyes and minds. The pimps with their girls stood out. So did the police officers. Most of the people were passing through, but quite a few of those present had made this place their home or workplace or something very much resembling one.
The pimps, at least some of them looked worried, very worried.
Liz and some of the girls grinned at them, and their worry, their anxiety took a visible turn for the worse.
The sound and stench of oiled guns were very noticeable to Liz's senses. Their sweat played pleasantly in her nostrils.
She sent Ted a tense, but confident smile.
I've got this.
She studied the men, looking for signs that they would crack and draw their weapons. Some of them revealed themselves to be close, and she steeled herself, making herself ready to act.
The moment passed. The world re-entered her vision, her primed senses.
Everyone kept looking at the details, in order to spot a less evident danger.

None revealed itself.

They moved further down 42nd street, further into Hell's Kitchen.

– You just saw one aspect of what is threatening us, Ted said. – I'm afraid there's a lot more, and the most dangerous is what isn't apparent. When the biggest or bigger threat strikes it will do so with a cunning and brutality those low-level threats are not even close at achieving.

– We didn't plan for all this to happen, Liz said. – True to form…

– Trouble keeps piling up when the two of you are concerned, Marlene grinned, with something akin to awe in her voice and stance.

– People will gather around you, Carla stated, – and they will be at risk. It's nothing new and it will keep happening. Those of us surviving will be better suited to aid you in the many years to come.

Ted and Liz and Eric studied her, but she was like a sphinx, unfathomable.

– You would have wanted to keep the children out of it, she kept going, – at the very least them, but how could you? You, meeting up with Lee and myself was inevitable, and when that happened you had already, deliberate or not set in motion almost everything else. It's what you do. Take pride in it.

She spoke to them, even when she wasn't. Something about her they still couldn't quite grasp related to them what was unheard and unsaid.

Strength coursed through them all when the ramifications of the recently spoken words dawned on them, strength and only a tiny amount of fear.

– Wolf speaks truth, Ted Warren told them. – And the truth of the matter is that you would all be counted as adults in virtually any pre-modern society, anyway. You may not be fully grown, but you're clearly more mature, far more so than most others considered adults today.

He sensed their pride, the way his words made them feel.

– You haven't been forced into adulthood, Liz added, – forced to grow up too early. You have *chosen* it, taken its power for yourself. Perhaps some of us have been gathered here by circumstances, but you haven't, not to the same degree.

Prevailing fire surged through them all, as they pushed deeper into forlorn streets.

– I grew up here, Abby said. – It hasn't really changed much at all. The basics remain. The population is pretty much divided between those admitting that its name is appropriate and those professing to higher aspirations. It makes no difference.

– But you experience it differently, now, Liz stated.

– I do, the young woman conceded willingly, looking at the other woman with the usual excited admiration. – You've opened my eyes, opened them wide.

– And that's nothing compared to how you will end up seeing the world, Liz said.

They stopped by the harbor, on an open spot, where they would be extra vulnerable in case of an attack. They stood there for minutes, calmly scouting the terrain for snipers and possible enemies.

– Someone is photographing us, Liz grinned. – I can hear the clicking.

Eric tilted his head. There wasn't really doubt in his voice when he spoke.

– I don't hear anything.

He studied her, without attempting to hide it.

– Someone is definitely using a camera, Ted said, – and I take for granted that we're the focus of their interest.

Liz focused and zoned in on one of the buildings. She closed her eyes and suddenly she saw so much better the movements in the air, practically the sound moving through it.

– They're both on the upper floors to the left and to the right, she reported.

– Let them, Ted said. – Let them be, for now.

She - and most others didn't need any explanation in order to understand the finer points of his words. He didn't speak to her, though, but to their companions.

Carla nodded to herself. Ted and Liz saw it, even if no one else did.

Liz turned and looked across the Hudson River, unable to really see much. She could not hear anything across it, any sound originating from there hopelessly muddled with the general city noise.

They turned around, returning to the deeper parts of Hells Kitchen. Liz heard those watching them move, change position. Carla did as well. Liz noticed that, as an afterthought. There was some kind of dynamics involved there, faint, but unmistakable. Liz and Ted walked ahead. Eric and Carla guarded the rear. Marlene and some of the others walked the sides, even though it was mostly for show. There was no way they could guard effectively against a sudden attack.

– Carla is hard to grasp, isn't she? Liz said.

– She is, Ted confirmed.

– I'm pretty certain she can hear us speak, Liz said.

They didn't turn their heads, but they still focused on the woman they couldn't see. Liz glimpsed her, as an indistinct shape back there, partly hidden by the larger group, partly standing out in her mind's eye.

The city wanderers passed the building with the apartment Ted and Liz had shared with Lynn and gained many a nervous glance. They had abandoned the place a while ago, but those living there and close by still remembered them.

That wasn't hard to determine, not hard at all. Even the workers doing the repairs seemed to have picked up on their identities from the locals. The wide grin came easy on the wanderers' faces.

A band played, played hard rock not far away.

– That's loud, Liz said pleased.

They stopped for a while, listening to the music. It was from a basement nearby. The rumble, the sound rose from the ground or seemed to do so. Liz was very aware of the fact that loud noise made it harder for her to notice critical sounds in their surroundings, and that it would be a good moment for a given enemy to strike at them.

The lead guitarist and the drummer went overboard and engaged in a long duo play. The musicians hadn't really managed the critical game of mixing properly, and there was a lot of unwanted distortion.

– That *is* loud *and* noisy, Eric said and shook his head. – They can probably wake the dead.

He actually had to raise his voice a bit to be heard…

– The enthusiasm of those guys alone will bring them far…

They walked on eventually, with a certain regret. The guys in the basement kept playing.

Ted frowned. Liz noticed immediately. Ted's frown grew deeper as she watched. She studied him with keen interest and anticipation.

– Wake the dead… he mused.

Then he got it. She watched while it happened, and a pleased grin flooded her face. His excitement, when he turned towards her was downright visible and she couldn't wait to hear what he had cooked up.

5

The room at the hospital had been completely transformed from how it had been only a few hours earlier.

A big battery of drums had been placed by the wall. Jesse Coleman sat behind them with the sticks in his hands. Linsey Kendall with his guitar and Alvin Draper with his bass stood in front of him. Huge speakers pointed at the opposite side of the room.

Diana McKenzie, Helen Cumbes and the rest sat still there in their straitjackets, looking at the world with empty eyes.

Ted, Liz and Ethel Warren stood in front of them, holding hands, the very image of witches, past, present and future.

A little behind Carla stood, clearly out of place, still clearly complementing the others.

The nurses looked at the entire spectacle with incredulity and stark fear, even in their imposed stupor. They were not really there anymore either. Ethel had taken them away with a gesture and a spell sounding like a curse.

The pressure in the room, in the entire building and even outside it increased significantly.

– This is a ceremony of awakening, Ethel stated. – It should work. We will prompt memories in brutal ways, force them to the surface.

She turned to Linsey with her direct stare.

– Use your Voice and your Sound, she told him, – use it to the full extent of your power. Cut a path through the mist of their mind. If you hold back this may not work, and you will be responsible for the continuance of their unending suffering.

Liz and Ted sensed how he struggled with her words, with their caustic truth. She did cut to the bone.

There was a buildup, a slow-moving train speeding up, until it shook and almost tipped over in each curve, until it raced the rails and smoke rose from the metal as if it was on fire.

Linsey Kendall struck the first chord on his guitar. The first riff erupted from the speakers and thunder filled the room. A rumble spread throughout the building.

Then… the shaking began.

Linsey began singing. His voice penetrated every eardrum and piece of flesh it reached. Ethel smiled. She waved her hands and added her voice to his, a chant not as loud, but just as piercing. Guttural words flowed from her open mouth and vibrating throat. The room… changed further, turning into something unrecognizable and strange beyond words. Shadows reached out through the windows and showed outside. Day turned to night. Ted and Liz got caught up in their study of Ethel and almost forgot to participate, to consciously contribute in the ceremony.

They felt it, deep within, how the five of them, Ted, Liz, Ethel, Linsey and Carla shimmered in sync and influenced their surroundings, and the people caught in their bubble of mist and shadow. Jesse and Alvin played hard, but they couldn't help but staring at the spectacle with incredulity in their eyes. Carla, Liz and Ted joined the chant. Ted, Liz and Ethel let go of hands and moved to their designated spots. The five witches formed a pentagram, and that very moment lines formed on the floor, and all five burned in dark fire and shadow.

Ethel's presence burned Liz and Ted, but they also sensed how their presence burned her. Features twisted and changed in suffering flesh.

The jungle revisited them yet again, stronger than before, the impressions far more powerful. The visions visited them with a greater potency. Ethel gasped, her face lit up in something very close to ecstasy.

You're such a marvel to behold, she told them, saying that and keeping up the spell-casting simultaneously.

Focus! Carla cautioned them.

You're correct, of course, Aunt Carla, Ethel grinned.

The storm gathered strength and momentum. A frown appeared on Diana's brow. Awareness seemed to supplant the emptiness in her eyes.

Diana McKenzie began screaming and it seemed like she would never stop. Then, not many seconds later Helen's even louder and more piercing scream joined hers. Both cut through those assembled in the room like knives. It was like a dam bursting, bursting, *bursting.*

The music stopped, with a few strikes on the drums extending the ending. Screams from almost everyone in straitjackets added themselves to those first two. Every new sound added cut everyone present like the sharpest of blades.

Then they stopped, from one tiny moment to the other. Those shaking in their street-jackets stared at those gathered in front of them with the clearest of eyes, expressing themselves with features soaked in sweat.

– T-ted?

Diane McKenzie met Ted Warren's eyes across an abyss deeper than forever.

He walked to her and knelt before her, removing her straitjacket. Her arms free after being bound a long time, she started touching his face, her movements painful, slow.

– What happened to your *eyes?*

– I will tell you, he said. – I will tell you everything!

She glanced around her, expanding her attention. It rested briefly on Liz that removed Helen's straitjacket. Everyone had their harness removed. Helen crawled to him as well. They both started shaking in his arms. Everyone shook hard.

– Where are we? Helen asked. – What *happened?*

He didn't manage to reply before countless unpleasant memories abruptly returned to her. He watched it happen. Forgetting himself for a moment, he attempted to reach out with his mind. Then, remembering, he grabbed her and held her, embraced them both.

– It's over, he insisted. – *Over!*

Some of the others screamed a bit and wailed loud enough to scratch sore ears. The two in his arms didn't. They kept shaking in distress, but slowly

calmed down.
– It feels so good to be in your arms, Diana said, and Helen nodded in solemn agreement.
He and Liz looked at Ethel. They made no conscious decision of doing so. It was instinct or better.
– Congratulations, Phoenix, you woke up the dead, Ethel mused. – Is there no limit to your power?
They didn't understand that. At some level they did. Yet another chill burned their skin.
– What was it you wanted to tell me when you called in DC? He asked Diana. – What was so urgent?
She looked puzzled at him.
– I don't know, she said. – I can't remember!
He saw how her distress level rose and potentially skyrocketed.
– It's alright, he said hastily. – It will come to you. Don't think about it, now!
– You're so warm, she whispered. – I've felt such a chill for so long, so long that I can't remember how long it has been, but now you're here.
He made sure their eyes met. He saw reason there, and at least a faint echo of the girl he had known.
– You look different, Helen said abruptly.
He didn't comment on that, but attempted to convey calm.
– Yes, you look different, Diana remarked. – It isn't just the eyes, but… *you.*
Their attention spread from him to the others, and stopped at Liz.
– That is Liz, isn't it? Helen said, her voice rising an octave or two. – Little Liz.
He didn't have to say anything. They saw confirmation in his constantly shifting, burning eyes.
– How long time has passed? Another asked anxiously. – What year is this?
– 1979, Ted replied.
Their shoulders sagged. They bowed their heads. Tears flowed down some of the cheeks.
– Those doing this to us, where are they? Helen raged, making him feel relief.
She would be a valuable addition to their tribe.
– Dead, or in prison, Liz said. – At least surprisingly many of them. This was too big to cover up.
She turned to Helen, to her alone.
– We cut off David Gidman's head and burned it and his carcass. Whatever is left of that is rotting somewhere in the Amazon jungle.

A stunned mumble, an eager acknowledgement flowed between the newly awakened.

– You've changed, Diana said softly and touched his cheek, – changed so much.

– So much water has flown down your river, Helen said, sounding very native just then.

He easily recognized the rage flowing through her.

She grabbed his hand and kissed it.

– Teach us, she implored him, demanded. – Teach us everything you've learned.

– I will! He heard himself assure her. – Don't you worry, I will!

They packed their gear and left the old, dusty building, both the visitors and the particular group of former patients. It was like a strange migration. Doctors, nurses and orderlies watched them with fear in their eyes. Ted knew they would not raise any stink about it. They had signed all the release papers with shaking hands.

– Did you look at them? Liz said with excitement in her eyes.

She knew he had.

– They looked at us as if we were demons, minions of Satan himself.

Her laughter was harsh, loud and free.

– We did what they couldn't do, Linsey mused, – and actually helped people recover from their ills, and they look at us with suspicion and distrust. That's so weird!

They looked at him with fondness in their burning eyes. He was still naive.

Everyone helped with carrying the gear to the bus. It was a great catharsis. The exhilarated good mood grew even more.

– They will remain troubled, Ethel remarked to Ted. – Some of them may be impossible to salvage, but I'm confident you'll deal with that, with that, too, in stride.

– We will! He assured her. – And once again, thank you for your help.

– I will always be there for you, Edward, she said, and he noticed stunned that there was a catching in her voice.

She remained one of the most enigmatic people Ted had ever met. That word was hopelessly insufficient concerning her.

The work was done. Everyone gathered by the bus, ready to board it and leave. Ted and Liz standing together noticed that Ethel whispered something in Carla's ear. To their astonishment Carla nodded and grinned.

Liz and Ted sort of stood apart from the rest, a subtle thing not easily discerned.

The two of them did, and so, they realized did Ethel and Carla.

Ted looked at the gathering dark clouds, and knew it was significant beyond the moment.

– I'm, ready, now, Phoenix, Jane told him, somehow appearing in front of him in an endless line of faces and determined expressions. – Ready to follow you on your path, wherever it may lead.

There was thunder, and blood, and passion in all those faces in the half moon circle forming in his line of sight.

Somehow Liz and Ted, exchanging anxious glances found themselves holding hands in front of everyone gathered in that tiny spot of the world.

– The once and future queen and king, Carla cried aloud.

Everyone cheered. Behind half closed eyelids images began forming. Sensations filled them and the images and sensations began forming a narrative. Gasps and sighs broke from open and closed mouths.

6

The room had been transformed since Abby had last seen it. Oozing candles and torches cast shadows everywhere. She knew it was Justin Bieber's bedroom, the place where she and the others had suffered so long and hard, but it didn't look like it. It reminded Abby, with its decorations and changed general appearance much more of her perception of a magickal place, a place where a witch resided, and there, at the center of the pentacle sat the witch, sat Liz Warren.

Some of the candles levitated in the dense air, moving along the circle, leaving a streak of mist. Their flame flickered, but kept burning strong.

Liz beat a shaman drum. It sent waves through the timid girl approaching her.

– Sit down, apprentice.

Even the voice sounded different compared to how it usually did. It sounded put on, but Abby knew it wasn't.

She sat down in front of the witch, the beyond imposing sorcerer or shaman.

Liz stopped beating the drum and used her power to put it away into a far corner. She studied the other young woman with stern eyes.

– So, what have you been doing lately?

Abby hadn't seen her for a while. She and Ted had stayed away from the old warehouse since the visit to the hospital.

– My group reached another level of the physical training. Carla and Eric keep pushing us beyond endurance, to levels I never imagined were possible. But I've also done the mental exercises you wanted me to focus on. I've been preparing, just like you told me.

Excitement and anxiety warred within her, mutually strengthening each other. She looked at the young girl of the same age as Abby herself sitting there, the woman so much older than her.

– Where have you guys been? She wondered. – We miss you!

– We've been preparing, too, Liz said, clearly distracted.

Abby wanted to ask what they had been preparing for, but the fireeyes lit up in clarity again and set their hooks in Abby, and speech failed her.

– Your training as a witch begins now. You started on your path long ago, and you will never leave it. No witch ever does!

Abby nodded and nodded again.

– Take my hands and hold on.

She did, and felt it as it happened, felt the charge, the pain, as if Liz's very skin had become claws. Dizziness, weakness grabbed her, and wouldn't let go.

– I will not hold back. I will teach you everything I can.

Fear struck Abby, forgotten in the next burst of excitement, rekindled in the next flow of fear.

– It hurts! Abby whimpered.

– It's supposed to, weak girl, the witch snarled. – Pain is a good teacher. You better learn!

Abby writhed in the witch's grip, but could not escape it.

– Relax, Liz whispered loud and soft in her ears, in her increasingly attentive mind. – Breathe in, breathe out, repeat and keep repeating.

An open mouth drew breath, exhaled, and drew breath again.

The dark fire in the witch's eyes intensified.

– That's my girl, my good girl…

Abby started sweating. She gasped, heaving for air, her breathing turning labored, a wheeze more than a breath.

– What's happening? She mumbled, shaking her head in distress.

– You're reacting to my intrusion, attempting to fight off my influence. It's what's supposed to happen. You're not a slave taking any given indignity from a master anymore, but your own woman, not taking shit from anyone.

Two bottles rose from the floor. They floated through the air until they levitated between them. One contained water, the other some weird-looking seeds at its bottom. The bottle containing water tipped slightly, and the fluid fell on the seeds. They began swelling, expanding in the bottle.

Abby stared at it with dull eyes. She watched as the swelling pushed itself out of the bottle, and Liz harvested it in her palm, and began smearing it on Abby's skin.

– You're untrained, unskilled and therefore in greater danger. You do need a guide, a protector from the potentially bad effects of your Journey. I will be your shield, but you need to be your own sword. I can't stab for you or be the rage rising from your core. I will gut you, cut you open, and you will become a flower with fangs and claws, a rose with thorns, and be equal to the blades wielded by the ancient gods.

Abby looked at the young girl. Liz looked at herself through Abby's burning eyes, at the ancient being sitting there with her legs crossed.

Existence… shifted, and shifted again in their eyes. A waterfall of sweat broke on Abby's brow and flooded her eyes and cheeks, and sweat and tears intermingled, becoming one, singular flow.

– I can feel you, feel your power through my own, now. Identify that feeling within yourself, and know your power.

The echo of each and every one of those words lasted forever. They sat there on the floor, facing each other, but they also stood side by side in a shimmering landscape without end. Vast ruins and growth surrounded them in equal measure. Abby - Abigail Draper - blinked again, yet again, and fear and awe touched her. A shadow surrounded Liz, flapping its already mighty, but incomplete wings.

Its incomplete wings.

Phoenix was still a child, still not mature, not quite ready for its task.

Its vast task.

Hearts beating like one struck like sledgehammers in their chest. A plane wreck surrounded by a vast desert burned and released black smoke seen across the Earth. The two and twenty-one survivors made their way on an invisible trek of dry, dry sand.

Abby's throat was just as parched. There was not single drop of moisture anywhere.

– You see me. I see you.

– You see me, Abby breathed. – I see you.

– In the brightest sunlight, I walk in moonlight.

And just like that, the brightest day transformed into the darkest slivers of gray and violet. Repeated gasps attempted in vain to draw air into straining lungs. They walked through burning streets, but the flames weren't red, but blue, light blue. Reality shifted and shifted again.

She died and he grieved, and he couldn't change that no matter how many times he tried, and eventually he began seeing beyond the event itself for a solution, and a much wider tapestry began revealing itself. The man in the cave finally saw beyond the chinks of his cavern.

Liz grinned in excitement. Abby brightened and felt a hard, hard catching loosening in her throat.

– Liz, I remember. I *remember!*

Then even more clouds parted and revealed more of what was concealed. Caskets filled with flowers opened wide, and energy began dancing in the witch's eyes.

Abigail Draper seemed to join with the clouds, with the mist surrounding them. Sometimes she felt like she was just floating away, but she always managed to rein herself in. She shook in a storm many times stronger than any battering her body. Liz sat there with her, seemingly unaffected, a statue in the whirling vortex submerging them.

Abby beheld her, the fireeyes reaching out to the surrounding skin, the wings burning with dark fire and gasped in fright, in awe.

You're so beautiful, so terrifying. I will never behold anything like you.

You will!

The fire flared, and Abby got a glimpse of what it might one night become and she gasped, and everything got away from her, and she became smoke drifting through the Void.

She felt so light, light, light, like dust drifting through an unending night. It made her experience such peace, such riveting unrest. She, the dust danced in the warm flow she had become a part of, the deep, deep chill she couldn't and wouldn't escape.

Then the pain came, and she felt like she was burning herself. First her face solidified and then her body. She sat gasping on the floor, facing Liz, staring at her through a haze of clarity.

Liz studied her like a bird of prey would do. Abby got the chills, at least until she noticed the interest, the dark, dark curiosity, and then she got stronger, far stronger chills.

– Your power is smoke, Liz stated, – and perhaps a bit mirror. You will love it!

Abby held up an arm, both solid and not. At one moment, she saw Liz from her position on the floor, and then it was as if her head rose a bit, and she had gained headroom without trying.

They were back on the floor, and the world slowly returned to normal, or what she had perceived as normal. She kept gasping, even as she looked absolutely astonished at the other young woman.

– The moment you get conscious of using your power it inflates, go poof, Liz said. – That's perfectly normal. In time you will master it, both consciously and subconsciously.

They rose, Liz as supple as ever, Abby a little awkward, rigid.

– Thank you, the girl said, – thank you, thank you, thank you…

She grabbed the witch's hands.
– I'm better prepared than *ever,* now, Phoenix, she told her, – ready to follow you on your path, wherever it may lead.
– You may regret those words, Liz joked.
The other looked like she hadn't heard the words, but kept looking at her with boundless, ongoing awe in her smoky eyes.
Liz started moving, and noticed that the girl fell in behind her, preparing herself to walk behind her. Liz made a deliberate move to slow down and allow Abby to catch up. An even bigger smile cracked the girl's face.
They left the room side by side.

7

A truck waited for them when they entered the hall one morning.
– You need a different kind of training, Eric told them, – one closer to real life.
All the youngsters looked curiously at him, waiting for him to say more, but he didn't offer further explanation. They walked into the large space. The large door closed behind them. The roaring engine started, and the truck drove off. They sat there in the semidarkness, in the cramped space, unable to look out, clearly itching with impatience, realizing that was a part of the training.
– It's a funny feeling, Christy said, – not knowing where we are going.
– Soldiers get that all the time, as they are shipped from place to place, Carla said, – But you're not soldiers, so we expect more from you.
There wasn't any condemnation when she spoke, only a quiet confidence she relayed to her charges. Christy and the others nodded.
– Reach out, Ted said. – Go beyond the noise of the engine. Get a sense of yourself by getting a sense of the space you move through.
They did, and it felt easy, like putting on a new coat. Their senses sharpened, tuning in on what they were focusing on. They looked at the teachers with more awe in their already bright eyes.
The sound of the wheels changed, more than suggesting that the quality of the ground they rolled on had changed.
– Are we… are we on a bridge? Abby wondered.
The others looked envious at her.
They sensed the changes outside, even though they couldn't properly identify them, by using their five senses. She could sense more. Some of her smoke seemed to… drift outside, and she was able to see the road, the Brooklyn Bridge, the water far below.

She pulled back into herself, a little startled, but not afraid, not anymore.

– You aren't merely mist, Liz remarked, – but partly Dust as well, the kind of dust that can penetrate anything.

Everyone noticed the special way she pronounced «dust», one clearly different from common pronunciation.

– I think I know what you mean, Abby mused in wonder, – at least to a point.

They reached Brooklyn and the sounds shifted again. The sounds and shouts of drivers blowing their horns by a traffic light reached them in their muted form.

– It sounds completely insane out there, Christine mumbled more than a bit disturbed.

But she and all the other recruits clearly looked ahead and forward to today's activities with interest and eagerness. They sought patience on the long drive through the city, even as it eluded them.

The truck eventually reached what could only be described as uneven ground. There were lots of bumps. The vehicle groaned under the abuse. The drive seemed endless after only a few seconds of that.

It finally came to a halt. The engine was turned off. The hydraulics began humming as the backdoor opened and the bright light flooded the cargo bay.

They stepped outside close to an industrial park that had definitely seen better days. It was hardly more than ruins. Roofs were completely gone on some structures. Nature had long since reclaimed huge part of it. Floors were covered by grass, and trees had started growing inside buildings.

– This is the perfect place to train urban guerilla, Marlene breathed excited.

She looked back at the uneven field they had crossed, at the distant city.

– We will start off in modest ways today, Ted said, – and return from time to time to refresh and further sharpen our skills.

He inadvertently flashed his fangs while saying it. They groaned good humored.

The recruits gathered before Eric, attentive and anxious.

– Fighting urban guerilla is basically the same as fighting in nature, – he said. – You take advantage of the terrain in order to gain the best possible position. You flow through the fighting area like water. The trick is to spot the enemy before the enemy spots you, to fire in the split second before it does. Hesitation will get you killed. Sticking your body out from a corner or window makes you vulnerable. It's a matter of taking advantage of the margins as they reveal themselves, to become like an oiled machine, a unit working at peak efficiency…

Not that much later the first shots thundered between the walls. They used rubber bullets, knowing that being hit by them wasn't exactly pleasant and also potentially dangerous. And also paintball gear. They were being hit and big bruises grew on the skin where the bullets hit. Some of them fell unconscious to the ground. Carla checked them to be certain, breathing a big sigh of relief when she convinced herself that they would live and weren't seriously injured.

Scouts kept an eye on the surroundings. No one approached the place. There was no sign that anyone had heard the noise and was on their way to check it out.

Lewis was hit in the arm when he stuck his arm out from a corner. He released a loud shout of pain and lost his gun. The arm turned numb.

Carla rushed forward and began massaging it.

– It will be useful again in a few minutes, she said unconcerned. – It will be blue and black and sore for a while, but that won't keep you from using it.

He looked at her with a hurt expression in his eyes. She ignored him.

She seemed colder, warmer… different, compared to the girl he had learned to know, as if she had shed skin and more. He wondered if this was how she truly was beneath her exterior.

He had always wondered what she was hiding, and he got some inkling of it now.

The next time he exposed himself, he was much faster and much more focused. He felt it, almost as if he had been given an injection or something. The notion distracted him, to the point of him almost being hit again, but he wasn't. It pleased him to hear a scream from the opposite corner of the square.

Ted and Liz stood on a roof, watching their surroundings, their eyes even bigger than usual.

– It's exactly like we… we saw it, she mused. – It's uncanny.

Images and sensations from their visions mixed with reality, becoming one.

– I saw you get shot, she said stricken.

– I saw that, too, he reminded her of.

She looked aghast at him.

Other images and sensations from New York they hadn't actually experienced in real life yet assaulted them. They saw themselves chase five cars in Jersey. Patrick and the others were there with them.

Ted watched their tribe train below, and suddenly the image, the movie shifted in his head, as the memory of his vision, the one he had experienced for months raged through his head. There were fewer of them, and he was right down there with them, and real bullets were exchanged with a relentless enemy persecuting them.

He realized he experienced it differently from Liz, since she still experienced the visions and he only the memories of them.

They watched Marlene. She had cut her hair short. Her inborn ruthlessness made her a natural for this. She had no qualms about killing, no initial barrier for it that might restrain the others. She learned faster the art… the art of the hot metal, the one surging through the Warrens' blood and self.

Jane had already learned it all, in the care of the Abraxas Omega, like Ted himself. It was just a matter for her to… remember. He saw her by his side.

He saw himself standing by her grave.

– We don't see the future, he repeated what they already knew. – None of us do. No one does. We see its potential.

She rubbed her lips at his cheek.

The day seemed to rush on, and dusk arrived early. They packed their gear and returned to the truck. Liz and Ted stood outside and waved them goodbye.

– We will take a detour and join you shortly.

They sent the two curious glances, but didn't ask any questions. The door closed. The truck drove off. They ran across the field and reached the buildings on its other side. The once distant city returned to them, to their senses.

It didn't take too long to reach what they were looking for. They ran through familiar streets they had never ventured before, except in their feverish minds.

– We just backtrack, he stated.

She nodded excited, not burdened with the same unrest… fear he was.

They located the unassuming building without making major mistakes in direction, only almost making a mistake twice. It felt amazing, even though they couldn't let go of the fear.

– It feels so familiar, she marveled, – almost like we actually grew up in the neighborhood.

– We've walked through here a million times, he said solemnly.

She nodded, squeezing his hand.

They rushed up the stairs and entered the house, rushing down the stairs to its basement, running through the tunnel concealed by a simple dark sheet, a cover so effective that few would even spot it in the semidarkness. The tunnel looked old and forgotten. Perhaps children ventured down here occasionally, but they would bet much that the traffic wasn't heavy.

It was completely dark in there, not a single light anywhere. Their radar kicked in and served them well. They reached a hatch, opened it and climbed through a short crawlspace to the next hatch. Ted opened it and they could run through a long hallway in another basement. There was a heavy door, one they struggled a bit to open, but managed well enough. There was a staircase. They spotted a room through an open door. There was a circuit-breaker there. It was on, but they still saw no light. They walked up the staircase to what was clearly the ground floor.

The entrance door practically glowed in their vision. She pushed a button by the door, and electric light flooded the large hall. He remained. She returned to the basement and turned off the electricity. Everything turned dark again. She turned it back on. The light returned. He pushed the button. Total darkness flooded the place. There were no windows, no sources of light anywhere.

He watched her as she appeared from the corner, her features just as clear to him as if he had seen her in bright daylight. They opened the door and stepped outside. There was no one there. The door slid close behind them.

They stood there for a while that felt like forever, breathing in the night, looking at each other with inevitable excitement.

– There is a subway station not that far away, if I'm not very much mistaken, she said upbeat. – I'm willing to bet that we will find it fast.

– I am, too…

His memories from the river of time mirrored hers.

Loud laughter echoed between the buildings. They ran off between Brooklyn's low buildings.

8

Liz led her warriors to the warm, humid room.

Nude men stinking of sweat and shit crouched in the cages, the skin surrounding their eyes swollen and unhealthy.

– Hello, slaves, she greeted them.

– GREETINGS, MY GODDESS, they choired dully.

They knelt before her, their eyes cast down. She smelled the stench of fear on them, on him. In her nostrils, it wasn't overpowered by the stench of shit.

She grabbed Bieber around the jaw, smiling cruelly to him. He whimpered like a scared little boy. She grabbed the arm full of needle marks, pleased by the drug-induced need in him, very aware that the first withdrawal symptoms would kick in in a few hours.

– You had quite the stock of smack. It will take time before that runs out. It will serve us well long after you and your gallant knights are out of here.

Her voice was thick with wicked spite. The paralyzing terror that had shaken them like ragdolls the last few weeks since she had appeared in their lives added a bit more to itself. They shrunk in her presence, they always did.

She squeezed her nostrils shut.

– The boys stink, she said with contempt. – They need cleaning!

Frances opened the hose, and ice-cold water hit the men in the cages, a relentless flow keeping up for minutes. She walked around the cages, cleaning them from all sides.

They crouched behind the bars afterwards, gasping and heaving for breath.

– You're a sorry sight, aren't you? She said softly.

All the locks on the cages opened simultaneously. The doors slid open. She slammed the whip against the floor. The dull look in the prisoners' eyes didn't go away, but the loud sound still made them jump out of their skin.

Liz deferred to Frances.

– ON YOUR FEET, WRETCHES! The tall and big woman shouted, and slammed her whip at them.

They were slow, so very slow. The other women started using their whips on the slackers. The men stood there swaying soon enough, shaking in fear, shame and something totally surpassing terror. They stumbled off, driven like cattle, surrounded by furies working up their rage every time the lash hit long since inflamed skin.

A truck awaited them below. They were pushed brutally inside. Liz and her furies joined them there. The truck rolled through the New York streets. Justin Bieber sat there, a sorry sight among sorry sights. He looked even worse off than his men. His eyes cast constantly at the floor, he hardly even dared glancing around him. He still saw Liz's eyes, couldn't avoid seeing them, no matter where he directed his attention, knowing beyond knowing that he would always see them, for the rest of his existence, no matter where he went. Abby stared at him, too, he knew she did. In some ways, she looked exactly like the old, cowed Abby he had known. In other ways she, more than the others added even more to his constant shaking and whimpering.

They drove across the George Washington Bridge on Hudson River well after midnight. The traffic was light. Sore eyes became more so, as the hunger for heroin grew in the boys' bodies and minds. Fort Lee traffic was equally light. The city appeared like a ghost town this late at night.

– New Yorkers dump everything bad in Jersey, as I understand it…

All the women in the van chuckled wickedly.

The light from neon signs played on sweaty skin for a little longer, until they reached a somewhat remote area. Her nostrils picked up the stench from far away. She could practically have led them by the nose to the giant garbage heap, but there was no need for that. They didn't need to look for it, but found their way without trying.

A bumpy road led the last stretch to the top of a hill and a cliff. The garbage heap reached almost all the way to the top. Frances stopped the van just a few steps from the edge. She looked like quite the accomplished driver when she swerved and parked with only one hand on the wheel.

The human wrecks were dumped on the ground. Liz snapped the last few photographs and film footage. She handled the big film-camera like it was nothing. When she handed it to Frances, she had considerably bigger problems handling it.

Liz Warren turned towards the men gasping in fright and despair on the ground.

– I could have done much worse to you, but I don't want you in my sight or have your scent in my nostrils anymore, and killing you would have been the easy part.

She bent down and in one easy move she had grabbed one man's feet and lifted him up. He hung upside down. She started swinging him around. The centrifugal force made him gasp even harder for air. Limbs and sinew, subjected to the hard pressure threatened to break.

She let go of him, and his whimper faded to a scream. He landed near the top of the heap. They saw his body move, half buried in the organic smoking mass.

– Trash buried in trash, she spat. – How appropriate!

She turned to Abby.

– Your turn.

Abby took one step forward.

– No, Liz instructed her. – Grab him without moving close. Your reach has grown considerably. Use it!

Abby hesitated, reaching out with an arm, seemingly hopelessly far away from her chosen subject. Then the flesh of her arm turned transparent and misty. Only the hand stayed solid, as it grabbed the man's collar and lifted him high up. She laughed giddily, and in one swing of her seemingly intangible arm she threw him down on the heap.

The other girls joined in, in a frenzy, working two and two to somewhat keep up with the two witches. Loud screams of fear, loud screams of savage triumph echoed the fairly remote Jersey landscape.

Only Justin Bieber remained. Liz held him up in a casual grip.

– Goodbye, she told him. – Pray to your Goddess that we will never meet again.

The scream in his mind was far stronger than the weak whimper he released from his throat.

They watched him as he hit the soft tissue of the organic mass below, watched as he, weak in body and mind began crawling through it with his previously so fearsome men.

– Will they ever be able to get out of that shit? Abby asked with slowly sparking eyes. – They're pretty worn down after weeks in your care.

– That's not our concern, Liz shrugged. – We've given them a change. That's far more than they deserve. We're done with them. They're merely the first stones of our painting.

They looked beyond curious at her, beyond eager. They were hers.

She turned and returned to the car. Her furies joined her. The car drove away, fading into the night, and the changed forever New York urban landscape.

Chapter 8

Elizabeth Warren and Abigail Draper walked on light feet down Broadway. The path stretched out forever before them. Liz whistled a happy tune. The subsequent haunting humming reached every ear and every mind on the busy street. Abigail joined in, literally euphoric in her joy. They were quite the pair, creating a stir wherever they ventured.

The man surrounded by his stable and bodyguards, somewhat discreet sat by a table at a sidewalk cafeteria close to Port Authority. Everyone froze slightly when the two approached.

They slowed down as they got closer, moving in a very non-threatening, almost to the point of cautious way, almost.

Liz grabbed a chair from a neighboring table. Abby grabbed another. They kept moving slowly, practically telegraphing their intentions. Liz put down her chair and sat down, facing the man across the table. Abby joined her on her right.

– Hello! The dark girl greeted him brightly. – May we join you?

Parker Redman didn't point out the obvious: that they had already done so. He frowned.

– It's a free country, he shrugged deliberately.

– Is it? She countered.

A thin layer of sweat formed quickly on his forehead.

– I thought we could just sit here and settle for a pragmatic, intelligent conversation, enjoying the pleasant afternoon, so to speak.

Liz said.

The bright sunshine surrounded them. The dark fire stayed pronounced and very visible in her eyes.

– That sounds reasonable.

He said, unable to keep the hoarseness from manifesting in his voice.

– I want you to leave the city forever and give the money you've earned to your victims, she said, – share it equally among them. It will give them a fighting chance, at least to leave behind the horror you have visited upon them.

He wanted to speak, but a sudden constriction in his throat kept him from doing so.

– I'm fully aware of the fact that others will try to take over your slot, she said, – fill the vacuum you've left behind, but I will deal with them as well. It won't be very smart of them. I will make them see reason as well, you can be certain of that.

– You have a sniper somewhere! He stated incredulous.

She didn't reply in any way, not with her voice, not giving any indication that she had heard him speak at all.

He stared at her, and at the eerie, smoking (not smoking hot) girl by her side. Everyone present did. In one way, Liz Warren looked perfectly normal, unthreatening, in another like the most horrible demon of the abyss. She seemed to grow in her chair, into a creature of shadow and cold.

Parker Redman grabbed his right hand in order to keep it from shaking. He couldn't speak, imagining that someone had transplanted a giant ball pushing at his throat into his neck.

– We have both conventional and unconventional means at our disposal, Abby said casually. – We can snap our fingers and you will be *gone* like a puff of smoke. Will you truly risk bringing the entire wrath of *the Janus Clan* upon you?

The name spoken aloud echoed up and down the street in impossible ways, both inside and outside both frozen and shaken minds.

One of the men snapped. He jumped to his feet and drew his gun, pointing it at Liz's head. They all watched him, beyond fascinated. He pulled the trigger, or tried to several times. They saw how his finger twitched and twitched and twitched and nothing happened.

He suddenly froze completely, standing there totally unmoving. Then, like a mannequin his arm twisted and turned, and the barrel of the gun pointed straight at him. Sweating like a pig and with huge, bulging eyes he stuck the barrel into his mouth and pulled the trigger. The loud crack shook all the tough guys present. One of the light-clad girls screamed. Pieces of his brain spread all over the place and landed on practically everyone present. The body fell to the ground, crumbling like a sack of flesh.

– Yuck!

Liz Warren cried out with disgust in her voice and expression.

Parker Redman stared at his very dead henchman with distant eyes and looked like he wasn't quite present at all.

Liz turned to her companion in a relaxed move.

– I think that pretty much concludes our business here, don't you agree?

– I think you're very much correct, Liz, Abby nodded in a very relaxed manner.

Liz turned to Redman.

– I will not hunt you to another city, she said offhand, – but if we should meet by coincidence somewhere, it wouldn't be healthy for you if you stay in the business. It would, in fact be a very bad move on your part.

He didn't reply, as if he hadn't heard her.

– You girls are now free, like you were all the time, to strike out on your own or to join us. Know that you're welcome. We have plenty of room, both when it comes to physical space and in our hearts.

The two witches rose. Liz brushed a piece of brain mush from her thigh. They left. No one made any move to stop them.

The two of them walked back the same way they had come. Abby could hardly take her eyes off the other.

– You showed him! She said with savage triumph in her voice and eyes. – You showed the cruel and bad man how insignificant he is, and it was nothing to you. One thing is what you did with Bieber and henchmen over time, but this is something else entirely. Words of your exploits will keep spreading, and the relevant parties will shake even harder in their *pants*.

She spat the last word, in a kind of cheerful contempt.

Her words comforted Liz and cheered her up, even as she wasn't really listening much.

She stopped on a corner. Abby, having learned to know her, at least to a point saw that she wasn't really that cheerful.

– Help me understand, Liz said, making Abby frown. – I think I do, but help me anyway.

Abby nodded her consent.

– Did you see those girls? They were more threatened by me than by him, their molester, the man beating them every day. I know I'm scary, that's the entire point, but they knew I came to liberate them.

– The abuser becomes the anchor of their existence, Abby said cautiously. – It's so easy to defend him… or her, and see any kind of… interference as the threat. It's like you and Ted point out in your… classes.

– I know, Liz said. – I know we're raised to be slaves. Both men and women are. It's so easy to slip from the general, non-localized slavery to a more personal. We all need drastic methods in order to shake us up, to empower ourselves, liberate ourselves from our chains.

She gave the other girl a hug, trying not to overdo it, to harm her. Abby looked astonished at her.

– You're right, Liz said. – I did show him. We both did. But we need something more, a qualitative difference adding to our brute bullying tactics.

She started walking again, speeding up so much that Abby had difficulties keeping up.

They returned to the warehouse where Justin Bieber had resided like a king, to the others anxiously and eagerly awaiting their word.

They did tell them, retelling the events with both soberness and triumph, stressing what they had concluded with on that random street corner.

– I truly feel like I can't breathe sometimes, she sniffed. – Modern society is that bad. It's strangling us all slowly.
They comforted her somewhat, drying her dry tears, equally excited and distressed, as their friend and mentor.
Liz stood alone on the balcony, watching the streets below, zooming in on any tiny movement or development. There was no sign of hostiles.
She returned to the warm apartment, to what had become her current place of power, her brief home, unable to shake off the feeling of… of…
Then, one tiny moment later she knew someone was in the room with her. She turned in a rush of motion.
The old woman looked totally unthreatening, but still gave Liz the willies, and that, in turn made her feel even more threatened.
– I'm not here to fight you, but to offer you aid and guidance. My name is…
– I know who you are, Liz snapped, unable to contain her surprise and sudden anxiety. All her alarm bells were ringing.
– My name is Rachel Dalhart, the rather infamous brothel madam of Paris, New York and the world, and I think I can be of some modest assistance to you.
– I *know* who you are, Liz repeated.
– I've watched your recent exploits, Miss Dalhart said. – Very impressive!
– Thank you, Liz heard herself say. – And now you attempt to turn the tables on me, to be proactive?
– Not at all. As stated, I'm only here to offer you advice, to illuminate your path.
Liz's heart was racing on a slow beat. Droplets of sweat emerged on her brow and she remained unable to quite pinpoint the reason.
It dawned slowly on her that she felt exactly like a prey facing the predator.
– Bieber and Redman were no match for you. Nor will others of their kind be. Leaving them in the gutter isn't enough for you. You need more, need… an outlet, a particular kind not including physically punishing your enemies.
– And you have… a solution in mind?
– I have the *perfect* solution in mind, one that I believe will benefit us both. I have a club, fairly respectable on the Upper East Side, one screaming to be scandalized, where you and your brethren can act out as you please.
Liz began pacing the floor, not once taking her eyes off the old woman.
– Do you think, she growled, – you're protected from my wrath because you're a woman?
– No, I don't think that, don't think that at all. I know that you know that the world isn't divided by sexes, and that one isn't any better than the other.

Dalhart seemed totally relaxed. Liz didn't get anything from her, anything at all… except that there was something there, something just below the surface.

– Feel free to check out my boys and girls at any time.

The kind old lady offered.

Liz snorted in contempt.

– It isn't that easy. Even if there's no coercion, mental, physical or financial, you still support the system of it.

– I'm just running an enterprise, Dalhart shrugged. – Anyone should be entitled to that, don't you think?

– An…

Liz never quite managed to complete the incredulous outburst and snarl, to respond to what was clearly a deliberately condescending statement. She felt, finally felt how the rage filled her and she welcomed it.

Before she managed to do anything, a dark flashing shadow rushed her. It happened so fast that Liz hardly managed to acknowledge it before the huge, lethal creature with features twisted in rage had grabbed her and pushed her at the wall.

She felt dizzy, nauseous and her powers didn't work, no matter how hard she tried.

– I can kill you now, the creature hissed, – and you won't be able to prevent it. I can certainly slice you badly. Perhaps you *deserve* to be taken down a peg?

A hand with huge claws entered Liz's cloudy vision.

The other hand around her throat let go. The creature pulled back. Except for the two normal legs Liz looked at something very much resembling a mermaid, a young such, hardly looking any older than Liz. She stood there exposed, her clothes in tatters and the dark fireeyes pulsing and burning.

Liz heard the sound of running feet. Almost like an afterthought she reached out with her powers and made sure the door stayed closed. Anxious hands hammered it.

– Is everything okay in there? Frances asked.

There were others there with her.

– Everything is fine, Liz replied. – I just had a moment.

They understood what that meant, having witnessed her bouts of rage often enough.

The two tall women faced each other across an abyss wider than years.

– I don't suppose you have any clothes I can use, Rachel said.

– I can ask Ethel to send some over, Liz said, shaking her head.

– Don't bother!

They watched each other, their stares burning holes in the other.

– My offer still stands. You should consider it, youngling.

One more condescending statement, one more provocation. Liz didn't reply.

In what seemed like one step, instead of a series of them the creature rushed to the balcony and was gone the next moment. Liz didn't bother to rush to the balcony to look for her, knowing beyond knowing there would be nothing to see.

2

He woke up from yet another waking dream.

– They killed all the men and older males and youngest children, and took the females as slaves. The somewhat able boys were incorporated into his army.

Lee looked aghast at Carla, the memory suddenly raw and painful in his awakened mind.

– That's his method of warfare, his creed, she stressed. – He conquers the world tribe by tribe, nation by nation, crushing people's spirit to dust, doing so repeatedly, in order to become master of the world, on his path to true godhood.

He looked at Eloise. They both shivered in the warm sunshine, unable to help themselves, shaking in despair and rage.

A woman at the other side of the street cried out in a foreign language to the man meeting up with her. Lee thought for a moment he understood what she was saying, but the meaning eluded him.

– «I'm so happy»… Eloise frowned, excited, startled and apprehensive, – «so happy to see you again».

– «I'm so happy to see you again, just as I've been a thousand times before this», Carla translated.

Lee looked at her, at them both with fondness and frustration.

– What can I say, she joked. – I have a knack for languages…

– You must have learned all the tongues of the Earth by now, he said sourly

He realized startled that he had spoken Old English to her.

– I always travel extensively to catch up with old friends, but sometimes I don't have to.

– Sometimes, they come to you, he stated.

She put her arms around his neck and kissed him softly, passionately.

– We're all learning to remember. We will keep doing that for the eternity to come. Only the professed master of the world and a few others and all those he has made his supporters wish to keep that bounty from us.

The shiver passed down his spine like an electric charge. He returned her kiss with equal passion.

– Sometimes there are riders, he mumbled in a foreign language he couldn't identify.

A raven screeched somewhere. He saw it, not with his eyes, but with his spirit, a sight far clearer and more haunting.

They approached a playground, not quite there yet, expecting to see a bunch of children, but those playing there were adults, adults moving like children in a circle, choiring, singing, chanting.

Twenty-one, they were twenty and one.

– *Join the circle, the wheel turning, and let it burn,* they sang heartily.

He understood, even as understanding eluded him, comforted by Carla's soft smile.

He realized that they weren't quite adults, after all, but late teenagers, only a few years older than himself. They had looked older at first, then younger, then older again, until settling in their current form in his blurred vision.

Someone, somewhere played a xylophone. The dance matched its rhythm perfectly. The dancers clearly had agile bodies, their moves that of far more than mere dancers. A girl, the lead singer stood out to Lee. She practically glowed in his more sensitive eyes.

He glanced at Carla. She teased him with her usual enigmatic smile, but didn't speak.

There was something eerie about the entire scene, the stage (if a stage there was), both unfamiliar and not in front of them. He spoke a name. The girl looked at him, clearly confused.

Not all the dancers were siblings, but most of them clearly were and of mixed blood, half Asian, half European. They were tall and big, contrary to most Asians, even bigger than most of European ancestry, almost as tall as Lewis himself. It was a startling, amazing sight.

The twenty and one stopped their dance, but kept dancing.

Lewis caught the eyes of the girl with blonde hair.

– There is something very familiar there, Eloise whispered, – but I can't place it.

– Hi, he heard himself say. – I loved your dance.

He remembered it, remembered every step and turn, and he realized startled that that thought didn't startle him.

– Thank you, the girl said. – That's sweet of you to say.

She stepped forward and reached out a hand.

– Hi, she greeted him, – I'm Kimberly Russel, nice to meet you.

Her abundant snarl of a smile overwhelmed him. The flash of her fangs blinded him.

He knew where he had seen her face.

– Your father is Victor Russel, Eloise yelped, unable to help herself, blushing deeply.

– Guilty as charged, Kimberly said with a strange expression of shame and pride she shared with most of her siblings.

She crouched, touching her midsection and pulled back the hand that had touched his, as if in pain, suddenly sweating profusely.

She looked at them with what was now distinct fear.

– I'm sorry, she said. – We must go.

– Go? Lee said puzzled.

She turned and walked away with quick steps. One of the boys sent them a smile of regret and blocked the path for Lewis when he attempted to catch up with her. Lewis didn't attempt to contest the matter, but stopped his forward motion more or less voluntarily.

All the twenty and one rushed off. In a matter of moments, the three stood there alone.

Lewis stood there, facing Carla.

– I felt…

– You felt a kinship beyond blood with her, Carla interrupted him, – something practically tearing you up inside.

He stared open-mouthed at her.

– The reason will reveal itself in time. Be content with that.

Carla Wolf said.

– That was absolutely bizarre, Eloise stated.

It was as if he and Carla stood there alone, as if Eloise wasn't present, and the circle, the wheel around them speeded up and turned faster than ever.

The world turned blurry and unreachable before him.

3

Ted and Lynn patrolled their given area for the day. They knew others were close, less than a block off on all sides, but still felt to a certain degree vulnerable and isolated in a street filled with potential hostiles.

– They will come for us, right? Lynn said, cursing her loud and weak voice.

– They will come for us, he confirmed. – If we let them, they will come for us all, so we will stop them long before that happens.

– Stop them cold! She stated with passion and venom, making him smile in acknowledgement to her, the snarl of a smile she loved so much.

His eyes moved constantly back and forth, up and down, to all sides. It didn't unnerve her anymore. When he turned his head, and cast a glance behind him, it looked like the most natural act in the world.

He felt it easily, how she experienced him. It took no effort at all.

His eyes turned distant, even as he kept walking, even as his footing stayed firm. She attempted to draw his attention, in vain. Waving her hand in front of his eyes brought no reaction at all.

– Are you here? She wondered.

– I've always been here. He frowned. – I've never walked these streets, until recently, but they were intimately familiar to me long before I set my foot here.

He blinked one single time, and far older streets of far older cities revealed themselves to him.

He shook his head.

– Current human society is even more insane than I previously believed, disregarding the most fundamental truths about life and eternity.

– I know what you mean, she whispered. – I've learned so much since I met you, all you guys.

He kissed her, a soft kiss still filled with fiery passion.

Even as his eyes kept moving and scouting the surroundings.

A figure materialized from the surroundings and approached them.

– She's exactly where you said she would be, Lynn said excited, beyond excited.

The woman looked confused at first, before brightening.

– Ted? She asked perplexed. – Ted Warren?

She had known him as Ted Cousin. He looked at Margaux Thompson across an Abyss that felt far wider than eleven years.

– Hello, Margie, he greeted her.

– You've changed, of course, she said nervously. – You were hardly more than a boy when I last saw you, but I… *heard* you were in town, and once I knew that, recognizing you became child's play.

The snarl of a smile crossed his lips again.

– Look at you! She marveled. – I thought the newspaper and news coverage were impressive, but they didn't really do you justice…

He took a bow, and looked at her with steady eyes.

She was the one who was blushing, not him.

She caught herself, becoming more intense, anxious.

– Hugo Manning is here, she said.

– I know! He shrugged.

– I figured you've already encountered him, she said insistent, – but he's preparing something very sinister against you and your followers. A friend of a friend is a disciple of his, and my friend heard some very disturbing shit.

She fell more back to the hippie lingo. It made him smile.

– I haven't forgotten, she stated. – Most of my former friends have, but I never will!

Ted gave a signal. Lynn noticed, but Margaux didn't.

He started moving. They followed him with quick steps. He walked a little faster than usual, but didn't seem to be in a hurry. Margaux looked anxiously at him. Lynn sent her a smug grin.

The path narrowed before him, into one single point, only a few possibilities. He had experienced that before, even though he hadn't been this aware of it before. It always brought nausea to his mind.

He didn't sense Liz, not in more than a rudimentary way, but he still knew exactly where she was at that moment in time. The labyrinth drew itself in his overactive, feverish mind. He had dreamed of himself walking through it many times.

Liz sensed him, sensed virtually everything in her close and far surroundings. Suddenly, startled, he realized he had been wrong. He did sense her, did sense her in a completely new way, now, in this state of… chrysalis.

The Port Authority was not far away. The narrow path before him stayed narrow, even at the swirling center of the station, where people crossed back and forth, in all directions.

– It's strange how we always seem to end up here, one way or another, Lynn mused. – I feel so different from when I first arrived here.

He pondered her words.

– I don't really find it strange at all, he mused. – This is a crossroads, and we are of the crossroads.

She pondered his words.

– It's true. I've always felt outside everything. I guess that was one major reason why I came here, here to a city of crossroads in the first place.

He measured her reaction and his own, knew she was jittery because he was, knew that nothing showed on the outside, but she knew him well enough now to see when he was distracted, when he moved his eyes even more than he usually did.

He studied the surroundings, the added security level. The hall seemed to change around him, becoming something threatening and foul, closed off, instead of the somewhat thriving crossroads most others perceived.

There was a commotion, a slight disturbance as the woman and man emerged from the gates. He had never actually seen Martine Rubleaux and Morgan Lombard in the flesh before, but he still remembered them from a thousand unrealized dreams unfolding before him this very moment.

He heard cries in the night. It didn't seem to matter that the sun brightened the entire hall. He heard insane howls of pain and terror, and he saw the sister and brother chuckle pleased. The two of them and their visible and not so visible bodyguards crossed the hall. He knew she had spotted him. Very few others noticed or were close to noticing, but he did.

They walked out the front exit. Several cars waited for them out there. They stepped into the third car in a row of five, cars that started moving as if on cue. The activity surrounding the cortege picked up, picked up considerably. Ted visualized it in his mind, how the resident Janus Clan members jumped into cars in the area around Port Authority, and started tailing the cortege with Rubleaux and Lombard. Ted rose as well. Lynn and Margaux followed him an instant later, as if being acutely attuned to him.

The visuals changed in his perception, turning dark and foreboding. The darkness had become his friend, his companion in recent years, but not this. The sense of menace and impending doom had become all too real.

He zoomed in on the young man, the bald boy sitting by Rubleaux's side, on his face, the lack of expression, the empty eyes, and he saw a row, an endless row of smiling dolls, his brethren and humanity as a whole. Cold sweat broke on his brow.

Lynn noticed, of course. She had learned to know him well enough for that. His dogged expression became hers. Two pairs of feet picked up speed, and Margaux had to compensate in order to keep up.

Eric drove the van stopping, or rather slowing down in front of them outside. Ted opened the door and he and his two companions jumped into the moving van, Margaux with some difficulty. Eric speeded up, and they were on their way.

The city and every piece of it moved around them, even more than it usually did, through Ted's heightened senses, his constantly higher level of consciousness. Time itself seemed to be speeding up, in pushes and pulls. His attention was fully focused on the hunt, on the ongoing event developing, but one part of his mind was still taking in the streets and the people walking them. He was multitasking as always. He didn't mind. It made him more focused, not less.

It became part of the bigger picture he needed… in order to… to understand and anticipate possible hurdles and traps.

One crucial piece was missing. He noticed it in numerous ways. The entire scenery seemed… awkward, out of place. Then he spotted Patrick joining them from the adjacent street and everything fell into place.

He was driving and Caitlin and Sylvia were passengers.

– What is it? Eric wondered, as astute as ever.

Ted closed and opened his eyes, speaking with his downright spooky, ghostly voice.

– For the first time in my life all the pieces of the puzzle… fit.

Everything was coming together, like neat little pieces of an ever-changing painting.

It was exhilarating to the point of being over the top, and he had to pull himself together, deliberately toning down his raging emotions.

The seething fire within remained and flourished.

Patrick almost collided with another car and it seemed like a pure miracle, a startling chain of coincidence that he didn't, evading it just in the nick of time.

– Everything comes together here, Ted stated, – before parting again.

Patrick's face changed briefly in his vision into Ethel's, before shifting back.

Eric looked startled, with a glimmer of understanding at Ted.

Then the moment was lost, and the present caught up with them.

Patrick's unique perception ingrained itself in Ted, how he saw everything in moments… or between moments they shared. Another moment visited Ted, where he felt he almost regained his missing power, but then that moment was also lost. Reality continued its race.

The cortege with Martine Rubleaux and Morgan Lombard drove on ahead. Ted blinked slowly. He still remembered the visions, remembered them vividly, even though he could no longer bring them forth except as memories.

The walls of the tall buildings on both sides seemed to shift and shake, and once again he was tempted into believing that his powers were returning.

He focused on the task, on the ongoing event making sweat pour into his eyes.

Just like that, in successive flashes of moments they found themselves on the bridge, on yet another dangerous bottleneck.

– This would be a good place to take us out, Eric remarked.

– It would, Ted acknowledged.

He knew he didn't seem particularly worried.

They reached the Jersey side and Fort Lee just as the first signs of red started showing in the western sky. The route unfolded in Ted's expanded mind. The unfamiliar, familiar urban sprawl spread out before him. He spotted the welcoming committee from the no longer dusty warehouse awaiting Martine and Morgan and loyal and brainwashed men and women, even though he couldn't actually see them with his half-closed eyes. He saw more of his long-time visions turning solid, becoming real.

– They know we're coming for them, right? Margaux said, slowly grasping the situation, the setting. – They must know.

– They know! Lynn nodded vigorously. – It won't be pretty, but they won't know what hit them.

She sounded and seemed totally calm and confident, the look she sent Ted filled with trust.

He didn't notice or didn't reveal that he noticed. His attention stayed on what was happening outside the car, on all the whirling movement in the streets they rushed through.

Patrick and the others crossing the bridge after him, had now reached Fort Lee, and were firmly entrenched in its streets and the upcoming conflict.

– Everything is in place, Ted said. – We're set to go.

He knew he sounded casual, almost indifferent, knew it distressed the others.

The sound of gunfire echoed in his ears, but he knew from the others' lack of reaction that it wasn't real, wasn't actually happening yet.

It mixed with his hammering heart, with all the close and distant hammering hearts.

– Turn left, they heard Patrick's casual, insistent voice.

– Is he insane? Eric cried. – There are…

Ted took the wheel and turned the van sharply to the left. They managed just about to avoid a car charging them from the right. It missed them with a hair's bread.

– … lots of cars in the other lane.

There were lots of sounds of screeching tires and of other cars crashing. They drove on unscathed.

– That was just a test, Ted said. – They wanted to take our measure, and they did, did learn something.

A dark mist drifted through the street, practically following them down the dark, dark path, and startled he realized that it was something new. Their path turned into a river, or he perceived it that way. The river, the river of time was familiar to him. It didn't surprise him when its water slammed the car's doors.

They drove through an unfamiliar street, a long, long tunnel with the shadow at its end.

It… began. Hearts beat faster, fingers twitched around triggers, skin slipped around metal. The open space he had seen a million times in his dreams and visions appeared through his physical eyes.

The moment the car with Martine Rubleaux and Morgan Lombard reached the center of the large square the machineguns and grenade launchers played up from both sides, from the buildings where Liz's squad had waited. The onslaught and inferno of explosions and the roar of a thousand bullets shook the air and the ground.

All the cars were armored, fortified to stand against such a barrage. While cars and people around them were blown to pieces, the cortege drove on.

A direct hit made one car crack and stop. Another had one of its wheels ruined and slid from side to side before crashing with a lamppost. People present on the square ran off in full-scale panic. Abby, leading one of the squads in one of the buildings had turned pale and sweaty, but she kept firing. A couple of the others had stopped, but she waved to them, commanded them to keep it up.

– Everyone enslaving others will pay, she snarled.

It worked. Rage once more supplanted the reluctance in Penny and Cathy's eyes. They fired one more grenade each.

The people in the wrecks still alive and kicking rushed out of them and started returning the fire. They fell in a hail of bullets.

Total chaos ruled. Large holes appeared where there once had been even ground. The cars on the heels of the cortege reached the square. They drove close to the buildings, where there were no holes. Ted, Liz and Patrick arrived and everyone not already there arrived with them.

Blood and a hot draft filled the plaza. A large garage door opened in a building ahead and the cortege drove through. The moment the large car had entered the building a heavy wall fell down and blocked the access.

Memories of what had never happened kept assaulting Ted as he led Patrick and several teams rushing in from all angles in front of the building through an alternative entrance. He saw the chopper on the roof crystal clear in his mind, and also Liz scaling the building on the outside, how she practically dragged herself up by the hands and only occasionally used her feet to support her. It was like watching an ape climbing a tree, and people stared astonished at it from the ground.

Rachel was scaling another wall. Her method was different from Liz's, but just as fast and agile. It seemed to those watching that her entire body was moving, was stretching and bending in order to find the most effective path to the roof.

– Ambush, Patrick said relaxed, almost offhand.

Those charging the stairs stopped by a corner. A murderous salvo that would have hit them right in the front if they had not stopped in time whistled past the corner and penetrated the wall behind. Ted and several others stepped forward and fired at the exposed shooters. They were hit and fell in pools of blood. Ted and Eric charged forward and took care of those awaiting them behind the next corner. It was like they had always worked together, as if they knew each other's moves before they made them. More enemies fell in murderous crossfire.

– These are just expandable muscle, Ted said almost relaxed. – We need to get to the roof fast.

The chopper had started up there, if its engine had ever been turned off. The rotors spun without sound in his head, round and round and round.

His left arm burned. He had been hit. Irritation flared.

He ignored it, leaving it behind as he rushed on, as he led his people higher up in the building. Excitement flushed his veins, the blood burning wherever it reached. He ignored it.

The long dark tunnel existence had become stretched on just a little longer, but that stretch was littered with danger, with rough edges and pools of blood.

He fired around a corner. Screams filled the air and bodies dropped to the floor. They ran on.

The fight proceeded floor by floor. Rubleaux and Lombard's dedicated racists fought without concern for their own safety, with an obsessive zeal bordering on the insane.

– Die, mutants, DIE! A woman acting like a lunatic parody of a mutant hater screamed and fired a barrage at Ted and those around him.

Several of them were hit. Patrick hit her with a round of bullets also hitting many behind her, just as they stepped out to fire a follow up.

– Sorry, he said, responding to Ted's scowl. – I was too late. Her act was totally random, impulsive. Such acts are always harder to determine.

Ted started running. They heard the snarl rise from his throat, from his very being.

– We're moving too slow, he shouted. – MOVE! Don't stop for anything!

They followed him, following him straight into the next nest of enemies. One fired a round of bullet right into his chest. Ted stumbled back and hit the wall. Patrick and Eric, calm and collected fired at all the exposed enemies. Ted recovered quickly and started running again, driven by something both encouraging and terrifying to those following him.

Rubleaux, surrounded by four of her dedicated disciples and protectors with machineguns stepped out on the roof. They moved fast and decisive towards the waiting chopper. There were no hurdles in sight. Everything seemed solid, seemed set in stone.

Then, there was movement, a whirl of moving air, of flesh and bone and burning eyes moving. Elizabeth Warren had decked two of them before they had even reacted. She took out the third the next moment and the fourth seemed to be hit by invisible air. Liz jumped at Rubleaux and struck her down. Five unmoving people rested unconscious on the roof.

Then there was more movement. Two arrows hit the fireeyed woman. There was an electrical discharge. Liz screamed and collapsed. She stretched out on the roof. She didn't move.

The door to the roof opened. Martine Rubleaux and Morgan Lombard stepped through it. They were rushing forward, surrounded by eight of their most loyal guards.

Rubleaux stopped by Liz, looking down on her with a triumphant grin.

– I have a stand in, she chuckled. – It has proven useful on so many occasions.

She who had looked like Martine Rubleaux began shimmering. Her features changed and the body turned bigger.

– We had to sacrifice a few pawns. Martine said filled with triumph. – It's regrettable, but our reward is great, is immense. We have captured at least one of the People, one of added value to you, and there might be *more*.

Her eyes and very being were practically glowing with pride, as she addressed her half-brother.

Lombard nodded to her, to the guards, ignoring the wicked jibe.

– Into the chopper, he barked. – Fast!

One of them grabbed the unconscious Liz and put her on the shoulder. Then, it was as if she began shimmering as well. Her features changed, and her body turned bigger, with a body covered by hard skin.

It seemed like the chopper was lifted up by a mighty hand and that a swat by that hand threw it across the roof and into a wall. The explosion rocked the building, the very air surrounding them.

The neck of the guard holding the unconscious women broke like a twig. He and his load dropped to the concrete ground. Several others followed suit. Martine Rubleaux and Morgan Lombard stared frozen at the spectacle.

Liz jumped up on the floor, landing on light feet. She walked casually toward them.

– You're not the only one with shape-shifters at your disposal, she stated completely relaxed.

Rachel was already coming to. She looked at Martine with cruel, staring eyes.

More shots were fired inside the building. Then silence reigned. The door opened, and Ted and a number of others stepped outside.

– I told you I was coming for you, Morgan, Liz cried. – I'm even more pleased we managed to make it a family affair. Congratulations, my guess is that no one of your ilk has ever stood face to face with so many members of the Janus Clan before.

Martine and Morgan went for their guns. Ted shot her, while Eric filled Morgan with lead.

Both fell to the concrete floor. Morgan stared up with dead eyes.

Martine was still alive. She gasped, as she attempted to speak, stricken and hateful to the last.

– How could you do it? She gasped. – We had covered all the bases, meeting you with superior forces you couldn't possibly overcome or easily overcome. All projections told us we would get away with you, at least with you.

She spoke to Liz. Liz just chuckled softly. She felt so good, so immensely great!

– We had won, Martine Rubleaux shouted. – Won! Witches burned in the millions. They were nothing but ashes. And we were victorious.

– Just like you thought you had, now, Ted said.

The dull light in her eyes faded.

– We will never fade, Ted stated calmly. – Kill a million of us, kill billions. We will always be there, facing you.

– You don't truly know us, Liz said patronizingly. – You only think you do, think your collected biological data covers all the bases.

Martine Rubleaux stared at them with unmoving eyes.

– Now, you know it doesn't.

The patronizing snarl rocked the dead woman.

– You still don't get it, do you, Liz said softly to the shimmering air, – still don't get the truth about your own existence? How sad!

She severed Martine's head from her physical body with a slight focus of her power. A moment later she had done the same with Morgan. Ted took a photo of the two heads levitating in the air.

Eric held out a large plastic bag. Liz dumped the heads there.

– This was one pivotal moment, she said softly. – It has burned in our minds for months. Not all moments do. Our journey through this particular dark tunnel has come to an end. Everything is opening up, now.

Rachel was gone. They had looked away from her one tiny moment, and lost sight of her. Liz shook her head.

They picked up the five unconscious and bald people, and carried them on their shoulders. The load felt light.

The warriors left the roof, walked down stairs splashed with blood and remains. Two stakes had been stuck on the small lawn outside. Liz put the heads on top of them. Ted took another picture, a whole series of them.

– Too bad these won't ever be appreciated by an adoring public, he said and shook his head in regret.

– You never know, Liz chuckled. – You never know!

They jumped into the awaiting cars and left the place with very relaxed driving. The dust and drops of blood in the air had still not settled and wouldn't for hours.

– It won't be shown on the nine o'clock news and other fake news programs either, Ted said with a long face.

– The news of it will spread like wildfire, Liz stated with immense pride and confidence.

Everyone passed by a particular car heading back to Manhattan heard the dark laughter. They couldn't state with absolute certainty that it was real, but they kept hearing it in the days and nights to come, far into dreams and nightmares and what was beyond.

4

Liz stood there barefoot, fairly well dressed in red and black, but with no panties. Everyone could glimpse what was hidden by the miniskirt, if they made an effort. Her curves pushed at the tight fabric. Dark shadows twinkled in the fairly large, but still intimate room. Smoke drifted in the air. She smelled the Dust, drawing it in from the very ether surrounding her, and the sweaty, excited people present.

This was Twilight Shadow - the somewhat exclusive club on the Upper East Side owned by Rachel Dalhart. It was more or less packed. Rumors of tonight's performer had circulated for weeks, until they had finally been confirmed only two days ago.

Behind her Linsey and the drummer and bass player stood playing. They played a low-keyed instrumental. Liz just stood there, a hood covering most of her head.

She began humming, humming their song, singing the lyrics, the words she had no difficulties recalling, and the music changed to accommodate her.

Fly
The bird can fly
Fly in fire, fly in shadow
It doesn't need to fear anything
Except perhaps death
The walking death
I see a valley

A circle of fire and shadow
And I dance in its shade
On the edge of its abyss

Her feet moved, as her dancing began. They watched her, and it didn't resemble any other dance they had ever seen. She seemed to be floating, more than moving her feet, even though her feet clearly, firmly touched the floor, doing so like silent drums, like thunder.

The thunder lingered, clearly present in the room, like dark clouds a hot afternoon just after the first lightning.

She removed the hood, her long, dark hair instantly flowing around her body, one sizzling with energy with each new intense move. The dark, golden skin seemed to be free of sweat, but if one looked closer, there were tiny droplets of it on her brow. Alvin Draper went apeshit on the percussion. She moved even faster in order to keep up with his rhythm. The visions once again assaulted her. She saw other dancers around tall fires, saw the dance unfold in many different lands and ages. It, with variances basically stayed the same. She didn't have to strive hard to keep up. It came to her naturally.

The dance, at least its purely physical aspect ended with the fading of the music. The communication between the dancer and the players remained.

She turned towards the spectators, to everyone present on this particular venue tonight, easily catching their expectation and badly concealed excitement.

– This is an ancient dance, she said, – from an age where women's sexuality could be displayed without fear.

Her silky, intense voice reached everyone within hearing range, all over the building, not just in this hall.

– Today is different. Today all humans are taught to repress their emotions and expression of it from an early age. Girls are taught that they are worth less, that they should submit to male authority and demand less, a lesser position in society and in relationships. Just because it feels right, doesn't mean it is. Women are socialized into accepting, even enjoying or preferring male dominance. Girls are raised to cater to fragile egos of men, to make themselves *less* than they are. *Enough!*

The after-image of her fist spread through the room and hazy visions.

– Yes, it's still like that, even after a decade of supposed women liberation. It started many centuries ago, as religion rose from virtual obscurity to a dominant position in human life. St Augustine, a typical christian stated the following words of wisdom: «Women shouldn't be educated in any way, but segregated as the cause of hideous and involuntary erections in holy men».

I recognized early the profound hypocrisy and malevolence of Christianity and religion in general. Religion is one of the major poxes of mankind.

The drums picked up again, slowly, shaking the ears and the bodies and minds gathered at this place this night.

She started shouting, unexpectedly and shocking.

– «I DO NOT WANT TO BE THE LEADER. I REFUSE TO BE THE LEADER. I WANT TO LIVE DARKLY AND RICHLY IN MY FEMALENESS. I WANT A MAN LYING OVER ME, ALWAYS OVER ME. HIS WILL, HIS PLEASURE, HIS DESIRE, HIS LIFE, HIS WORK, HIS SEXUALITY THE TOUCHSTONE, THE COMMAND, MY PIVOT. I DON'T MIND WORKING, HOLDING MY GROUND INTELLECTUALLY, ARTISTICALLY; BUT AS A WOMAN, OH, GOD, AS A WOMAN I WANT TO BE DOMINATED. I DON'T MIND BEING TOLD TO STAND ON MY OWN FEET, NOT TO CLING, BE ALL THAT I AM CAPABLE OF DOING, BUT I AM GOING TO BE PURSUED, FUCKED, POSSESSED BY THE WILL OF A MALE AT HIS TIME, HIS BIDDING».

Everybody held their breath, in the sudden silence following her words.

– Anais Nin said that, in passion and reason.

Slowly, only slowly they exhaled and started breathing again, still unable to take their eyes off the mirage on the stage.

– Anyway, I certainly don't agree with her. Politics and everything else, really, are just too important to leave to one half, the stupid half of the population…

The grin, the devil-may-care glow in her eyes drew them in, pulled them to her like flies to sweets.

– I agree with her in what she said at another occasion, though: «How wrong is it for a woman to expect the man to build the world she wants, rather than to create it herself?» I guess she said those very different statements at different parts of her life.

She danced some more, an enticing, sensual dance. They couldn't take their eyes off her.

– I learned that dance and this way of dancing in the tribal community in the Amazons. They don't mince word or emotions there, and neither do I anymore. When I get down on my knees, it's not to pray or beg.

The mumble rose yet again in the hall, pushing at the ceiling.

The music picked up and rose and fell with her moves and the intensity of her words.

– To the guys saying they want a girl who will fix them a snack after sex: If she's capable of walking you haven't earned a goddamn sandwich!

Uncertain laughter spread throughout the room. She returned the laughter, making it potent and powerful. She snarled it at them, like a curse.

– I want you to come and rape me and have me RIP YOUR BALLS FROM YOUR BODIES

Cries of horror and astonishment filled the moist room, spreading far beyond the walls.

She jumped to Alvin Draper's side, relieving him of the sticks. He gave in to her desire without resistance. She began drumming, and each hit on the drums echoed like thunder, exactly like thunder. The young girl played as if possessed, and no one present had ever heard anything like it before.

Gasps rose from wide open mouths, doing so to such a point that they filled all spaces between flesh and mind and spirit. The final beat on the drum was so hard that both the stick and the drum broke, fracturing like a landslide. She stood up and walked to the front of the stage again.

The thunder faded, the drums faded and the music as well. The room and everyone in it had fallen completely silent. She stood there in front of them again, so very close to each and everyone present. Every word and syllable hammered them.

– Yes, be afraid, like modern society is afraid of woman sexuality… or stand on your feet, taking on the world head on.

And that was it. It stopped, but didn't end. It echoed in their feverish minds forever.

Chapter 9

She walked among them afterwards, taking in their scent and mood, interacting with them on both a conscious and subconscious level. The drums still played in her head, opening her up further.

They ceased being drums, or only drums. The music rose within and without, playing all kinds of sensations in her deep self.

She sat around a packed table with Frances and Abby and several others. People flocked to her like rivers to the sea.

A young woman stepped forward.

– You're saying we should never have a prolonged relationship with a man?

– No. Liz shook her head. – I'm not saying that, not saying that at all. I'm simply saying you're not there to serve him or his ego. If he isn't okay with that, he isn't worth your time.

– But, what if it feels good being with him in spite of that?

– As stated, Liz shrugged, – even if it feels good, it might not be. If you aren't on equal footing, it's your upbringing and its imposed sensibilities speaking. Trust truth, not empty illusions and deceptions!

The woman glanced backwards, at her companion, the scowling man.

A man stepped forward and spoke up.

– I want to thank you, he said. – You've made everything so much clearer to me. Men are just as much trapped as women in this system of oppression.

– I would agree with that, she Liz acknowledged. – If you come to one of the meetings, you will indeed see that we explore that angle as well. Boys are told from an early age that they aren't men if they aren't bullies, aren't oppressors, and many women attempting to compensate for being oppressed overcompensate to the point of becoming oppressors themselves, emulating the bullies, not fighting them. Current society, in various overt and sneaky ways is oppressing everyone.

She held court for quite a while, while emotions seethed and burned all around her.

If they had initially entertained the idea that she was inferior because of her youth, they quickly forgot that there was a twenty-year old girl sitting there.

– You're just one of those disgusting feminists, a man snarled, practically spitting saliva from his open mouth.

– Thank you, what a kind thing to say, she grinned.

Laughter filled the room.

– Many men can't handle facing truly independent women, she added. –

Some males, as incredible as that sounds or should sound see feminism as a threat to their manhood. They're not very confident or mature, I guess.

The laughter turned wicked.

– We're raised in a patriarchal society, with its twisted view on human relations, Abby said. – Equally insecure females are afraid that they will not appear to be sufficiently «feminine», as if feminine means being weak and subservient and dependent.

– The bottom line is that sex and everything, all human interaction, should actually come from mutual interest and/or respect between two or more people, Lee said. – Is the word «mutual» really that hard to understand?

– You snotty little shit, the man with saliva flowing from his mouth shouted, finally finding an outlet, a direction for his frustration and anger.

Lee rose abruptly, towering above the grown man. The grown man backed off and kept backing off, pushing himself through the tight crowd in an attempt to reach the entrance as soon as possible.

The scene shifted again. It felt amazing how fast the mood turned more relaxed. More males and females approached Liz, doing so in far nicer ways. She spoke to them, exchanged thoughts with them and felt good about it.

She was dancing and Ted was dancing with her, even when he wasn't. She glimpsed him between the moments. They were holding hands without being physically close, touching constantly without touching. It was the most intimate act she had ever experienced.

Many joined her on her street walk later. The considerable number of people, people walking the night caused a stir, even among others of equal bent.

The smile kept playing on her lips. It did so naturally, without any effort on her part.

– New York City changes from area to area, from one block to another, she mused. – It's quite fascinating!

One single step could bring them from one world to another. Even though nothing overt changed, other, more subtle things did. One part of a given street could be fairly safe for people walking there, another could be downright unsafe the moment a person crossed an invisible demarcation line.

They observed it as it happened, catching people's nervous, jittery glances.

But the Janus Clan walked everywhere with impunity and no one bothered them.

– Rape isn't illegal, really, she spat at a few police officers standing on a corner. – Only a few rapists are punished.

They looked sullenly at her, glaring at her with something bordering on hatred. Fear and a fundamental insecurity festered deep down in them all. Liz and her people walked on, crossing several more invisible lines.

– We're such a remarkable sight, Frances marveled, – to friend and foe alike.

The laughter shook flesh and concrete and the very air they breathed.

– In a few months, you will look back at yourself as you are now, and laugh yourself silly, Liz remarked. – This has only been the modest beginning for you.

The laughter turned uncertain by her kind, condescending words.

– To those watching us through their shivering hearts, this day will live on in infamy, though.

The laughter turned hearty again. Liz grinned or rather snarled, her fangs very visible and distinct.

– I was only seventeen when I and Ted turned New Orleans on its head, she said brightly. – New York City should be a piece of cake, a nice, relaxing holiday.

She was glowing in anticipation.

Young black women and men stood on a corner. Liz had heard them speak for quite some time. She smiled. The others smiled as well. The young women and men approached them almost before they entered that particular street. Liz and the others had stopped well before they were in motion. They waited patiently, studying the others exchanging glances.

A tall and big woman, clearly the leader, the leading force stopped.

– I had your speech referred to me, she snorted. – It was quite the nice speech… coming from a white girl.

– Perception is a strange and funny thing, isn't it, Eliza? Liz mused. – You may not have noticed, but my skin is actually far darker than yours…

She couldn't keep her voice completely free from the patronizing tone exhibited by the other, and didn't care to. The open smile crossed over into the familiar snarl. Her voice kept a taint of soreness the other lacked, though.

– I know black women are at the low end of the totem pole in the white patriarch society. You can skip your speech. That's certainly one of the things we're set to change. I know you're no one's toy. I love that!

– You're awfully confident, Eliza said, visibly taken aback.

– You know there are cracks in that confidence, Liz said softly. – You've read up on me. You know I seek aid, seek other seekers.

The silence lingered between them.

– What do you want? Eliza asked, not really asking.

Liz's wicked grin made her shiver a bit, just a bit. She caught herself with an effort. Liz walked on. Those following her did as well. Eliza hesitated only a few moments before following her. Eliza's charges joined in.

Eliza hurried to catch up with Liz, anger and puzzlement warring within and without.

– You snapped your fingers and made us follow you, she said, clearly shaken.

– Was that what happened? Liz countered.

– Oh, you're good. You're very good…

They moved on, penetrating ever more unknown and hostile streets, the two groups not quite mingling. People kept staring at them, stared even harder than before, but kept their distance, making no overt move against them and their mood improved further.

A man had been following them, stalking them for some time. It didn't really worry Liz or felt like it concerned her, not even after she had identified the man.

Especially not then.

She identified dimly the man with graying hair at his temples, recognized Logan Dysart. The group turned a corner, became hidden from his hazy vision. She stopped and turned not long after that, signaling the others.

He stumbled around the corner, freezing as it dawned on him that they were waiting for him.

– Hello, Logan! She greeted him softly.

The years had not been kind to him. One glance had told her that, the next and everything following that confirmed it.

– I couldn't go back there, he choked. – I wanted to, wanted to get back to you, but I just couldn't.

She nodded, sort of understanding.

– You need to pull yourself together, Logan, she stated calmly, – need to pick up your pieces.

– I… tried, tried all the time.

– Now, you will have help, she told him. – You will have *lots* of help.

She smiled to him and knew it reminded him of the snarl she had given him years ago in the Colorado wilderness.

She walked on and he joined in with the others in her slipstream. Frances caught up with her, an eager girl filled with questions.

– I did a number on him, Liz shrugged. – He was my first fuck. I was like a savage beast, a great crazed witch and hardly cared about him at all. He was nothing but a convenient outlet for my desires. I pretty much liberated myself from personal mainstream concerns that day.

The special trickle of heat and cold, anxiety and excitement so common in

Liz Warren's presence passed down Frances's spine.

– This is a nice walk and all, but… what's its… purpose?

– This is a tour the force at the current boundaries of our territory, Liz replied both intense and calm. – We will expand it significantly in the coming weeks.

They did understand and nodded to themselves. She smiled brightly.

– It won't be pretty, she stated, – but that was never the objective.

They reached familiar ground, the inner circle of their territory. Abby began shedding more mist, but more than that was happening. She and Liz's power interacted somehow, making mist and shadow even more distinct around them.

The big, no longer cohesive group turned a corner, and there, not far ahead awaited them Port Authority.

– This is a natural center of our operations, Liz told them, – from where we can easily expand our reach.

Everybody could practically see that, how one of the city's major way stations stretched its web to a large area.

– It's too bad we haven't a resident telepath available, Liz mused, – one who could show you everything I can see.

They could, sort of see it, or at least glimpse it, in the presence of the seething shadow in their midst.

Her words alone did that, and there was more to it than that, much more.

They spread from that central point across Manhattan and New York City and even state, and further.

– We will never stop expanding our reach, Frances cried, – never stop doing this!

Many echoed her sentiment.

Liz smiled to her, and she felt a warm, warm flow fill her body.

She saw them, saw their walk as it happened. It took no effort at all. They were glowing in her mind like the great shadows they had become. Lines of fire flowed from that central point and left glowing embers across a vast area.

Frances and Marlene walked on one of the shrinking East Coast shores. The redhead stared at the other with hard eyes.

– I couldn't see it at first, she remarked.

Frances was rocked from what held most of her attention, her never resting eyes keeping a nervous eye on the surroundings.

– What?

– I couldn't see what it was about you that Liz would appreciate. You seemed hopelessly inadequate in reaching any requirement that would benefit her.

Frances frowned and turned towards her.

– Gee, thanks!

– But then, it dawned on me. I saw the determination, the slowly hardening steel, the desire to achieve wonders in your eyes. For what it's worth: I think you will do great!

A warm, warm wind surged through Frances. She blushed hard. Marlene smiled.

They both took that crucial step forward. Marlene grabbed her head and kissed her on the lips. Frances froze momentarily before softening in the other's grip and eagerly reciprocating.

It felt like minutes, hours had passed when they pulled away, pulled away just a little from each other.

– Do you think she paired us… on purpose?

– Of course, she did!

They held hands as they continued their beach walk, giving away kisses and caresses without pause and consideration.

Marlene chuckled softly. Frances looked at her with inquiring eyes.

– I used to see this… as a weapon, and I was damn good at it, until Ted showed me how empty my existence was, and I… crumbled, and I started using, using hard. I had seen myself as so strong, so hard. I was revealed exactly as weak and dependent as the chicks I had drawn into prostitution.

– I was there when you told your story, remember? Frances said softly. – I remember thinking you were so strong, much stronger than I, for having lived through that.

They kissed and fondled each other some more.

The world slowly imposed itself on them again, and they allowed it.

Sounds and movement ahead of them caught their attention. A group of people, predominately Asians did martial arts training at the far end of the shore. Frances and Marlene rushed forward and put themselves straight ahead of them, duly presenting themselves with fast and dangerous moves. The two of them sparred with each other in a continuous movement so much faster and skilled than what any individual in the large group had demonstrated.

Everyone in the group stopped and stared at the bodies moving so fast that they could hardly be seen. The two women hardly touched each other, hardly made contact. It resembled far more a dance than it did fighting, even though anyone with an untrained eye would think that they were engaged in hostile combat and not performing.

It went on for minutes, the intensity never letting up, until they quite simply stopped and sat down on a bench nearby. They sat there, evidently having a low-keyed pleasant conversation. Two, a woman and a man of the more extensive training group split from the main body and approached the two women.

The stopped at a respectful distance, hesitating.

– We watched you train, the woman said, unable to hide her excitement. – It was awesome, such a great sight to behold.

– Thank you, Marlene said.

– You don't teach, do you? The man wondered. – We would be very interested in joining up.

– We could teach, I guess, Frances pondered, – but we have teachers at our disposal that's so much better at it.

– We… recognized your style, the woman said hesitant. – It's quite distinct.

Frances grinned at her.

– If you know who's teaching us, you must also be aware of the harsh and intense training program you will be joining, and its purpose.

The woman and man exchanged glances.

– Only come if you truly wish it, Marlene shrugged. – We certainly won't force anyone. We won't even accept those not burning with dedication.

Her quiet intensity got to the couple, dug into them far more than shouting would have done.

– You, you guys alone can teach me so much, the woman said. – I can hardly fathom what… those teaching you can do. I'll come!

– I will, too, the man said.

Frances and Marlene exchanged glances, deliberately postponing the confirmation.

– Okay then, bring everyone from your class.

– Everyone?

The couple blinked.

– Indeed. Those that don't belong will quickly reveal themselves.

– You know where to find us, Marlene said. – Come to us, rise from your sore knees and come into yourself. In the group, you never truly revealed your skills, revealed yourself. With us, you will be unable to hide from yourself.

The shadow without visible eyes moved on, refocusing its attention. It was easy, exactly like turning its head.

Jess Parker, wearing suit and tie looked at his watch again. He sat on a sidewalk cafeteria with a coffee slowly turning cold.

They were a strange pair, the female and male he spotted as they turned a corner. One seemed impossible tall and the other like walking mist.

Abby sat down opposite Parker, staring him right in the eye.
– Your date, the petite blonde you ordered won't be showing up today, I'm afraid. In fact, it's safe to say that she won't be showing up - ever!
– I realized that the moment you showed up, he said, unable to keep the nervous twitching in his mouth from revealing itself.
– You recognize us? Very good, that will make this easier, will expedite matters.
The smile practically danced on her face, the red, red lips rocking up and down. Sweat covered Jess Parker's skin. He fought to keep his calm, his cool.
– You will help spread the word to all the customers you know, Lewis stated. – I imagine there are quite a few of them.
– I can do that, Parker said casually. – In fact, I'll be happy to help out.
– That's very nice of you, Abby said. – In fact, it's downright commendable…
Her mask cracked.
– How can you do it? How can you help people prostitute themselves?
– It's a business transaction, he shrugged, – excellent for both parties.
– So, you enjoy buying people?
All pretense, if there had ever been one, was gone from the conversation. Her smoke was no longer hot, but ice cold.
– What are you doing to me? He gasped. – Don't think your trick will work on me.
She moved closer to him, her face suddenly so close that he feared the breath he felt on his skin was real.
– I won't exclude completely my own role in my downfall, but know that the young, innocent and suggestible girl that I used to be was made a drug addict by my pimp. He seduced her in all important ways and changed her to fit his sinister purpose.
The smile widened.
– Then Liz came along and showed my pimp the error of his ways. She showed me how I had denigrated myself and also how my choice had consequences for others. You see, it doesn't really matter that much whether or not you buy a hooker or call girl truly volunteering her services…
– That «business transaction» you speak of is a matter of supply and demand, Lee said curtly. – You, by your demand help keep in place an extended system of degradation, violence and enslavement.
The boy seemed very adult just then, becoming a snarl shaking the grown man from head to toe.
– We could cut off your balls, Abby said abruptly. – I could! It wouldn't cost me shit. I wouldn't feel bad about it at all.

– We can do anything we want with you, Jess, Lewis said.
– You will become an anti-prostitute advocate, Abby said softly, – and all the time you're doing that, I want you to picture yourself on that giant garbage heap, a hopeless drug addict selling your body and soul for one more heroin shot. I want you to have nightmares about it every night, for the rest of your sorry existence.
She rose slowly. The boy had one more word for the grown man.
– You might drink yourself to death as well. That will work, too. It won't be a big loss to mankind.
They pulled back, fading into the background, but to the shaking man they would always remain. Their presence would stay with him, doing so for as long as he was walking and breathing.
And beyond, far, far beyond.
The shadow without visible eyes moved on, doing so many times, observing her charges do their tasks, eventually moving beyond them
A woman wearing a hood and a blind covering her eyes began haunting the streets of Manhattan, of New York City entire. She became a ghost, a shadow, a terrifying reality to those she encountered, those she set her eyes on.
Invisible eyes, very visible eyes penetrated everyone they cast their eyes on, and those people shivered, shook like leaves in their frozen hearts.
Joseph Carrington returned to his penthouse, discarding his driver and two bodyguards as he unlocked the heavy door and it slid open. He walked inside. The door slammed close behind him. He walked to the drawer, found a bottle and a glass, and poured himself a drink.
The cold draft struck him like the chilliest of winds. He turned around in a whirl of motion.
She stood at the other side of the room. She didn't move. No matter how much he studied her, he couldn't spot a single discernible move.
– How did you get here? He asked baffled.
Clothing hid every piece of her. There wasn't single piece of her skin not covered in dark clothing. She seemed to be cloaked in shadow. The bright light in the room didn't seem to be reaching her at all.
– I know who you are, what your objective is. You won't succeed with me!
The fabric didn't really conceal her features much. He saw her mouth twitch, saw that she was smiling. She was looking forward to this.
He drew his gun and fired at her.
She didn't move. The bullets stopped in midair, as if losing all forward momentum. They dropped useless to the floor. He started sweating, glancing at the door. It didn't open, as it was supposed to. The two bodyguards

hammered at it. The loud sound hardly registered as anything but dull bumps in his ears.

He wanted to charge her, but couldn't move, couldn't move an inch, not in either direction, as if he was contained in invisible concrete or something. Panic swept him. It did him no good.

The big windows broke. They didn't seem to be broken or anything, but quite simply seemed to collapse. They fell to the floor, in the living room and on the balcony.

His attention was drawn to the big, human-sized metal statue. His head was moved by an invisible hand and his eyes made to look at it, and he had no choice in the matter. Then she moved, ever so slightly. She held up a hand and an index finger, like a mime doing her silent art.

Behold! He thought, chilled to the bone.

The statue rose into the air. It floated, like a balloon. It floated out on the balcony and beyond that, into open air.

He could see it crystal clear out there, bathing in the distant city lights. It turned round and round and round.

It dropped.

He felt the beyond sinister pressure at his throat. It was just there for a tiny moment, but distinct, irrevocable, and when he could once again breathe, he felt a stark relief beyond any he had ever felt.

The door opened. The bodyguards rushed inside with drawn guns. Carrington looked back at the woman. She was gone. He had only looked away for a moment, but she was nowhere to be found. He could move again, but stood there like frozen, unable to move, to do anything but shake violently.

Liz moved through the streets like a ghost, fire and ice in one package. She was spotted occasionally, but only in glimpses, at the edge of the eyes. Only those she deliberately sought, friend and foe and neither got a good look at her, at the black fabric coating her.

She hardly felt the fabric pushing at her skin, not the tighter fit of the band covering her eyes either. Her walk had been a bit awkward at first, but she had quickly regained the firm and confident stride she easily recalled from the last time she had walked around in complete darkness. The radar, always working, always there grew to the fore of her attention, and pretty soon it felt like she had never done anything but looked at the world this way.

The flock of ravens rose from the rooftops and spread through the city. She heard the distinct flapping of wings.

She expanded her reach, expanded herself, filling the streets, the very city she roamed with her presence. Her reach spread, until no one, no one in all the near land could avoid her touch.

2

– I will always be here!

The voice hissed at her from the darkness.

Sometimes it sounded just like a boy's cracked voice, other times like a mix of adult voices, a man and a woman, and sometimes like a mighty shout echoing everywhere she was able to cast her keen attention.

The tower fell silent with the night, most of its inhabitants sleeping. Ethel wandered through her aerie, preparing the spell in her mind. The shaken, determined smile played on her shivering lips. She stepped into her sanctum, her cave. It welcomed her, smothering her like a velvet cloak.

Ethel sat down at the center of the pentacle and crossed her legs in front of her with practiced ease. The sounds and the visions came to her before she had properly begun. She heard gunfire. Experience told her that it wasn't real, wasn't current. She knew it came to her from several, from numerous sources. The visions assaulted her, even as she began casting her spell, began chanting words current, old and ancient. The words flowed from her lips, her fast-moving lips. She saw a skinny young boy tied to a bed. Another boy, one looking like his twin was beating up on him, beating him to pulp. The boy screamed in horror, but beneath the horror she glimpsed rage, glimpsed a glowing determination vanquishing all fear. It was years later. The boy and the girl with black hair had grown up and the snarl rolling from their mouth had become thunder, had become something to command respect and fear. She could not help but shake under the onslaught of that ruthless scrutiny.

Liz and Ted studied Diana as she supervised several new groups of recruits. She noticed and waved to them. They returned the wave with a catching in their throat.

– She's good with them, Liz said. – She has recovered well. We've done a great job with her and the rest.

He nodded in acknowledgement. Her words found an echo in his mind. Hands sought and found hands, and squeezed and found the contact they both had desperately sought.

Liz held a speech to their people, their current present warriors.

– To say that those in charge are failing is to give them too much credit. They're not failing in anything, not from their perspective. They're succeeding in keeping the population subjugated. In order to counter that we must become even fiercer and bolder in our approach, and when that happens you will become even more targets then you currently are, and you will need to step up accordingly. Remember:

She took a small break, pausing, allowing her words to linger and gather momentum.

– All acts of conformity, however minor, are damnable. All acts of rebellion, however futile, are glorious. Remember this, in the many cold and hot nights ahead.

Ethel sat in her aerie, weaving her magick.

The fair haired girl and dark-haired boy exercised in a park in Chicago long ago. The same boy and girl, adult and powerful, joined with the black-haired woman exercising in the vast desert, as if they had always done so, as if they were born to do it.

An old woman rested in bed. She looked frail and tired at first glance, but not at the second, third or tenth. Her body withered and died, but not her spirit. A young man or a seemingly young man with fireeyes glowing like a thousand bonfires sat with her.

– You go to New York, he told her. – Go there when the time is right. I won't be there, but many of the others will be. The rest of us will gather in time.

– In time, she breathed.

Nick Warren stood by the bed until Carla Wolf drew her last breath, and her spirit, her soul, her Shadow rose from the spent shell.

Ethel Warren sat there mumbling, swearing her spells.

– I wish you into existence. You become my creation, my intended.

The dark voice filled the room, the apartment, spreading beyond it, seeking its targets of flesh and mind. Silent whispers reached ears and thought.

Patrick and Jean stopped the moment they stepped outside and caught each other's eyes.

They both frowned a bit, as if listening to a sound they couldn't catch.

– You needed… fresh air, too, huh? She said coyly.

– I did, he willingly conceded. – They're mostly kids in there. It can be a bit too much sometimes.

– They're quite mature, though, she mused, – and are fortunate in the sense that they have had the blindfolds removed from their eyes early in life, and in a fairly gentle way as well. They will never close their eyes again.

The passion in her voice and eyes… moved him. It dawned on him that they were talking to each other, but not really being that aware of what they were talking about.

– Let's go to the river.

He heard himself say.

She smiled, revealing a sudden happiness she was unable to hold back. It was exactly what she had wanted to do.

He noticed (again), as they walked off side by side that she was half a head taller than him. It surprised him how little that mattered.

They sat down on a bench. The thought striking him that they now seemed to be of even height hardly registered in his mind at all. She was blushing when he looked at her.

– It can't have been easy for you, he began cautiously.

– It certainly wasn't! She replied softly. – I can hardly recall a moment in my life when that word would have been fitting. I catch myself in wishing that I would have had a support group like we have when I grew up. I catch myself envying them, until I tell myself to be happy for them.

– I had no one, he stated, – except Ethel.

And a thousand willing bedsores, he thought.

– Poor rich boy, she teased him without malice.

She reached out with a big hand and touched his cheek.

– I see it as a miracle that I'm still somewhat anything approaching sane, she said passionately. – I'm not sane, you know, not sane at all.

She grabbed his head and pulled it close and kissed him, kissed him hard on the lips, leaning back a little, gauging his reaction.

He grabbed her hands and pushed them back on her back. She allowed it, relaxing her beyond powerful muscles and limbs. He moved close. Suddenly, they sat with their mouths near enough to share breath. Lips found lips. He saw seconds ahead without trying, and in his vision, they were still making out. He pushed harder at her. She gasped and chuckled softly.

– I didn't exactly seek to involve myself with another Warren, she said and sent him a dark glare, – but you're nothing like him, nothing like him at all.

He began fondling her. She began breathing faster almost instantly. He saw her becoming eager, needy. In his eyes, she was already there.

She freed herself from his grip easily enough. She grabbed him and began touching him as he touched her, with pretty much the same result. He found himself enjoying her turning the tables on him. She grinned wickedly. A big hand grabbed him below. An even wider grin touched her lips.

– You will have great staying power, she teased him some more. – I know that. Every Warren has. You guys could have impregnated hundreds of females in no time if you had set your mind to it.

That word, that word alone made him go frantic. He pushed at her, pushed harder at her. She softened in his grip, surrendering to his advances. He began touching her, fondling her in earnest. She relented quickly, without any real or visible struggle.

Their hearts began beating as drums, even as they became synchronized, began beating as one. He undressed her. She writhed impatiently beneath him, even as she undressed him, as they joined in violent pulls and pushes, in long, uninterrupted flows.

One touch brought another, brought the next and the next and everyone following. They both came with a shout, with a scream, as if in pain. Silence slowly, only slowly returned to the quiet and abandoned street. Both kept up the caresses afterwards, the kisses and touches, the thousand tiny, tiny touches of affection.

Ethel smiled in her cave.

3

The low laughter of the women drew him like a beacon. He walked the streets somewhere with Lynn and Margaux. They looked both like a part of him and like distinct individuals. It was a startling effect that he knew affected others watching them profoundly. They just couldn't cope with the apparent dichotomy.

Margaux laughed aloud because of something he said. He couldn't tell what, no matter how much he tried catching it moments later. It was lost in the summer heat, in the seething, shivering air.

– I must confess that I never forgot you, Ted, Margaux said softly, – not you and not your sister. You were just children, but you made such an impression on us all, beyond shaking that oaf Hugo Manning to his shaky core.

He watched as a dark cloud covered her sun and she tried embracing herself by putting her hands on her shoulder.

– Manning kept working tirelessly in order to achieve his goals in all the years since then, though, and he has pretty much amassed an empire preying on people's gullibility and prejudice. Millions watch him on TV every day as he rages against «immorality and sin», and he has a loyal pack of two-legged wolves doing his dirty work for him. We, a group I belong to and others have been helpless to stand against his crusade against anyone different and not acting within his narrow definition of accepted conduct and morality.

– My bet is that he still acts like the typical religious nut and hypocrite and don't even attempt to follow his own edicts, Ted remarked.

– No bet! Margaux chuckled and kissed him eagerly on the lips in further excitement.

They visited the storefront office giving legal aid and support against religious and sexual discrimination. Frances and Marlene and Eliza were there as well and some of the others. Liz wasn't.

Well dressed people stood across the street and photographed everyone visiting and even passing by. Ted photographed the photographers in return. They grew visibly restless.

People visiting the office grew wide-eyed and stunned by his presence. It was a moral boost to them that would even reach the mainstream media in the coming days.

– Manning and people like him have always been tyrants, he stated aloud, his voice and words carrying far and wide, – using any opportunity to fan people's prejudice and lining their own pockets doing so. Manning is one of those people echoing any horrible racist statement and bias, gaining lots of new, fanatical followers in the bargain.

His words would be repeated often in the days and nights to come. They already were. He watched as those watching and listening to him moved their lips and spoke in a quiet voice, one that would quickly rise to thunder.

An anxious woman stepped forward.

– My name is Adriane, she said. – I was one of Manning's concubine's before fleeing from his order. It wasn't always like that. We were all on equal footing at first. Hugo started out pretty much as the rest of us, just like one more member of our gathering, but he kept asserting himself, gaining more and more power within the group, until he eventually dominated us completely. Some of us left, fed up with his antics. Those remaining gave in to him and submitted to his tactics and domination.

She rushed forward and kissed Ted on the lips, before pulling back, into the shadows.

– Thank you for stopping by. Please come again anytime.

One of the men shook his hand, pumping it up and down to the point of embarrassment.

– You made it look so easy. It's such a great thing to behold, such an inspiration. Thank you, thank you!

Lynn and Margaux, Marlene and Frances all looked at him with desire in their eyes as they moved on, and he found himself appreciating that, feeling it beyond denial.

– You turned the table on him, on them magnificently, and as the man said; doing so as easy as breathing.

Marlene gloated and glowed, the red hair dancing freely in the many-directional wind. Both she and Margaux seemed to be on fire in his mind, and he caught himself wondering if it was caused by the color of their hair or something else.

– I'm impressed as well, Eliza said pointedly, making his grin grow wider.

They returned to Port Authority. It had become their way station of choice, a place where all the secrets of mankind could be glimpsed, in a glance or a stare. It was such a pleasure just sitting there and drinking coffee or enjoying spiced food, and watch the travelers arriving and leaving in an uneven stream of flesh and consciousness.

It had become the intersection he and Liz had imagined, where they spread out to the surrounding areas in New York state and beyond.

He didn't need to look at the clock on the wall. Carla and Maeve, with their squad and fresh recruits appeared from the trains. Carla sent him the unnecessary signal, her version of a thumbs up that their mission had been successful. They didn't visibly acknowledge his presence or revealed that they knew the three sitting there, but proceeded straight to the entrance. Ted knew there would be others later. He sat back in his chair, enjoying in full the company of his two companions, as he kept studying the small events in the giant hall.

They were young, but well beyond fully grown. Both their flesh and minds attracted him. Five young women sat by a table at the far end of the hall. They were a curious and rare bunch, with five distinct heritages or cultures involved. One black woman, predominately African, one Latina, one Polynesian, one tall mixed Asian and one Northern European.

– That's Ted Warren, one of them stated with a shaking voice. – I'm positive!

All of them cast long, stealthy glances across the hall. He had no trouble following their conversation. His hearing remained sharp as a nail.

– He's such a hunk, another sighed.

The others chuckled softly.

– Did you guys… did you guys read about the *orgies?*

They exchanged awkward glances, shifting uncomfortably in their chairs.

– Most of the stories are clearly exaggerated, the tall, big black woman stated decisively. – If only half of it was true, it would… it would…

He rose and approached the five women with the five women in tow.

They saw him approach, at least just before he and the other five stopped right in front of them.

– I heard you speak about me in fear and curiosity and burning interest and thought I should be kind, resolve the conflict in you.

– You… heard us? Pauline asked stunned and visibly shivering, noticing herself nodding. – But surely not…

– You were at the other side of the fucking hall, Toni stated empathically.

– I like women that have trained well and have curves, he said, as if they hadn't spoken.

– Your… cousin is far more so, Stephanie giggled, looking at him with tinder in her eyes. – She looks amazing. What's the matter, isn't she… enough for you?

– I like variety and diversity, he shrugged.

The five glanced at Lynn and Margaux and Marlene and Frances and Eliza.

– But surely you aren't that… shallow? Viola, while retaining the stars in her eyes couldn't quite keep a stint of anger from her voice. – Only finding interest in outer appearance?

– I look at both what's outside and inside, he shrugged. – And the spirit, at least to a degree does sculpt the body.

They found themselves nodding, in doubt and clarity.

– You aren't insecure girls that need to be *comforted* by a strong male, are you? Lynn teased them. – You do know your own worth without needing others' affirmation?

They nodded, clearly uncertain and timid.

Ted and his five companions grabbed chairs from the nearby tables and joined the other five.

The five insecure girls glanced at him, unable to meet the intense, direct stare.

– So, you guys are musicians, right? He prompted them.

They looked at him, stunned by his casual approach, his relative normalcy.

– We're a «girl band», they say, Stephanie the Polynesian said with sarcasm in her voice.

– We, on the other hand see ourselves as a band, Pauline the African American stated.

– I think you've reached an important conclusion there, he said.

They grew emboldened quickly in the company of him and the other women, not really noticing the moment it happened, but awareness struck after a while, a timespan they couldn't quite determine.

– The music business is so fucking misogynist! Rita the Latina said with contempt in her voice.

– And that's just for starters, Ted stated empathically.

– That's so true! Ashley nodded, pondering it, and nodding again.

– They do call us a multicultural band, «with many different influences», though. They're not wrong about that.

– They still appear confused about it, as if they can't quite decide what to think of us, or what they think of us.

The five band members looked stunned at each other. They had opened up in just a few minutes, in a way they never had in the company of other strangers.

– You shouldn't feel bad about being stonewalled by a Warren Eliza mused.

– You're not the first and won't be the last.

She looked like something important dawned on her then.

– Here's to multiculturalism, Ted said and raised his cup of coffee.

Five faces brightened some more. Ten fair voices echoed empathically his sentiment.

– TO MULTICULTURALISM!

Eleven drank. The coffee flowed into their mouths and down their throats, and they felt every drop.

– It tastes different… somehow, Ashley the Asian mused.

Ted felt it, how they all felt it.

– Multiculturalism has been a great benefit to any society where it has flourished and caused widespread changes, Margaux said. – No wonder those in charge frown at it.

The North European blonde stretched lazy and content on the chair. He got a good look at her and didn't hide his interest, in any way.

– Gertrude, called Gerdie is a junior champion in cross-country skiing, Stephanie said gleefully. – Look at that butt and those thighs.

He looked at her, and her eyes turned hazy and remote. She writhed uncomfortable on the chair. He grabbed her hands. She had indeed a laziness about her attracting him. He fondled her hands, massaging them.

– That's a new trick, she said dazed.

She wore a white, tight sweater and nothing underneath, her pants snug around that butt and those thighs. He watched as her nipples, easily revealed under the thin fabric rose hard and sore. The gasp pushed itself through her open mouth. She blushed quick and deep.

– You don't feel intimidated by my touch? I don't cross a boundary you don't want me to cross?

– No, she replied weakly.

She caught herself, straightening into a passionate, fiery posture.

– No, you *don't!*

She practically jumped him, jumped into his lap and kissed him fiercely on the lips. One moment she seemed to hesitate, before relentlessly continuing her pursuit.

He grabbed her, holding her in his grip and returning her kisses, his hands wandering her big, curvy body.

She slipped down from his lap, looking at him with dazed eyes.

Her mouth moved, but no word was spoken. She was breathing hard, practically gasping, looking at the empty chair to his left. One moment, two passed before she rushed forward and sat down by his side. She blushed deep once again, lowering her eyes one moment, raising them stubbornly the next.

He took her hand and lifted it to his lips, giving it one single, prolonged kiss. A deep moan escaped her open, her wide-open mouth.

– We will get arrested if we continue this here and now, he said casually. – I don't mind spending a night in a cell, though. It's certainly worth it.

She looked incredulous at him. Then she giggled and giggled louder. She took his hand and drowned it in wet kisses.

– Anticipation is half the fun, isn't it? She heard herself say.

– They say so, he willingly acknowledged.

She cast stolen glances around her. Then, one moment or two later her eyes dwelled on him yet again, and they stayed there. She returned to his lap and stayed there, sighing, her body softening, forming itself after his.

– It feels so good, she said softly. – I want you. I want you very much.

– I want you, too, he said. – I want to fuck you to death!

A huge, expectant grin transformed her face.

They made out some more. Her increasingly loud breathing sounded like a storm in his ears. The others started shifting uncomfortably in their chairs.

She glanced at Lynn and Margaux, Marlene and Frances, but they looked totally relaxed at her, at the display, and her brief anxiety and unease faded quickly. Eliza, on the others hand, being fairly new to the extended group didn't.

– You've fucked a lot of sizzling chicks, I gather?

With the words «sizzling chicks» her English turned a little thick, enough to expose or at least suggest, for the first time that English wasn't her native language.

– That is an accurate statement, he shrugged.

– I don't mind, she stated, sounding a bit too convincing. – I don't mind at all.

He felt it before it happened. His experience revealed it to him, not whatever power he still possessed.

A girl passing by looked at them, only taking her attention off her very possessive boyfriend for a moment. He noticed in an instant. Ted practically saw how he changed from calm to rage during the time it took to blink.

The man walked straight to the table where Ted sat with the girls.

Ted rose with a casually and seemingly relaxed move. The man stopped as if he had been slapped. His rage persisted.

– Were you looking at my girl?

– No! Ted shook his head and shrugged.

The move seemed to enrage the man further.

– You were! I *saw* you!

– No, I wasn't looking at your girl, since she doesn't belong to you, doesn't belong to anyone.

Ted witnessed how understanding turned from suspicion to certainty, when the other realized what had actually been stated.

– Smartass, huh? The boy snarled.

He looked pretty much like a kid to Ted.

The fist rushed forward like lightning. Ted easily avoided it, taking the necessary step to the left without effort. The enraged man left himself wide open for retaliation, but Ted didn't take advantage of it, didn't exploit that obvious option.

The man threw himself forward, hitting only more air, almost losing his balance. Ted stood behind him, now, awaiting further action with an expressionless face.

– You think you're funny, huh? The man snarled.

He rushed forward once again - and collided head on with the column behind where Ted had just been standing.

Saliva flowed from the man's mouth as he rubbed his aching head. He jumped. Once again Ted stepped aside. The man landed on the table and a chair. There was a loud crack as a leg broke. The man screamed in pain. He crouched on the floor, holding his broken leg, whimpering and snarling bewildered at the dark cloud towering above him.

Ted stepped back, visibly distracted, as if what had just happened didn't concern him at all.

– I would reconsider your aggressive behavior if I were you, he said. – It will only bring you trouble.

He turned to the girl staring speechless at the spectacle.

– I would consider a change of boyfriends if I were you, he said.

– You stink, she said with contempt, suddenly erupting in rage. – I'm willing to *bet* you haven't had a shower for days.

– I could have told you that I like everything about you, he said, – but that wouldn't be true.

Gerdie stared at him.

– That was *amazing*, she said with glowing cheeks. – I don't believe you touched him a single time.

The girl knelt by her suffering boyfriend.

– You poor baby, she cooed.

Ted walked away and the ten women keeping him company followed him.

– Why didn't you fetch the poor, timid girl as well? Marlene inquired.

– My heart wasn't in it, he shrugged.

She giggled wickedly.

– You're such a tool, Ted Warren.
The others laughed as well, a bit uncertain.
They approached the entrance. He froze just a few steps from it. The others noticed his reaction. They looked where he looked, at the two police officers suddenly blocking their path.
The police officers' intentions spoke to him almost in plain language. He almost smiled. The cops sensed it and felt an anger they did not fully understand.
He heard the sound of the sledgehammer in his ears, felt it pounding his head.
– You will come with us, cop one said.
– On what charge?
He said casually, visibly unconcerned.
– Assault, cop two snarled.
Gerdie stepped forward with an incredulous look on her face.
– Are you serious? That guy attacked him. That the clumsy shit couldn't even touch him and harmed himself in the process shouldn't matter… right?
She stepped close to the two men. So did many others, those both curious and angry present in the hall. It happened so fast, from one moment to the next. They didn't see it coming, until it had blown up in their faces.
– I saw what happened, a man said, – and I will certainly testify about it, no matter how much you threaten and intimidate us to stay silent.
Loud shouts accompanied his words.
– Most people are sheep, Marlene grinned, – but those few wolves left and even some of the sheep get angry when they smell the stench.
Eliza looked at him, shaking her head, then taking an even closer look.
More loud shouts sounded all over the giant hall. It was amazing, really. Ted's grin, already present, widened to an uncanny degree.
The two cops took one look at the unfriendly atmosphere and pulled back with vicious stares. They faded quickly from the scene and from people's attention and memory.
– That was fantastic, Eliza cried, suddenly filled with excitement. – That was absolutely fantastic!
She rushed to him and kissed him passionately on the lips.
Both she and Gerdie looked at him beyond endeared.
The life in the Port Authority returned slowly to normal, or at least something resembled normal.
And just like that, it was over and done, a brief event leaving only chuckles and echoes and dust and a slowly fading noise, as the excited murmur in the large hall faded in Ted's ears.

Chapter 10

They, one man and ten women moved through the streets like a group, an organic, living breathing entity. Everyone watching them or casting them a glance found the sight odd. Most didn't ponder it further in a busy city, a stressful existence, but some did and wondered, and the sight stuck in their mind.

– Maybe some of those watching us and wonder entertain the idea that you're a pimp, Marlene chuckled. – Wouldn't that be funny?

She displayed herself to him, signaling that she was available, not exactly an unknown act to him. He snapped her picture just then, and knew he got it, got her slutty expression and acquiescence to whatever he demanded of her.

The five band-members moved themselves in various positions as he directed them on and around a green bench. They posed behind it. One stretched out on the bench. He stood on the bench, photographing them from above, knowing it would give a startling effect compared to how most people would experience that particular place.

He stood and stopped using the camera for a moment, allowing for the visuals and experience to sink in.

– Everyone should try changing perspective now and then, he remarked. – It's such a simple but effective way to gain additional insight, to achieve contact with your creative inner self and make it bloom.

The last word sounded different, stretched out, like a rubber band.

Blooom

Blooooom

He stepped down, the considerable step seemingly no more a trial for him than any smaller down a staircase. He landed easily, casually on the ground.

– Now, you, he told them.

They all did and all had that expression of wonder grow on their faces, Gerdie's even more pronounced. She jumped back down and had her attention locked on Ted with stars in her eyes.

A poster began circulating among the New York crowd. They spread it further and also put it up on lampposts and walls.

Art and music night at Liz's Place
The Multicultural Bombshells
And Mystic play music
Ted Warren displays his photographs
Come like you are
Not as a pretender

It hadn't always been called Liz's Place, but had been unceremoniously rechristened after her recent notable performances there.

He could practically see them come from all corners of the big city, migrating to the small spot in the quiet street. They were subjected to the both disturbing and more conventional images from the moment they stepped inside and walked into the entrance hall and hallways. The place filled up early, and many had to be rejected by the entrance and return home with disappointment burning in their gut.

– Be bold! Ted told them backstage.

They nodded, practically shaking with excitement and anxiety, pushing themselves at him, kissing him as if there was no tomorrow.

The five young women stood on the stage, fairly well dressed, not more or less undressed, like most female performers.

The organ sneaked up on the audience, seemingly coming from nowhere or everywhere. Five voices choired the intro, before the first guitar riff brought the rest of the instruments into play.

Stephanie, the lead singer began her performance, and it was as if she grew every second she spent up there, each new chord she cried out at the quickly shivering audience.

– They're good! Linsey told Jesse Coleman and Alvin Draper. – They're really good. We have some standard to uphold alright.

The music was slow, but aggressive, intense nonetheless. Stephanie began swaying on the stage and people in the audience began swaying with her. The play grew rough. She started a guitar orgasm making everyone present turn both immersed and wild in their movement, their eyes vacant, as they dreamed themselves away.

The music ended to an unexpectedly strong applause.

Stephanie stood there with blushing cheeks.

– Good evening, she cried. – We're the Multicultural Bombshells, and we celebrate multiculturalism in all forms.

Cheers filled the room.

– We want to thank Ted for the gift he has given us. Take a good look at his art. It's marvelous and deep beyond words.

She turned an even deeper red.

– The next tune is called «Swaying».

The music started up again.

And now Stephanie was indeed swaying, to the point of almost toppling over.

Sway with me
Writhe like a snake

Coiling in the air
Without gravity or thought

She intoned her passionate song. Her voice started fluctuating between levels more, as she let herself go, as she and the band and almost all the people present started responding to the increasingly savage rhythms shaking them. Swaying turned to dancing, dancing to swaying and swaying to dancing again. The floor turned to a ground, a constantly shifting pattern of moving flesh. Powerful emotions grew even stronger as the intensity of the music picked up.

The mood... grew ever more in intensity, and stayed that way, a seemingly endless ladder descending into deep shadows and hissing, flickering fire. Sweat turned to steam and the steam lingered as a haze beneath the ceiling in the large room filled with gasping, celebrating people.

They played five songs. Everything was documented on small, portable sound recorders, and also on strategically placed cameras.

Helen operated one of them. She looked at Ted with a hot stare.

– This is an event worthy of being saved for posterity, she grinned, a grin so wide that she couldn't and wouldn't diminish it in any way.

Ted, felling inspired went up on the stage and danced with Stephanie at the end of the last song. She played one chord wrong, frowned with irritation and shrugged, and kept playing. She danced with the guitar held above her head. Ted held it for her as she kept playing. They danced tight and hot. The mood in the hall changed even more towards a passionate rumble.

The music ended with one, disharmonic riff making the speakers groan in pain. She stood there soaked in sweat. The other band members joined her. They stood there and waved to an ecstatic participating audience.

– Thank you, she cried. – We love it here!

She jumped into Ted's arms and kissed him fiercely on the lips.

Warm laughter and heat kept rising towards the stage.

The five left the stage. Ted remained. It turned quiet. He turned off the microphone.

– After a brief period of unrest, humanity is descending back into rest, obedience and submission, he cried. – The wind of change has stopped blowing. It's our task to reignite the flame, to fan it until it becomes the inferno it's meant to be.

There was applause, both wild and somber.

– Our ideal must ever be those fighting with their dying breath, doing so their entire life and never let go. We're in this for the long haul, and the sooner we realize that, the better. The true human life of true justice and freedom will come, perhaps tomorrow, perhaps decades or even centuries from now, and even when it is achieved, it isn't achieved once and for all. We will keep fighting for it throughout existence itself.

Linsey and the band started strumming their instruments. The people gathered under this shimmering roof hardly noticed. They kept hearing Ted Warren's voice loud and clear. He knew they would always hear it, and the warm, warm ember within ignited once again.

– You will not forget this, not when you go home tonight, not when you return to your dreary work tomorrow. It will stay with you wherever you go, for the rest of your life and beyond. That's my promise to you.

He pulled back, but in more ways than one they felt it as if he remained. When Linsey stepped forward and turned on the microphone again, the image of the man with the beastly eyes stayed superimposed on the new lead band member.

– We are Mystic, he shouted at the audience, clearly inspired. – Hear our song, our nightly cry of pain and blood and joy!

There was something about him, about him as well. Ted sensed it easily, how he worked his audience, how he made them listen, made them hear his song. His power had grown as well, and as with all powers, it was at its strongest when its wielder was passionate and inspired and angry and filled with all types of emotion, of a beyond emotional rainbow raining down on everybody.

The mood was already volatile, and it didn't grow any less so, as the evening progressed.

Marlene sat there, drying her brow in vain. Francis and the other women operating the equipment also kept writhing on the stools, unable to keep their growing need in check. Marlene began rubbing herself. No one noticed or cared.

The first number was more traditional hard rock, but not exactly. There was something about it, something about how the instruments were handled and the resultant music clearly making it a departure from mainstream songs.

The first tune ended with one strike of the cymbal seemingly lasting forever.

– Good evening, Linsey said, clearly conveying the impression of a man on top of himself, of aggression mixed with calm personified. – We play mystical rock, taking music back to the Stone Age, playing rock the way it was always supposed to be played…

A girl unbuttoned her blouse and started fondling her breasts. No one noticed or seemed to notice.

– This is one of the first songs we've written, he cried. – It's dark. Let the ShadowWalk begin. Listen to and experience *Witchsong.*

Lights were dimmed. All the shadows in the room turned more pronounced. People shivered in visible delight. It sparkled in the shoulder length red hair. Rough, soft and hard heathen moods slipped close to them all. Like with the previous band, there was something incomplete, raw about how Mystic played, but the daring and passion and energy in their music more than made up for that.

Pulse quickened. Sweat poured from skin already soaked in sweat.

We walk
Through fire, through shadow
From the night we are born
An owl howl between
The dark trees
The Hunger of Life
from the newborn

Ted started dancing. It, the inception and the dancing itself felt perfectly natural, like a burst of energy. He imagined that Liz danced with him, as if they were two sides of the same mirror image moving through that so very special landscape of mist and shadow. They were both there and here, and there was no distinction between the two places. They were one and the same.

Frances visibly hesitated, but then, in a move making her gasp in shock and delight, she jumped in front of him, and it was as if there was no people, no people at all blocking her path to him on the cramped floor.

He heard the music, not just of this room, the here and now, but also of another, vastly different place. There was no disharmony, as if the people playing did so in concert, actually heard each other… and each chord echoed the other.

Mystic's music had always had a pagan and/or medieval quality, but tonight it approached that even more. The electronic modern instruments didn't sound like that *at all.*

Frances and Ted kissed, and it felt completely natural, as if they had done so many times before and didn't do it for the very first time *right now.*

– You look so much like her, Frances mumbled, growing more excited by the second.

Beneath the music, there was… more, sounds of the forest, of the marches and the castle, the besieged castle. The two of them stood at the palisade overlooking the marches, the dawn, the gathering, blood red mist.

– You are her, she whimpered in joy. – You are!

A forest with trees covered in mist appeared to him, to her in a blink lasting forever. Two women, two young, wild women danced at the early dawn. There was a vast forest covering the land behind one of the frontlines of the war converging on Eboracum, Jórvik, Old York.

The riders came at dawn, crossing the marchland surrounding the two rivers Ouse and Foss.

The two rivers, Ted thought startled, sweat breaking on his brow.

Swords were raised and blades fell, cutting flesh. Cries of pain and a beyond deep fear and boundless defiance met the riders coming at dawn. Both the rivers and marches and the women and men fighting there drowned in blood.

He closed his eyes, he opened his eyes, it did not matter. He saw only the girl, the two girls enjoying pleasures, desperate pleasures in the forest, those images, those sensations juxtaposed with the war, the eternal war.

Mystic started on one of its more intense songs, playing it better than ever. Everyone saw and felt, knew beneath the skin how it worked, how it worked on them all, as they rocked up and down and danced tight on the floor.

Frances pushed herself at Ted. Hands moving without conscious thought opened the buttons of the shirt exposing her breasts. Several others echoed her act. People sought to the backrooms and wardrobe dressing rooms, and no one kept them from doing so or told them not to do it. Ted walked with Frances, with Marlene and the five members of the Multicultural Bombshells in tow, one smaller group of many moving in the dark river of human passion and seething emotion.

Ashley gave him both an affectionate and pointed stare.

– You don't feel awkward and intimidated surrounded by women?

– I feel pretty good, actually, he shrugged.

It chuckled and giggled around him like a well in spring.

They found a large bed in a cramped bedroom somewhere. It was occupied, but it didn't seem to matter. Women and men stood lined up by the wall, the growing desire darkening their eyes. Some of them had long since started on the fondling and invasive touching, echoing the two couples on the bed.

His presence in the room caused a stir. He noticed that easily, knew how it worked and felt.

– Perhaps we should find pastures elsewhere…

One of the men on the bed waved and called him, called everyone to him.

– There's no need for that. There's more than sufficient room here.

That wasn't quite true, not on the bed or in the cramped room in general, but suddenly it didn't matter.

Gerdie, never taking her eyes off Ted moved her hand, pulling his between her thighs, gasping in delight before the deed was done. Everyone present in the room tumbled down on the bed or the floor, and they could no longer tell the two apart.

The music from the outside hall faded at some point, even as the band played on, even as Ted glimpsed Linsey in the ocean of flesh surrounding him.

Ted sensed it without trying, sensed how Linsey's presence electrified an already electrified crowd. The slow explosion spread from several points and mingled and joined, and grew further. Analysis faded, thought faded, except for the strays that would always roam his consciousness. Everyone leaning on the walls fell on the floor, the soft and warn and enticing floor.

Marlene rode him, writhing beneath him or in front of him. She was not the first and not the last, but he paid more attention to her, for some reason. Her hair danced like flames on sweaty skin.

He dived deep, and then deeper into it all, not holding himself back in any way. There was the faint worry that would always be there. He felt no rush, no transference of energy, even though he couldn't be totally confident about it, since it always had been an integrated part of sex to him.

The warm, warm, ice-cold sea awaited him down there, he knew that, but he pushed, pushed, pushed on, almost as if… as if he wanted the flow of life to return to him.

The flow of life was there, floating in the air and between all the sweaty bodies. He felt it, even as he emptied himself in Marlene, even as he grabbed Gerdie and just continued on her, even as he caught the deep devotion and worship in her eyes.

But he couldn't grab hold of it, couldn't catch it in his wide, wide net.

Frances cried out a name as she moved beneath him. Stephanie chuckled content and wild as her desire waxed and waned, as she closed her eyes, her consciousness fading into sleep after the boundless and continuous burst of passion.

The word «passion» was so hopelessly inadequate.

Liz and Carla and Ethel stood there, watching him from afar, stood in Ethel's aerie, and Ethel pulled away the veil to another place, as if it was nothing to her.

They watched the carnage, the orgy, the group mating and the low-level arousal rise to an even more pleasant level in their loins and mind.

– You're aiding him, Ethel said pleased, practically gloating.

Liz nodded in acknowledgement. She dived, through no active action into the ocean there in the quiet darkness at the place that had her name.

– He's letting go, she said softly, – and taking advantage of the fact that he, for a limited time, doesn't risk sucking anyone empty of lifeforce.
– The risk is always there, of course, Ethel said with a wicked grin.
They all felt it, how his infinite power rested just out of reach, just as potentially lethal as it always would be.
– You're both letting go, Carla remarked, – even though none of you are quite there yet.
– A drop of blood is all it takes, Ethel said, – to set you free.
– Is that figuratively or literally, Liz inquired.
Ethel didn't reply, at least not in an obvious way.
They stood there, mesmerized, as the dance continued, swaying with all the sweaty creatures on that close and distant place… as the savage dance continued into the night and beyond and the loud moans filled the streets of New York City from the deepest cellar to the highest tower.

2

He felt the sword penetrate him, felt it time and time again. There was only the blade, coming from nowhere gutting him. He didn't see the attacker, didn't see anyone, but he heard the screams of rage and pain from the ongoing battle, and smelled the stench of blood in his nostrils, and its taste in his mouth as it gushed up his throat and life left him.
It didn't really bother him. That didn't. It was like watching a movie or something, even though it was like sitting close, very close to the screen, everything reaching him undiluted.
But then, as he felt life leave him, felt life leave that other him, a veil fled from his eyes, and he saw the man with the long braid down his back as he truly was, and everything, *everything* came rushing in on present day Lewis Talbot as he sat up in bed and he opened his eyes, with cold sweat covering every single piece of his skin.
He found himself awake, on his mat with all the others in the large hall, waking up like one of the last. Eloise had just woken up as well. He caught her studying him. She reddened.
They both rose and began dressing. The nudity no longer bothered them. They felt nothing special when they covered themselves. He imagined he could sense her emotions, her interest, and he reddened as well, and she rewarded him with a grateful smile, her own shyness and embarrassment lessening somewhat.
The two of them, with a few other stragglers sought the dining hall, and sat down around the long table. She sat down by his side, looking at him with

stubborn determination. A smaller hand sought his. She reached up with her lips and kissed him. There were a few cheers and jeers, but nothing loud or major. Showing affection openly had long since stopped being an issue among them.

They all fed, doing so as most of them always did, practically gorging, devouring the food, but obviously enjoying it immensely.

Eager conversation reached them from all sides around the table, the long, long table. Lee heard the words with a clarity he could only dimly remember having experienced before. He looked into Eloise's eyes and his hearing seemed to improve further. Shaking his head in amazement, in wonder, he attempted to focus on the girl and not grow distant, not lose himself in what wasn't there, what couldn't possibly be there.

– This is all so exciting, she breathed. – I didn't even imagine it would be like this. The life we used to live, everything before feels like a dream and this, *this* is the reality.

She believed it. He saw, sensed that. There was doubt, but faint, unconvincing compared to the moment, the here and now.

Others nodded and cried their consent and that pleased her. That pleased her to no end.

Her skin turned a deep shade of red. He watched her moment by moment as she grew aroused, as her arousal grew from low level, manageable to inevitable. She had become so immediate, so different from the shy girl he had used to know.

The shyness was still there, but muted by her new, determined confidence. She rushed her meal or at least speeded up her feeding just a little, revealing her impatience. He did as well, as he felt himself hardening below. Her triumphant smile brightened his existence.

She devoured the last few pieces on her plate, remaining on her seat a bit longer than she had to, just for effect. He had no trouble seeing how she displayed herself to him, when she sat there, when she rose and walked off. He jumped to his feet and followed her, striving to keep himself in check, to not making his eagerness too obvious.

The low-level laughter from behind did make him redden, but didn't really affect him that much, didn't make him stray from his objective.

He caught up with her in the dark hallway, the one with all the bulbs missing. One hand grabbed her shoulder and turned her around. She looked at him with calm eyes, calm eyes burning. He recognized that. She puckered her lips, and he recognized that, too, that act, that characteristic. A name he couldn't remember echoed in a vacant hall of his mind.

She looked pretty much like the girl he had known for years, but not quite.

Something had been added. The expression in her eyes, a subtle thing beyond the physical had changed notably.

He bent down and kissed her, and she responded instantly. Her lips burned against his. They both pulled back a little. She smiled in excitement, in her obvious desire.

– Let's go somewhere, she told him in hoarse whisper.

He hesitated a bit and felt stupid about it, but he couldn't help himself.

– Are you sure?

– I'm not a child, she hissed. – Don't treat me like one!

He wanted to speak, but couldn't quite do it.

– I know I can't compare to your… your other lovers.

Her show of insecurity calmed his. He grabbed her and kissed her again. She squealed in delight, and rewarded him with a bright, seductive smile.

Her hand sought his. She grabbed it and led him down the final stretch of the dark hallway. There were smaller rooms in the building where they could find solitude. They walked there, ever lesser aware of their surroundings, more and more seeking the intimacy of the other.

They reached the room with the mat at the center. It made her blush yet again. She had trouble looking at her old boyfriend, even as she kept giving him that sweet smile, showing that she trusted him.

He kissed her on the lips, forcing himself to be rough, to not hold back, and she cast him a grateful glance. They took one step back. He began removing his clothes first. She was clumsier, but he knew she wanted him to look at her, and he did. The young girl's uncertain smile gained a determined quality. She studied him deliberately. He pulled down his pants. A gasp escaped from between her gritted teeth. She pulled her top above her head, exposing herself. The determined smile grew uncertain again. He smiled to her, and she looked grateful at him. She displayed herself to him, daring him to look at her, to study her, and he did. Hands sought her hips, the belt holding up her pants. She bit her lip.

– It feels… feels so good, she gasped.

She turned and wriggled her hips, swaying, dancing, never taking his eyes off him. He was aware, on some level that it was raining, raining hard outside, but he didn't really hear it, except as if from a distance, not even through the open window.

– I'm a young squaw. I danced jump the stick with other young, untouched squaws earlier today, and now I'm ready for my warrior, giving myself to him without reservation and regret. I don't know regret.

Her voice had turned hoarse, her eyes increasingly hazy. She fell on her knees in a somewhat controlled move, even as she kept swaying, kept drawing his attention to her growing need. He took one step forward, and had to crouch in his fervor. She lay down on her back on the mat. He hit its edge with his knees. She kept urging him on. He crawled on top of her. They began moving against each other, pushing, pushing. He pierced her. She cried out in pain. They kissed and moved and touched, their hands all over the other.

He moved on her, as she moved against him, pushing her hips at his, squeezing them around him. Her face changed in his vision, changed back and forth. He glimpsed those features in moments of half closed eyes. She looked older, more experienced, her fierce expression far more pronounced compared to that of the girl.

He bit into her shoulder muscle. She scratched him on the thigh, drawing blood. It dawned on him that she didn't have long nails, but still scratched deep. She smiled sweetly to him and swore at him, urging him on. He came a bit before her, but kept moving, kept touching and fondling her, and then she came, abruptly, violently, crying out in her aggressive climax.

They collapsed in each other's arms, as they kept kissing and fondling the other, as their bodies slowly descended into rest on the both hard and soft mat.

She chuckled softly. They rested on their side, face to face. The smile didn't leave her face. She kissed him on the lips.

– My, oh my, that was fucking something! I had no idea, really, no idea at all, but now I know, know what the big deal is.

She shook her head in awe.

He didn't ask her if she was okay, even if a part of him was tempted to fall back on that rather stupid angle. He stayed quiet, enjoying their closeness, the feeling of the soft, hard body against his, of the girl's excited smile and joy.

They rested there, face to face, touching and fondling each other without pause, but doing so slowly, enjoying the prolonged close contact of mind and body.

– I always had a big, sick crush on you, she mused, slightly ironic, caustic, her enthusiastic smile in place, – always knew we would end up together.

They pushed their lips forward and kissed each other simultaneously. Her temporary solemn features cracked in a big smile.

– Everything is so great here, she said, – so easygoing. We can take new lovers, experiment as much as we want, and it's just one more day of our lives of struggle and joy.

Her words… echoed within him, making him nod.

Sounds… reached him from seemingly every angle in the room. He imagined they transformed into whispers. Her face changed. One turned into many, and they were all the same.

– You perceive what's hidden, right now, aren't you? She said happily.

She looked at him with an open, eager expression moving her entire face. A catching formed in his throat.

The stirring began once again in both of them.

– We will not be joining the training today…

She whispered seductively in his ear, still the young girl, still reminding him of a far older woman.

He imagined he heard chanting, and loud cries of pain and rage. Soft flesh moved against his. He saw raised swords dripping of blood, felt the blade gut him. A loud moan made him move harder against the writhing female. He heard a choir of moans rise in the deep night.

The here and now faded before his eyes like daylight. Two rigid bodies froze and fell into the deep, deep night with content smiles around the pairs of lips locked on to each other.

3

The atelier was big and bright, with windows bringing light from every side. It could be controlled by covering the windows with dark curtains and several other constraints.

Ted Warren controlled the environment and everyone within it, a ruthless photographer moving his objects around like puppets.

Everyone was fully dressed, placed within cages, clutching the bars with despair in their eyes. He snapped photos from various angles, from virtually all possible angles, really. There were contraptions aiding him in establishing control, making the controlled environment.

He walked to Frances. She stood there with her face pushed between two bars. He began examining her, more than touching her. She started blushing again not long after that.

– Stand still, he ordered her.

He grabbed her jaw, appraising her, making her dance to his tune, letting go the moment he was pleased with her stance, her expression, not a moment before.

– Yes, Ted, at once, Ted, she said meek and timid.

– She's hopelessly smitten, the others chuckled.

He took two steps back and pushed the button on the camera. The burst photography began. Through a series of clicks, he killed an entire roll of film in a few seconds.

He used another camera, taking one and one photo, using different settings, working very deliberate, close to obsessive. It felt strange, even eerie indulging himself to such a degree, doing so without risk.

– We grow up and exist behind bars, he said. – They're everywhere, keeping us from expressing ourselves, from the very act of living.

The black and white photos displayed on the walls at the gallery on the ground floor below showed rows and rows of females and males looking through the bars with empty stares. People visiting the exhibition, and there were quite a few of them shook their head in distress.

– It's so…. disturbing, a woman said to her companion.

Another hall displayed photos with strong colors. The photos depicted the same people, but they looked completely different. Some photos were clearly staged, while others were taken during protests and during meetings and activities in the no longer abandoned and dusty warehouse.

Ted watched his models while taking those photos and he saw without trying how they brightened, how they came alive with color, and he felt the fire within.

When he studied Frances and also some of the others, he realized that he could do pretty much what he desired with them and could take them wherever he wanted. He realized startled that the risk was very much there, very much present, just as much as ever, just as sneaky and dangerous as ever. Cold sweat broke all over his body, and he imagined he felt the power rise in his hands, in every cell of his body.

Powerful emotions kept surging through him as he walked through the gallery and had a conversation with some of the visitors, grinning like there was no tomorrow, knowing that it was disturbing to them.

His coconspirators grinned with him, and he felt even better.

– People know, are very much aware of the fact that the world, current human society is fundamentally wrong, he told a group of people admiring his work. – They feel the wrongness everywhere, have felt it since their earliest memory. Most of them, having forgotten what they once knew by heart feel the solution is to work within that fundamentally wrong system, but that is not the right thing to do, not the right thing to do at all.

– You use people from all cultures here… a journalist mused almost incredulous, as if the very thought was alien to him.

– Why shouldn't I? Ted retorted. – We're all suffering under the current system of oppression.

– You say that after having spent years in the *jungle?*

– The jungle was great, the jungle, the wilderness is the place, the human place to be.

He directed his sole attention at the journalist.
– We returned here, to dead civilization in order to live it up, he grinned.
The «journalist» turned a distinct shade of pale.
The crowd walked into the third hall, the walls exhibiting the photos from the jungle.
– They're so… graphic, a man practically choked.
– It would be strange if they weren't, wouldn't it? Marlene commented brightly.
She and Ted placed themselves by one of the walls, overlooking the crowd. While he needed a certain brazen confidence in order to perform, it was clear she thrived in the attention and limelight, at and by his side.
– The temporary… unpleasantness we experienced was due to the issues we carried with us from civilization, he told the attending journalists. – We found peace and life and true humanity in the jungle. It was only when we touched civilization again our troubles truly began.
The queues kept lining up outside the building.

4

He felt a soft hand on his shoulder and turned to face her, face Eloise Sargeant.
– You had the dream again?
She wasn't really asking. He nodded, numb all over.
Fear touched him. He couldn't avoid that, only lessen its impact.
– Poor baby.
She pushed herself at him, kissing him softly, with growing fervor, the fifteen-year-old girl he had once known fading further by the second.
– I remember, too, she whispered, – remember the sword in my hand, the blood flowing from its blade. We were fierce warriors making our mark on the world.
Her voice echoed in his fevered mind, doing so even more as she climbed on top of him and turned beyond eager in her efforts.
– We were lovers then, are lovers now, fighters in the eternal war.
It was like she had flipped a switch. While he earlier had seen the ancient warrior in Eloise, he now had to strain in order to glimpse Eloise in the young face, in the very expressive eyes.
He could practically see her remember more and more and more with each passing second, every time she rocked up and down on him. She, for some reason remembered far quicker and far more than he did.
Later that day, he watched her during the sword practice. Lester and Eloise

fought and she vanquished him, destroyed him in a few fast moves.

– I need to be careful, she acknowledged. – This body isn't used to the strain of intense fighting yet.

She knew her limitations, knew how to work around them, as the experienced warrior she was fast becoming.

Guns were clearly harder for her, but she handled them better as well, instinctively gaining an understanding of their use.

He worked hard to keep an expressionless mask, to hide his deepest self from her. It seemed to be working. Her face kept the excited, youthful expression and show of devotion. They walked along the river, holding hands, walking close, being close, no more than a hair's breadth away.

The next morning, he once more woke up soaked in cold sweat. A chill colder than any winter shook him. She was there, comforting him. He could no longer pretend it was working or working well enough to calm him. The words forced themselves out of him.

– It hurts, now, hurts like a true blade buried in my gut.

– We should tell someone, seek help from Carla or anyone. This has gone on long enough.

But Carla wasn't there that day. She was nowhere to be found.

– She said it was only a short trip, Eric shrugged, – and assured me she would be back soon.

– She… assured you? Lee said perplexed.

– That doesn't sound like her at all, Eloise frowned.

The two of them searched harder for her, with a zeal bordering on desperation, but she was nowhere to be found.

They joined today's training, mostly teaching recent recruits, but also throwing themselves into the fighting, the beyond intense exercise. It didn't help, but did, on the contrary focus their waken dreams into razorblades.

– I feel so powerful, so beyond great, a newly arrived dark-skinned boy cried to those around him.

He had only been there a week, but had showed vast progress. Almost everyone present had that experience, and walked around with a proud smile painted on their features, but he clearly excelled in it.

When Lee watched them fight, he saw them raise their swords and fight for real on the battlefield, one of moor, mist and Shadow. It faded only slowly, threatening to become real, become present tense.

Lester and Eloise fought. She was creaming him. He had been better than her as late as yesterday, but now there was no contest. She had become faster, more skilled and more vicious.

He watched her savor her victory briefly. It didn't take her long to move on to the next opponent or rather target. Most of the others applauded. He found himself unable to do that. The frown on his brow grew bigger and bigger. She stepped up her efforts further. He could practically see how pearls of sweat formed on her already sweaty skin. Her face changed, twisted in rock-hard concentration.

He watched her remember, awaken from the cobwebs of time. It happened in the middle of the hardest exercise, the roughest moves. Shock froze her features. Their eyes met.

She struck down Immogen. Immogen stayed down. Eloise rushed off the fighting area and out of the room. He walked after her, practically chased her down the hallway, until she finally turned and faced him. The sight of the naked, exposed expression startled him, startled him beyond words.

– I… killed you, she gasped. – We were lovers, but I… I betrayed you. I knelt before the master of the world and joined his cause.

The sword in his gut got an arm, a face and a memory. What he had strongly suspected and feared proved true.

He tried speaking, but failed.

– Kill me! She implored him abruptly. – Kill me, now, this very moment. Return me to the Dark River.

She pushed her throat at his blade. He realized that he had raised it in defensive position without being aware of doing so.

– No, he replied, gritting his teeth, choking on each syllable, pulling back the blade. – No!

He looked at the girl in front of him, the two somewhat distinct creatures in one body, the indistinct versions of the same person.

He reached for her, but missed, grasping nothing but empty air.

She ran off. Three, four steps and she was gone around the next corner.

He stood there for ages, unable to move a finger. The sword lowered itself because he quite simple was unable to keep it raised. He leaned against the wall with half closed eyes.

Lester and Eloise fought, fought again in his mind, his inner vision, his third eye, one growing more and more distinct in his consciousness, his growing awareness.

He caught the moment the distinctive change came upon her, and despair and shame replaced the spirited glow in her eyes.

And he felt very much like being stabbed in the gut.

5

They spotted one of several graffiti drawings of themselves on walls, as they walked through the streets. There had been a few since before they arrived in the city, but their numbers had picked up quite a bit lately. Ted snapped photos of each one. It slowed down their walk considerably.

It was raining that day, at Palahoa Cemetery in Queens. Liz and Ted walking ahead of Ethel, Patrick, Jean, Carla, Linsey and Lee crossed through its outer gate and into a vast area of tombstones.

– I'm concerned for Frances…

He offered casually.

– I told her she needs to pull herself together, Liz said unconcerned.

The newshounds followed them around, as was their want. It was very tempting to *do* something to them. She was close to go ahead with it several times.

– Let them have their fun, he suggested.

– As you wish!

She glanced behind her, without revealing it to those chasing them. Wise by experience the newshounds kept their distance, didn't walk close enough to be upgraded from nuisance to annoyance. She nodded to herself.

– You handle me so well, My Lord, she teased him.

He didn't take the bait.

They approached a distinct, disclosed part of the cemetery. It stood out to them, in more ways than one. They stepped through another gate, entering the Warren family tomb in New York City.

There was a system to the tombstones, moving from left to right.

Joseph Warren

1841 – 1897

was the oldest.

– My great grandfather, Ethel remarked casually. – I've been told he was some piece of work.

The youngest, most recent stared them in the eye.

Rachel Dalhart

1912 - 1979

– I don't need to open the grave to know she isn't there.

Liz snarled.

– She isn't there, Ethel remarked. – There's nothing there. That could be said about many of them, though.

They studied her, like they always did. She didn't sound and seem ironic or obscure… or did she?

Other names, Tanya Orbov, Cynthia Warren, Dalilah Warren, Nell Warren, Susan Warren, Desmond Warren, Catherine Martin, April Powell, Joel Warren and Nick Warren paraded before their eyes.

Their eyes gathered, in undivided unity on one tombstone.
Nick Warren
1890 - 1952
– Nick is most certainly a fake, Liz stated. – He's shown to be dead years before he visited the Kendall ranch.
– He was very much breathing and vibrant the last time I saw him years later, Carla, being obscure told them.
– Everyone believed he died in the fire, Ethel said. – In a way, he did. He finally said goodbye to his old, mundane existence forever.
– So, he's still alive? Ted asked her pointedly.
– I believe so, she shrugged. – I can't be certain, since I haven't seen him since that day.
He wanted to push her further, but saw no point in doing so. She would tell them exactly what she wanted to tell them and nothing more.
The extended family left the enclosed, private area and returned to the larger cemetery. The newshounds confronted them almost immediately.
– Rachel Dalhart, the infamous brothel mama is your *grandmother?* They asked, mostly directing their question at Liz.
She gave them a bright smile.
– I'm surprised you didn't know that, that you haven't dug it up.
– And she has left her entire fortune and business to you?
Liz grinned some more and shrugged deliberately.
– Life hands you great irony sometimes.
She split her fortune between her grandchildren, but left the business to you. Do you care to speculate on why she did that?
– No, I don't!
The grin stayed in place.
– So, what will you do with her… business?
– That's a fair question, she replied, seemingly unconcerned. – I guess I'll have to get back to you on that.
– The rest of you are okay with this arrangement?
– We're more than confident in Liz's ability to handle it, Linsey said.
The newshounds wondered a lot about his tone of voice, whether or not he was being sarcastic.
– Excuse us, Ted told them with a smile, – we need to get going.
They made no attempt at pressing the issue, pretty content, relieved that they had received any response at all.
The extended Warren family left the Palahoa Cemetery in Queens somewhat at peace.
– Do you care to speculate on Rachel's motives? Ted asked Ethel.

– I don't need to. It's pretty obvious that she deliberately left her mundane existence behind, just like *he* did.

She granted him a sweet, sweet smile, looking very young in the process.

Liz gave her a slight nudge, catching her attention.

– I need a favor, she said casually. – I need to inspect and impress my overseas holdings. Can you help me do that?

– Of course, Ethel replied lightly.

– I need to return to my atelier, Ted said, a little too fast.

– To your abundant number of models, Jean teased him.

He didn't blush, but did feel a little hot under the hood.

– It's such a smorgasbord, he remarked.

– Poor boy…

There was laughter, more than a bit wicked.

– One Janus Clan male can easily create an entire people, Ethel said, – a nation, an army of fierce warriors single-handedly.

He glanced at Liz. She seemed totally indifferent.

– You should go for it, she shrugged.

She grabbed Ethel's arm in a light grip. Even through the clothes she felt the power.

– I and Ethel have a more important task on our hands, she declared.

The two tall fire-eyed females left the group. Liz kissed Ted on the lips. Ethel did as well. Something did happen. The air lit up between them like invisible fireworks. Liz had no trouble seeing it. Ted sensed it. Ethel smiled her enigmatic smile.

Ethel's driver waited with her car just outside the main gate. The two of them sat down in the spacious backseat. It started with an acceleration so soft that Liz hardly noticed that they had started moving. They quickly left their suitors in the news business far behind. There was no need for Liz to blow one of their tires or anything.

– I like this setup of yours, Ethel, Liz remarked.

– Thank you, Liz, Ethel said. – You can soon afford the same or even better accommodation, though. Rachel was loaded. She hasn't exactly been lazy since she walked out on James that day in 1944.

– I haven't decided if I'm going to keep it, Liz shrugged.

– You will keep it! Ethel stated.

Liz heard no doubt in her voice.

– I'm not tempted by wealth or its luxuries, she pointed out. – I put that behind me with Regina Forester and especially with the man that wanted to be my husband.

And that time in South America when I was a goddess, she thought.

But that hadn't really been her, had it? That had been Ted's dream, his vision, his experience of a possible future. He had discarded Power, not she. She had dreamt of being a lowly slave groveling at her master's feet.

Ethel's coughed, very telling and deliberate.

Liz set her eyes on her.

– You discarded wealth as a necessary tool for power, Ethel pointed out, – not Power itself.

– Don't you think I know that, Liz cried, – know that I will always struggle with it?

Ethel's expression remained stoic, noncommittal, the snide smile only visible as a pale shadow on her lips.

Liz crouched in her seat, unable to hide her shame, her shattered pride for her relative.

You don't struggle, she thought with scorn on her mind. You have chosen long ago.

They arrived at Justin Bieber's old building, the place that had become her bigger place, her aerie, her eminent domain. Abby and a few of the others met them downstairs, the floor they had baptized the «reception area», strangely apprehensive and respectful.

– We have important matters to attend to, Liz told them sternly. – Do not let anything or anyone disturb us.

– The lawyers are here, Abby pointed out cautiously.

– Let them wait, Liz shrugged. – Let them stew in their own fat.

The two of them took the elevator up to the office, to her place of power. Liz visualized how her people cleaned every room up there for people, how it became an empty and abandoned realm.

The two Janus Clan females appeared from the elevator. Liz felt how the domain greeted her, comforted her and strengthened her.

– I like what you've done with this place, Liz, Ethel said. – I can feel your presence, your power seething in the very air.

– Thank you, Ethel, Liz said. – I appreciate that.

They sounded like two distant relatives having met after having spent years apart.

– You're so young, Ethel remarked, – and have achieved so much already. That's a Janus Clan female for you.

Liz didn't even consider verbally replying to that.

They reached the inner sanctum. Liz felt even more welcomed. Ethel's discomfort was quite evident.

– Do you think it will work?

– Huh?

Ethel looked disoriented, distant at her.
– Us, siring an army of Janus Clan warriors?
Ethel shook her head.
– It never has, and we've made repeated attempts. They easily become unruly, unmanageable, representing an added risk to us, not improved safety.
– What about Nick?
Ethel smiled, somewhat back in control of herself.
– Everyone believed he had perished in the fire, but I knew better. I was just a child, at the start of my ascension, like you are now, but I knew him like a song in my blood.
She crossed the line to the circle, to the pentacle.
– Shall we stop with the third-degree interrogation, now, and get on with our task?
– Very well…
Liz crossed the boundary as well. They both gasped, as their combined power surged through them.
They sat down on the floor, sitting face to face, crossing their legs in front of them.
– There's no need for anything… extra at this time, Ethel instructed her, in her snobbish, overbearing way. – We just touch each other and combine our power, directing it according to our will. I will graciously submit to yours.
Liz pondered that word, tasted it on her sensitive tongue.
They grabbed hands, unceremoniously, and it was happening, just like that.
Melinda Mercier froze as she looked at the Eiffel Tower through the window in her office. She turned slowly, and Liz appeared in the air in front of her.
People in other offices around the world experienced the same, staring at the ethereal creature, the bird of prey hovering above them.
– Call in everyone on the premises, Liz bid them. – Do it now!
It didn't take long, a few calls through the intercom, and women and men filled the room.
– I'm the new owner of the operation, Liz informed them. – I assume you've been given notice.
– We haven't received the confirmation yet, Melinda gasped. – We…
– You will!
Melinda fell silent.
– I will keep this short and sweet. I assume you knew about Rachel's… peculiarities. Know that I am far more powerful than she ever was, and you do not want to cross me.
– This is highly irregular…

A woman objected. A moment later she gasped and fell to the ground shaking in pain.

– I can't do much from here, the creature shrugged, – but I, my physical form can be on site in just a few hours of flight. You don't want to cross me, don't want to face my full power.

– That won't be necessary… Liz, Melinda whispered. – We know our… our place.

– Very good!

She faded from their view, but they didn't feel like she did.

She didn't exactly open her eyes face to face with Ethel, but it felt like she did. It felt more like she was closing them, closing her eyes to infinite possibilities. They unclasped hands, broke contact, and the shared power, the far stronger force than the mere sum of their parts faded.

It took forever to rise and reach the outside of the circle. She imagined she crossed an immeasurable distance.

– Thank you, she said graciously to her relative. – That was certainly fast and efficient.

– Our combined power glowed dark beyond words together, Ethel said, unable to conceal her… her excitement. – I had expected some fireworks, but nothing like this. I'm more confident than ever that your contribution to the family will be immense, my dear.

Nothing like this...

The words echoed in Liz's distracted mind, taking a backseat to a more pressing concern.

She started pacing the floor, wearing out the carpet, with her arms behind her back, an image she had always seen as ridiculous.

– Selling it is no solution, it just isn't.

Ethel looked good humored at her, quickly catching, regaining herself, as she straightened her clothes.

– You have some quandary on your hands here, she grinned. – Well, good luck with that, I must be going.

She turned in the door, giving her relative an appreciative look.

– You handled your subjects well. I look forward to see how it will turn out.

The door closed. Liz was alone. Ethel returned to the world, no doubt more eager than ever at stirring up trouble.

Liz froze.

Stirring up trouble… She brightened as a brilliant idea dawned on her.

Then the image, the potent presence of Ethel re-entered her mind.

Thought and action were one.

She rushed out of the room, feeling like the door, the distance between them was hardly there at all, catching up with Ethel in an instant. Ethel looked puzzled at her.

– I must know! Liz said…

and grabbed Ethel's hands.

Chapter 11
The Queen of New York

She squeezed Ethel's hands, did so with her claws, like a bird of prey. Ethel whimpered and crumbled in her grip. Liz kissed her on the lips, acting on impulses, instincts she had always known were there, but that she had rarely acted upon, closing the circuit. Ethel whimpered, the banshee scream of pain, of boundless pain dying in her throat.

Power rose in Liz like an inferno.

And it was just a tiny flame at the tip of her finger, easily controlled.

It took her only seconds to tower above even that.

– Oh, *my,* her mighty voice hissed in eternity.

She stepped back, letting go, not letting go of the limp body and mind caught in her cruel grasp. Saliva flowed from the other woman's open mouth. Her empty eyes stared at nothing.

– Come here, sweet girl, let me care for you, take care of you.

She kept the carcass floating in the air, and it was nothing to her. It floated behind her as she returned to her sanctum and the pentacle.

Whatever was left of Ethel was alive, somewhat, was breathing, but barely, in tiny, helpless gasps. Liz strung it up inside the pentacle, bound it with thousands of invisible threads. It hung there like a corpse, a breathing corpse. The even flow of power from it and into her continued. Touch skin to skin endured. It felt so pleasant, so beyond pleasant. She savored that pleasure, allowing it to linger a bit, just a bit, before moving on.

What did a god first do when gaining its power? It didn't need to reveal itself to its worshipers, not exactly. A power like that didn't need to be demonstrated, but needed to be used, like a dog pulling the chain.

An urge filled Abby and the others below. They didn't think, didn't reason, but stepped into the elevator and rode it into the castle in the sky.

Ten moments, one moment later they faced the goddess and fell to their knees before her. Abby and all the others gasped in endless awe. Liz looked bigger, even though she probably wasn't. She emanated irresistible might. They didn't even consider resisting it.

Abby glimpsed the shrunken figure suspended in the air behind the goddess, but even though it was one more detail adding to the reverence, it didn't seem important, somehow. Liz sensed their thoughts, and a moment later she heard them, just like that, able to follow them like trails on an endless chain of shiny shadowy pearls.

– My ascension has started, but we will take it slow. Even though my ascension is felt everywhere only you will know at first.

– YES, MY GODDESS, they choired, using both mind and vocal chords.

– We have important tasks ahead of us.

YES, MY GODDESS

She pretty much ignored their prattle, their show of devotion after that, delegating it to a tiny piece of her expanding, already vast consciousness.

She signed the papers. It felt like one more meaningless act.

The moment between then and now seemed like nothing more than a blink. The power kept growing in leaps and bounds, pretty much like Ted had described it. Her path stretched out like an eternity before her. Even with Ethel's prescience added to her own she could only glimpse what she would become. The lawyers became hers, her vassals without effort, without conscious thought.

A tiny move or nudge and Abby placed herself by her side, offering herself and her services unconditionally to the Goddess.

A casual thought brought her to the New York branch of what had been Rachel's holdings. One moment later she had returned to all the brothels world-wide simultaneously. This was a far more powerful presence than during her previous ethereal visit, almost solid, material, even though it wasn't quite like that.

Pieces of the building loosened from the main body, staying afloat, rising in the air, falling upwards like dry dust in the warm wind.

They knelt before her. There was no reluctance or hesitation. They bent their neck and will to her. Their lips kissed the ground she walked on.

The rush of time slowed down now and then, when something she deemed curious or interesting displayed itself to her.

Eloise knelt down in her path. Liz knew what made her different the moment she set her eyes on the girl. Eloise didn't speak or raise her eyes from their cast down position. She waited to be acknowledged. Liz obliged.

– This warrior presents itself to her king.

Liz didn't speak. She looked amused at the fierce, humble creature.

– This warrior must serve someone, and since she doesn't want to serve him, she will serve you.

She bowed her head again.

– I… regret my actions, My King. I will do whatever penance My King requires.

She waited for what Liz knew felt like forever for the reply.

– Chop off your little finger, she shrugged. – That should suffice.

There was hesitation, but so brief that only Liz had a chance of noticing it. Eloise drew the sword from her back and proceeded to execute the royal command. She did release a tiny sound of pain and looked ashamed at the floor.

– Have someone attend to that. We don't want the queen's personal guard to catch an infection.

– Yes, My Queen, Eloise cried happily. – No, My Queen. Thank you, My Queen!

Liz walked away. Eloise didn't follow her, but not long afterwards, a blink of an eye to Liz, she had caught up, appearing with a bandaged hand and a film of sweat on her forehead.

From then on, she stayed at Liz's side all the time, every moment of her life. She became a tail Liz hardly noticed, a grain of dust at the back of the head.

The Goddess walked the streets, with the entourage tailing her. They were like driftwood on the stormy sea, like dust in her vortex. She wanted to see with her eyes what hid behind a given wall, and just like that, the wall vanished like smoke. Her casual action weakened the structure, and she had to quickly restore the wall in order to save the building. She watched as the material rebuilt herself, smiling and shaking her head in wonder and indifference.

An impulse could be enough to make her act, make her execute a desire. She had to watch herself.

Or not.

The laughter shook flesh and mortar alike.

She noticed every single piece of flesh and bone and concrete and everything around her, in an ever-wider circle.

The chrysalis cracked and Ted woke up prematurely. She felt it as it happened, the seconds before and the many moments after, like a froth on her ocean.

Then she felt the butterfly flapping its wings, then she felt the gathering storm.

They stood face to face, every angle to every angle. She smiled radiantly to him.

– I dream, a dream of power, and I want you to join me. My gift to you. Are you a bird of prey taking what you desire?

There was only a moment of hesitation before he nodded, before he agreed and embraced her offer, the offer he made to himself. She nodded exalted.

– We're the same, you and I. You will catch up with me.

They approached the shell hanging like a ragdoll in the pentacle. He touched Ethel. She screamed again, rocking the world.

Liz watched him grow in mere moments, to match her, and her happiness soared.

They turned to their ragdoll, watching her with lupine eyes.

– I believed myself to be the most powerful, she choked, – but that was just a convenient delusion. I can't possibly imagine what you are.

The two of them stood on the top of the highest twin tower.

– We could drain her. I didn't think we could drain our kin, but we can. We can!

– *We* can! He stated.

The warm, warm trickle up her spine spread across the high spires, high and low.

They began changing their clothes, transforming their environment.

– Not… this, he said hesitatingly. – Let's try something different this time.

She could draw on his experience from the jungle and nodded in agreement. They had been gods once, and it hadn't worked out.

They walked the streets again. A horrible sound from a drill and construction work nearby was silenced promptly, an act utilized by a casual thought. The machines just stopped, from one moment to the next. Those in their company looked at them with even stronger awe.

Liz and Ted (Ted and Liz) saw with a glance how the workers attempted to restart the engines, but doing so in vain. There was nothing there anymore, no spark, the spark needed for the engines, the very Machine. It had become nothing but a useless construction of metal, a piece of art more than anything. It, its pieces looked the same, exactly the same to ordinary eyes and senses, but it wouldn't work. The two pondered what their casual action had wrought.

– Even the laws of nature will bend to our will, she marveled.

– People are more complex, he mused, – but we could easily change them, too.

They both remembered that other world, their kingdom in the jungle that had spread to the entire world. Everyone had worshiped them there, everyone.

– What are you doing? Carla asked them, or had asked them days ago.

She remained an itch in their presence, one not letting go, unbowed and free. They allowed that, relishing it in an environment where everyone else fell in line.

The city changed, in subtle ways. It was a slower process than during their previous attempt at godhood, but just as inevitable. They noticed, even if few others did. Faces raced through their attention, their inner display window, never sticking around long enough to leave a lasting imprint, but each still lingered, and could be picked from that long hall of paintings if the need presented itself. The city changed and so did its people. Other cities and places also felt the effects, particularly the cities where they had holdings, where the other whorehouses had been.

– It's so liberating, isn't it, Liz told him, – to free ourselves from all preconceptions, all pretense of humanity.

She sensed his approval as if it was her own. There was nothing between them anymore.

Port Authority and other waystations became, even more than before one of many methods of spreading their influence, their word. They could easily observe the lines advancing on the map, the map drawing itself in their heads. They chose to work through intermediaries, emissaries this time. It was a slower, but in some ways a more satisfying approach.

They could follow each emissary, following him/her/them closer by focusing ever so slightly on the individual or group of individuals in question. They zoomed in on them, and on the determined group of pimps they confronted. Machineguns played up, their sound spreading like ripples in water. Flesh and bone fell like dummies on a shooting range, but they bled, and couldn't be mistaken for dummies. The unmoving figures bathing in blood crouched on the ground, moving just a little longer, before moving no longer.

Emissaries of the gods moved upstate New York, to a large estate up there, and more blood was spilled, and more dummies leaked blood and decorated the floor in the large house, one tinier piece of the giant canvas they painted.

The emissaries, having vanquished the opposition moved into the house, using it as a springboard for further conquest. An icy gust, a fiery wind and events moved on from there. The gods could catch the moment if they bothered, but usually they didn't.

Fireeyes watched and studied and assessed, and then the two of them acted or didn't act. It was that simple. Everything had become the equivalent of ones and zeroes.

The next moment they focused on was Liz walking up to the stage in a hall filled with people, with some of the most influential movers and shakers in the city. Flashes brightened constantly her eyes and her surroundings. In her inner eye Ted walked up the isle in another hall with more movers and shakers gathered.

A woman shaking in awe met her as she stepped up on the platform.

– Thank you for coming, Liz, Marcia Harden greeted her, gushing in her presence. – You're only twenty, and have already accomplished so much. I hardly dare speculate at where it will all end. You're such a wonderful being, so exquisite, so… perfect.

The older woman curtsied like a young girl would do before an older, respected authority figure. She rushed then to the microphone and cried out her dedication.

– Ladies and gentlemen… the Queen of New York…

Liz stepped before the microphone, even though she didn't really need to. She started speaking. Every word went straight into people's ears, right into their mind.

– We need to start the reeducation of our children, teaching them critical thought, teaching them true independence and stop those constantly brainwashing them from continuing their undue influence.

The applause echoed through the hall. The long, long moments stretched to become even longer as she continued speaking, and gave them more food for thought. Her speech ended. She smiled to them, as she stepped down from the platform and walked among them. She kept speaking to them, and they listened, even though they weren't consciously aware of doing so.

A narrative played in her head, one coming from her depth, her deepest core, choiring with Ted, in imperfect harmony, a great discord making them hum and swell. Patterns revealed themselves to them, creating one major tapestry. They could follow it like strands of day and ash, and see the night and fire beneath.

There is hope, she rejoiced. They need only a bit of pushing and pulling here and there, and they will bloom, becoming flowers with fangs and claws.

This is only a city, he mused, no different from any other throughout history.

They prowled the streets, the buildings, the entirety of the seemingly vast urban area. Sometimes they even used their feet doing it, and it felt good in a way.

[Frustrated], she frowned.

Of course, he shrugged, creating ripples in the air and concrete miles away.

I never imagined that. We can basically do anything, and we're still… limited.

That thought, that stray thought was all it took, and…

They were all over the places simultaneously.

Port Authority, Times Square, The Central Park forest, the top of the Empire State Building, everyone at Port Authority taken in by a glance, a casual probe, not even a probe. Everyone became extensions of their being.

– Don't be silly, sweetie, she told someone she couldn't identify. – The way you look at her, leaves no doubt about what you're feeling.

They stood at Times Square for the second, tenth or first time.

The ravens rose and swarmed people like insects, their beaks stabbing like knives. Bricks and pieces rose from the rooftops, rose into the twilight.

They began transforming their surroundings again, unable to tell if they wished to do so, or if it just happened.

Ethel gasped once, twice, and gasped no more. She turned to dust before them, the dust falling slowly to the floor, the dust they ingested and felt to the tip of their being, and power, *power* flooded the two.

Time stretched out to eternity, space to infinity. They drew breath. One breath was… was…

Their surroundings folded in on themselves, and stayed the same. They caught everything forwards, backwards, sideways, upwards, downwards like a giant fist in the gut strengthening, not weakening them. It imploded and spread outwards, and it was a giant dust cloud and the cloud was stars and… and…

We held back, she breathed, and now it's getting away from us. I… I…

A deluge, flooding everything.

They crossed vast expanses, not only meters, not only miles but seconds, minutes, weeks, months, years, centuries, millennia. The fairly small group of people joined with the land, with the planet itself. They walked and kept walking, wanderers without any hearth or home, except everywhere they happened to find themselves.

Earth - a tiny elementary particle in the vast universe. The sun - hardly any bigger. A sun exploded, not this one, but another, far out in Space. Ripples spread from that pinprick into the vast Universe and actually made a mark on it. Earth as it would become, a dead rock in the Void, and nothing more. Earth as it had been, alive, vibrant beyond words, filled with life.

Each blink brought not one image, one sensation, but a number higher than infinity times eternity *squared.* And there were too many blinks to count.

And

and

And…

2

She was back at her sanctum, pacing the floor. Ethel had just left. She had yet not reached the elevator.

Liz had returned to her cave, to her old, limited self. She had trouble remembering it like it had been, as if centuries, eternities had passed.

She remembered vividly a reality where she had been queen, where she had reigned supreme.

Liz rushed into the other room, catching up with Ethel just as she was heading into the elevator. The older woman, the same person that Liz dimly remembered, turned to face Liz. Liz studied her with triumph in her eyes, unable to help herself.

Ethel would never know.

– Thank you, Liz said.

– You're welcome, Ethel said.

She stepped into the elevator. Its doors closed. The sound of it leaving the floor faded slowly.

Liz's experience faded quickly, the memories turning dim.

They would always be there.

And threatening to become real even as she pondered them, and cold sweat kept soaking her brow and only slowly stopped flowing from her sore skin. Her eyes kept burning.

Abby and the others saw Ethel step out of the elevator. She looked at them, ignoring them with her usual condescending smile as she left the building. They took the elevator up to the top floor, to the aerie, eager to hear the news.

Liz waited for them in her sanctum. They came to her, eager, enthusiastic, capable. It was enough. It had to be!

– We have important tasks ahead of us. We will use everything and everyone, all assets at our disposal in order to achieve our objectives.

– You will… sign the papers? Abby asked, unable to hide her resentment and concern.

– I will! Liz replied.

She looked good humored at them.

– I admit I needed some serious soul-searching first… until it dawned on me that accepting the goodbye present from granny didn't have to be a burden at all, but a true gift. I realized what I should have seen instantly: how easy it is to turn it around, to use it to help those we aim to help and stir up trouble for those we want to harm on a level we could not have done without it.

They got it. It slowly dawned on them. An uncertain smile turned to a full-fledged grin so wide that it threatened to leave breadcrumbs in their ears.

She signed the papers. It felt like one more meaningless act. The lawyers kept glancing curiously at her, never quite able to grasp her or her motives.

– Thank you, Miss Kendall, the very formal senior lawyer said as he filed the papers in his briefcase. – Will you also retain your grandmother's account with us? We can offer…

– I think I will, she grinned. – Everyone needs good lawyers in today's unfair society. I would appreciate it if Peyton and Fallon could be permanently assigned to me and the firm.

She didn't leave room for rejection in her voice and stance. The two mentioned looked stunned at her.

– That can be arranged, the senior lawyer coughed.

He kept himself in check, not asking the question burning on his lips.

– Very good, Liz said. – I foresee major legal difficulties for the firm in the near future…

Peyton hid a smile behind a hand. Fallon attempted desperately to keep a straight face.

The group of lawyers turned to leave.

– Now, Liz stated curtly. – I want them here from this very moment.

They froze. The young woman no longer looked the part, no longer looked the part at all. Peyton and Fallon parted from the group and walked to Liz without waiting for approval from the senior partner.

– That's a good girl and boy, Liz said pleased. – It's a good thing that you listen and learn to listen. That will be expected from you without exception from now on.

She focused on her breathing, on controlling, at least to a point the raging, demanding storm within. She recalled without effort her time as the Goddess, when her word had been law.

The senior partner and the rest of the team nodded and left. She even glimpsed approval in his eyes.

Peyton and Fallon stood straight and attentive before her. Abby and the others paid attention as well.

– We will pay a visit to the New York branch, Liz informed them.

– Very good, Peyton spoke up sharp, eager, – I'll have a car ready in ten minutes.

– No can do, Liz said. – Haven't you heard? We walk in our circles. At least fairly short walks like this one.

It would take them at least an hour.

– You will need lighter clothes, of course, Abby cued in, – and high heels are out.

Peyton looked very guilty when she glanced down on her high heels.

– Come with me, both of you, Abby bid them.

They followed her.

– It will take us close to two hours, Liz heard Fallon complain, his shrill voice even more elevated, no matter how much he fought to keep it down.

– More than that in a car, Abby responded unconcerned. – You know New York traffic is a killer, right?

They were given light clothes and good walking shoes. Abby transformed them in mere minutes from the people they had been. She gave them a critical look when they stood before her. Not quite pleased she roughed up Fallon's five-hundred dollar haircut and loosened Peyton's hair so it fell down on her shoulders and back.

– That's better, much better.

She presented them to Liz shortly thereafter, daring a grin at the woman she had trouble recognizing. Liz nodded her approval and Abby's grin widened.

Abby had certainly experienced Liz's cruel and pointed demeanor before, but now there seemed to be added something to it, another layer.

The dark one didn't speak, but just started walking. They followed her to the elevator. It opened up to them like a mouth. They felt like it welcomed them with a hot breath. Her eyes burned on a low flame, and it kept doing so. The elevator descended. They felt it, like she did, as a startling effect in the gut.

The somewhat chilled storage building gave way to the sizzling heat of the streets. Liz didn't sweat or showed any visible discomfort. Most of the others started sweating and gasped in the heat just a few steps after having left the building.

Liz kept walking at a murderous speed. They were just about able to keep up with her.

Peyton rushed to her side.

– I'm doing hard exercise, she stated eagerly, – doing a long run almost every day the opportunity presents itself.

– I do as well, Fallon joined in. – The firm encourages a healthy mind in a healthy body.

– Today and from now on, you will learn what hard exercise and a long run truly entail, Abby told them, giving them a cruel grin.

They passed a construction site. Loud drills surrounded them on all sides. Liz frowned, easily identifying the irritation boiling within, forcing herself to stand it, to suffer in silence. Frustration didn't really add to her suffering anymore.

Everything stayed slow, insufferably so. Things she wanted done in an instant had to be postponed or wouldn't happen anytime in the foreseeable future. She did sweat, not because of the physical hardship and palatable heat, but due to the boiling cauldron within making its mark on her appearance.

She experienced the walk as a kind of catharsis, where she slowly, still unstuck realigned herself with… herself. Second by second, minute by minute it filtered through her experience of godhood, of a might she could once more only dream of.

They reached the New York branch of what had been Rachel's holdings, entered the cool, pleasant entrance hall soaked in sweat.

The light-clad girl sitting behind the desk and two others sitting on the coach became short-breathed the moment she spotted them.

– M-miss Kendall, she said stunned, – we didn't know you were coming.

The three girls rose and stood straight, practically presenting themselves for the other young woman.

– I wanted it that way, Liz said, a bit distracted.

– Of course, the girl mumbled.

– There is video surveillance here? The boss can see us right now, right?

– She can, Miss Kendall.

– Call me, Liz, Fireeyes said, still distracted.

– Of course… Liz.

The door locked behind them. Everyone present in the room heard it.

– I want you to call in everyone not on the premises, make them come instantly, without delay. If there are any guests, get rid of them immediately, also if they have paid for any services.

She spoke about it all in a totally indifferent tone, as if she was speaking about the weather.

An older woman, in her early thirties, Adrienne Sherman appeared from the elevator.

– Good evening, Liz, so good of you to come.

She did attempt, at least to a point to talk down to the young woman, even if she was shaken and remembered their earlier encounter.

Liz didn't say anything, but just stared, good humored. Adrienne blushed.

– We are first and foremost an escort service, she added.

– Yes, it makes everything easier, doesn't it, makes everything run smoother?

– Indeed, Adrienne whispered, cowed before the sparring even began.

– You will arrange everything according to my specifications and gather everyone in the hall. Tell everyone they will be staying for a while, for as long as it takes.

«The hall» was a luxurious living room upstairs. Liz remembered it vividly.

– Yes, Liz, Adrienne straightened, as if at attention.

– Don't bother calling off any appointments. Let the «customers» stew in their own fat. Don't make any new.

Adrienne repeated her acknowledgement.

The sweaty wanderers took the elevator upstairs, emerging into its lush

surroundings.
– It looks like a paradise, Peyton breathed.
– Yes, Liz snarled, and it makes me sick to my stomach.
They felt her rage. It burned them, burned them hard.
She dismantled several lightbulbs, creating a darker, sinister mood. Those not used to it looked wide-eyed at her as she did so without being near them.
People, pretty women and men began gathering in front of Liz. She sat on the couch, studying them as if they were prey, and they felt like that.
– Everyone will stand or walk, she commanded, – displaying themselves to me. You will keep doing it, until I say otherwise.
They were good at that, even while being shaken by apprehension and insecurity. Others arrived and fell in line easily, getting it without further explanations.
The first couple of times they stopped in front of her, the professional smile was in place, but eventually that smile and attitude turned frazzled, frustrated.
But they kept doing it.
Liz appeared indifferent, to the point of bored. Only in the edge of her eyes, they caught the darker parts of her expression, and that eventually filled their entire attention. They began sweating, even sweating hard, but kept moving.
The last two, one of each sex arrived, getting it, joining the rest, in just minutes sweating and striving like the rest.
Everything turned into suffering, like one, endless stretch of repetition and agony. Those present then recalled the demonstration she had given them during their previous encounter. The others had heard the stories, and any disbelief faded to zero.
– You may stop!
They did, hardly remembering anything before they had started parading before the creature relaxing on the sofa.
She rose, and towered above them.
– It would be so easy, wouldn't it, to turn you all into pretty slaves, into pretty girls and boys, and nothing but.
– Yes, Liz, Gail whimpered.
The others echoed her statement.
– Well, you are not whores, not prostitutes or anything like that, anymore, not in my employ. You will require extensive retraining, of course, but we have the adequate facilities for that.
A heat lit within them, a relief and joy they couldn't hide.
– In the old warehouse? Gail said brightly.

– Precisely. You will join the others there, becoming one of them, becoming free, independent people, human beings, or die trying. We will turn all this shit around, making it into something truly memorable. If you ever wanted your actions to echo in eternity, this is a good start.

– We will not leave here for a while, though, Abby spoke for the first time, making them look at her as if she was a ghost or something. – Someone should order some food. We will be here for quite some time.

– I will interview you all, Liz stated. – The questions will be invasive and thorough. You will probably experience it as an interrogation, even if it will be nothing like that, nothing like a true interrogation performed in prison camps or such.

– This is the beginning of our boot camp, Adrienne said inspired.

She felt herself being grabbed by invisible hands and lifted into the air. Everyone stared.

– That is not an altogether wrong comparison, Liz shrugged, – even though it will be far harder than that.

She let the woman back down.

– I will perform all interviews. I require adequate facilities.

– We have the perfect place available, right here, Adrienne choked.

– Very good, you will be first.

3

After some finetuning, what remained was a small room with a bed and two chairs and a table. Adrienne Sherman shook face to face with the dark girl.

– Your eyes, Adrienne whispered. – They are so… your face… so…

She just faltered under the intense stare, until she stood there quiet and timid.

– So, where do you see yourself in ten years? Liz said casually, like an executive interviewing a young, hopeful candidate for a job.

– I'm not certain, not certain at all, not anymore.

Liz slapped her, and she fell on the soft carpet.

– Good answer!

– You didn't have to do that, she said with an eager smile. – You're a goddess. I'm yours.

She spoke in an eager but even voice, telling Liz everything she didn't know.

– Perhaps that's why I did it.

The smile faltered, faltered just a little.

– Undress! Liz said casually.

The smile returned. She remained on the floor, and began removing her clothes, began something clearly meant as a classic striptease, performing for the woman in the chair.

All the clothes were gone. She displayed herself further, signaling in all ways that she was available.

– You've had customers, I take it?

– Yes, a selected few, people able and willing to pay more, a win both for me and the company.

– But you never allowed the other employees to enjoy that, did you.

– No, I impressed upon them I would be most vexed if they did. I had the opportunity to demonstrate that a few times.

There was pride there, and menace.

– You've kept your charges on a tight leash, Liz shrugged. – Very good!

Adrienne lit up like a torch catching fire.

– On your knees!

Adrienne rushed to obey, lowering her eyes. Her scent changed in seconds. She grew notably excited.

– Don't move, not a finger.

She grabbed a breast and began fondling it. Adrienne started breathing even faster. The breast swelled in Liz's hand, the nipple grew and hardened.

– This is fun, Liz remarked.

Adrienne glanced up at her through a haze.

– Fate has placed you in my care, and you better step up to that fact.

– I do, Liz, Adrienne insisted. – I will obey you, do whatever you wish me to do.

Liz slapped her once, slapped her twice.

– Your reeducation has begun. You need to be reprogrammed. You believe you exist to serve men.

The kneeling woman looked aghast at her, unable to keep herself from doing so.

– I don't believe that!

– Don't you? The way you smile and display yourself to them?

– That's just playacting, pretense.

– Is it? I don't think so. I think you, beyond your tough exterior long to belong to men, to submit to them.

– I smile and display myself to you, Adrienne sniffed and insisted.

– I am a man. In your eyes I am.

What had been a suave, sophisticated woman crumbled before the creature towering above her.

– You will now tell me everything you know, the goddess stated calmly.

Adrienne began talking. She didn't resist the impulse at all. It flowed like water. She shook as she spilled her secrets.

– I whipped her and kept whipping her, she breathed. – and enjoyed so much the sight of her blood on her lovely body.

She felt empty after just a few minutes, and it just kept going. The confession continued forever.

Liz emptied her insides, excavated it, until there was nothing, nothing at all left.

– I skimmed from the firm, she confessed, feeling nothing in particular while doing so, – taking a little here and a little there. No one ever noticed. If Rachel did she never told me.

Liz held out a hand. Adrienne grabbed it and drowned it in wet kisses.

The door to the interrogation room opened. Adrienne was thrown through it and landed on the soft carpet by the sofa. She landed hard, but it still seemed like something cushioned her landing. Everyone looked shocked at the nude, humbled woman crouching on the floor.

– Next! Liz shouted.

A man rose, clearly hesitant at first.

He was a big, muscular man with a steady stare and calm exterior, one he was now unable to keep from wavering. The door slammed close behind him. He jumped in his tracks.

– So, your name is Andrew Morton?

– Yes, he replied hoarsely.

– It isn't, of course. You took that name from a tombstone in Miami two years ago.

His heartrate picked up instantly. His breathing turned labored. He couldn't quite keep up appearances either.

– Do you read my mind?

She made no verbal reply, making his fear reply to him.

– Undress, she bid him.

He did, clearly not unused to do that, to display himself to a woman. He got caught in her eyes. It froze him to a point of him hardly being able to move.

– You love women's attention. The fact that you're paid for it, is just a bonus.

She grabbed his jaw. He froze in her ruthless grip, under a relentless stare he didn't find comforting at all.

– The truth of the matter, of course, is that you're just as much a whore, a prostitute as the other dolls.

He was almost as tall as she, but felt small, felt insignificant in her presence.

Her eyes grew to giant globes in his vision, in his shaken beyond words mind.

She grabbed his cock. She started examining it, like she would a specimen in a laboratory, revealing nothing but a cold, clinical interest. It swelled and hardened in her grip. She gave him a cruel smile. He crumbled in her ruthless grip. She placed him on his knees, and he was helpless to resist her casual treatment, as if he was indeed nothing but a doll in her hands.

– Speak!

The words didn't come to him. He opened and shut his mouth several times, unable to utter a single sound. His mind felt like wool.

She let go and started circling him, never taking her predator eyes off him. He felt them on him every single moment.

– You will do my bidding, she said evenly. – You will obey my every command.

She resumed her examining. She squeezed and stretched his arms, his hands, bending his fingers. It hurt. She had full control and he had none. He began breathing faster, began panicking, unable to act on it.

– You are a well-equipped stud, she remarked. – Don't let anyone tell you otherwise.

He heaved for breath. The ever-faster breathing made him lightheaded. He writhed in her grip, struggling hard in his attempt to move, to free himself from the cruel and strong hands.

– You will not struggle, she said casually. – You will not even entertain the idea of doing so. You will not risk provoking my rage, not if you know what's *good* for you.

She continued her cruel touch, ignoring his resistance to it. He choked in despair and helplessness. His struggles ceased. He turned limp in her grip. Tears started dropping from his eyes.

– Please, My Goddess, he sobbed. – I'm yours, yours in all things.

The wicked grin filled her face. She let go of him. He didn't move, didn't make any effort at doing so. He started talking and didn't stop. When he finally did stop, he still didn't move, but just knelt before her with lowered eyes.

– It feels good, doesn't it, to unload your burden?

He nodded eagerly, like a kid that had been punished and was grateful for it being light. She sat on her heels by his side. He leaned against her and she comforted him with kisses and kind touches.

The door opened again. One more wet rag ended up on the soft carpet by the sofa.

– I love your eyes, Liz told the girl in the chair.

– I love yours! The girl said eagerly, apprehensive.
Liz circled her like a vulture.
– You're just an overgrown China doll, Liz insulted her.
– My family is from a place in China where everyone is tall.
It sounded like she was apologizing.
– I know that. What do you take me for, stupid?
Lin Chi blinked.
– You're deliberately provoking me.
Liz grabbed her wrist and squeezed. Lin Chi shouted loud and sharp.
– You were saying?
The Chinese girl attacked her. Liz struck her down and kept striking her, until she crouched dizzy and frightened on the floor.
– On your knees, China Doll! Liz spat with a dark, dark face.
Lin Chi obeyed promptly. Liz looked at her with cruel, lupine eyes. The kneeling girl started shaking. Liz chuckled in contempt.
– Fear is a good teacher. Fear is the key.
The heap on the soft carpet and surrounding floor grew and grew. It dragged on, a prevailing ordeal taking its toll, both physically and mentally.
Everyone confessed. They opened up and confessed like a waterfall. Some of them couldn't stop talking. They had to be stopped from doing so.
It ended slowly. Everyone having suffered through Liz's interrogation sat or crouched on the floor. She rejoined them in the living room. Everyone looked attentive at her.
– You misunderstand most gravely if you believe this is the end of your ordeal, she enlightened them. – This is just the beginning.
She turned towards Peyton and Fallon.
– The two of you will have a disadvantage at the boot camp, though, she informed them.
– Because you haven't given us the… treatment? Peyton wondered.
– Aren't you the clever one? Liz grinned darkly.
– Then, give it to us, Peyton urged.
Liz looked at Fallon. He nodded, apprehensive, but stubborn.
– Okay, then, I will do you both together. It looks like we will be here a bit longer.
It sounded like the threat it was.
She returned to the enclosed room. The two lawyers followed her.
The door slammed shut behind them. Both jumped in their tracks.
– So, where do you see yourself in ten years? Liz asked.
– With you! Peyton replied.
– With you! Fallon replied.

– Good answer!
She slapped the girl, slapped the boy, not very hard, but it still burned.
– Undress!
They obeyed, shaking a bit, but stubbornly going through with it. She gave them her relentless stare. They reddened.
– You're just as much prostitutes as the rest here, of course, she told them.
– We're not, Peyton said. – I'm not!
– Haven't you *prostituted* yourself in order to reach your current position within the firm? Haven't you worked like a slave in order to be promoted and accepted by your superiors?
Fallon attempted to speak, in vain.
– On your knees!
They obeyed in a rush, casting fearful glances at the towering inferno in their midst.
She grabbed their jaws and squeezed. The boy and the girl froze to ice in her grip.
– You better step up your act, or you will be *useless* to me.
She let go of them, didn't let go of them, as she pulled back and sat down in one of the chairs.
– This is fun, she gloated. – Have you any idea how much fun this is?
They lowered their eyes in shame.
She used her telekinesis to rub his cock and her cunt. They looked stricken and horrified at her.
– You should be honored, she spat. – The Goddess grants her gifts sparingly.
– G-gifts? Peyton stuttered.
Fallon's cock grew and hardened. Peyton turned wet and warm below. A moan they desperately attempted to keep contained rose from two open mouths. It was as if she touched every single piece of their skin simultaneously.
– Oh, my… my GODDESS, Peyton cried.
– This is… *abuse*, Fallon gasped enraged.
Liz slapped him with a contemptuous laughter.
– Do you think one such as I care about right and wrong, about such trifles?
– No, Liz, Peyton breathed. – You don't, and you don't need to. There is no right and wrong anyway.
Liz chuckled even louder.
– What a stunning grasp of the obvious.
She rose and sat down on her heels, filling their vision completely. They

crumbled in her overwhelming presence.

– The Goddess's servants will now confess their sins, will now tell their Goddess everything.

– I c-cheated at bar exam, Peyton sniveled, her nose suddenly filled with snot. – I cheated and was so proud of my accomplishment.

The confession hardly shocked her. It felt like it was happening to someone else.

The Goddess rewarded her with a soft touch on the cheek.

– We're loyal to you, Fallon cried, – not our official employer.

She rewarded him with a petting on the head.

Peyton kept speaking. The Goddess stopped her now and then, leaving room for Fallon. They both rambled on and practically competed in the spilling of secrets and previous unvoiced thoughts.

They felt completely spent when they were done eons later.

Liz kissed them on the forehead. They looked at her in awe and gratitude.

She discarded them on the soft carpet with the rest.

Everyone rested there, skin touching skin.

– Any trouble? Liz asked Abby.

– None whatsoever, Abby reported what Liz already knew. – They're all such well-behaved children. It has been such a pleasure caring for them. I would say they're ready for further trials.

– I would agree, Liz said. – They're poor excuses for the warriors they need to be, but who isn't at first?

She turned to them all, catching their eyes with a casual glance.

– Bring the clothes, she commanded.

Several large boxes were brought in.

– Dress!

They opened the boxes and found what was basically training gear.

– These are basically solid, simple clothing, she remarked. – Your time of wearing expensive couture is forever behind you.

The clothes had in common that they were simple design, but aside from that they weren't uniformed in any way, with a true variety of colors and form and everything. They noticed and nodded to themselves and looked even more attentive at her.

– You get it, she said pleased. – Very good.

She led on, down the elevator and through the lobby.

– Janus Clan members basically move through New York on foot, she stated in a low-keyed manner. – This probably sounds like a monumental task to you right now, but not that far into the future, it will feel like the most natural thing in the world.

She started running the moment she reached the street and was far off before they could react. They looked for Abby, but she was gone, too, not that far behind the wind they glimpsed down the street. Everyone moved in the slipstream of the storm they all felt pull at them.

Liz and Abby returned to them, just as their charges feared that they were gone.

– You may start running, now, Abby informed them.

Liz and Abby ran back and forth constantly, running twice and even thrice the distance of those chasing them the best they were able. Throats and limbs burned already. Sweat soaked every piece of skin. Loud horns and engines sounded distant in everyone's ears. Tunnel vision focused almost exclusively on the two shapes moving like lightning ahead.

The large groups of clumsy runners chased the two in front, making their very best effort at catching up with the wind, knowing beyond knowing that they never would.

4

Liz returned to her aerie, with Abby and a few others. She easily noticed and would always notice its special quality, the feeling of coming home. It welcomed her. She acknowledged that with half closed eyes. It would always be a place of power, where a witch could reside in something resembling harmony.

She watched Eloise as she approached, wondering briefly what made her different from everyone else.

Eloise knelt down in her path on the ground floor. Liz studied what looked pretty much like a western version ninja warrior from films and stories. Eloise didn't speak or raise her eyes from their cast down position. She waited to be acknowledged. Liz obliged.

– This warrior presents herself to her king.

Liz knew then. She remembered enough of her past life centuries ago to make the connection. The words set in motion a long chain of buried age-old memories.

She didn't speak, looking amused at the fierce, humble creature.

– This warrior must serve someone, and since she doesn't want to serve *him*, she will serve you.

She bowed her head again.

– I… regret my actions, My King. I will do whatever penance My King requires.

She waited for what Liz knew felt like forever for the reply.

– Chop off your little finger, she shrugged. – That should suffice.

There was hesitation, everyone saw that, but not for long. Eloise drew the sword from her back and proceeded to execute the royal command. She did release a tiny sound of pain and looked ashamed at the floor.

– Have someone take a look at that. We don't want the queen's personal guard to catch an infection.

– Yes, My Queen, Eloise cried happily. – No, My Queen. Thank you, My Queen!

Liz grabbed her jaw, squeezing brutally hard. The personal guard made no attempt at freeing herself or protesting.

– You're happy in your servitude, Kwaiala, and that was why you so easily succumbed to his will all those years ago. We'll see what we can do about that.

She let go and the physical body and the spirit of the person kneeling before her crumbled to dust.

– Come with me, Kwaiala, Abby bid her.

– Aye, Kwaiala, the girl responded promptly.

She rose, and followed the misty shape out of the hall.

Liz took the elevator upstairs alone. She knew there was no one there with her, but she still imagined that there was. The air was filled with familiar and unfamiliar spirits. She was met by others of flesh and blood the moment she emerged from the elevator, and there was no major difference, not to her. They greeted her with happy, exuberant smiles.

– I would like to be alone, now, please, she informed them.

They pulled back, a little startled, a little hurt, but still nodding in understanding.

She entered the room with the bed and the pentacle, stepping into the circle after a little hesitation. The memory of it all was stronger here, lingering like eternal echoes of a sound that never was.

She heard it. She knew she always would. The non-existing, beyond potent Dust filled her nostrils. It spread so pleasantly through her body, her self. The vacant stare became a happy smile.

Abby and Eloise entered the room a timeless time later, knowing that they would never have been granted access if that wasn't the Goddess's will.

Eloise had a bandage on her hand and a film of sweat covering her forehead. The pain and the drug made her equally drowsy and off-center.

– Your new Kwaiala is ready to serve you… my queen, Abby said.

Eloise stepped forward, presenting herself, humbling herself.

Liz didn't speak, but knew they heard her still.

Abby stepped forward as well, imposing on her sphere.

– May this Kwaiala ask, the Queen seems…

Liz made an impatient gesture, unable to keep it back.

Abby caught herself, in fear and relief.

– You seem different, Abby wondered apprehensive and excited. – It isn't immediately obvious, but it is there. Something… happened, didn't it?

– It did! In one sliver of eternity, I saw everything that ever was, is, will be and might be… and might have been. It opened me up like a flower, like one more flower in an endless chain.

The two Kwaiala breathed faster. They stared at her with shiny eyes.

– I learned impulse control.

The familiar shrug and grin were both there, in her response.

She stepped out on the balcony. The two Kwaiala followed her, did not follow her. It didn't matter. They were still there.

The balcony seemed different, somehow. She experienced it differently.

She imagined she stood at the top of Empire State Building.

The Queen of New York beheld her holdings.

Chapter 12

Nude, sweaty bodies occupied the long row of showers. Water comforted sore limbs. Exhaustion kept shaking them, all the new recruits.

Adrienne glimpsed everything caught in her vision through a haze of shifting clarity. The massive nudity made her excited, and she could easily see, with her experience others affected by it. The males were easy, of course, but the females affected were easily found as well.

She watched Eric with his partly hardened limb. It didn't seem to bother him at all, and that held true with pretty much everyone that had been here a while. Everyone approaching instructor level was obviously unbothered, both by the nudity and the hard, horribly hard exercise. Eric was clearly a special case, but the others weren't that different, not seen through a newbie's eyes.

I'm a newbie, she thought unprompted. I'm inexperienced like a virgin.

She felt very much like that, exposed, vulnerable like a teenager.

He did cast her more than a passing glance. She knew she was probably his type, considerably bigger than most of the younger girls. She did spot insecurity in his eyes and felt a pleased smile coming up. He had a reputation as being quite… emotional. She displayed herself to him without being obvious about it, a result of her long call-girl training. He ignored her, like she had more than suspected he would do.

The group dried each other with large towels, an act clearly designed to be one more bonding experience. She was very aware of the fact that it could change into an orgy any moment, but also that it probably wouldn't. Everyone here, for various reasons needed an extra incentive in order to succumb to low-keyed arousal.

She faced Carla, and bowed her head in an obviously submissive gesture. Carla ignored it.

The giant boy towered above her. He didn't have the fireeyes, but he still made an impression on her. She noted that he was still inexperienced and could be handled more easily.

Marlene looked at her with a patronizing smile.

– You're still seeing yourself in the cutthroat environment you profess to have left behind, the big and sassy woman remarked, – looking for vulnerabilities to exploit.

Caught! Adrienne thought stricken.

– Don't worry, you will come to see yourself as a young girl again, the redhead instructed her, – eager to learn the secrets of life.

– Yes, honored teacher, Adrienne replied humbly.

– I love the sound of that, Marlene grinned wickedly.

Everyone moved into the dressing room. There was no separation of the sexes, not even a suggestion of it. They mingled without visible embarrassment or shame. The clothes were the same or similar simple and varied type that Liz had given the former sex-workers, uniforms not uniforms.

They followed Marlene into the informal classroom, sitting down on the floor in front of where Marlene sat down. She appeared completely casual, calm, relaxed, waiting patiently for everyone to choose their spot.

– They claim that human society can't really be changed, but that is clearly false, Marlene began. – It changes all the time. We're surrounded by changes. The question is who's doing them and for what purpose. Carla will tell you in detail, in one of the advanced classes how it's possible to completely transform a given society in a generation or two if the circumstances are right. It's mostly a matter of attitude, of believing it can actually be done. There will most certainly be hardship and setbacks, but you will learn to handle those, to deal with despair and personal crisis. The most important thing is to keep fighting, to learn that the fire within is worth any pain to keep burning.

They watched her, her quiet passion and determination, the smile lurking around her mouth and in her eyes. She had a very expressive face. They imagined they could see every single mood in her features.

Lee trained with Lydia later. She kept looking at him with excited and eager eyes.

– You shouldn't be concerned about me, she said brightly, stubbornly. – I'm nothing like her.

He nodded to her, to himself.

They moved, and they had a connection, one clearly beyond this life. Every move, every glance brought familiarity and deeper understanding. Every time their eyes met brought faint memories.

The repeated chills and ravages of joy mixed within them both.

Eric sat in his small office in the practically refurbished warehouse, sat there typing without pause or distractions.

He had moved out of his hotel room early on, after starting on his tenure here. It was quiet, in spite of the frequent sounds of fighting. Journalists had better access to him here, but even that didn't feel like a bother. Inspiration kept surging like a fire in dry summer grass.

The words kept flooding him. He could no longer stop them, even if he wanted to. The tapestry appeared on the back of his eyelids whether he closed his eyes or not.

Adrienne brought him coffee. He noticed at the edge of the eye, where he noticed everything, everything not the keyboard and sheet.

He kept tapping monotonously. Time just went away for him. He knew the coffee turned cold, but didn't touch it. Adrienne brought him a new steaming cup, and removed the old and cold.

The light had changed notably outside when he grabbed the cup and sipped the coffee and discovered that it was still hot. He turned towards her.

– How many times did you refill?

– Only about fifteen times, she joked.

She stepped forward with stars in her eyes.

– You write about them… about her?

He nodded with a parched throat.

– She's a Goddess, she breathed.

– Yes, she is, he nodded.

She nodded as well, when studying him.

– I guess he and the others are gods, too, but I haven't yet had the pleasure of seeing them in action, so I'll stick with worshiping her, for now.

She kept studying him, looking him up and down, as if assessing him.

– You are her scribe, one of the foremost priests in her temple. You will bring her word to all the heathens. This humble priestess salutes you!

His eyes followed her as she stepped back, as she walked to the couch, the big and pleasant couch. They narrowed as she began removing her clothes. It was an easy process.

– I'm yours to do with as you please, she stared, – but you don't need me to tell you that. You know it with every glance you send me, with every move you catch.

He knew, with one glance that she was telling the truth. She rubbed herself, eager and ready. He rose abruptly, knocking over the chair in the process. She fell on the couch, displaying herself to him, signaling with every move she made that she was ready for whatever he wanted to do to her. He walked to her, removing his equally easy to remove clothes as he did so. She writhed there on the couch, constantly whispering her loud litany of surrender, and it filled his ears, until he could hear nothing else.

2

They visited a bar off-Broadway. Ted recognized it the moment he stepped inside, recognized the huge cactus by the entrance, the worn globe in the far, opposite window. They played Credence Clearwater Revival and that, and the decor reminded him of New Orleans.

And with that thought came a rush of memories of another day. Margaux, Lynn and Gerdie looked attentive at him, the smiles on their lips warming his chilled bones.

– I can always tell when you zone out, Gerdie said. – Your eyes grow distant, and even bigger and more beautiful.

Her accent became notable again, as if the subject of her speech actually affected her throat and lips and tongue.

She pushed herself at him, mauling his lips, practically glued to them.

All four walked to the bar. Ted bought a bottle of whiskey. The others grinned and didn't buy whatever they had considered buying.

– May we have four glasses? Lynn asked the bartender.

He granted her wish without comment.

They sat down by the wall opposite the bar in a half full room. Almost everyone present stared at them, but they had become used to that by now, and didn't allow it to affect them much.

Ted opened the bottle and filled the four glasses.

– Cheers!

– CHEERS! The women choired.

The four of them drank. He didn't cough. They did.

– It burns, Gerdie giggled.

He drank faster than them, even as he took his time, even as they all did, enjoying the numbness growing slowly in their limbs and lips and mind.

He waited patiently for Bad Moon Rising to be played and it was, of course. All four, one thought and one mind rushed out on the limited dance floor. Everyone moved according to each other in a manner impossible to misunderstand. The other guests stared harder than ever.

– Look at them, Margaux mused, – they're all so… prosaic.

She worked hard at keeping the contempt from manifesting in her voice, and didn't quite make it.

He frowned at the thought that wouldn't come, the trail of reflection still missing.

– BAD MOON RISING, they sang. – BAD MOON RISING, BAD MOON RISING

The dance took yet another turn for the wild. The song ended only slowly in their minds. They returned laughing and chuckling to the table.

It was the strangest thing. He noticed, even as he enjoyed himself in the women's company a kind of second reality buzzing at the edge of his consciousness. The buzz overwhelmed him for a moment. He watched the street outside, as if from a different vantage point. A man stumbled on the sidewalk and fell. Ted turned around and he was inside the bar again. A woman stumbled across the room, returning from the restroom, bumping into virtually every chair and table, every piece of furniture she passed.

She collapsed on the floor. They watched her as she crawled across the room to her table, and climbed back on her chair. She started drinking from the bottle, and it was clear to him that she would never stop.

A man approached their table, a man Ted knew was very much present in the here and now. He stopped very close to Lynn, his stinking breath almost making them all faint on the spot.

– Hi, would you like to dance?

Sounding and appearing like a parody of a drunk.

– Thank you, she replied cheerfully, – but no.

He grabbed her unceremoniously and pulled her up from the chair. She allowed herself to be pulled on her feet. Then, she struck him in the face, once. He fell unconscious to the floor.

– One dance, she mumbled, as she dragged the unmoving figure to the space between the tables.

She danced and swayed, a lone figure on the limited dance floor, moving around the unconscious man. Wicked laughter echoed all around the room. Ted relaxed. The danger, if there had ever been one faded.

Suddenly, the deep chill was notable and very present, as the extensive trickle flowing down Ted's spine spread to his entire body.

He watched the door as Jane stepped into the room. He knew she wasn't there, wasn't there yet. Closing his eyes did him no good, of course. He watched her as she was hit by several bullets.

One moment it happened, the next it didn't. No one had recently stepped through the door. No woman, not Jane. She didn't fall to the floor. The pool of blood did not spread from her ruined body like a rose. He realized it was the memory of the vision he had suffered through several times the last few months, not the vision itself, even as he wondered and kept wondering what the difference was.

The sunshine shifted on the floor. The moment ended.

The others rose from the chairs when he did, as if they could somehow anticipate his wishes and actions. They left the bar and headed into the hot and dry street.

– Look at them, Lynn chuckled. – They just can't stop looking at us, can they?

Ted nodded. The eyes were there, all the time.

– I've come to accept that, he said. – So should you.

His three companions nodded empathically and solemnly.

They walked to what seemed to him like ghostly streets, with ghoulish entities crossing back and forth on all sides. There wasn't merely one more layer added to his vision, but several more, too many to count.

A man stood on the corner with his gun drawn, pointing at Ted and the lone woman by his side. Lynn and Margaux looked concerned at him, with eyes filled with trust. The vision, the recording of the vision in his head didn't go away.

He closed his eyes. His walk didn't turn uncertain. His feet remembered exactly where he was supposed to tread.

Returning to the warehouse, his current brief home felt like an easy, grateful task. He said a passionate see you later to his three companions and walked upstairs. Liz waited for him on the top floor, standing with her back to him, looking out the large window, totally exposed to whoever would watch her from the outside, even the far outside. He walked to her and grabbed her shoulders, kissing her on the neck. She turned and faced him.

– Hi, she said softly, – how's your day? Have you had fun?

She looked at him with her large eyes. They had always looked large to him, like his own, but now, for some reason, they looked even bigger and more mesmerizing.

– It hasn't been too bad so far, he shrugged, striving to keep a jovial tone. – Lynn beat the living bear shit out of a poor guy that wouldn't take no for an answer. We laughed a lot about that.

– I bet you did.

The smile transformed her face.

One, two second passed.

– It is the right place, he insisted.

– I think so, too, she nodded. – I'm convinced it is.

– But the sunlight on the floor is wrong, he pointed out. – Whatever will happen won't happen for weeks.

She nodded again.

– Have you experienced anything more? He asked.

– I haven't, she replied, – and it isn't for the lack of trying. You know as much as I do.

– She doesn't know the place, he said. – I walked past there with her, and there wasn't even a shred of recognition in her eyes.

– But now she does know about it, Liz said, – at least in her subconsciousness. Chances are, she would never have come close to it without us, without us saving her from the hospital.

– Perhaps we should tell her? He wondered.

– Perhaps her… her fate is set, no matter what we do, she mused. –

Perhaps we just can't save her from that encounter in Samara. Perhaps everything we do will assure that it will happen?

Something rose within him, something he still couldn't explain. She felt it and nodded to herself.

– We know time, but time says that she will die, and I can't, won't accept that.

– You should be careful, she told him softly. – We don't know the repercussions of tampering with… with probability.

She shook her head, disagreeing with herself, knowing his shaking before it began. She took him in his arms and kissed him on the brow.

– Did you, he began hesitant, – did you feel as helpless when you lost your powers?

– If you're asking if I felt insecure and useless and everything, that is a sure bet, she said good humored.

– You should be there when it happens, he said, – not I.

– We know I probably won't be, she pointed out, totally unnecessary. – We don't know why, but I'm not there in any of our visions.

– Why do we see her and not… all the others?

All the others of his old friends that had been with him in the squatted building in London.

She felt very mature and confident compared to the young boy in front of her.

– I saw them dead, he choked, – but I saw no details, only felt the overwhelming certainty that they would die, that they wouldn't be alive some years into the future, that I would survive them all.

– We know that the future isn't set, she stated, – know it is… malleable, and even if this seems different in a way we can't explain, we can change it, I know we can, know *you* can, if it comes to that.

The pep talk worked. She nodded pleased to herself when she saw how he straightened, how he pulled himself together.

They both shook and kept shaking in the seething heat created by the warm, warm sunlight bathing them through the large window, both convinced, convinced beyond doubt that destiny had caught up with them.

3

Diana McKenzie woke up soaked in sweat and dread, and a rage breaking all boundaries.

She kept her emotions somewhat contained while she dressed, while she headed for the breakfast table with the others. It felt hard, like being a cage others rattled. She kept it together until she spotted Ted standing with Jane in the hallway. She couldn't keep the shaking from manifesting when she rushed forward and stopped abruptly in front of them.

– I must speak to you… both of you, she insisted.

She grabbed them and practically dragged them with her. He didn't need to look closer at her in order to see her state of mind, and Jane followed his lead. The distraught woman brought them far away, into the still more or less abandoned parts of the building. She pulled them into a room and closed the door.

They looked attentive at her. Ted couldn't help but feel a chill when he met her eyes.

– My… father was… is a member of the Thousand Feet, she spat.

Jane released a shocked yelp. Ted found it amazing that he could stand there without visibly reacting.

– He was an integrated part of the operation before we were all kidnapped, Diana said with a dull voice. – I saw the written plans and also overheard him talk to his colleagues. It was what I wanted to tell you, what I should have told you that day in Washington DC.

Ted wanted to ask her if she was sure, but held his tongue. He had no doubt that she was.

– It was there, all of it, when I woke up today, half in, half out of dreams, she said. – Everything became crystal clear.

– Oh, Diana, Jane said, – I'm so sorry!

Diana evidently didn't hear her.

– I have no idea what happened between them later, whether or not they had a fallout or what the reason was…

– They tried to kill him, Ted said. – Stewart and Caine saved him, and he joined up with them.

– I *know*!

She grabbed his collar and squeezed. He forced himself to let it happen.

– Perhaps he broke with them when they kidnapped you? Janet suggested. – Perhaps they did it in an attempt to make him stay in line?

– I appreciate you attempting to comfort me, I do, Diana said, – but it is misguided. I know he was there later, before I was rescued. I saw him, heard him.

Jane gasped.

– He was *there*, when they attempted to make me forget everything, brainwash me. It worked for a while, but didn't take. I *remember*! I remember the plans in detail. He was an integrated part of the plans and was there when you guys were taken. I heard them talk about what a great job he had done, how he had delivered you to Gidman on a silver platter.

Saliva flowed from her mouth. Ted wanted to take his sleeve and dry her, but he couldn't move. Jane had to do it. Diana hardly reacted to her fuzzing.

A crystal-clear memory hit Ted as well.

– Fitzallan, he said slowly, hardly hearing himself speak.

That made Jane stare at him.

– There was a man there, a professed tourist guide with a giant red beard. He led us astray, fooling us to walk far into the mountains, where they had complete control of the situation. We believed they had hired a fucking actor or something, but that doesn't make sense, of course.

– My father tried acting in his younger days, Diana shrugged.

Her rage didn't abate, but picked up further by the second.

– But now he will pay, she swore. – Now, we will expose him and all his works. Now, he will pay!

Ted grabbed her, catching her eyes. She looked astonished at him.

– We have a weapon, now, he stated, – one we can use a like a blade, the sharpest scalpel… if we stay quiet about it, about what we can't possibly prove.

He could hardly recall being this astute, having experienced such a massive clarity of mind, not ever, and to him, that said a lot.

The two women glanced at him, at each other and nodded, understanding beyond understanding what he was actually *saying*.

– We don't tell anyone, Jane stated, – not *anyone*.

Diana nodded.

– A secret shared is no secret, she acknowledged. – No one must know.

They looked at Ted. He nodded as well.

Hands grabbed hands and held on. The bond was confirmed. The pact was set.

4

The creature without eyes roamed the New York City streets, both alone and in the company of other enigmatic creatures. A woman dressed as something resembling a ninja warrior from a film was spotted close to her. So was another emitting a different kind of mist and shadow.

The smoke stretched and bent, and often seemed to float more than walk, but never quite lost its human form.

People studying the ninja and the eyeless shadow swore they hardly touched the ground at all. They were movement without substance, forward momentum without air, without friction.

Liz felt her two companions without effort, also when they were fairly far away. Each step registered in her mind like a soft, comfortable pressure. It wasn't only sound. No matter how her radar worked, it certainly didn't only have to do with soundwaves.

Linsey and the band played at markedly improved venues these days. They held a concert tonight with hundreds of listeners and watchers applauding their music.

Helen sang on a couple of songs. All the pain and longing of life seemed to be present in her magnificent voice and intense features. The audience went bananas, clearly feeling like they were a part of the performance. Linsey, and thereby everyone present, grew more inspired and excited. Liz felt the power of the deluge many blocks away. Passing it at the nearest point, she imagined she actually got wet on her feet.

Eloise moved in Liz's shadow all the time, never wavering in her commitment, an ongoing presence in the dark one's sphere, just as much a part of her as a piece of dust or the air she breathed.

– Thou were crushed by the onslaught of thy ill-advised decision, Liz told her without looking at her. – Thou must return to what you once were and recommit to the cause you once served or must find a new center, something beyond the beliefs once crumbling to dust within your shaking figure.

It remained strange to hear herself speak like this, speak Gaelic, its ancient, archaic form. She felt both outside herself and closer to herself than ever.

– This humble warrior feels something when moving through these streets, My Queen. There is something here she can only recall as a faint itch in the ashes of her existence.

– There is a secret here, Liz said, – the same that is present everywhere. Jahavalo took you in your moment of despair, when you were down and vulnerable, and made you his creature. He took from you what he takes from everyone: our very ability to live as human beings.

Eloise shook hard. The name Liz had spoken lingered between the buildings for eons afterwards.

– I wanted so to please him, to serve him, Eloise whispered, – beyond anything, beyond myself.

– And now, you wish to please and serve me beyond dedication, beyond anything, Liz shrugged.

Eloise shook, even as she frowned, even as she understood or struggled to understand.

Abby approached a group of pimps and working girls. Liz noticed, and Eloise noticed when she noticed.

– You good folks should really stop what you're doing, she told them in a calm manner.
They fired at her. The bullets passed right through her body, but she pulled back.
– We will get back to you…
Liz stood ready to intervene, but there was no need. The men made no attempt to chase Abby back into the shadows. The three of mist and shadow met and moved away, returning to the aerie.
– I guess they were very determined in their defense of their chosen lifestyle, Liz joked.
The other two laughed with her, dark expectation lit in their eyes.
The activity at the aerie had picked up lately, and had become just as pronounced as at the former warehouse. They used it to relieve the pressure from the main site, but the recruitment had picked up to such a degree that both places together had trouble handling the influx of new people eager to take part.
– I guess we need to be pickier in our recruitment, Liz mused.
– We should at least not do any active recruitment drive, Abby acknowledged. – It's too bad, but we don't really have any choice in the matter.
– It's really funny, Liz chuckled. – I and Ted were set against doing the usual gathering of forces when we arrived in the city.
– That is funny… My Queen, Eloise giggled cautiously.
– She Liz, you Eloise, Abby joked, not joking.
The activity stopped or at least paused a little the moment they stepped inside. Everyone glanced at the three, as they proceeded to the elevator.
– How can she *see* anything? Liz easily heard just before the door to the elevator closed.
Peyton waited for upstairs. She jumped from the coach, eager and zealous.
– Your eyes, she gasped. Your *eyes!*
– You can see them?
She nodded, both subdued and excited.
– They are actually glowing.
– Your power is perception, Liz enlightened her. – You can see what most others can't.
– My… power?
Liz didn't voice a reply, but only looked at her with those burning eyes that to Peyton's exchanged senses looked like small dark suns.
A big, excited smile brightened Peyton's face.
– Uh, I have drawn up the papers. They're ready to be sent to all major and

minor newsrooms.

– That is good, Liz said. – Good work!

– Are you sure you want to do this? It won't exactly be pleasant.

– It will be! Liz grinned.

Peyton felt warm and appreciated.

– I've thought about it long and hard, as you know, about our entire approach to this and other stuff, and this is the right call. In fact, it's long overdue.

– Yes, Liz, Peyton breathed.

Liz took the folder and skimmed through it one more time, the list of former customers, but also a network of pimps, of the competition. Rachel had been very thorough.

– It is almost as if she knew you would need this one day, Peyton mused, her eyes widening as she spoke, when she realized what she was saying and its implications.

Liz's grin widened. She knew it was unnerving for people to see her like this, to see her and not see her, even for the three women in her presence that should have known better.

– At attention, she said casually.

The three instantly straightened before her.

She stopped in front of them, making them look at her.

– We are ready for this, well prepared and trained for all of it. Give the word to everyone you speak to within our extended clan. Speak both comforting and enticing words. Our warriors will need both, as the unrest and body count pick up.

– Yes, Liz, they choired eagerly.

They drowned in the huge fireeyes, the chill touching their heart.

– I dream, a dream of power. You will, too.

– The power needs to be used, Peyton acknowledged and breathed, – or it will leave a void sucking you dry.

Liz acknowledged her statement with an almost imperceptible nod.

The documents were sent with couriers to all relevant destinations, even many abroad. The reactions began ticking in almost immediately. The phones began to ring. Peyton and Fallon took them and replied to question and made appointments about interviews and such.

– Yes, Fallon said amiably, very amiably, – Liz will be available for interviews on the twenty-third. Yes, she will definitely be willing to do an in-depth interview. No, she has no need to see the questions in advance.

He took a break several hours later, and left his spot to someone else.

She walked to him and gave him a wet kiss on the cheek.

– Good boy.
He turned deep red again.
– Yes, I can confirm that «Miss Kendall» will be holding a press conference in the backyard outside her home at 4.30 this afternoon, Adrienne enlightened a reporter. – No, sweetie, there will be no further communication before that, either public or private. I should point out that Liz prefers to be called by the surname of Warren. She doesn't exactly look kindly at those not respecting that.
She put the phone back on the receiver. She blushed when Liz gave her an encouraging smile of approval.
Journalists and TV-crews began gathering in the backyard not long afterwards, rigging and testing their equipment. A few tried the doorknob on the solid door. It remained locked, no matter how many times they tried to open it.
– Good thing we had food and supplies delivered this morning, Peyton said and rubbed her earlobe anxiously. – We're talking a siege here.
– Don't be nervous, Liz encouraged her.
– I'm not, Liz, Peyton assured her. – Honest!
She was so zealous, so eager to prove herself that it was almost touching.
– It's time, Liz grinned, – time to pay the piper.
Everyone prepared, readying themselves, far more than she did. She smiled good humored at their zeal. Only a short stretch of time passed as they took the elevator down, as everyone but her made the last few corrections in their clothing and appearance.
She stepped out in the hot, arid air surrounded by her loyal guard, acolytes, associates and accomplices. The giant smile seemed stuck on her face, the very expressive face. She wore jeans, a jacket and a top, appearing as ordinary as she possibly could, demonstrating that she never would be.
Elizabeth Warren stopped in front of the gathering of journalists and reporters, standing in the open, not protected by anything like a high dais or an array of microphones most famous or infamous people making a public statement had at their disposal. They had made one such for her, but she ignored it.
– Early this morning, she began with a loud voice, – we sent copies of my grandmother's «customer» list to anyone that might be interested, publishing it in full, not hiding anything or leaving anyone out. We included notes and customers' preferences, a very detailed description of what they paid for. I will be reading juicy excerpts for a while, and then I will speak a bit more, and then I will answer your questions.
She pulled what was clearly a notebook from her pocket. A loud murmur

of expectation rose from a crowd of newshounds.

– The first section is about Lester, Lester Carmichael. Lester is a man of excellent taste, Rachel writes. He prefers them young or at least young-looking, and just loves punishing them in many inventive ways, including but not limited to birching, spanking and whipping. He also loves calling them names while doing so, pleasant designations like whore, bitch, slut, tramp, harlot, hussy, cum dumpster, nympho, vamp, flirt, tart, floozie and a number of designations that certainly would have made me blush in my preteen days. He put several of the girls in hospital. We did report him to the police, knowing it was a failed venture, but made sure we got copies of the official and unofficial police documents. I barred him from admission, but there is no doubt in my mind that he found what he wanted from other sources.

It went on and on. The journalists imagined she read every single word in the notebook. The shadows grew long as she spoke.

She stopped, lowering the hand holding the notebook.

The questions began as a deluge.

– So, now that you have done what you set out to do, any early regrets?

The loud laughter shook them just as hard as her other actions.

– I remain very happy about my decision. It was the right call and long overdue. Someone should have done this shit ages ago. I will stress that I just don't want to focus on the brutal «customers», but on all of them. I know you won't print or relay important details in your excellent papers or broadcast stations, but you should know that everything will come out, also your role or lack of role in keeping the info from the public. It has already.

She *touched* them, not holding herself back at all. She used her powers to rub their cocks and cunts, making them writhe in discomfort. The smile grew even more enthusiastic.

Questions and answers continued for a long while, clearly hostile, but much of it lost its bite early, and even more so as the seance progressed.

– What about your fellow squatters? One asked a question obviously designed to embarrassed her. She shrugged it off with yet one more act of sequential elegance.

– The others are certainly a part of this campaign, but we work on many things, many aspects of the modern community, the list of horrible wrongs to be corrected is horribly long.

– Garrett from the Post, ma'am, he presented himself.

– It's so nice to meet you, she responded sweetly.

The frown on his brow grew visible and deep.

– Isn't prostitution merely an exchange of funds and services between two consenting adults?

She did pause, pretending to ponder the issue.
– That's certainly one of many myths that have prevailed for a while, one we will keep cracking like the overblown balloon it is.
She shook her head decisively.
– No, it's a process where the one receiving the funds is the weak part, a very unequal part. Prostitution is happening on many levels and variations throughout society, but the version where people are sort-of fucking is our main focus right now. We will certainly return to the rest at a later point.
Something happened then, a darkening of the very air no one could put into words. She seemed to grow, to suddenly stand very close to them, towering over them like a giant.
– We are told, pretty much from the cradle that we should accept every single injustice and indignity visited upon us. It is time we give a loud FUCK THAT in response to such horror.
It only grew in intensity from that point…
The people shook, shook hard in the warm sunshine when they left the enclosed space and reentered the busy New York City streets. Liz moved with them on their shaking legs and parched throats. She stood there with half-closed eyes. The others looked at her, practically jumping up and down in excitement.
– I can sense them, she mumbled, – sense them fleeing like rabbits before the predator.
– I can, too, Peyton said excited. – They are like an open *book* to me.
She turned towards the younger woman with a childlike expression on her face.
– You showed them! You showed their superiority down their throats like nothing. You made them lick your hand.
– It will make you even more famous… infamous, Abby said.
They all looked at her with that look.
– Please don't think I will allow myself to be seduced by the fame and glory, Liz said. – It's so unimportant that I can hardly even pretend it matters.
– We know, Liz! Abby insisted. – We know!
They all gathered around her, touched her, touched her deliberately, willingly, eagerly skin to skin. She felt the instant power transfer, felt it strengthen her in a very personal way, strengthen her resolve, the very fire burning within.
– Goddess… Peyton whispered.
That word… affected her. Even as she attempted to conceal her emotions, she knew she couldn't quite do it. Elizabeth Warren felt an even stronger

heat, one that no physical touch could provide.
– It's time to take the next step, she said, catching their eyes yet again, – taking it to the next level.
– There is a next level? Abby joked, feigned a gasp. – I would have thought we reached the ceiling long ago…
Liz… appreciated that.
Her surroundings dissolved around her, changing into another. It wasn't like she had experienced it when she had been a goddess, but at least faintly resembling it. It was close enough.
She found herself in another office, facing yet another arrogant prick of a man attempting to intimidate her.
– Yeah, I want you to…
He stopped talking in midsentence. The kitchen knife rose into the air. He froze and stared tantalized at it. Suddenly, it flew across the room, and buried itself in the opposite wall. It shivered with a deep, troubling sound. It kept shaking, not showing any signs of stopping.
She showed him the creature, the dark shadow and he shivered in the bright sunlight. To him and others like him, she would be the Goddess. They didn't deserve any better.
– You're gonna withdraw the suit, she instructed him, – and you will start using all your resources to aid centers for battered women, and programs to truly aid poor people in the city, not with charity, but with true aid, with unconditional support.
He laughed incredulous.
– If you don't, I will take your children away from you. I will take everything from you, and you will never be able to prove anything. It will fade away before your eyes like a mirage, as if it was never there, but you will remember.
He stared at her with insane eyes, with cold pearls of sweat appearing on his skin.
– Your meek wife may wish to leave you, anyway, and if she does, you will let her and let her have custody of the children. At least you will have them during weekends.
She turned to walk away.
– Know that the Goddess chose to be merciful. Know that that can change anytime.
– Merciful? He choked.
She broke his little finger. It was nothing to her. He screamed in pain and shock. She broke his wrist. It snapped like a dry branch. The scream stuck in his throat. He couldn't quite get it out.

– On your knees! She ordered casually.

His knees hit the floor, hardly a conscious act on his part at all. She walked to him and patted his head, drying some of his tears.

– That's a good boy. Some people grow emboldened faced with hopeless odds. Let's hope, for your sake that won't be the case with you. I give you this one chance, and no more. If you take that as a sign of weakness, it is on you. If you do anything, anything to hurt anyone from this point on, I will come for you, and your death will be one long scream.

She walked off. That office faded as well.

A big hall faded into her vision. She recognized it. She recognized the woman welcoming her.

– You're only twenty, the woman gushed at her, – and have already accomplished so much. I hardly dare speculate at where it will all end.

Liz made her speech, an imperfect version of how she recalled it. She received thunderous applause.

– What a bunch of hypocrites, Peyton snarled.

Liz looked at her with appreciation.

Her entourage gathered around her, following on the heels of Peyton's fast feet. They walked the street afterwards, in full view of the newshounds and the public.

Something touched Liz, making her itch somewhere she couldn't identify. She turned and looked up. A man, a man with fireeyes stood on a balcony far above street level.

– I see him, My Queen, Eloise said instantly. – There is no way any of us can reach him in a span of a reasonable timeframe. If he wants to, and I imagine he would, and don't want to… *talk* to us, he will be long gone by the time we get up there.

Liz nodded. Eloise's reasoning was sound. If he had wanted to talk to them, to her, he would have just approached them. Liz nodded again. If she had been able to levitate, to fly, she could have been there in seconds, but that wasn't an option anymore.

It wouldn't have been an option even if the ability had been there, of course, and he would know that.

She didn't sense him, didn't feel his presence at all, aside from actually seeing him with her eyes, seeing him up close, as if they stood face to face. He resembled Ted and Mike and herself quite a bit, looking distinctly different from Patrick and Lee, more than suggesting that he was from her part of the family. She recognized him, recognized him from her childhood vision. A chill penetrated her spine.

A sound from the left, a coughing engine made her turn her head. She caught the sight of an old car driving by.

One moment of inattention on her part, and he had vanished when she looked up there again.

They reached her building, her aerie. She unlocked and unbolted and opened the entrance door with her mind. It closed behind them as they stepped inside. Eloise locked and bolted it. The others present there greeted them with hugs and affectionate kisses. Liz enjoyed the touches, the skin against skin. They noticed her distress, had learned to know her, the small signs of various emotions hard to hide. She sighed and relented.

– There was a man on that balcony, she told them, – a fireeyes, a wicked mirage I know briefly from before. He made quite an impression on the child I was, but only as a shadow, a presence without a face. I still recognized him. There's no doubt in my mind that it is the same being.

The others nodded. They caught the nuances of her wording, like they caught those of her emotions.

Sixteen. She had been sixteen. It was only four years ago.

– I am convinced that first impression was essentially correct. He wishes me or no one nothing good. I'm not sure if he was actually here this time either, or what he actually wants, if he actually wants anything, except announcing his presence to me.

– He wants something, Peyton stated passionately. – Men like him always do.

– I guess he wants to play with his prey a little, Liz shrugged. – I thought he was done with me when he didn't get what he wanted from the weak-willed girl I was, but that's clearly not the case.

She had felt a sinister presence in South America as well, one she had later assumed was David Gidman, but perhaps hadn't been.

Perhaps he had sensed the soft spot within her, her recent vulnerability, the crack in her armor, and decided it was worth exploiting, worth making another attempt at catching her in his net and reining her in. A… being such as him would have easily noticed her shaken self-confidence and decided to take advantage of it.

They came to her and touched her again, giving their energies to her, comforting her. The strength swelled at her core and she felt bloated and released the mental equivalent of a burp.

She stayed below with the rest that evening. They made dinner and gathered around the long table. She chose deliberately an inconspicuous spot between the head and the center. Everyone cast her glances. They always did that, moving in her sphere, blowing in her wind, and tonight was no different. The wine didn't work on her, but that and the strong spices combined did burn in her stomach.

– Cheers, Fallon cried and raised his glass.

Everyone echoed his action and drank. Laughter filled Liz's ears and mind and sphere.

There was some low-keyed conversation, but most did not bother with that. They knew she could hear them, anyway. Most spoke one and one, to the entire table, to her.

– You actually did it! Gail cried. – You did it!

– We did, Liz said. – We're still only in the initial stages, though.

– If that was your initial effort, I can't wait to see your follow-up, a boy said excited.

They knew, of course, or had an idea, most of them, but he didn't mean that.

– It will take years, and our continued effort, she stated with quiet passion, – and then we might see some lasting results.

– We see that already, Peyton insisted in her innocent zeal.

The gathering echoed its agreement.

– Look at this as a first wave, Liz stressed. – Picture a step-by-step escalation, until it becomes a deluge, until we no longer allow those in charge to have any say on our lives.

They nodded eagerly, not put off at all by her words of caution, and that encouraged her.

Dinner ended. Someone put on some music, and everyone stayed put. They began dancing, and she joined them. There, surrounded by sweaty bodies, she was able to enjoy their ambient energies in a more relaxed manner. The music and mood from the Sixties, from yet one more lost age filled their consciousness and encouraged them further.

She watched them laugh. Their laughter echoed in her ears. A different kind of awareness grew on her, a kind of unpleasantness she could not avoid.

It dawned on her slowly. She would never fit in. She would never be one of them.

They stopped almost before she stopped, sensing her mood as if it was their own. There were more comforting kisses and caresses. Abby grabbed her hands, and held on, also after she started feeling faint.

– Please stay, she implored her. – You shouldn't retreat to your cave like a wounded animal.

Liz nodded, relenting faced with the quiet wave of support.

Some of them stayed on the floor, but most returned to the couch with her. The good mood lingered, but subdued, not quite reaching the surface.

She sat there with them, laughing with them, joking with them, somewhat enjoying their company, beset with dark dreams she couldn't discard.

Glowing fireeyes looked at each and everyone of those surrounding her. They couldn't meet those eyes, but still made an effort at conveying eager support. That made the warm feeling grow within, but she still saw blood and strife when she closed or half-closed her eyes.

– She's alone, Lucas whispered into the ear closest to him.

– Shhh, she might hear you, Rosalyn hissed at him.

Liz kept her face impassive, confident that they didn't notice her brief slipup.

– Most people today concern themselves with trifles, becoming irritated by those, she stated abruptly, – virtually ignoring the truly important issues.

She spotted the same expression of devotion and breathless agreement in their eyes and features.

They had more wine. She had much more wine. Even if it didn't really affect her much, she still enjoyed the pleasant burning in her stomach.

She studied them, doing so even harder than before, evaluating them constantly, their reactions to the smallest hint and claim. Abby looked at her and smiled. Liz saw her dressed in black and wearing a mask, saw only her eyes and mouth. Others, like Peyton and Christy and Lin Chi and Gail and Adrienne and Eloise and Eliza revealed themselves the same way in her vision.

– Tomorrow night will be crucial, she told them. – It has to be only the females of the pack, but you males should know that your time will come.

Eyes burning with trust and awe kept warming her.

The world changed in her vision before it chanced in truth. She had sort–of grown used to that by now. It still felt unnerving, as if she wasn't really either here or there or anywhere anymore. Her recent touch with godhood had upgraded her once again, and she couldn't quite get a grip.

The van rushed through the night. She registered that, even as she wasn't positive tomorrow night had come.

– I trust you to go through with it, to commit fully to what we need to do, she told her charges in the back of the van, or what felt very much like it.

They looked very determined at her, as they clutched the machineguns in their hands.

– We will do it, Lin Chi stated, – will execute the operation f-flawlessly. We won't get s-squeamish.

– No, you won't, Liz shrugged, – because if you do, you will die.

– Just remember your training, Carla told them. – It isn't that difficult. You quite simply kill until there is no one left to kill. For the record, I think you will do well.

The more or less inexperienced among them glanced at each other. Sometimes, she scared them even more than Liz did.

– We, the two of us could take out the people tonight easily, Liz said, – but you need to do it. It must be your kill, your victory. If you survive, you will come out of it changed, transformed. Your hands may shake tonight, but the next time, they won't!

The mix of experienced and inexperienced warriors approached the house in upstate New York. Liz recognized it and the surrounding area through her haze of clarity. The attack force dropped out of the van two and two and spread out in the terrain, moving like they had never done anything else. Liz and Ted and Eric had taught them how to use the terrain to their advantage and they used that, making Liz shake her head in amazement. Lin Chi and Gail sought the nearest high ground and hid with their sniper rifles. They began taking out guards. There were ten of them, spread out around the building. The others began firing at those seeking shelter. Christy and Peyton readied their bazookas and fired at the house. It blew up and pieces of it spread all over the area. People stumbled outside. They were shot down fast and efficient. There weren't many left when the enemy finally began returning the fire. They were caught in one crossfire. Those escaping that were hit by another hail of bullets from several angles.

– Short bursts, Gail mumbled. – *Short* bursts!

There was hardly anything left of the suave, elegant woman Liz had met only weeks ago. Liz thrived on watching and sensing her ongoing awakening.

It ended slowly, with the attackers walking around and killing off those still alive. The woman with her entire head covered watched it all from the nearby mound, feeling very close to it all. She felt the girls' elation and triumph, felt each and every one on the ground dying and soaked death up like a sponge from the shimmering and tasty air.

Lin Chi approached Carla with feverish eyes. She was bleeding from a wound in an arm. The wound wasn't even approaching dangerous or lethal.

– I think at least one escaped, she remarked.

– Very good, Carla nodded pleased. – He will be our messenger.

Everyone returned to the car, looking at each other with shiny eyes, years of accumulated rage still ravaging their insides.

Everything fell silent, as even the echoes faded to nothing. Giant flames danced in the hot night and stretched and embraced them all. Ash and blood and dust floated in the air and showed no signs of ever falling.

Chapter 13

Ted, Margaux, Lynn and Gerdie had become a mainstay at the off-Broadway bar. They had their own bedroom on the second floor. Ted stood nude by the window, watching the street below.

The three of them woke up. He sensed it as it happened, as they turned from vivid dreams to awakening and a different kind of awareness.

They spotted him standing by the window and came to him, greeting him like they greeted the bright morning. He felt every touch like one distinct contact, and he returned their kisses and caresses with the special remote expression in his big and dark fireeyes. They looked softly at him.

He walked the streets with them by his side, a part of the whirlwind coated in flesh that would always be a part of him. The thought brought comfort, further heat and rage.

He heard the silent thunder, both distant and close.

Another loud scream echoed between the buildings. They didn't see anything or anyone, but certainly caught the boundless fear and desperation in the scream.

– Cities should be called places of screams, Gerdie shuddered, – of horror and desolation beyond sanity.

She sought closer to him. He put his arm around her and squeezed her softly. She was certainly no frail flower, but she clearly needed comfort, now.

He granted it without further hesitation and thought, and it felt good.

– That's a good one, Margaux remarked after giving it some thought. – We should definitely use that.

They turned another corner. He frowned. Something was… off, even more than usual. He couldn't put his finger on it, but it was there, a tangible quality or lack thereof in the air. It reminded him of something, but he was unable to recall what.

A woman with blonde hair and blue eyes stood at the opposite corner. She stared at them with wicked eyes. He blinked, and she changed, her hair turning dark, her eyes brown. He recognized startled Maria Jimenez. She smiled and pulled back, walking down the street with fast steps. Her presence affected him like a kick in the balls. He put on speed. The three accompanying him followed him breathlessly.

– What is it? Lynn wondered, easily sensing his distress.

– Can you see the woman across the street, he asked. – How does she appear to you.

– Of course, I can see her, Lynn said. – She's blonde and fair-skinned…

isn't she?

The other two nodded wide-eyed.

Maria turned a corner. Ted and his three companions crossed the street on red light. They reached the corner. He stared down the street. Maria was nowhere to be seen.

A hot poker stabbed him in the back. He turned around in a rush. Maria stood there, grinning darkly at him, startlingly familiar and unfamiliar at the same time.

– Hello, Ted, she greeted him softly.

– Hello, Maria, he replied curtly.

– Seek me out, she told him.

And then she was gone again.

Obsession rode him like the twisted storm it was. He glanced around him. He sensed her. She was close. He looked up and down the street. One building shimmered in an eerie color, easy to identify. He walked there, knowing that his three companions joined him. They had just a general idea of what made him agitated, but they squeezed his hand in support and looked around them with alert eyes, preparing themselves for violence.

The old building actually looked ominous in their eyes, in all four's eyes. The sunlight didn't reach it. As far as the building was concerned, clouds, dark clouds covered the sky.

– You know her, I presume? Lynn inquired.

– I know her, he confirmed.

He had never truly forgotten her, he knew that, now, with all the old feelings of resentment and desolation and the overpowering sense of helplessness resurfacing.

They walked up the worn marble stairs to the entrance. Two giant fires marked the threshold, their smoke ripping into his nostrils. They walked between the violently hissing, dancing flames and into the building. Reality itself seemed to be transformed the moment they did. They found themselves in what resembled Maria's home in Colorado, with a beyond confusing mix of Greek and Roman and Egyptian style.

Two lines of lightly clad women and men marked the stairs leading further into the building.

– Someone wants to impress someone, Gerdie whistled.

– Intimidate is more like it, Margaux mumbled.

They walked up the stairs. The women and men, the sentries didn't move, giving the impression of being statues more than creatures of flesh and blood.

A giant hall appeared to them. A woman sat on a throne at its other side.

Ted recognized the adult Maria Jimenez at a glance. She had appeared to him like the girl he had known outside, but not here.

He also recognized the chained and kneeling and nude and collared old man by her side, the man she held on a leash.

The four crossed the room, walking down the red carpet. They stopped before the throne, before the imposing being up there.

– Hello, Ted, she greeted him softly.

– Hello, Maria, he replied curtly.

– It's so good to see you again, she said with a huge grin.

It reminded him of that of a shark in a Disney animation.

He caught himself glancing at the man. Emilio Jimenez was covered in welts. He had been whipped so much that he looked like a man covered in raw, exposed flesh. Ted suspected the man didn't have a single untouched spot of skin on his body.

– Don't mind papa, Maria said. – He doesn't count anymore. I rule here.

There was imposing insanity here, thinly veiled, if veiled at all.

– I am a Goddess. These people are my subjects. This is my kingdom. What do you think?

Her very presence sliced him like the sharpest of razorblades.

– I think it leaves a lot to be desired, he shrugged.

Her ragged laughter echoed between the walls.

– You guys are old friends, I take it? Lynn stated more than asked, clearly getting Ted's cautious approach to the situation.

– Yes, we are, Maria brightened. – What a great observation!

Ted felt even more sweat break on his brow. He felt the intrusion in his mind like a red-hot nail. She did that. He recognized the buzz in his frontal lobe, now. It was similar to, or at least it reminded him of the report he and Liz had shared with Laurie Isherwood, but was wicked, sinister, twisted.

– So, what have you been up to? He asked lightly.

– I left papa and traveled with you to Denver. I left you, after your rather disappointing performance. Papa found me and had me brought back to him. He wanted to run my life, all parts of my life, and was very cross when I resisted. I found myself during his kind tutelage and decided that I would take over as head of the family. He resisted, and I had great fun showing him the errors of his ways. I looked for you, but you were stuck in the jungle for years, and I had to find other pursuits while waiting for your return. It worked beyond expectation, as you can plainly observe.

All the scantly-clad people present in the hall looked at her with blind worship in their eyes. He nodded. Her grin widened.

– I watched you and your puta cousin establish yourselves in this beautiful city, how you gathered forces and pawns and how you wasted it on trifles.

– You should join up, he heard himself say through the loud, silent buzz. – You might be surprised.

Her laughter reminded him of a rusty saw blade scratching metal. The laughter stopped, and she looked at him with the wet, insane eyes.

– Why would I do that? She spat. – Why should a Goddess fraternize with mortal men except as their absolute ruler?

She smiled and calmed down again, somewhat, but certainly not becoming less dangerous.

Ted spared a brief glance at his companions in order to see how they were faring. Lynn and Gerdie seemed okay, while Margaux was clearly frazzled around the edges.

– Can you imagine what it would have been like if I had awakened earlier?

He could pretty much imagine it.

– You don't want to experience what I experienced in order to get there faster, he said.

– I know, she smiled. – You poor boy…

The madness intensified. Reality seemed to dissolve around him, briefly, before correcting itself. The constant, pervasive pressure on his mind didn't ease a bit.

– You're absolutely correct, of course, she remarked. – Your suffering can actually match mine. We do belong together.

– You certainly have a way with words, your highness, Gerdie said, not making any attempt at hiding her sarcasm.

– That's my girl, Maria said pleased. – You will certainly fit in well in my court.

He imagined he spotted hissing snakes in her eyes, and that felt like nothing compared to how her mental assault made him feel.

She rose to full height.

– You will stay here, as my honored guests, she decided, as if revealing a great secret or boon.

– That's a kind offer, Ted said, – but we must regrettably decline.

There was a rustle in the congregation. All of them suddenly seemed to stand that much closer.

– The Goddess insists, she giggled. – The Goddess's will be praised.

The man standing closest to them made a threatening gesture. Ted struck him down with one blow.

Another man stepped forward, and Ted struck him down with one blow as well.

She frowned and looked at him with a puzzled stare, and he realized with dismay that she got it. It had been a test, and she had found him wanting.

– You've got no powers.

She laughed incredulous, filled with spite.

– It waxes and wanes like the moon, he said. – Fortunately for you, it is at a low ebb right now.

– How horribly impractical! She exclaimed with a voice sounding like a shriek.

Precisely at the end of the last word, her court made their move, attacking them like one single mass. The sinister mood in the room was finally actualized.

The four defended themselves fiercely. Ted didn't hold back. He kicked the first attacker in the face, killing him instantly. The three women also took care of those first in the line of attack easily enough. Then, they were overrun and could no longer utilize their superior fighting prowess in full.

The attackers clung to Ted like leeches, keeping him from moving properly. One opening was enough for him. He ripped apart the throat of the woman in front of him. They grabbed his arm and hung on to it, and started beating him up. He hardly noticed the first hits, shrugging them off like they were nothing. One fist hit his head from the right, another from the left. His upper body was hammered from all sides. One brutal strike in the ribs made it hard to breathe. He gasped even as the red rage overwhelmed him. They pulled him to the ground, and kept beating and kicking him. He kicked upwards, practically splitting a body in two. They held him down and hammered him, beating him to a pulp, keeping it up long after he could no longer effectively defend himself. The red rage changed into a red haze of weakness slowly turning dark, and the pain turned dull, and he could no longer sense anything, except the vast darkness surrounding him, and he lost all contact with himself.

2

He woke up in a state of delirious daze. Opening his eyes was hard. Keeping them open was hard. One stayed half closed because of a major swelling. He touched it with a finger. More dull pain charged through him. He found himself nude on a mattress in the throne-hall, but he was also alone in a quiet room, where no outside sound reached him at all. Lacerations and swellings covered large parts of his body. He glimpsed Lynn, Margaux and Gerdie nude on other mats. They looked fairly good compared to him. Everyone in the hall was nude. Tall fires grew even taller, making everyone sweat and burn. Drums beat in a constant rhythm, adding to the confusion and fever assaulting him. He couldn't move properly. Every time he tried, he was overwhelmed with dizziness and fatigue.

Maria spoke in tongues, in wild ravings reverberating through the ether, sending shivers through the air and making everyone present her subjects. She had grown powerful in her insanity, powerful beyond words.

Her spells invaded him, making him confused and constantly rattled. Every time he tried defending himself against them, he was pushed further into delirium. A heavy boot hit him in the face, and he didn't see it coming. He still didn't see the man doing the kicking when he scouted for him after pulling himself up from the mattress again, no matter how he turned his head and looked around with bewildered eyes.

His surroundings became… unset. He couldn't find a fixed point. The more he tried, the more unset everything became. The latest man to kick him in the face… he glimpsed the twisted, demonic features. He felt fear, even as he attempted to fight the irrational emotion. But every new thought brought pain, brought despair, brought a confusion cutting him up inside. A big, stupid grin grew on his hammered face.

The silence of the night, when everyone else slept or seemed to be sleeping brought more noise, more dull pain. The giant drums kept beating. They could be quiet one moment, and rise to a roaring crescendo the next. He whimpered in his prolonged suffering.

– Poor beast, she said softly.

She towered above him, looking down on him with cruel eyes. He looked up. Everything else in his vision appeared like a twisted haze, but not she. She appeared in immaculate detail, undressing as he watched, as he squinted his eyes and stared at the Goddess descending on him. His cock began twitching, growing, hardening, until he imagined it would burst anytime, and he gasped in sharp, sharp pain.

– That's my boy, she chuckled, a study in malice. – That's my good, good boy.

They were alone in the quiet room, even as the drums kept ringing in his sore, sore ears. She fell on him with her entire delicious body. A hand struck his ribs and he choked paralyzed, not getting enough air. She squeezed his cock, studying it like a predator would a prey.

– Very good, she said with a hoarse voice, clearly growing aroused.

She sat on him, rocking up and down. He pushed himself up and down within her, within her tight cave.

– My stallion, she breathed. – My eager and skilled stallion with your remarkable endurance. You will always be available to me, stallion, and wish for nothing elssse.

Her voice turned into a serpent's hiss. He shook in his sweat and pain and torture. She made certain it hurt. A wail rose from his sore, sore throat.

He emptied itself in her. It never seemed to end. She kissed him softly with her giant lips, smothering him with their fire. It began again, as if it had never ended. She licked his face, her large, versatile tongue seemed to be everywhere at once.

– Lick my breasts, *boy*, she snarled. – Suck your mother's nipples.

He did, and whimpered when the burning juice flowed into his mouth. Everything, everything but her went away for him. She rubbed herself on him, moving up and down on his body, drowning him in her sweet, sweet enthusiastic smile.

He had become a four-legged creature, a tame dog. She led him around in her leash, proudly showing him the sights, displaying him to her court. A sea of wicked eyes and a choir of cruel laughter surrounded him.

Gerdie rested on a mattress. One giant, cruel eye on the wall studied her. She whimpered in her delirious slumber.

– I am a giant and you are a gnat, the triumphant voice giggled darkly. – I am a giant and you are a gnat.

Gerdie shrunk to nothing before the cruel eye. The sentence repeated itself endlessly in her feverish mind.

Another eye looked in on Lynn. She floated, surrounded in waves, in a space without walls, ceiling or floor.

– You are nothing, except a grain of dust floating in my universe. I am everything there is, and you are just a fleeting thought I will soon forget.

Lynn felt fleeting, unable to catch a thought, floating away to nowhere, nothing, less than nothing.

– I'm so inventive, Maria bragged to Ted. – My creativity knows no bounds. You will see, you will know!

Margaux suffered in a torture chamber without boundary or end. She spotted no one else there, no matter how much she strained herself. She was screaming, she knew she was, but no sound reached her ears or vibrated her skin or shook her larynx. Her body, her very being still shook in beyond violent pain.

A burst of powerful wind pushed her at the vertical table. Many needles attached to thin cords penetrated her skin and bound her tight, the cords surrounding her body like a cocoon. Each tiny sting hurt like a stab by a much bigger pointed tool, a knife or a spear. She didn't die, and couldn't fathom how she didn't. The banshee-like wail filled the space, and her consciousness, her entire being.

– She is a spy, Maria told Ted, – sent to you by Hugo Manning, in order to gather as much discriminating info on you as possible. He got to her. She used to be very critical of him and his actions, but she gave in to his charm and became a part of his group of eager, brainwashed disciples.

He didn't need to ponder her words, to truly test their validity. One look at Margaux and her guilty expression told him everything he needed to know.

– I'm sorry, Margaux sobbed, – sorry, sorry, sorry…

She descended into never-ending ramblings and self-recriminations.

Maria brought Ted back to the quiet room, even as he kept wondering if they had ever left. She rubbed his cheek and petted his head.

– We will expose all liars, all hypocrites, she said softly, – make them all rot to ashes in the bright light of day.

The twisted smile burned him. She, in her insanity sounded supremely confident.

– Father is ready to confess, she told him, – ready to confess everything, not only to his priest, but to the world. It will be so much fun. I can hardly wait.

She smiled again. Her lips felt like fangs. She grabbed him below and squeezed. He turned hard, and she grinned in triumph. He was ready for her. She put him down on his back and rode him again. She struck him with bloody fists. Blood flowed from his mouth.

– Yes, she shouted. – YES!

She drowned him in her juices. He came then. It hurt. The pain made him weak and nauseous. She smothered him in soft, wicked kisses. Even her laughter hurt. When it turned dark and wicked, it hurt even more.

The four of them knelt before her with several others. All of them swayed, almost unable to keep themselves steady. They swayed back and forth, back and forth.

– Do you swear allegiance to your queen? Do you swear to serve her and forego all other considerations?

– I do, My Queen, Margaux whimpered. – I so swear!

Maria's powerful laughter shook everyone present.

– You're already broken. It isn't strange that you would jump from one master to another.

Ted and the others were dragged to a room looking very much like a dungeon. They were thrown into cages. They sat there on their knees and clutched the bars, creating an emotion not at all unfamiliar to him. Memory assaulted him like a lukewarm wave.

But this was also different. He felt like dust floating in the wind, totally unable to affect or change his fate. His head hung so much that it hurt. The dull pain kept surging through him in waves.

He looked around him. Nothing seemed solid, no details fixed. He tried speaking and heard sounds, but no coherent words formed. More timeless time passed. His face felt sore to the touch, swollen like meatballs. Every piece of skin he caught or glimpsed with his eyes looked like raw meat. He should have healed by now. A big frown of confusion crossed his brow. He didn't understand what was *wrong* with him.

There was a buzz in his frontal lobe, something he hadn't felt for quite some time. He waited, but nothing more happened. Time crawled. He was unable to tell how much. Sleep claimed him, claimed him twice. He imagined it claimed him many times. Maria returned occasionally, with her gloating and wickedness and abject cruelty. It eventually felt like one, prolonged horror.

He slumbered in a daze, totally unable to tell if he slept or was awake. Awareness eluded him, he knew that much. Everything felt like one unbroken jigsaw line of suffering, and he moaned like a wounded animal in his horrible sleep.

3

Activity picked up from early in the morning in the no longer dusty warehouse. Liz arrived with her people well before most of those sleeping on the mats woke up and gathered around the long dining table. Everyone gathered around it, using all available chairs in the building. The people not getting a chair stood behind those that did. The mood was visibly uplifted, excited.

– Today is the day, Carla said.

– Today is another great day, Liz grinned.

– I see all of you before me, and see great promise, Carla said. – It looks like the Sixties didn't end early after all.

There was a catching in her throat. Those knowing her best knew why, but everyone present picked up on her ambiguous mood, her longing and sorrow and hope.

– We will fill the streets, Abby stated. – Everyone will be given tasks designed to maximize our efforts. We will make our presence known. They will not ignore us.

Breakfast ended. The devouring of food made them even more energized. The final instructions were given in private, on an individual basis. Faces lit up in excited smiles and anticipation.

They hit the streets, flowing into them like frothing rivers. People on Manhattan began noticing them almost immediately.

– What is Ted doing? Eric wondered, catching up with Liz. – He should have been here by now.

– I guess he just celebrated a bit too much last night, Liz shrugged. – He has become quite fond of that cozy tavern.

– We should check up on him, Eric insisted, – in case it isn't just a case of him and the others oversleeping.

– You're right, of course.

She signed for Lewis to approach her, the signal meant for him, and he and his squad appeared in a rush of movement.

– Go to the tavern, she instructed them. – Return here as fast as possible. Insist that Ted and the others accompany you.

– Insist? The boy swallowed hard.

– Stress that I am the one insisting, she grinned.

She frowned.

– What is it? Eric was there in an instant. – Did you see or sense anything?

– Nothing conclusive…

She had felt a momentary dizziness, as if she had been drugged or something… and a profound sense of… dread, sorrow, grief.

– You go with them, she told him. – There's no need to take any unnecessary risks.

He nodded. A moment later, he led the youths down the street.

Abby studied her.

– Better safe than sorry, Liz shrugged.

Abby waited patiently.

– There is something, Liz said irritated, frustrated. – I've known that for quite some time, but I still can't pinpoint it. It's like a large, hidden truth is lurking behind the next corner, but I can't access it. When I turn the corner, there's nothing there. Fear touches me. I'm walking down a long hallway, and at its end… waits the dragon.

She imagined that a… a presence entered her surrounding, entered her and darkened her vision.

– The dragon, Abby whispered.

Both shivered in the warm sunlight, and they couldn't make it stop.

The large mass of flesh split into smaller parts. Liz marveled at how well it worked. The flesh and mind surrounding her heated up her frozen parts. The chill lingered in those frozen bones.

One smaller part of her, one group of her envoys reached Washington Square and joined the others already there. A choir, one choir of many rose at the heavens, fell into the Abyss. She was there with them, even as she walked on with Abby and bunch.

Other small parts of her reached other sites, swarming Manhattan and New York City like locusts.

The distant music reached them as they approached their destination. It… affected her.

Her smaller part, the part where she was physically present reached Fifth Avenue. Other groups arrived as well, filling the road, blocking traffic. This was a major protest, a gathering of many disparate groups and political directions, all of them radicalized through the recent actions of Elizabeth Warren and her companions. A great shiver of emotion passed through her body and mind and deeper self.

The drums began beating louder. People ran into the middle of the road and began dancing. Everyone began swaying with half-closed lids, with eyes slowly opening.

– We… brought this, Abby said excited.

– We, too brought this, Liz stated. – Many of those present did!

Abby nodded. She understood.

A ring of flesh, of hand clasping hand clasping hand, formed around the center stage. A second and third ring formed inside the outer and strengthened it. Everyone on the outside, from angry drivers to the first approaching traffic cops was kept from entering. More people arrived all the time, most of them actively aiding the protesters. The snarl of a smile crossed Liz's face. Anticipation rode her repeatedly. A thousand warm and cold waves rinsed her body and mind.

Her senses worked overtime and handling it felt like nothing to her. Liz and Abby walked to the quickly assembled stage with several others. The final preparations moved forward quickly. Equipment was connected to portable batteries. There was a hum from the speakers. The first speaker cried into the microphone.

– The enterprise in the building behind us has for a long time profited from human misery, the man stated. – The people there have become wealthy beyond words by exploiting others, by earnings from slave labor and yes, from selling women into base slavery. They have hidden it from the public for a long time, but now the truth is out. They have become rich, become respectable by paying little or nothing at all. Theirs are not merely one crime, but many. The government won't act against them, but *we* will. Society doesn't care how an enterprise, or a person turn a profit. If they do, it doesn't care how, but we do. We have been fed up with such a sordid state of affairs for a long time, and now we act on it.

Cheers and angry cries rose from the street in uneven intervals. There was a great, but anxious mood. They imagined that distant sirens grew louder, but couldn't verify that.

A woman stepped in front of the microphone.

– New York City was alive ten years ago, she cried. – Now, it's waking up anew.

The cheers grew loud.

– So much is happening, so much is happening simultaneously. It's such a beautiful experience, is it not?

She grabbed the microphone, released it from its confines and held it closer to the crowd. They responded promptly. The speakers shook.

– It inspires me, she said, excitement visible in every single line of her face. – Everything that has happened since certain someones arrived in the city inspires me. We've seen everything turned around. Establishment media and centrist politicians are either running for cover or rushing to hide this remarkable development from the general public. And do you know what the best part is?

She paused and waited. The cries of the crowd rose in anticipation.

– They, at least some of them have even ceased their lies and deception. They fear it is no good anymore, and they are correct. New York City has woken up and many of its citizens with it. The rotten apple is no longer dying on the vine, but grows fresh and with a delightful taste. My friends, we will no longer accept what they say we cannot change. Everything has become possible, EVERYTHING!

Her face, covered in sweat glowed in excitement, an excitement beyond words.

Time passed in something resembling a vacuum as one by one of the speakers stepped forward and spoke their piece. There was a nervous energy visible in them all, but that usually aided them instead of holding them back. Liz felt the exchange of seething air between those on the stage and those below and around it. They were all participants.

– Ladies and gentlemen, the current ceremonial master said with a mocking, ironic but admiring tone of voice. – Our next speaker hasn't been with us for very long, but she has made an undeniable impression on us all. I give you… the Queen of New York.

There was something resembling a drumroll, or they imagined there was. It hammered them hard and they rejoiced. Liz felt it.

The other woman stepped back. The dark creature standing behind her took one step forward, and that was all it took for everyone present to focus their attention on her.

– CAN YOU HEAR THE MUSIC? Liz shouted.

Her voice pierced reality itself and all the powers of the Earth heard her loud cry. She paused a bit, allowing the anticipation to grow, blood to flow faster through already heated veins.

– Grave injustice has been visited upon us, upon the world, she shouted. – For time immemorial big and small horrors have been forced on mankind by human beings setting themselves up as lords, as gods. The many have suffered under the yoke of the few. The power hungry has ruled aided by their eager accomplices, and the rest of us have accepted it. What happens here today is merely a modest start of our rejection of that.

She smiled, she snarled, her fangs flashing in the bright light, flashing in shadow, distinct in every vision, every single pair of eyes present.

– The company residing in the high tower behind me has major interests in slavery and subjugation, and we have come here to protest against that, but that is almost incidental in the greater scheme of things. This company is merely one of thousands world-wide. They are just one symptom of many of the decease, the decease destroying humanity, destroying the world. The decease is modern society itself.

She held up one finger, and they imagined they heard her whisper «one».

– Justice has been asleep. Humanity itself has slept for so long. Our fire has been dormant, has hardly been more than embers for many generations. Civilization puts us to sleep. Our awakening is doomed to be rude, but remains so very necessary. Those in charge, the oppressors of the world believed they had won when the Sixties started fading in people's immediate, short-term memory, but they were very much mistaken. We show them that and will keep showing them that every day of our lives, show them that the human spirit is still alive.

The cheer grew loud enough to make the surrounding buildings shake.

– The cities are an unnatural construct, she mused, – but some of them, just a few give the impression of being a jungle, in both good and bad ways, a place where great, savage mankind may still thrive. I experienced the true life of the human being in the jungle, in the most savage wilderness we know. It felt so right from the first moment we spent there. Years flowed like seconds. Time itself became immaterial. Only the certainty that the bigger world haunted us and would continue to do so and would sooner or later find us made us break with that life and find our way back here. We returned to civilization to live it up, and you ain't seen nothing yet.

The sirens grew ascendant, and there was no longer any doubt that they were on their way here, carried by the four-wheeled coffins, the metal beasts. Everyone present knew that way before they turned the nearest corner and became visible to all.

– Resist them with all your might, Liz instructed everyone, – but do not fight back with violence. Let's show them how reasonable we can be today. Use only your fists if you feel your life is threatened. It might come to that, but do not act before that becomes obvious. We are not afraid of them. Let's show that beyond certainty, beyond doubt.

The first large group of police officers appeared from vehicles arriving on whining wheels. They charged the circle of flesh and calm rage forming the protective shield around the protesters on the stage.

The arm locked to arm was very effective, very hard to break. The police punished the protesters hard, to the point of sore limbs and bleeding noses, but they held on. Folded hands locked the chains of flesh even more effective. The officers needed to break that first, but even as they broke it once, the folded hands refolded only moments later.

– The police are the tyrants' bullies, Liz said. – They are among the most eager servants of the establishment, and are almost beyond reproach and clearly above the law they claim they are set to uphold.

One by one the parts of the human chain were pulled away from the iron circle and carried off, into the waiting vans. The ground was slowly covered in blood.

– They're allowed to kill with impunity, Liz continued. – If you want to kill people and get away with it, become a cop. The courts will never hold them accountable. We must do that, like we must do so many other things.

More cops arrived. More protesters were carried away. Some managed to free themselves and return to the circle. The cops kept carrying them off.

The uniformed thugs entered the small stage, and grabbed those standing there waiting for them. Hands were forced behind their back and handcuffed. Liz resisted, slowed the process down, but didn't stop it. She felt the cold metal around her wrists, and also felt her senses become muted, her powers diminished. Photographers rushed forward. The police gave them more than sufficient space to document the event. A constant flow of flashes blinded the handcuffed people as they were pulled and led away, more or less unkind.

She felt a stirring in her frontal lobe. Eric and Lewis and the others entered her vision, her immediate attention. Lewis spoke. She heard him well enough.

– Ted and the others weren't there, he shouted. – The owner said they hadn't been there for days.

– Look for them, she cried, – but don't make a production of it. They can take care of themselves.

A hand struck Liz. Blood flowed from her mouth. She kept holding her head high.

– We will put you away for good, a female officer snarled into Liz's ear. – Lots of powerful people want to get even with you. You will stay quiet, if you know what's good for you.

She threw the prisoner into the dark van, on the heap of flesh already there. The door slammed shut. It drove off not many seconds after that. The sirens hurt her ears.

– Hang in there, she told her fellow prisoners. – We knew what we were in for.

They cast her admiring glances. They held their heads high.

A long row of dark vans drove down Fifth Avenue and headed for darker pastures.

4

There was a cry, a loud, piercing wail in the distance. He raised his head and stared into the mist. He didn't see anything there, but imagined he glimpsed something, some movement, some drifting shadows.

Embrace it.

He frowned, imagining he heard a voice.

Embrace the cold within, someone or something said, and he couldn't tell if it came from outside or inside himself. Embrace the fire.

He nodded to himself, nodded again.

– Reach deep within yourself, he heard the siren song. – You're a witch, an ancient being of power and knowledge. Nothing is beyond you, beyond your reach.

He brightened in his eagerness, darkened in his sick fear.

And then he realized that this wasn't Maria, but Tilla, her words to him in the cabin so long ago.

And then he caught himself wondering if this was pure memory… or if he actually heard her breathing it in his ears…

Right now.

He started walking. He rose and started walking. The bars dissolved around him. He walked on sore, sore legs, attempting to move forward with stiff thighs. He felt like he walked forever.

The mist split in front of him. He didn't imagine it. The air cleared. A vast landscape revealed itself. He saw ruins, tiny remains of what had been and himself towering above it all, and then… he saw the giant redhead woman.

– About time you showed up.

It was Tilla, but not Tilla. It was her, but also more, like he was more, a giant shadow covering far more of the vast landscape than it appeared to be covering.

– Greetings, Ror Ken, she/It said.

– Embeth, he/It greeted her. – Em Beth.

Clarity assaulted him, like it had never assaulted him before. Gasps rose and fell through his open mouth.

Voices weren't really voices, but impressions, sensations forming thoughts, words, consciousness. Lips moving weren't truly lips, but air or something resembling air forming sounds in the infinite space they inhabited.

She looked at him, and one single glance told him so much, communicated a thousand impressions in a fraction of a moment. Communication was instant, without impediment. Two shadows stood there, facing each other, exchanging a million soundless words in a second, or what seemed like a second lasting an eternity.

– You are open now, wide open, finally able to sense me beyond the rudimentary. I missed you, missed you so much.

He wanted to convey how desperately he had missed her. He knew he did. One moment was not merely one eternity, but many. The catching in his throat felt so real. He had a thousand questions, but knew he wouldn't get an answer to any of them, to what he already knew.

She looked good humored at him, very much like he always remembered her. It dawned on him slowly that this was real, that this was actually happening. What he experienced was no mirage, no deception. The awareness screaming at him made that absolutely impossible.

– You do remember, now, she said softly. – The memories will turn dim again when you awake, but you will never again forget.

He closed his eyes, didn't close his eyes, and the memories flooded him, his entire consciousness.

– We ousted him, she said, – but he managed to get away, to flee from our sphere of influence, and it became a stalemate instead of a victory.

He remembered a beyond cruel struggle, one even rivaling the many they had suffered against Jahavalo.

– He escaped our wrath, Ron Ken said slowly. – We searched for him our entire life, but we never found him.

– We died, but he didn't, she said, speaking in both his ears, in his beyond excited consciousness. – We couldn't find him because in a very true sense, he was no longer himself. He wandered the Earth, unable to recall his former life.

Clarity flooded Ted Warren.

– His name was Wharton, Reginald Wharton, and he was never called Reggie…

– Wharton…

– I guess he recalled dimly his old last name, she said, – and came up with a reasonable facsimile.

She stepped close to him. One step was infinity.

– He appeared on the battlefield in the North American war between Britain and France, without memory, without self, reborn in a forge hotter than the molten core of the Earth.

Her green flames flared.

– You weren't there, but I was.

He wanted to ask her, ask her about so much. He opened his mouth, his mind to speak.

She faded before him, fell before his eyes, into the vast abyss below where he couldn't reach her. He screamed in the void surrounding him, but there was no reply.

Ted Warren opened his eyes. Maria Jimenez faced him with wide open eyes and shaking lips.

– What are you doing to me? She whimpered, crazier than ever.

She took one step back on unsteady feet.

– I can't reach you, she whispered. – Why can't I? How can that be?

Another wave of her horrible insanity washed over him. It felt almost pleasant, even as it shook him to his core.

She turned abruptly and ran, fled the fastest her feet and mind could carry her.

Ted Warren opened his eyes, imagining that they had been closed forever. Pain stung his eyelids. His vision cleared, his surroundings only slowly turning distinct.

He found himself on an abandoned construction site filled with bricks and dust. There were bodies with cut throats all over the place. Both the bricks and dust turned red in his sore eyes.

Lynn and Gerdie sat up in front of him, beyond distressed and horrified. They choked and threw themselves at him, embraced him the hardest they were able.

He returned their affection, even as he kept scanning their surroundings. He didn't see, didn't sense Maria or Margaux anywhere.

– We are so small, Lynn whimpered, – so very small.

– You saved us, Gerdie sniffed, – *saved* us.

The abandoned construction site reminded him of the stately building they had been kept prisoner, somehow.

He realized that Maria's power wasn't exactly telepathy, but rather the ability to weave powerful elaborate illusions. Fueled by her insanity, it had become a force to be reckoned with.

The three of them rose, doing so more or less like one being. The two women clung to him, but distracted as he was, he couldn't give them his undivided attention, like he wanted to do.

He inspected his skin. The wounds had faded, as if they had never been there in the first place.

The stench of blood, the sight of all the decomposing bodies briefly overpowered him.

They stumbled forward on the uneven ground and broken stairs, and kept stumbling, even after they had reached the closest sidewalk, not looking back while leaving behind the crimson tide beating like a sick, scarred heart.

5

Liz touched exposed skin with her head and hands. The energy reached her, but only in an uneven, distorted manner. The handcuffs disrupted her power. She tried relaxing, tried to discard her unpleasant circumstances, but reality kept imposing itself on her and everyone thrown in the heap of flesh with her, creating a loop she had a hard time handling. She did her best to suffer in silence, to smile and give encouragement to those suffering with her in the crowded van.

– They will just keep us in cages for a few days tops, she assured them, – doing their best to intimidate us, scare us into becoming nice, obedient sheep.

– We know, Liz, a boy said. – Everything was explained in detail. We will persevere. Don't worry about us.

Many echoed his sentiment. It comforted her.

An abrupt turn made the van tilt, and everyone inside tilted with it. Two heads hit the wall. It didn't really hurt them, but it certainly added to their growing discomfort and anxiety.

– They do this, Liz explained patiently, – do things like this all the time in order to diminish us, to make us afraid, to make us mere shades of a human being.

Determination, if it was ever gone returned to their eyes. Someone behind her grabbed and squeezed her hands. Her power grew to the point of hurting her. She looked at all the shadowy faces, the familiar and unfamiliar features, feeling in powerful ways that she knew them all.

Their thoughts and dreams and yearnings filled her. She sucked them up like a sponge.

– I could have been out of these cuffs in seconds, she stressed, – but that is not how we decided to play this. We want to be martyrs, not fugitives.

They looked at her with even more awe. It mingled within her with all the other emotions, the jigsaw puzzle she had become.

She noticed well before they slowed down that they were approaching their destination. Tiny variations and changes in the air, in the way the driver and the shotgun looked at each other told her that. Ironically, the fact that she was weakened made it easier to focus.

The van slowed down. Everyone noticed what she had noticed several seconds earlier. They heard the sound of an iron gate opening. Anxiety spread among the prisoners.

– Where are they taking us? A girl wondered with a loud voice.

– They want to give us special treatment, Liz shrugged. – We have challenged Profit, the most sacred principle in this society. They look at us with unkind eyes.

Laughter relieved the gathering anxiety. She felt their admiration, their love, their fear. It strengthened her.

The van stopped, and its doors slammed open. A full honor-guard awaited them. Eager and insensitive hands pushed and pulled the prisoners out of the van.

– Welcome to our hotel, a caricature of a cop gave them a caricature of a greeting given by a brutal cop. – We will do our best to keep you entertained.

They were dragged into the worn building. Hands squeezed already swollen arms. They were brought into a giant hall with lots of cages. People already filled nearly half of them. They recognized quite a few of their fellow protesters.

– You will spend quite some time here, the caricature of a cop said gleefully, very pleased with himself and the situation. – You will spend days and nights in these pleasant accommodations, and I guarantee that you will ponder and regret your foolish actions and your entire life during that time.

This place, just called The Cage was infamous. Everyone that had ever been a protester in New York City had spent at least some time here. A pervasive heat filled the hall. A cold draft occasionally chilled those hit by it. Everything here was designed to be as unpleasant as possible.

– Listen to that kind man, boys and girls, Liz joked, – we will have a great time here.

Laughter shook the air. The caricature cop frowned deep. Liz sensed movement behind her and tensed, preparing for the upcoming strike.

It didn't happen, or it happened only as a light tap on her exposed neck. It was Liz's turn to frown.

Her vision turned fuzzy. The dizziness overwhelmed her in seconds. She would have fallen if they hadn't grabbed her, and she realized she had been drugged. Two cops carried her away. She sensed unrest around her and heard the sound of people attempting to come to her aid being beaten with bloodied clubs.

The drug was effective. She stayed half unconscious no matter how hard she struggled to resist it. Thoughts faded. Vision turned dark. She couldn't hear the excited chatter of the others anymore. The two cops carried her away, far away. She faded in and out of consciousness.

There was a sting on her left calf, hardly noticeable, but the addition of that drug brought her the final stretch into the seemingly endless darkness overwhelming her.

Oh, no, she thought, suddenly realizing why she wouldn't be there, wouldn't be with Ted in his long hours of tribulation, and a deep, deep fear touched her like a bullet grazing her heart.

Chapter 14

The room above the bar in the cozy tavern waited for them. Their recent riveting experience stayed fresh in their memory. Lynn and Gerdie remained shaken. He felt strangely calm. They didn't have his experience with dealing with strife and violence and death.

– That was something, Gerdie said, her accent very pronounced. – What the fuck happened?

– Maria has the power to create convincing illusion, Ted said. – To our perception it felt like we were truly in that building and not on an abandoned construction site.

– It felt so real, Gerdie whispered.

– We were drawn into Maria's mind, the nightmare she has made of her existence, Ted shrugged. – Whether or not she projected herself into ours or not doesn't really matter.

– It was both amazing and terrifying, Lynn breathed.

He studied them. They looked quite composed. He imagined they would be okay.

– So, what happened to her? Gerdie wondered.

– She bit over more than she could chew, he grinned, flashing his fangs.

They sought close to him, sought his heat. He frowned as they did, reexperiencing what still appeared clear in his mind. Even as he responded to their caresses and growing fervor, he stayed distracted. Tilla, his experience of her kept flooding his awareness and he couldn't sort out his feelings about what had happened, whatever that was.

He kissed the girls, a bit ashamed because he was unable to give them his full attention. When he stood by the window later, it was almost as if nothing had happened. He glanced at the bed. They were still sleeping. He stared out of the window, at Tilla's radiant face. The girls snuck up on him. The fact that they were actually able to do that told him a lot about how distracted he really was. They rubbed themselves at him, content and warm.

They walked downstairs later, into the dusty locale. The sun did shine through the window, but it was still in the wrong place. He could relax. They had breakfast, a very late breakfast. All three wolfed it down.

– I feel so… hungry, Lynn mused. – I feel so excited, as if everything happening in that awful place made me… *better.*

– I feel like that, too, Gerdie nodded eagerly. – I thought joining you guys had elevated my awareness, but that is nothing compared to what Maria did to us. She challenged us to grow in brutal ways. Margaux broke under the pressure, but we didn't.

He recognized easily the enthusiasm, the dangerous confidence. He masked his emotions.

– I can feel my heartbeat, Lynn whispered softly in his ear.

She rose and wandered out on the floor, and began dancing to the beat, flowing to the music originating from the speakers and that seemed to come from everywhere in the room. He knew she danced for him and for herself in equal parts.

– We grow and thrive in constant pushes and pulls under your tutelage. Gerdie grabbed his hand and kissed it. – I can hardly recall my existence before you guys entered it. You prepared us well for Maria, for all the Marias in the world.

The fire within him turned warm and pleasant. He gave her his complete attention. She realized that and blushed hard. He still saw Lynn move on the floor, still saw her sway and perform on the floor. Multitasking had never been hard for him. He saw two pairs of eyes even as he grabbed Gerdie and pulled her into his lap. She noticed the instant he put her down, noticed him turning hard again. Her eyes turned wet.

The frown hardly manifested at first. Sounds grew slowly in his ears. He signaled to them, gave them the danger signal before he was consciously aware of it. They froze. Gerdie slipped down from his lap. He caught the shifting of light on the floor. The imprint of the window changed, becoming exactly like he remembered it from his vision. He rushed to the window and made a sweep with alert eyes. Across the street, a bit to the right he spotted the difference, the change.

A window had been opened, just enough to cast the reflection visible on the floor behind him. A louder sound of the backdoor opening registered crystal-clear in his ears, his suddenly beyond astute mind. He recognized Jane's breath, her inflamed scent.

She stepped into the room, anxious and alert.

– I knew you might be here, she said out of breath. – I had to talk to you.

He moved forward before he knew he would, the sight of a rifle sticking out of the window across the street burned into his consciousness. He jumped and tackled Jane, pulled her with him to the floor. A bullet missed her, missed them with a hair's breath. The glass, the shards from the broken window fell to the floor, hitting it with a cascade of noise. He rushed to the opening and fired at the man on the second floor across the street. The sniper managed to fire one more time, but not before he was hit, and the bullet from his rifle went haywire. Ted hadn't told the three women to seek cover. There was no need for that. He jumped across the floor and joined them and the bartender behind the desk. The three women had drawn their guns, primed and ready. They looked at him shaken but calm. He looked at Jane with stark relief in his eyes. She returned the look, vibrant, alive, the image of her dead and cold on the floor no longer so imposing.

– We need a phone, he told the bartender.

– In the office down the hallway, the shaken man said.

Ted's eyes kept moving, not resting for a moment. The five-step distance to the hallway felt like a wide, wide scar of a divide. He turned to Jane.

– We will go together, he told her.

She nodded. Action followed words without delay. He moved on her left. Covering her from other possible snipers. They hit the wall in the hallway. Lynn and Gerdie followed suit without incident. The bartender stayed behind. They forgot about him as they moved down the corridor. Ted moved first. He opened several doors before he found the office and the phone. He lifted up the receiver. There was no sound. The phone was plugged in.

There was no sound.

– We need to get out of here, he said.

– Someone has cut the line? Gerdie asked incredulous. – Someone has actually…

He moved, and they moved with him. The training returned further to them with each new step. He watched it as it happened and marveled at it.

– You trained us for this, Lynn said, – trained us for urban guerilla. We'll be fine.

– We will still hold you back, Jane said.

– Do not be concerned with that, he stressed. – Focus on your survival.

He knew he couldn't hide the fact that he was haunted. He just discarded that, too, like everything else, except the situation they found themselves.

The street appeared crystal clear to him. Every single movement and detail in the flowing backdrop that had become his sole reality caught his attention. He spotted nothing instantly suspicious or potentially dangerous.

– It seems like the shooter worked alone, he mused. – That doesn't mean no one is poised to take over where he left off, only that they aren't close yet.

They walked down the street. The iron-hard focus made them sweat hard. There were cars parked the entire stretch, providing some modest cover at least. They reached the corner. He stopped there, and cast another look in both directions. He spotted nothing overtly dangerous. They kept moving.

Their surroundings passed by in a rush, more mist than visible and tangible matter. Their feet hardly touched the sidewalk. The pace of their breathing and heartbeat picked up, but they didn't grow tired. They rushed into the nearest alley, finally no longer out in the open, in the extremely vulnerable position.

Ted noticed the vagrant before his eyes spotted him, knowing beyond knowing that the others didn't, that his five mundane senses were in no way diminished. The man dressed in rags didn't move, but stared at the world with empty eyes.

They stopped running and changed to fast walk.

– There was only one lone gunman, Ted mused. – Why?

– We… lack information, Jane said. – Actually, that's the understatement of the year. We don't know anything, have no idea of the motive, who the target was or anything.

She stopped, noticing his miniscule reaction and turned cold.

– You were the target, he stated, confirmed calmly. – I have no idea why, not of the specifics, but I know that. I and Liz saw you being shot in a vision. I saved you from that, but changes are high that the danger persists.

She handled it well, didn't freeze up or anything. Her mind and body kept going.

– Why me and not you? She asked.

– At some point, somewhere, you saw something, he said, – or someone believe you saw something.

– But why *now*? She cried. – Why… wait?

– You wanted to speak to me, he said. – What is it about?

– It wasn't anything life-shattering, she said, frowning, – just that I thought we should tell the others, tell everyone. I had a heated discussion with Diana…

– Someone could have heard something, Lynn said cautiously. – It isn't far-fetched that we have spies, informants in our ranks.

She glanced curiously, but not really angry at them.

He looked at Jane. He saw that she got it, that she realized the frightening truth.

– I'm not safe anywhere, she said.

– We need to go deep, he nodded. – We can't return to the others. We must inform them, if an opportunity presents itself, but we can't go back.

He grabbed her in the arm, making her look at him.

– Nothing will happen to you, he stated.

She nodded, looking at him with gratitude and fondness in what had become her never-resting eyes.

They searched for empty buildings, any place they could hide, but they reached the end of the block without finding any. Busy streets and its people once more surrounded them. Every single person appeared threatening in their eyes.

A man advanced down the street. He didn't really walk and caught Ted's eyes almost immediately. Ted watched how his eyes sought the closest shelter. Ted didn't hide his interest at all. The man grew visibly nervous. He drew his gun. Ted shot him twice in the chest.

People fled. Ted watched them, and quickly identified one pretty calm man among them. His run stayed controlled, measured throughout the mass-exodus from the street.

– We've been spotted, he said.

He didn't look at the others while stating that, but he still caught their nervous reaction, their added anxiety, their hands whitening around the guns.

– Underground stations are out, he said. – It's likely they are swarming with enemies.

The way he pronounced the last word, like a snarl affected the others deeply. They nodded with a grim determination in their drawn faces.

They ran into the nearest alley, into a semblance of cover, an illusion of safety. One heartbeat, several steps. Repeat. The rising roar hurt his ears. He ignored it, distilled reality, ignored everything except what aided their survival. They approached a set of public phones. He pondered the quandary for a moment or two, before making a decision.

– Full perimeter alert, he instructed them.

The three women placed themselves in a triangle, with a view covering all angles. It happened fast, without hesitation or awkwardness, every movement economical, fluent.

He grabbed a receiver, put coins on the payphone and dialed a number.

Gail answered the phone at Liz's place.

– We are in major trouble, he reported. – Jane has been marked for termination. We need to go deep undercover, and won't be available for some time.

– Where are you? She wondered. – We are stretched beyond capacity here, as you know, but you need help.

– Don't send help. You may have a mole. That is, in fact highly likely.

He hung up. Almost before he did that, they were on the move again. They ran along a low row of moving cars breathing poison gas. The coughing started up after just a few breaths. He swore as his sensitivity got the best of him.

He heard it long before he saw it.

– There is a van approaching on whining tires, he said.

It pleased him that he didn't have to explain himself further. They got it. He saw how they readied themselves, prepared themselves a notch even above their previous level of alertness.

One more hard turn, and the car entered the road at the far end of their street. Others might not see it as anything but a car speeding a bit, but they easily saw more.

– The van is full, he said. – They're readying their guns.

He heard the clicks and the loading of clips and bullets.

The four kept moving forward at a steady pace, as if nothing had changed. They waited, somewhat calm, as the car rushed closer. The three didn't look at him. He knew that. They, like him kept their eyes and complete attention on the approaching vehicle.

The van came closer, even close. Gerdie and Jane glanced at Ted. Jane seemed completely relaxed. Ted pulled the trigger, and the other three followed him a tiny moment after that. Several bullets hit the front of the car, hit the driver and the man by his side. The van screeched to the side and hit a pole about thirty steps away. At first nothing happened. The four rushed closer. Three guys stumbled out, raising their guns. Ted and the other three kept firing as they ran. He and Jane hit the target every time they fired. The other two missed as much as they hit, but they did hit. Flesh ruptured, and blood flowed across the street. A man managed to fire once. The bullet passed Ted's head with ten centimeters to spare. The sound sang in Ted's ear. They fired into the van's back, both through the open door and through the wall. Screams of pain and death filled Ted's mind.

No one moved in there. Dead eyes stared at nothing. The four stood there, Ted and Jane composed, calm, the other two breathing in horror and excitement. They reloaded their guns like a reflex, one they were hardly aware of. Hands, fingers moved by themselves without conscious thought.

– That was… Gerdie said with shiny eyes. – That was…

Her loud laughter filled the ether.

– Your training… your training *works*, Lynn stated.

They rushed on.

– More cars are coming, Ted said, – from several directions.

– Someone is really serious about this, huh? Jane said.

– I'm afraid so, he nodded.

– Let them come, she stated calmly.

They ran into the nearest alley, between more low buildings where the sunshine didn't reach, into shadows. Ted heard the distant sound of vans stopping by the first, of doors opening and guns being readied.

– I think we can safely say by now that this is a major operation, he said. – Someone is really pushing for it to succeed.

His ominous statement didn't make the others change expression. They just registered it, as a matter of fact. He saw pride in their eyes, in every move they made.

Their feet moved lightly on the hard surface. They charged through the modern city as if their lives depended on it, they all knew it did.

He couldn't sense those pursuing them, and could only hear them occasionally, when they were close and checked their weapon or barked an order. In one of his long-time visions Jane had died in his arms on the floor of the tavern and that was that. Everything was different, had chnaged from that scenario. Dimmer, lesser images and sensations from the other, alternative vision surged through him.

The scenery changed occasionally around him, turning into an old pre-medieval town. He shook his head and those images, those sensations faded, even as they lingered. They penetrated deep within the modern city with the barking dogs on their tail, twilight and darkness slowly imposing itself around them.

2

They chained her. She dimly registered that at some point. The pervasive presence of metal disrupting the circuits of her power weakened her further.

A man squeezed her jaw.

– You are not so tough, now.

He was wearing gloves. Her dull mind wondered if it was due to coincidence or design.

– She is tougher than a rhino, another man said nervously. – A rhino would have slept longer with the dosage she was given.

She felt two stings, one on each thigh, and she went away again.

They fed her some timeless time later, just put a teat attached to a bottle in her mouth. She closed her lips around it and sucked it like a baby.

– That's a good girl, the man with gloves spat, filling her head with condescending laughter.

Shame and dull anger passed through her one moment and was gone the next, when they gave her two more dosages of whatever they injected her with.

She hung in her chains, her arms stretched above her head, her feet attached to the floor with a different set of chains. She was strung up like a…

She lost the thought. It just vanished like…

Like smoke.

That, the catching of the thought made her feel a little, just a little better.

She was sweating profusely and felt like shit. Time went away again. Everything went away. She heard the cell door being opened, but she hardly sensed anything beyond that, except the two stings on the thighs. Thoughts, if they existed at all didn't connect to anything. She fell in a void and had no sense of any bottom or ending. Vomit flowed from her mouth, wetting her entire front. The drug… the powerful drug destabilized her system. She felt like shit shit shit shit….

Powerful shakes rattled her. She couldn't stop them. Ted's face appeared in her hazy vision. One tiny second, it felt like he stood in front of her. Then, he went away, and she choked in further misery. The first thoughts of her situation began circulating in her drugged mind. She still couldn't connect them to anything, except a deep sense of dread and even fear.

There… there were no other prisoners here. Someone had picked her for special treatment. Dim thoughts wondered how special, what plans they had for her.

She heard birds, a jigsaw puzzle echoing like knives within her. She couldn't make sense of it, of anything, no matter how hard she tried. She saw Ted being hit by a bullet. She saw him being hit by another bullet and whimpered in distress.

– You don't need to be afraid, the wicked man chuckled. – We will take good care of you.

That made her laugh, even though he, based on his reaction probably didn't experience it like that.

She floated in water, in a cocoon of thousand bees stinging her simultaneously, and her mind, even in its current dull state kept analyzing and she wondered what kind of drug they used on her. The thought vanished or lost its potency a moment later. She once more floated and fell in the void.

Loud, angry voices disturbed her peace. She wanted them to go away, but they persisted. Ignoring them didn't work. She fought herself up from the abyss of her dull thoughts. Her eyes focused so slowly that she imagined that they would never get there, never clear, but they did.

She identified Fallon, Carla and Patrick and the two guards.

– She was quite frisky, the guard with the gloves said with a sleazy grin. – We had to restrain her, but she kept at it, and we had to drug her to keep her from harming herself.

– This is an outrage, Fallon practically shouted. – If you don't allow her to get lucid within the next ten minutes, I will make sure you get charged with abuse of power.

– It may take longer than that, the other guard said nervously, – but her

next dosage was up in an hour.
– Heads will roll over this, Patrick said, very, very calm.
The sound of his very sinister voice made her smile.
– She is awake, she heard Carla say.
– How can she be? The wicked guard said incredulous.
Liz opened her eyes fully, still woozy, dazed, weak.
– Open the door, Fallon snapped.
The guard obeyed. Fallon rushed inside and touched her face with his hand. She feared for him then, but the energy came to her slowly. Even that didn't work properly. She gave him a grateful smile.
The trickle became a flow.
– Enough! She mumbled.
He let go and stepped back, and she released a sigh of relief.
Patrick entered her field of vision.
– They gave you the famous round trip in New York prisons, he said lightly. – People have been lost for weeks within the system. But we found you fast, and we will get you out of here in no time at all.
– Define… «no time at all», she mumbled.
– You may have to enjoy the lousy hospitality of New York's finest for a bit longer, he shrugged.
– Ted, Jane, Gerdie and Lynn are on the run, Carla said. – They managed to call it in, but had to run before we got there. We have no idea where they are, now. Fortunately, they, Ted and Jane in particular can take care of themselves.
– I need to get out of here *fast*, Liz insisted.
They sensed the urgency in her muddled voice.
– We will stay here with you, Carla said, – while Fallon goes to court.
– No, you need to get out there, she said. – You *need* to find them.
The sense of desperate urgency didn't leave her, and she knew she conveyed that urgency to the other two when their expression changed from worry to deep concern.
– We will! Carla said. – Others can take our place here.
– Get her out of the chains, Fallon ordered the guards.
– The chains stay on, the wicked guard said stubbornly.
There was something about him, something raising their suspicion, beyond the image of the brutal cop, but they couldn't put their finger on it.
They left her alone. She felt lost, abandoned. Calming herself remained an effort. She hung there, in the endless void. Something formed in the darkness in front of her; a dragon's face. Its cruel grin mocked her.
The chains… she got a better sense of them, now. They weren't merely

iron, but strong magnets as well, disrupting even more of her power. Someone had truly done their homework. Every time she tried powering up, the horrible pain cut into her. The growing sense of helplessness made her despair deeper, deep as an ocean. She couldn't help herself.

Her eyes blinked. It happened suddenly, unexpectedly. She was no longer in the cell, but on the streets with Ted and the others. Ted was hit. Blood flowed from his body. He was hit again. He stumbled on, while firing his gun. The others were wounded, too, though not as bad as he was. Liz saw the enemy, a moving swamp of gunmen closing in on them, catching up with them.

Liz screamed herself hoarse.

3

They broke into a beyond well-equipped gun store and fetched shotguns, various other arms and loads of ammunition, and contraptions making it all easier to carry. A few minutes after that, they just walked into a pharmacy and fetched everything that might be useful. Their load didn't feel heavy, didn't feel heavy at all.

Jane crouched in his embrace, shivering like a leaf. He imagined there was a dark shape in the backyard, even though his eyes revealed nothing like that. The fan in the ceiling kept spinning in his head long after he closed his eyes, long after they the coming night kept moving through dim streets.

– My childhood memories are still vibrant, she said with a smile. – I remember the shooting contest in the mountains…

The smile faltered.

– I remember how they taught us martial arts and the handling of arms, how they made us deadly killing machines, and I'm so pleased they did.

The rage, the madness, thinly veiled found an echo within him. He understood her, they understood each other so well. They had a bond he could share with almost no one else. He understood, at least in part why she was so important to him.

– Remember, he stressed to them all, – if it becomes necessary, push at the back of my hand, so I can't grab yours. It won't guarantee your survival, but your chances will increase significantly.

A distinct chill passed down her spine. He felt it as it happened and nodded to himself. She nodded, too.

– I'm not afraid, Jane insisted.

– Neither am I! Lynn and Gerdie choired.

The laughter brought comfort, brought passion and anger, a devil-may-care attitude, more of the essential qualities so necessary for survival. They grabbed hands, stared at each other, stared into the upcoming darkness with defiance and death on their mind.

The night moved around them. This was his time, his turf, more than anything else. The brick and mortar surrounding them didn't really matter. The buildings could just as well be trees in the deepest forest.

They ran into an underground station prepared for trouble. There weren't many people there, not outside, not inside. People cast them anxious glances, but no one exposed themselves as spotters, as spies for the enemy.

– We need to change trains often. Two, three, four changes and it will be impossible to guess our whereabouts. I presume that they haven't placed people at all the stations. Theirs are a big operation, but not that big.

– You're funny, Gerdie grinned. – I love that. I just love that!

She kissed him hard on the lips.

Only two persons boarded the train with them. One chose a coach three coaches away. The other chose their coach.

– He looks nervous, Lynn said aloud, – but it would be suspicious if he didn't.

He left the train at the next station. They didn't laugh. The grin felt strange on their lips.

No one entered the train at this station.

– Let's check up on the other guy, Ted said.

He walked first. The other three followed. Everyone moved with drawn guns. They walked through the almost empty coaches. The few passengers looked at them with anxious eyes, everyone doing their best to mind their own business, not exactly surprised to see gangs or their equivalent on late trains.

The lone passenger sat pretty much at the center of the coach. Ted walked there and sat down opposite him.

– Nice time for a walk, Ted remarked casually.

The man left at the next station, very anxious, not exactly the image of a calm assassin.

Then again, he could just be an observer, hired to do just that.

They reached a nexus, an intersection at the next stop, and changed trains. No other passengers did. There were three other people entering the new train. No one looked overly suspect.

– I feel so astute, Lynn mused. – I've never felt more so.

– Neither have I, Gerdie said with shivering lips.

Jane didn't say anything.

The train charged into yet another tunnel. The lights failed, blinked and failed again. The periods of darkness felt longer, much longer than the periods of lights. He knew it to be an illusion, but he didn't really care. It was all just intermissions in the intermission. He knew where they were headed, and so did his companions.

– It didn't feel bad killing those people in the car, Gerdie said. – It didn't feel bad at all.

– Why should it? Jane said. – They were our enemies. They wanted to kill us.

She didn't hold her gun in a hard grip like the other women did. The skin on her hand didn't whiten around the metal.

One blink lasted another eternity. He remembered the torture, the brainwashing and the training, all of it mixed up in glimpses of exquisite clarity. When he glanced at Jane, he knew she did as well. Eric had cultivated their training during their time in London, making them remember, not forget.

– I feel grateful to Eric, Jane said, as if she could read his mind, – not angry.

They grabbed each other's hands. Gerdie and Lynn joined them.

– Eric is probably one of the best drill-sergeants around, Lynn joked. – US Army didn't properly appreciate his talents.

– He made us confront the horrors of our past instead of helping us run from it, Jane said. – I will always be grateful for that.

– A killing machine made us all into the killing machines we truly are, Ted stated. – Use that for everything it's worth, and never stop using it. The poor bastards coming for us will only find horror and death.

He saw them nod, even though they didn't move.

They changed train again and again. They finally left Manhattan and ventured into Brooklyn. Brooklyn would have been one of the biggest cities in the country if it wasn't part of New York City. Ted nodded to himself.

They stepped off the train at Union Street Station. They walked up with the same extreme readiness that had dominated their lives for seemingly forever.

– They've finally come through about the renovation, Lynn said incredulous, looking around with big eyes. – this station looked quite different the previous times I walked through it.

It wasn't complete, or didn't seem to be, but parts of the station had clearly received an upgrade.

Even before they approached and reached street level and moved on, they had their eyes on all possible angles simultaneously. It felt natural by now, to them all.

– We've become an urban guerilla group, Lynn said with huge, shiny eyes. – I imagined that would be hard, but it feels so easy, like removing an old, worn coat.

Brooklyn looked distinctly different from Manhattan. They saw no really tall structures, but mostly three-story buildings or close to that, as if they had moved to another city. With each new step they became an integrated part of that particular urban landscape. They moved with it, and it moved with them, breathed with them. Silent feet and silent mouths rushed through the concrete jungle. They communicated through signs and thus stood out from the other late birds frequenting the night even beyond the obvious of carrying guns openly.

Ted found a worn bull cap on the sidewalk and put it on this head. The others also began the process of transforming themselves. They found clothes in several dumpsters, both rags and not, and also lots of discarded food. Weapons were concealed beneath long coats. It took them only a few minutes to change their appearance.

– We look like completely different people, Gerdie marveled.

– Among other things, Stewart taught me how easy it was to disguise yourself, Ted said lightly.

Merely speaking the name brought back more memories. He let them come, but he didn't lose sight of his surroundings and their inherent dangers. Once again, he marveled at how easy multitasking had always come to him.

They found a derelict building with a door ajar. They rushed inside, pushing the door close with a little effort. Lynn rushed to the nearest window and took a look outside. No one kept their eyes on them.

This had also been a warehouse, which in turn brought back even more memories. They stepped into a world stinking of rust and decay. A staircase leading to the upper floor had several missing steps. They penetrated deeper into the ground floor, into what resembled an office with dry furniture and stuff. There was even a tap and sink that wasn't rusty. Lynn turned the tap and water flowed into the sink. The water was brown the first few seconds, but then it cleared.

Every single furniture had at some time, long ago been covered in white sheets, now gray with dust. The four removed them cautiously to keep the dust from spreading in the room. They were moderately successful and carried the sheets to another room and dumped them there. Small amounts of dust did whirl in the air, enough of it to create a special mood in the weak glow of the streetlights.

They sat down on the large couch and hugged in, devouring much of the food they had gathered. He saw her face and features shift in light and shadow, like he had done for so long. Her death mask and her lively expression changed back and forth. It was the way he recalled his visions, not anything happening right now. There had been times he hadn't been able to tell the difference, but now he easily could.

He wished for his powers to return, but it didn't happen. There might be some stirrings beneath the surface, but nothing conclusive. The dust only reminded him of Dust, a pale echo of the real thing.

He spotted it in glimpses, or he imagined he did.

Jane stared at him with curiosity and hunger in her eyes.

– Does a gun or a bullet feel anything?

He imagined he knew where she was going with this.

– No, it doesn't, he replied.

– Eric keeps repeating to us that we should discard emotion and become weapons.

Lynn's chuckle sounded like a bark.

– That is pretty ironic, she spat, – considering he wears his emotions on the outside like a worn coat.

– We are not weapons, then, Jane concluded. – We feel everything stronger, not lesser.

She began undressing. The other followed her lead only moments later. It felt completely natural and casual, like moving and breathing. They began breathing faster. The sight of nude bodies and hungry eyes and the way they moved excited them.

– We may die tomorrow or anytime. I want our final hours to… to be memorable. If any of you should die and I survive, I want a lasting memory of you.

She kissed Ted hard on the lips. He returned an abrupt, fierce response. The other two joined them. The three of them surrounded Ted and changed on being closest to him. Then, they began kissing and caressing each other as well.

– We don't expose ourselves, Jane stated. – We strengthen ourselves.

He nodded, the familiar catching forming in his throat.

– Everything we have endured, all the hardship has not ruined us, but empowered us, she insisted.

She began swaying in front of him, rubbing herself against him, and then he finally felt himself hardening and grow below.

The excited breathing around him picked up yet another notch.

– I'm wide awake, anyway, Gerdie snorted. – We need to sleep, and this is the best way to assure that.

Laughter echoed in the room and touched and bounced off flesh, making eardrums vibrate in pleasant ways.

She and Lynn rubbed each other, while also touching Jane and Ted.

– I love doing it with many people, Lynn breathed. – I just love it!

She demonstrated that, showed that with every move she made, every shifting feature in her face.

Ted grabbed Jane and held her, froze her in place. Her mouth opened wide. That image of her was juxtaposed with the image of the dead face bathing in blood. He kissed her fiercely on the neck, almost biting her, cracking skin. Her loud and longing moan filled his world.

– Normally, another male would be advantageous, Gerdie said naughty, – but this savage beast can easily serve us all.

She struck his butt, struck it hard, gaining his attention, his dark fire. Her dark giggle filled his world. Clouds filled her eyes.

The stench in the air after the firefight earlier today ripped into his nostrils, as if it was just happening now, and not hours ago.

He grabbed her and pulled her close. She yelped in joy. He put her on his knee and slapped her on the butt. She cried out in pain and wriggled helplessly in his grip. He slapped her again. She shouted and turned limp.

– The girl likes it, Lynn, wicked Lynn chuckled, – likes being punished.

She rubbed the girl between the muscular, wet thighs. Ted let go of Gerdie and she rejoined the other two pushing themselves at him.

– Cruel, cruel boy, Gerdie hissed and moaned.

Each touch felt different, felt new and fresh, as if it was the only one that mattered. Awareness soared with each of them, with the group as a whole. Ted heard drops hit the floor in another room and knew it wasn't his imagination.

He put Jane down on her back and entered her. Both froze, as the pain, the itch grew a hundredfold. He felt it, as he slipped into her, noticed, observed in a detached manner the first couple of thrusts. She grabbed his shoulders and burrowed her short nails into his skin. There was a sharp pain, but he forgot about it one, two, five heartbeats later. The fire within burned and spread. He dived into her, into her depths. Her eyes grew in his vision. He sensed the other two, swaying around them like snakes. Gerdie (or Lynn) bit his upper arm.

The fear faded, making his fear grow. Locked lips to lips, they moved and rocked on the giant bed. She squeezed impatiently his cock between her thighs. Mouths opened in a soundless cry. Thoughts faded. Rational consciousness faded. Awareness soared. A thousand sensations and impressions surged through his feverish mind simultaneously.

They fell. Bodies soaked in sweat and juices crouched close on the vast bed, keeping up the touches and caresses. Lynn (or Gerdie) impatiently began working on his spent cock, squealing in delight when it started growing mere seconds later.

Gerdie rode him. A moment later Lynn did. They switched places so fast that he hardly noticed the switch except like a flash of dark lightning behind his eyelids. Gerdie spoke softly to Jane in a whirl of wind and water.

– It's so silly. I was jealous of you, not because of Ted favoring you, but because you… you were targeted.

The dark giggle rose from her mouth like steam and he found the sight endlessly fascinating. She began moving faster on him, screaming and moaning in equal measure. Her expression, her expression froze in his vision, creating an endless afterburn of unmoving images. He tasted her long nipples, rolling them in his mouth, biting down hard on them. Her hot water burned his front. Her scream faded slowly, slowly, slowly in his ears. He forgot everything, except the three females with their savage demands. He pushed into Lynn from behind, moving brutally back and forth.

– Yes, she screamed. – YESSSSSSSSSSSSSSSSSSSSSSSSS

For some reason he still heard the droplets hit the floor in the other room. He saw the drop hit the floor and spread on that infinite spot. Then he forgot about that as well. He was no longer multitasking, but immersed in soft and hard flesh and eager whispers and sighs and moans and grunts.

There were no sharp sounds. Everything was soft. There were no soft sounds. Everything was sharp, like a drum. Flesh and mind fell like soft and hard rain. The four embraced on the pleasant bed. Joy and laughter kept teasing their sensitive eardrums.

Sleep, sleep was imminent. He watched Jane's sweaty face, her dissolved features and knew that the next moment would be the last before deep, deep sleep.

– Memorable, she whispered.

4

They had drugged her again. She had believed that they wouldn't dare do that after they had been found out, but she had been wrong, and she cursed herself.

She kept feeling the stings, as if they were still administered. Shame cursed her.

– Look at her, she heard one hoarse voice. – She's such a peach.

– Too bad we can't take her out of here, the other hoarse voice complained. – We just have to have our fun with her for as long as it lasts, and be content with that. We have all the protection we need.

You don't have protection from me, she thought.

It came off as a distinct, well-defined snarl in her stupor.

She wished their mouth would keep running and they would expose more of what this was about, but they didn't. That more or less confirmed to her that they weren't ordinary cops.

She began fantasizing about everything she would do to them the moment the opportunity presented itself. Hatred, deep and scary rose from her depths, and she was unable to put a stop to it. All the control she had gained over her impulses over the years just slipped away.

It hurt, but she didn't care. She allowed it to happen, to flow freely. The smile grew on her face in anticipation. She expected the rage to aid her, to push her out of the fugue state, but it didn't happen. It fizzled and died. A loud, pitiful moan pushed itself through her open mouth.

– Poor girl, he spat and slapped her hard on the butt, brutally striking her all over the body.

The pain helped momentarily, but it fizzled and died fast, delegated to the same Void of everything else in the horror her existence had become.

– You will be cute and compliant by the time I'm done with you.

The voice hardly sounded like a voice at all. She frowned. It hardly sounded like the same man. Fear cut into her. She realized dimly that she was in danger, in real danger.

The fear, the panic fizzled and died. She hung there, like butchered meat. The hunter had already caught his prey, and prepared it for… for consummation.

She imagined he carried her away, far away from preying eyes. It felt so real sometimes. The thought revisited her time and time again and scared her shitless.

Energy focused outward made her writhe in her chains, to throw herself back and forth as much as she was physically able in the air, the beyond clammy air.

The outward movement ceased, she knew it did. She fell calm like death in the landscape of the Void, and allowed herself to drift aimlessly. Her focus turned inward fizzled and died a thousand times.

Focus focus focus focus the word became nothing, just a soundless sound echoing in the void. Meditation, meditation, the lack of thought is the highest form of thought. It succeeds where nothing else does, where everything else has failed failed failed.

Come with me, he bid her. Fate brought you into my care. I will take your destiny, become you, a better you, a far superior you.

She didn't shake her head. She didn't move. She pulled away from him, denied him in his prize without moving.

Mist surrounded her on all sides. She walked in the park, in Central Park, and there was no one else there. She was all alone.

He was there, waiting patiently, like the predator he was for the prey to expose itself, to become vulnerable. She felt vulnerable, felt frightened beyond her wits. The horror haunting her grew to be everywhere.

The scream, the pain worked itself up her throat, erupting like a geyser. Pain cut through her as she ripped her top, the upper part of her clothes, exposing her breasts, shaming herself further, knowing she had succumbed to the use of female wiles in order to save herself, knowing it didn't matter, knowing that the ends justified the means.

The act hurt and paralyzed and drained her. She hung in the Void, drifted there like a speck of dust.

The Void… She gasped and heaved, knowing she didn't move, knowing she was just driftwood in the Void, knowing that the Void was a great place to be, that it was… was her home.

She felt his hands on her breasts.

– You are so beautiful, he said hoarsely. – I would love to see you dance on the stage, dance for me, and no one else, as my puppet, my doll.

She imagined it was the lesser man among them, the insecure apprentice not wearing gloves. Even as she feared she was imagining it, she felt his skin against hers. She hoped with a vast, black hatred that it was her true tormentor, her Enemy.

He squeezed her nipples and breasts, «fondled» them in beyond cruel ways. She felt the energy, the first, initial sparks. Then she felt…

The *Flow*.

It hurt. She bit off a piece of her tongue. He tried pulling his hands away, but she kept him from doing so. The first bracelet unlocked. Then the second, third and fourth and the collar in quick succession. He fell backwards. Her feet made contact with the floor. Her eyes opened wide, noting what she had known all the time: She was still in her cell.

He writhed on the floor, weak and drained. She forgot about him. She unlocked the cell-door with a casual thought. Her system cleaned itself. She vomited on the man, on the speck of dust in her path. She dried the vomit from her jaw. The sinister presence had vanished from her mind. She didn't sense it anywhere.

– Rise, she bid the wreck on the floor.

She helped him a little, making a thin layer of air between the floor and the

underside of his shoes. He hung there. She could easily see her dark fireeyes reflected on his skin.
– I threw up, she instructed him. – You feared I would choke to death, and intended to take me to the infirmary, but I recovered, and you never took me there. You decided I needed some fresh air. Are we clear?
– … c-clear, he mumbled, absolutely terrified.
– Then you will report yourself and that other guy for improper treatment of your prisoner. You joined in at first, but then you got second thoughts, but still couldn't keep your hands to yourself just now. You will confess and reveal everything you know about your fellow officer. He encouraged you, he was the ringleader. You have done this before, with other young female prisoners. I bet you have! On second thoughts, let's do that first. Are we *clear*?
He nodded and nodded and nodded, and she knew he would never stop nodding.
Her thoughts raced like wildfire. Her depth rose to her surface, and it felt so good, so beyond great.
She stumbled out of the cell-area, into the main hall where Marlene, Frances and Linsey sat. They rushed to her. She started falling a moment before they grabbed her.
– Is this real? She cried. – Please tell me it's real.
They showed her in all ways and none that it was, and she gave herself over to their care.
– We need to get out of here fast, she said distressed. – We need to find Ted and the others. We need to get out of here, *now*.
– Fallon and his team are close, Linsey informed her. – They did get a court order to release you, but for some reason, the news never reached the warden.
She liked, loved his dry wit.
Everyone stared at her mangled, swollen breasts.
– That man and the other guard not here abused me, she accused them. – They didn't physically r-rape me, but did almost everything else.
The catching in her throat wasn't completely fake.
Patrick took photos. Liz knew she looked very young and very vulnerable, very aware of the fact that it wasn't pretend. She felt very bad, very good. The prison doctor gave her a cursory examination with wide eyes. Joined by Marlene, they walked into his office. Liz undressed and displayed her beaten body, the numerous lacerations. Marlene took more photographs. The medical doctor grew visibly angry.
– I believed I had seen it all, he grumbled, – but this… this…

His voice failed him. He kept shaking his head.
– I did wrong, the guard told the guard behind the desk. – I want to give a detailed confession.
The sitting guard looked aghast on him, glancing at all the witnesses in the room.
The guard began his detailed confession. A secretary had been called in to write it down. Fallon and his team had arrived and made sure everything transpired correctly.
– Everyone else is out, he informed her with shivering lips and relief. – You are the last. I still have not been given any satisfactory explanation for your… special treatment…
– And you never will, she stated.
He nodded and walked to the bench.
– My client is the wronged party, he stated to the clerk. – We would like a copy of the confession/testimony.
It was clearly a demand.
The guard said the name of the other man. It didn't tell Liz anything, but it still sent shivers down her spine.
– We need to go, she repeated for the tenth time to Linsey.
– You're no good to anyone right now, Linsey rejected her plea.
The girl nodded, bowing her head, feeling only a little better, a little worse by his soft touch.
They left the doctor's office as quickly as they could before the effects of Liz's healing power became pronounced. Her skin marks faded one by one. Those on her mind didn't.
– The other man, she said with numb lips. – I didn't see him for what he was at first. It was as if he was able to mask himself, his true nature. He talked about… about taking my d-destiny, and it was no idle threat. He needed to break me first, but he was clearly capable of carrying out his threat. He forced me to fall back on my female wiles. I had no choice.
She looked at the other with insane, hateful eyes.
Frances comforted her. Liz allowed it.
They left the waiting hall, left the prison. Lee and quite a few others waited for them outside. Everyone embraced her in quick, comforting gestures. Someone handed her a gun and she checked it automatically, falling back on routine, feeling stark relief that she was actually able to do that.
– We have identified several hot spots where they have left their mark, but still have no idea where they are now, Abby said. – New York City is so *big*.
She looked more intangible than ever, clearly tense, marked by the gravity of the situation.

– We will find them, Lee assured her. – We have thousand eyes and ears in this city.

He hardly looked like a kid anymore. The girl by his side didn't either.

Eloise stepped forward from another angle, ready, eager to serve. She certainly did not look like a child. Liz nodded, to her, to them all.

They started moving, moving like the giant wave they were.

– I want to strangle him, she spat, – want to remove his head from his body, but I can't do that, at least not until he has testified in a court of law. Patience is, as usual paramount.

The wicked chuckle echoed between them.

She felt a little better.

Her eyes turned vacant, seeking distant places. They saw Ted and the others run for their life while fighting against an invisible enemy. A mist, a whirl of water and air obscured the immediate surroundings in her vision, like it usually did. She heard the firing of guns, the cracks of thunder in the horizon, the screams of pain nearby. The stench of blood ripped into her vibrating nostrils.

Chapter 15

Day turned to dusk outside. Here, in this dank building, the night never truly went away. They awoke without having seen the sun. Everyone exchanged happy smiles and touches and caresses. They devoured more food of the heap they had gathered last night, while the smiles slowly turned somber.

– We can look outside without people spotting us, Jane remarked. – It's so interesting to see them pass by.

– The windows look like mirrors from the outside in daylight, Lynn said. – People outside could stare right at us, and not see us.

They didn't turn on any lights. The street provided all the illumination they needed. They ascended more or less precarious staircases to the upper floor, gaining a better view of their new neighborhood. Nothing instantly suspicious revealed itself. They circled all four directions, but saw nothing suspicious.

He remained distracted, even though the others probably didn't realize it. He had long since gained sufficient self-awareness to know that ninety percent of him was far more intense than most people.

Liz spoke to him in that whirl of wind and water so familiar to them both.

– Masks haven't fallen and won't fall for some time yet, she mused. – We play the masquerade as well, but not among ourselves, and here lies our joy, our suffering. We don't pretend. We know!

She looked older, as if she spoke those words many years into the future, but he couldn't say for certain.

They advanced without guns in their hands on the nearest grocery store with a casual walk. Ted and Jane had no trouble with it. The other two would easily be made by professionals. They ignored that, ignored everything except their surroundings and the task they had set for themselves.

– I think we might have approached this slightly wrong, he mused.

– Slightly? Jane teased him.

She clearly understood, knew where he was going with this.

They entered the grocery store. People looked at them, like they looked at them wherever they roamed, but he spotted no one instantly suspect among them. They spent some time there, making their selections without haste. He studied Lynn and Gerdie for signs of elevated stress, but didn't see anything. They kept their cool, even in the queue at the cashier, where people fought to keep their hard-gained position.

All of them breathed easier afterwards, back on the street.

– Even shopping has become an ordeal these days, Gerdie remarked. – People are so wired up that they seem ready to explode at any time.

The other three gave her cheery smiles.

They returned to their hideout, their fortress, not really feeling any safer there, feeding with the same jittery movement and anxiety.

– I believe we need to take the initiative, he finally stated. – Pondering it a bit, I believe the risk of not doing that is bigger than doing it. We need to make a statement, telling interested parties that coming after us will cost them.

His words and mannerism made them think, made them freeze.

– You've held back because of us, Jane said softly. – You should do so no longer.

– We have enough arms to start a small war, Lynn said. – Let's do so.

Gerdie nodded once.

– I will take the point when we advance, he said, – and the rear when we retreat. I can run and move forever without getting tired. I can also take a few hits without being killed or suffer serious injury. I will draw their fire, and you will exploit that, exploit that gross disadvantage to wreck pain and death on our enemies.

Once again, it was the casual, confident way he made his passionate, fiery statement that made both cold and heat course through them.

They spent a few more hours in the building, going through strategies back and forth one more time, and one more time and more, until they realized the futility of it.

– They haven't encountered anything like us before, he swore. – Show them how that is like.

Burning eyes met burning eyes. Hands clasped hands. They stepped out on the street and closed the door behind them. Their walk felt light, natural, like feathers touching the ground.

– We've walked a gauntlet our entire lives, he said offhand. – This is no different.

He saw it, saw the ghosts, all the shouting ghosts standing on both sides, the bloodied carcasses behind them, the jeering faces in front with their sticks and sharp and dull blades.

They walked around, back and forth, familiarizing themselves further with the area, like tourists scouting for a nice spot. He carried one large bag, Jane the second, and the other two the third between them. The load felt light, like air doing nothing to slow them down. They visited an innocuous cafeteria on a corner, sitting down on a spot enabling them to look in all directions, cover all bases, except the back of the building. People looked at them, like always. All four of them had gotten used to that by now. People talked and exchanged words between themselves. Ted didn't notice anything instantly suspicious, any immediate danger. He imagined a person somewhere, somewhen rushing to the nearest phone and give the crucial report.

The four had their coffee, its taste beyond sharp in their mouth. They had a toast, and they drank. A timeless time later, they once again roamed the streets.

– I can see so clearly, Jane stated amazed. – What used to be mud is now a constantly analytical mind, nothing but clarity.

Ted nodded. That mind always brought immaculate detail to his surroundings, and now he felt that awaken within once more. Birds began singing, began screaming, their voices turning human, at least in his mind.

Two of the birds changed. They grew and turned into misty creatures, mixing, melding, until there were no longer two birds, but one, giant bird of prey, of fire and shadow.

It didn't ruin his sensory input, but turned it even sharper.

He once again could confirm to himself that his five ordinary senses were in no way diminished. The loud noise of the traffic, of the city didn't overwhelm him either. His senses adapted to it, and didn't block other sounds.

His experience of time faded, like it always did. His surroundings became timeless, any measure of it meaningless.

Existence was measured in events, in steps, glances, a loud horn from a passing car, not with the passing of time. He noticed Gerdie's glance.

– It's so fascinating to watch you, she giggled.

Suddenly, it dawned on him that she was also at risk, that they all were, and he found himself fearing for her.

– I killed, she remarked, frowning, – and I don't really feel bad about it. Is that… normal?

– I don't really feel bad about it either, Lynn shrugged.

– Neither do I! Jane and Ted choired.

– It's different with you guys, Gerdie said cautiously. – You have… experience.

– It might haunt you, Ted stated, – returning to you in dreams and in dark moments, but you shouldn't let it bother you.

He was leveling with her, and she acknowledged that. She nodded.

One of the men in the van died again in his memory, his total recall. He had no idea why he saw him and not the others, but there it was. It would always be a part of him.

They passed a laundromat. It was still open. People passed in and out of it. There was a queue. The number of washing machines in the facility was insufficient to handle the neighborhood's needs, even at this hour. For some reason, that… bothered him. The thought kept distracting him while they moved further down the street.

– Some people claim that everything would be alright if everyone minded their own business, he said. – They even persist in the thought when others challenge them on it, confronting them with the obvious discrepancies in their «reasoning».

– Yeah, such silly notions help keeping society the nest of vipers it is, Jane nodded.

She rubbed his back, understanding the reason for his outburst. The other two got it, too. The four briefly stopped and hugged each other, giving each other cold comfort at least.

– Your thoughts tend to wander, he eventually said. – It's no big deal. Let them, as long as they don't distract you from keeping a keen eye on your surroundings.

Gerdie and Lynn nodded, nodded empathically.

They sat down on a bench not far from the underground station, appearing to most people like they didn't have a worry in the world. Gerdie frowned.

– They will know that we know they are coming?

– If they aren't complete amateurs, Jane replied. – We're exposing ourselves, and all in the business somewhat experienced will realize that without a second thought.

– This will keep escalating until we end it, Ted said. – There's no reason to not call for help anymore.

He walked to the payphone by the underground entrance and dialed the number to Liz's place.

– Yes? Gail replied anxiously.

– We need reinforcements, he stated. – We can't return home. Chances are high that they have surrounded both places. We're by the Union Street Station in Brooklyn, but will probably not be able to stay here long.

– Liz and everyone are out looking for you, she said, her voice shaking. – They will make contact at even intervals, but I'll attempt to reach them before that. They have fairly powerful two-way radios, but it's hard to tell how effective they will be. They're everything from very useful to next to useless. It's so great hearing from you. Frances and Helen are here with me.

He heard their voices, just as excited and happy as Gail's.

– Anything else? He asked her.

– Nothing comes to mind, she replied.

He hung up and returned to the other three.

– Our enemies will assume that Jane has shared her «secret» with us, Lynn said. – We're all targets, now. You are correct. It will escalate.

Eyes met eyes. Hands grabbed hands. They nodded like one.

The enemy's hands didn't come rushing this time, but chose a more cautious approach. He could still hear them handle their guns. His three companions watched him and tensed.

– We take those coming from the underground first, he said, speaking so low that they could hardly hear him.

They weren't certain if he actually spoke aloud or used hand signs to convey his instructions. The three of them nodded without nodding.

– I feel so awake, Lynn whispered, – so extremely aware.

That went thrice, at least that. for him. He had trouble handling all the added input at first, but then his inner self calmed down, like that worn, familiar coat.

It was night. That was another thing working in his favor. He was nocturnal, was the night. He nodded to himself, not moving his head. They were correct. They did slow him down, and he couldn't allow that, except when he would draw fire away from them to possibly save their lives, and especially Jane's.

The entire street, the entire space painted itself in his mind. He saw it from all possible angles. A man turned a corner to the south, a very conspicuous man striving very hard not to look conspicuous. Two broke into a house, seeking higher ground. Ted Warren stood still one moment, and moved the next, and the other three moved with him. He was a gunman. His father was one, his grandfather had been one, and also his great grandfather and great great grandfather and probably far longer back. Iron, the touch of it, its stench and handling, was in his blood.

One, two, ten steps and he stared into the opening of the underground station with two guns in his hands, with Jane by his side. It felt almost like having Liz there, and he wondered if that was the answer to why she was so important to him.

Three men drew their guns. They died as one being in a hail of bullets, only able to fire a single stray bullet before drawing their last breath. A walkie talkie fell from one mean's pocket and hit the floor with a silent crack.

The two of them returned to Gerdie and Lynn. He heard the voice from the walkie talkie quite clear.

– What is happening? I hear shooting. Able, Krasner, Partington *respond.*

The four picked up their gear and walked away.

– I heard the rather distraught voice of their operator through a walkie

talkie, Ted remarked. – He didn't sound very professional.
– That is good to know, Jane said. – I guess they're not used to encounter this kind of resistance in their work.
The fast walk took them away from there. Their feet seemed to move by themselves, hardly giving away sound as they touched the ground. Their breath seemed silent in the noise of their ears. They rushed into an area with narrow streets and alleys. Their surroundings changed in almost shocking ways.
– They will know we're heading this way, he said, had said to them, – if they aren't total amateurs.
He fired just as a man stuck a face and an arm holding a gun out of hiding, and hit him straight in the forehead.
Jane fired at another man in a window and hit him in the chest. He lost his gun. It dropped slowly to the ground. They never saw it actually hit it. Gerdie and Lynn had sought hiding behind a car. They lay down suppressing fire and kept other gunmen behind the corner from firing at Ted and Jane. Jane found the bazooka. She readied it in fast and efficient ways, and fired it at the corner only seconds later. The corner dissolved in loud thunder, and screams of fear, pain and death.
They moved on. Feet hammered against the pavement. Jane carried the bazooka. It had three projectiles left. Heavy boots stamped on their hearts. A bullet struck the pipe, making Jane twist her finger and fire a second shot. Gerdie fired at the shooter. Her first bullet missed, but not the second.
– They're here with us, now, Ted told them, now, or in the distant past, when they had discussed strategy. – They won't go away until it's over.
The stray projectile exploded, now, or many moments ago, creating more mayhem, as the four advanced through narrow streets and alleys. Ted saw the bullet being fired. It hit him in the side, pushing him backwards. The other three fired at the man, but he had sought cover again behind a large truck. Ted was back on his feet. Jane fired the third missile at the truck. The explosion, its sound and fury filled the entire street up and down. The shooter and most of the truck were gone in fire and ashes.
Ted's body rejected the bullet, ejected it through the hole that had almost already stopped bleeding. The wound healed in five, ten, twenty seconds. They watched in wonder as it happened. He signed for them to get their act back together. They did so.
– This is nothing, he said, practically bragging, ignoring the searing pain for their benefit. – I can take much more.
Fearful eyes followed them and pulled back, as they advanced further through the war zone the streets had become, what they were fast becoming.

Ted heard the buzzing of the walkie talkies. He could not catch what was being said, but the intensity in the voices was unmistakable.

– Let's at least pretend to make it difficult for them to track us, he said.

They broke into a building. He kicked down the door in two hard attacks. They rushed into the hallway. He stopped by the first door. There was no one inside, no activity his sensitive ears picked up. He kicked down that door, too. This time it was sufficient with one attempt. They stepped inside. A new mirage of shifting realities imposed itself briefly on them. They ignored the backdoor and proceeded to the kitchen. It was fairly easy to climb out of the window. They did so with amazingly relaxed anxiety, Ted first, with the others following in a rush of efficiency. They emerged into a small, enclosed garden. He made a sweep and found no one waiting for them there.

The scent of the plants ripped into his nostrils like blades. It didn't surprise him. He knew well his own physical senses supercharged by now.

Lynn looked stunned at her bleeding arm.

– I didn't notice, she marveled. – I just didn't notice.

A bullet had grazed her and ripped open the skin. It did bleed quite a bit. Jane cleaned the wound and bandaged it quickly and efficiently. The bandage turned red, but the trickle stopped.

– Leave the gear, he instructed. – We need mobility more than added firepower.

They loaded whatever they could fit of light ordinance on their bodies. Among the items were a sword. He put it on his back, tied and fitted it until he was somewhat content.

Yes, he had iron, steel in his blood. The entire clan had, from an age long before there were guns.

There was a gate on a trail leading to the street. They were out there again almost before actually noticing, in one more whirl of movement. He experienced it like a succession of frozen images, each burning with immaculate detail in the so very familiar fire and shadow.

Then the dirt and the noise returned like a slamming door. A man stood across the street talking in a walkie talkie. He studied them with a thick layer of sweat on his brow. Ted returned the stare. The man began shaking. He lost his nerve and ran off. Ted shot him. He was pushed at the wall. Blood flowed from the wound as he hit the pavement.

– This is insane, Gerdie mused with a glee. – This is gloriously insane!

Her dark laughter echoed between the indistinct structures surrounding them. She was high with adrenaline and spirit. The buildings seemed both distinct and not simultaneously. They shifted constantly back and forth. So did the colors between pale and strong. His senses worked overtime. His perception shifted between the eyes and the radar, attempting to reconcile between them.

His telekinesis didn't return, though, and he stopped wondering if it ever would, and focused more than ever on the here and now.

His fiery analytical mind kept showing him angles, possibilities, outcomes.

– They are closing in on us, he confirmed. – I'm confident they are behind us, though, not in front or on the sides.

All his senses told him that, but he wasn't certain, not certain at all.

They raced across the square on full alert. A car entered the square at a slow speed. It kept its distance, not moving slower than they ran. They reached the giant derelict storage building at the other side of the square. He pushed down the handle and opened the door. They rushed inside and closed the door behind them. It was completely dark in there, no windows or light anywhere. Lynn pushed the button by the door and light flooded the large hall and the entirety of the building's vast labyrinth of intricate hallways.

He sensed them gather outside and smiled, and snarled quietly, to his three companions. They returned both expressions, confirming to him that he had succeeded with them, no matter the outcome.

The contingent of their enemies gathered outside. He heard the sound of many weapons being checked and prepared.

The four walked directly the considerable distance to the main circuit breaker in the basement. The easy switch-off/on system he and Liz had tested weeks ago.was still working flawlessly He exposed his fangs again, like they had done then. Jane, Lynn and Gerdie looked at him with adoring eyes.

Those outside spoke excited to each other, confident that they had caught the prey in a trap, unaware that it was they who had been snared.

His three companions donned the three infrared goggles. They giggled a bit, just a bit hysterical.

The entrance door opened. A smoke grenade was thrown inside, obscuring the invasion. He heard the sound of their feet touching the floor. The entrance door closed. The interior of the building became a world of its own, cut off from the outside. The gunmen spread out. The first doors were opened. Empty space stared at the intruders.

Ted nodded. Jane turned the switch. Every single space within the structure turned dark. The four were on the move. He no longer heard the sound of the feet. All of them had stopped cold. Excited, anxious chatter supplanted it. The four reached the ground floor. The first group of enemies appeared in their vision. They fired their guns. The shapes ten steps away dropped like props on a shooting range. Screams and thunder filled all empty spaces.

More intense chatter filled the air. There was movement. The four fired on the members of the first group exposing themselves. More enemies dropped to the floor. Red mist kept lingering in the air. More hysterical chatter followed.

– Can someone PLEASE open that fucking door?

Seconds ticked away. His sharp ears easily picked up on the sound of feet hammering the floor. Someone finally did open the entrance door. There was some noticeable light, but it didn't reach very deep into the building. The four killed more props on the shooting range as those people fled the dangerous pitch-black area.

The screams of pain faded. The screams of panic picked up. The four rushed forward, moving through more shadows, through more darkness. Someone fired bullets somewhere ahead, but the four quickly realized the aim was far off, that their opponents pulled the trigger in panic, firing at the smallest sound nearby.

They approached them from behind and shot them in the back. Some of them managed to turn around in a rush and return the fire. Ted felt a bullet graze his arm. He lost his gun. The sound of the metal hitting the floor sounded louder than the cracking of the guns. He tried picking it up, but his arm hung straight down, weak and useless. They ran on, fleeing from the enemies rushing towards the place of fighting. They fired at them as well from a corner down the hallway. More bodies already dead or close to death fell.

The strength in his arm returned. The wound stopped bleeding. The stench of blood didn't leave his nostrils. They stayed in the deepest parts of the building, away from the weak light from the open door.

– I'm out of here, a loud voice sounded. – NO amount of pay can make me fight that inhuman bastard.

There was a single shot, and the sound of one more body hitting the floor. Then, there were more shots, more screams of pain and rage, more bodies hitting the floor.

– You SHOT him, a voice bellowed. – You don't think we would STAND for that, did you?

They heard the sound of a boot hitting flesh, heard it repeatedly.

Several of those still standing rushed through the door.

– The pay is good, one staying behind said, very hesitant but determined.

It was at that moment the thought struck Ted. He, without his active powers could not scare the living crap out of these men. He would have to do… do the hard work.

The four moved before he had finished the thought. The three followed him through twisted hallways and dark corners. They met with resistance. They fired a murderous salvo at the enemies and sought cover well before the retaliation began.

– We're shooting at ghosts, a man that just had to express himself complained. – Ghosts!

Ted didn't have to have the men in the direct line of his eyesight to see them. He saw them around corners, behind walls, in all directions simultaneously. It was liberating, so much so that he had to pull himself together to not go overboard. The admiration in the three women's eyes and the glow of their skin grew stronger the longer they spent in his company. Jane had been taught to contain herself, to put a leash on her emotions during extreme circumstances, but the other two couldn't hold the flood of it back. He had to caution them several times. They got it, nodding serious-minded at him, assuring him of their loyalty and dedication and ability to follow his instructions to the latter.

He watched the enemy combatants. They clearly became more cautious. They moved smarter. He watched how they learned and got it, and closed in on them by limiting their choices. One option was closed off to them, then another, and another without the people standing against them exposing themselves. It was somewhat satisfying to him that his companions also got it, got how their advantage slowly evaporated, well before he gave them the sign of withdrawal. They moved down the stairs to the basement without being observed. They opened and closed a heavy door and ran through a long hallway. No one followed them. No one waited for them ahead.

The hallway went well below street level, below several buildings, obviously made as a last-ditch escape plan at some point. They reached its end. He pulled open a hatch on the wall, exposing a crawlspace. They pulled themselves up and in. It wasn't possible to move upright there. They did have to crawl, and they imagined they did so forever. It didn't really take them that long to reach the next hatch. They pushed themselves through the rather narrow passage and into what looked more like a tunnel than a hallway. It looked old, old enough for no one alive to remember it anymore.

Gerdic covered her mouth with a hand to hide her giggle of euphoria. She didn't really try to hide it, just to keep herself from being loud. She kissed him. The other two did as well. The heated moment felt brief, long, before their long run continued.

He remembered in flashes other runs, other times he and his brethren had fled from relentless enemies, long before Ted Warren had been born. In flashes, those memories were just as powerful as those Ted Warren vividly recalled.

A group of people where almost everyone had fireeyes crossed vast plains, massive land masses, always on the move, always on the run from people hunting them because their very birth had marked them as different.

Nothing, absolutely nothing had changed.

The rage, the drive that had always been there rose a couple of notches more.

A rumble rose from the ground, from the very Earth. They flowed down a raging river. He became the river. He always had been. The skin on the hand touching the gun burned. He squeezed it hard. The pain woke him up to an insane degree.

Ted brushed aside a dark sheet and they appeared in another basement bathing in semidarkness, in a house looking quite ordinary. He led them up the stairs to the ground floor. A man with a walkie talkie in his hand froze before them. Ted shot him down.

– We don't have much time, he told them.

The three of them nodded with burning eyes, filled with pride and joy and a fighting spirit beyond anything mundane. He felt boundless pride on their behalf.

– We have more time than we would have had if you hadn't shot him, Jane pointed out.

– That is true! Lynn said.

And thus, they confirmed his impression of them. They rushed through the door and down the stairs, advancing down the street before they actually noticed on a conscious level that they did.

He glanced to the side, and imagined he glimpsed Liz there. Another catching rose in his throat. He quelled the distraction at its inception, focusing beyond focusing on his surroundings. A click of a gun reached his ears. He pushed his three companions beyond a cover. A bullet hit him in the thigh just as he reached temporary safety. Jane fired at the man with the rifle in the window, taking him out with one bullet.

Blood flowed from the wound. The bullet had hit the artery. He imagined, feared that the wound took longer to heal. A pool formed on the pavement. His body discarded the bullet through the puncture. He felt faint. The wound stopped bleeding. He wondered if he approached his limits.

– I'm okay! He assured them.

They exchanged anxious glances, before nodding vigorously, giving him uncertain, encouraging smiles. He could stand easily enough. Closed eyes easily saw the surroundings and those breathing there, breathing harder there.

He moved, walked and ran. It didn't prove difficult, in any way. There was no pain, nothing even suggesting a stiff thigh or anything. He stopped thinking about it, disregarded it with an invisible shrug.

If anything, the experience had sharpened his senses, sharpened them to an uncanny degree. He had to restrain himself, fighting to not give in completely to his instincts. They screamed all over the place, threatening to overwhelm everything else within the range of his perception.

One man waited in hiding and Ted and Jane fired simultaneously, fast enough for him to miss his fairly easy shot. They threw themselves on the pavement and rolled to safety. The enemy fired again. The bullet bounced off the wall around the corner.

Ted stood there, listening. He signaled that there was just the one man and that he would take care of him. Ted stood there, breathing, ignoring his beating heart, focusing on breathing even.

There, the sound of the man moving, of his heel rubbing against the pavement, his slightly elevated breathing and a thousand other factor exposing him. Ted had already him in his sight the moment he stuck out his arm and exposed part of his upper body. The heavy bullet hit him in the side and graced his heart. He was already dead.

More foes were approaching. He signed to his three companions. They nodded without nodding. The four fired at a group advancing down the opposite sidewalk. One died with a bullet to the head. Another was hit in the belly. The rest managed to reach safety. Another assault group advanced down an adjacent street towards the four. Ted pulled back. The others followed on fast feet. He marveled at how they had become a unit, how they moved like one entity, how detailed vocal communication had become unnecessary, how communication without words had become rapid, instantaneous, far superior.

He drew a map in his head, one already there, one leading to another familiar spot, a modest fortress in the midst of the stone city. He conveyed that as best he could with hand signals, and he knew they got it.

The fingers and hands moved fast, too, as if they had never done anything else, as if they… remembered.

He frowned over how effortless he did it, how he had made quantum leaps without his most powerful talents. It didn't make him pause, but he did marvel at it, at least in his fleeting thoughts.

– You seem to know… where you are heading, Jane remarked.

– I do! He assured her.

He heard the music, the strike of the drum every time his feet touched the pavement, heard it even as they charged across a field with soft soil, towards the abandoned industrial park. One of the walls in the nearest building had a large hole in it. More amazement brightened Gerdie's face.

– We trained here. We actually spent several days and nights here.

– We learned the topography and shit, Lynn said. – We learned to use all of it to our advantage.

It dawned on them what it actually signified. All three of them shook their heads and looked at him with deepfelt awe.

He heard the whispers in the street, the buzzing of insects in the ground and in the air, and this was now, when he was limited.

He caught the sound of four, perhaps five guns being cocked.

– Roll on the ground, he told his companions.

They did so, just as the bullets started whizzing around them. The first salvo missed by a mile. They got back on their feet and spread out in totally unpredictable patterns, as they returned the fire and kept rushing forward towards the temporary refuge.

Lynn was hit in the side and went down. He picked her up and carried her almost like a reflex, an automatic function. They charged into relative safety between the derelict buildings. A bullet had hit him in the back at some point. He had stumbled, but kept moving.

His hand moved by themselves, exposing Lynn's wound. It didn't bleed too much. She pushed a cloth at her skin.

– I'm okay, she insisted.

She wasn't. He didn't speak.

A car erupted out onto the field from the opposite cluster of somewhat whole buildings. Then another, and another. Ted nodded to Jane. She used the last rocket grenade in the bazooka. Her keen eye and analysis made her aim true. The grenade exploded and took out two of the vehicles simultaneously. The third moved on. Another revealed itself. The two vehicles moved against them from the left and the right, firing from shielded positions as they moved.

– They have hired lots of fighters, Jane said frustrated. – They have lots of money behind them. This is insane!

The four moved further into the derelict buildings. They had been here and trained here before. The path was lined out before them like a second sight.

A door slammed in the wind. There was no wind. He heard the sound of rain. There was no rain. He realized that it, one way or another was a phantom memory.

They spread out, preparing without thought, with all thoughts in the world for what was coming. Lynn placed herself at an easily defendable position, and one where she could easily withdraw from. She gave him a thumb's up in a display of deliberate euphoria, one that would inevitably fade as the effect of the wound became pronounced. They placed themselves in a half circle facing the path the enemies would take, constantly seeking viable alternatives for shifting of position.

– There is no… easy escape from here, Gerdie frowned.

– There isn't, Ted agreed. – This is the end of the road, one way or another.

– This is more than suitable, Jane remarked, – and the best of all: Liz will be here.

– The question is how soon, Lynn wondered.

They fell silent. The cars stopped on whining tires outside. Boots hit the ground. He pictured it in his mind. There was really just one entrance. They would have to enter through that before they could spread out. It happened not many seconds later. One group took cover behind the wall and fired at possible hiding places. The other rushed through the opening.

And was met with a rain of bullets. Those that could, those not penetrated by hot lead pulled back to the relative safety behind the wall. Jane and Ted kept firing with both hands. There were many, too many behind the wall. They could coordinate easily and keep the four from firing. Ted stuck his head out and fired, killing two more enemies as they rushed forward. He felt the pain in his shoulder. He was pushed backwards.

Another group took the long road around. They were not hard to follow as they approached the battle, approached it fast. The situation for the four became untenable. They retreated like a unit, fell back to the next easily defendable position, crossing a ruin between two somewhat whole buildings. Ted rushed to a window and fired at the group advancing across the yard.

They moved in the terrain practically made for urban guerilla, one they were also intimately familiar with. Jane and Gerdie rushed forward and were suddenly behind the attackers. They shot them down with a massive salvo. It worked, worked beyond remarkable. Gerdie was hit in the leg. Muscles strengthened by years of hard exercise kept her moving, running, moving. Ted saw the pain, the strain in her features, how she ignored it. He killed those following the two. Ammunition faded like moisture a warm summer day. The thought struck him one moment and was gone the next. They kept running, kept moving.

– Eric told us, Gerdie mused, the haze of pain covering her eyes. – He was shot in the leg on Aphrodite and just kept moving, even through the streets of London days later. The leg threatening to give in didn't.

Pride glowed in her feverish eyes.

– I know dangerous wounds can feel like nothing, like a fleabite at first,

Lynn said. – My eyes are open.

The words echoed in his mind. He tried closing them out, but he failed.

He felt lightheaded. The shoulder was still bleeding. The wound closed as he watched. Him focusing on it made it close faster.

They hid in yet another somewhat safe pocket of reality, a hideout of hideouts minutes, hours, an eternity later. They looked attentive at him.

– We're being overwhelmed, he stated. – There are limits to how much we can do against superior numbers.

They nodded, smiling in affection. Such a statement was so typical for him.

– I will take them on, he stated. – I will kill and keep killing until they are dead or I am.

They looked shocked at him, even as they nodded to themselves.

– You can do it, Lynn stated firmly. – You are a wild beast of the Earth. They are nothing to you.

She looked at him with staggering confidence.

He looked at them, gathering them in his vision, pulling them into it, and they shook in passion and overwhelming emotion.

– You must run away, he insisted, – whether or not I return.

– No fucking way! Jane swore.

She kissed his lips, practically biting them to shreds. He hardly noticed.

He checked, double-checked his body loaded with guns, with lethal tools. The load felt light, as if it wasn't there at all. He felt the berserker rage rise within, and he welcomed it, making no effort whatsoever at keeping it at bay.

He nodded once, and then he was on his way.

Wind rushed against his face. There was no face. The wind turned to fire. There was fire. He felt it peeling his skin, even as his skin kept repairing itself.

– I did it for you, Liz choked in that now so familiar whirl of water and wind.

That was the final distraction. Lynn, Gerdie and Jane fired the moment he jumped, fired himself into the passage like a projectile. He rolled on the ground firing against those suddenly so easy targets behind the seemingly far away corner. They fell like bowling pins. They pulled back, withdrew. He chased them. A bullet hit him from another angle. Jane fired at the shooter and hit him. He fell from a window and hit the ground with a dump sound. Ted reached the next corner on his path, somewhat safe.

He reloaded his guns. His three companions and the enemies did as well. He was done well before any other and continued his run. His three allies fired at the enemy stronghold just as he rolled on the ground and fired his guns again.

– HE ISN'T H-HUMAN, a beyond shaking voice whimpered.

Ted killed him just as he turned and ran off, as he exposed himself.

Then the storm of flesh and bone was right there, in their midst. He shot the first two. They went down. He kept firing. A bullet hit him at close range. It slowed him down. Another bullet hit him. He grabbed a man and shot him in the head, holding him up as a cover. Several bullets hit the already dead body. Ted let go of one gun and drew his sword, cutting two in one brutal sweep. The sword served him better at close range, making him even more unpredictable. The enemies hit each other, but not him. He cut a thigh, hitting the big vein. Blood flowed into the air like from a hose, painting everything in the already pervasive red mist.

Several combatants fled in panic. He followed them, covering himself behind them. They were hit by extensive fire. He was not. The red blade kept flashing. He killed them just as they reached the cover. There was no one else there.

He jumped into a window on the second floor. It took those firing at him by complete surprise. Their bullets didn't even come close to hitting him. He put the sword away and loaded the gun. The room had a somewhat solid floor, like he remembered it. The walls lacked everything except the original concrete. He ran up the stairs to the upper floor, another level to the roof. One glimpse was sufficient to get a sense of the entire field of war below. One group, moving with a notable purpose basically ignored him and focused on closing in on the three women, on Jane. A loud voice shouted commands. He recognized it. A hot chill flooded him, but did not make him stop or hesitate. He jumped across the divide, landing safely, far onto the other roof.

A walk in the park, he thought.

The taste of blood stuck in his mouth. It kept bubbling up his throat. A sharp pain in his chest made him stop momentarily. An abrupt dizziness made him sway, but he stayed on his feet. He rushed on.

Another divide appeared before him. He jumped and landed safely on the other side. The pain fired up stronger inside him. He ignored it and kept moving. There was no door down on this roof. He climbed down on the outside, sliding much of the way down the water drain pipe. It squeaked and groaned, but held.

He sensed the closest group of enemies. They were moving away from him, still closing in on Lynn, Jane and Gerdie.

On Jane.

He still didn't understand, still didn't

He fell at the enemy, or so it felt, fell from high up, into the gray swarm of flesh and bone no longer far away. He was right there, in their midst, killing with steel and led, and he was nothing else beside that. He shot Peyton in the chest. She stumbled backwards. He shot her again. She fell. It didn't distract him. Some of her men sort of relented when she fell. She was clearly the leader here. Ted kept killing. He was hit from two sides. His blade cut off heads and arms and penetrated warm flesh. His empty gun was long gone, short moments ago from his hand. He picked another from a cold hand and kept firing and swinging his soaked blade. Rocks floated in the air, and he realized startled that his powers were awakening. He felt it.

A bullet hit him in the head. Fear touched him, as he went down. He rolled on the ground, cutting legs, shooting the gray shapes flowing in his blurry vision in the gut, but he couldn't make his powers work. The headwound made him dizzy, close to unconscious. Three bullets, three hammers hit him in the chest. Two of the men firing at him were practically ripped apart by the power of his mighty mind. Then everything turned black.

Jane, Lynn and Gerdie arriving at the scene fired at the few men still standing. They fell and fired useless bullets at the ground. One bullet went high above them.

Everything… turned quiet. They looked at the slaughterhouse around them with wide eyes.

– He really made an impression on them, Lynn whispered.

– Peyton is still breathing, Gerdie reported.

She kicked the gun out of the other woman's hand. Eyes on the ground kept failing in their attempt at focusing on the fury standing above her.

– Let her croak, Jane snarled.

She looked down on Ted. He was not moving. There was no movement at all down there, not a single twitch.

– Stand guard, she told the others, drying her tears. – I will touch Ted.

– I will do it, Gerdie stated. – You… you must live.

– All three of us will do it, Jane said. – That makes it less likely that any of us will die.

All three nodded. They knelt around the unmoving body soaked in blood and pushed their hands at the outside of his hands and at the uncovered skin they could find. A unison gasp rose through three open mouths. A horrible weakness overwhelmed them. They collapsed, fell back from the man between them.

2

Liz, Lewis and the others made their way across the field. She was far ahead, her steps being giant leaps. Several people with guns erupted from the cluster of derelict buildings ahead. They threw away their guns and knelt in terror. Liz disregarded the fastest of them, broke the slow ones to pieces as she passed them. Some of them tried, in their panic to fight on. Lewis chopped off an arm with a sword. Blood flowed from the stump. The man crumbled and bled out on the ground. Lewis moved on, the sight already delegated to distant memory.

Liz felt like she walked the last few blocks, imagining she was unable to pick up speed. Frustration surged through her. She appeared on the open square where heaps of bodies covered most of the ground.

Jane, Lynn and Gerdie crouched around the still body, gasping for breath, fighting to move, to once again touch the man, unable to do so. Bouts of weakness kept riding them.

– Stop, Liz told them, somewhat gently.

They obeyed her reluctantly, overwhelmed with sadness, unable to meet her eyes.

She sensed it before she bent down and touched Ted's skin. He didn't breathe. There was no discernible pulse.

– We did as he said, Jane whimpered, – followed his instructions to the latter, and we did feel faint, felt weakness when we touched him, but he didn't wake up.

She clearly had a strong need to convey that to the tall wraith crouching above them.

– His powers were returning, Lynn insisted. – We observed floating stones.

Everyone nodded to each other. They knew well the significance of that.

– They were, Liz agreed, allowing herself to hope. – I felt them.

She looked at him, at the bloodied face, his expression so peaceful, almost serene. She hardly caught anything beside that. She strove to feel, feel anything, but was unable to do so.

– I reach out a hand for you, but you are gone, she whispered.

She shook him, shook him hard. He moved when she did, stopped when she stopped, resembling a ragdoll in her eyes, and she almost lost it that very moment.

– He wanted to save me, Jane choked, – and he did. I'm yours, in all things.

Liz knew, in the back of her mind that the child meant it, meant it from the bottom of her heart, from the very core of her being, in a far deeper sense than she could ever convey in words.

She saw her, saw her in their lives, a mainstay, one that would never fail them or betray them.

Them…

The still body moved, ever so slightly. There was a cough, and then…

– He's breathing, Gerdie said choked up, – *breathing.*

She was close, too close to actually throw herself at the still almost unmoving body in front of her.

The bullets seemed to push themselves out of the mangled skin, an amazing sight even for the jaded group still standing in the extensive ruins.

Liz bent forward and kissed the bloody lips, licking them, tasting them.

There was a cough a few steps away. Liz turned. Peyton moved or tried to move. Liz rose and walked to her. Peyton tried speaking, releasing painful gasps with each attempt.

– Yes, I know, Liz said dryly, – you didn't cheat on your bar exam, but used one lie to cover up another. I wondered what that was about, of course, but decided to let it play out. I had no idea it would lead to such… drastic results…

– I… visited every shady shop in the city, Peyton gasped, as if she had a desperate need to explain herself, – in an effort to find a drug that could affect and weaken witches and was left with three choices. We used all three.

Liz looked like a goddess of calm, of serenity, the fireeyes glowing ever so slightly.

– The firm cheated on Rachel, Peyton coughed, – embezzlement and worse. I was charged with making that secret stay a secret. I overheard Diana and Jane speak about a secret. Jane said Ted had to be told «at once». She even told the name of the bar. I acted immediately, and called people the firm had used in the past. I…

She coughed one more time. Her body shook and froze. Dead eyes stared at nothing.

– What a waste!

Liz shook her head in contempt.

She watched as the spirit fled, fled into the shadow world the fastest it was able.

– It's over, Ethel said. – The special circumstances threatening Jane's life no longer exist. An *amazing* chain of coincidences created them, but they're no longer in play.

She looked very amused, almost serene.

– Both Lynn and Gerdie will be okay, Carla reported. – They will just have to take it easy for a while, that's all.

– I will be happy to do so, Gerdie laughed.

Ted sat up, feeling dizzy, feeling more aware than ever before. It rushed slowly at him like the storm it was.

Liz threw herself at him, suddenly a storm of emotion, of relief and joy.

She kissed him ten thousand times in a second. Laugher bubbled in his and everyone's throat.

He rose. She helped him, and he let her. His features, covered in blood, glowed with power. His eyes burned like never before. She knew, and the smile widened.

They both sobered, even as the wide, wide grin persisted.

– Peyton got close to us, Liz said, – close enough that she imagined she knew our weaknesses, and she did.

A chill passed through both of them. It couldn't block the joy of the moment, but it was there, inevitably.

Jane threw herself at him, too, at them both. He touched her face with caution. Nothing happened.

They both saw her, on their path, a shadow never really leaving their side.

Dawn revealed its ugly mug in the distant horizon. The first signs of morning brought another chill in their bones.

– So, what do we do with all the bodies? Eric asked, not really asking.

– We leave them here, Ted shrugged. – It will be just another gang-related New York City shootout, one more riddle confounding the population and the authorities of the modern metropolis.

– We will express grief if anyone asks us about Peyton, Liz mused, – but also say we didn't really know her… which is the mortal truth.

They left, never to return.

Liz and Ted exchanged glances, looking ahead, in their newfound awareness at the long dark tunnel that was their life, feeling, knowing beyond knowing the familiar chill passing down their spines.

At the end of the long hallway… waited the dragon.

Chapter 16

She slapped him without being near him. They heard the slaps of what sounded like hands hit his cheeks, but Liz stood several steps away. A deep chill dug deep into them all.

– ON YOUR KNEES, BITCH, she yelled at him.

Everyone imagined that she grew to a giant of cold and shadow in their eyes, even though their eyes showed nothing of that. He gasped and dropped to his knees. Big, big tears jumped from his eyes.

– You know what you just did, right, she said with her quiet snarl. – You treated Caroline with disdain, as if she was your property, not your fellow human being and sister in arms.

– I'm sorry, he choked.

– You have forgotten something, she said icily.

– Sorry, he said, turned to Caroline.

– I accept your apology, she said.

He turned towards Liz again, wanting more than anything to regain his perceived lost favor.

She let him stew in his own fat for a few moments, until she let the matter go, at least for now, and turned towards the others present.

– He had obviously misunderstood the teaching, she shrugged. – He's new and entitled.

The training hall in the old warehouse had turned absolutely silent. Now, the hectic activity and its noise resumed.

Liz felt the energy. Ted felt the energy. It had grown, both individually and combined. It soared in the busy hall. It soaked it like warm, hissing rain. They gathered in the mess hall, and it was there as well. It was everywhere they went.

Caroline approached Liz afterwards, respectful and humble and awestruck, everything simultaneously.

– Thank you, she said. – I couldn't defend myself against him. He is stronger and faster than me.

– Hopefully, he will learn his lesson, Liz remarked, – or he will have no future with us.

The girl bowed and pulled back.

Liz stopped her with a hand sign. She froze and paid attention.

– He will always be stronger than you. Whether or not he will remain a better fighter is up to you.

– I will heed your words, Goddess.

Liz dismissed her with an impatient movement she couldn't hold back. Caroline pulled back, clearly stricken, frightened.

– You can sense us, can't you, Liz said abruptly.

– I can, Goddess, you sing loud and beautiful like a storm in my depths.

– Then, you are like us.

– I may be like some of the others, Goddess, but none is like you, the two of you.

Caroline faded like dew in her vision. Liz had some inkling that she had once again dismissed the girl, but she wasn't certain.

Liz spotted Ted by the door. She tried keeping herself somewhat composed, but failed. She rushed into his arms and flooded his lips with kisses. He returned them as best he could.

– I was so scared, she whispered, – so scared when I saw you lying there. I was paralyzed with fright. I sensed nothing from you, nothing even resembling life, and I was dead inside, and then the power of a thousand suns returned to you, and I was frozen with stark relief. All kinds of horrible thoughts raced through my mind, and I couldn't catch a single one.

He did his best to comfort her, making an effort of it. She crumbled in his embrace, unable to keep herself from trembling.

– They are looking at us, she kept whispering, – but I don't care. Perhaps they will finally see us as human beings.

It felt so peaceful standing close like this, almost like they were alone in the room. The thousand voices surrounding them didn't penetrate their shield.

They smiled and turned towards the others, letting them in. Everyone present rushed to them, and embraced them in fierce hugs choke-full of emotion.

The power grew as they did, and everyone noticed. The two took a little from each touching them. It felt natural and right. Fear faded to a tiny glow in their gut. The Fire pulsed and grew, piercing the ground, the walls, the sky above.

She looked at him with her big eyes, her twinkling flames.

– I feel so warm, he mused. – I've never felt so warm.

Then, from one moment to the next something haunting found its way from her depth to the surface. She shrunk from his touch, and he knew why in an instant. The past revisited her, reached out with its talons and bloody claws. It was an easy, foregone conclusion.

– I still remember it vividly, she said aloud. – Alanis had shot Richard in the chest, a deadly wound, but he still managed to return the fire. They kept firing at each other, beyond life, beyond death. That is the power of hatred.

He looked at her. Everyone did.

– What you did was the exactly opposite, she stressed. – You risked everything to save one life. I feel such pride.

She kissed him again, and this time her lips lingered. They still burned, but he hardly noticed that.

He pulled back. She waited patiently, waited with uncanny, unfamiliar patience.

– Mark and David went at each other like rabid dogs, he stated, he stressed. – It doesn't matter who started it. They destroyed each other. And Mark was eaten away by something even worse most of his life. I don't want that.

Liz nodded as if she understood something.

And she did.

– We did take care of it, though, she remarked, – took care of what stood against us.

He waited, just as patient.

– We *vanquished* him, she chuckled, – *slaughtered* one of the most dangerous beings in existence. There *was* a treasure at the end of the rainbow, and we found it, found our true nature, undeniable, forever and ever.

The emotional rollercoaster, the vast ups and downs surging through them lessened, but didn't fade away. It would always be a part, an integrated part of them.

The rest of the day pretty much faded in touch, in warm embraces and eager pushes and pulls. It faded like a dream even before it ended.

The dreams ripped into them, like they always did, like a waterfall they had to ride out, endure.

Jane was there, with them, even when she wasn't.

The unknown man kissed her. She allowed it, allowed him to step close to her and take her in his arms.

He grabbed her hand, studying it with undying curiosity.

– Most women's hands are soft. Easily crushed in a man's hand, but yours is strong as iron.

– It can be soft, too…

That was one. Two others approached her a little later in the heap of warm, twisting bodies.

– My name is Jim, I will serve you tonight.

– My name is Tim, I will serve you tonight.

– Yes, you will, Liz stated.

They reddened like tomatoes.

Then she was back with Ted. She rode him, rode him hard. Her moan rose like the thunder it had long since become. Two shouts sounded like one.

A long moment became silence, became the quiet darkness soothing them.

The quake beneath their bodies persisted and grew. It never ceased.
Regret faded to nothing in their elevated consciousness. Eyes closing never closed.
They woke up in one heap of bodies somewhere before dawn, unable, unwilling to sleep a second more, their acute, sensitive vision easily catching the invisible light very few others would notice.
She smiled and met him with soft kisses.
I feel so good, she told him, so incredibly great.
Jane and Caroline approached them with cups of water, respect and love in their eyes.
– Thank you, Kwaiala, Liz said with a voice tinged with condescension, more like her old, cynical self.
She and Ted drank the chilled, tasty water deliberately slow, savoring every drop. They breathed, and it was like everyone else present breathed with them.
She embraced him from behind, kissing him on the shoulder, and then she froze.
He sensed how tense, how apprehensive she had suddenly become, and he didn't understand it.
– The scars on your back, she mumbled amazed. – They're gone, finally totally gone!
And then he felt her joy, as she traced invisible lines on his back with her fingers and lips.
– Your skin isn't exactly smooth like that of a newborn baby, but there isn't even a trace of the scarring anymore.
And he did feel like an invisible weight had been lifted from his mind. It didn't exactly disappear, but its… significance noticeably lessened.
They prowled Manhattan after their ravenous feeding, their early breakfast of common food and drink. Carla was there, Caroline, Jane and many of the others. It was like one step brought them thousands of miles forward.
– The buildings look so small, Liz remarked.
She recalled her time as a true goddess, the age of horrible wonders that would never be.
They walked through Grand Central Station.
– The sun used to shine here, Carla said. – It doesn't anymore, because of all the tall buildings outside.
She sounded like she recalled an actual memory, not just something she had read or learned. Everyone among the wanderers caught that.
– We watched the comet together, all of us, in the cold spring night, on the great southern plains, under the constellation of Phoenix near Tucana and

Sculptor.

They saw it without closing their eyes.

Fallon appeared with those guarding him, approaching them with fast, determined steps. He was there a heartbeat or ten later.

– Everything is in order, he reported. – All the necessary papers have been filed. If there is anything left of the firm after the criminal courts have had their say, you will receive the spoils.

Liz touched his cheeks in an affectionate caress, knowing that it meant the world to him.

They invaded Greenwich Village, changing it from one moment to the next. Their very presence worked as a time machine, returning, by the blink of an eye, the area to what it had been ten years ago. They gave what remained of truly progressive stores and venues their business and their support, giving them invaluable free advertising. Some people stared and left, backed off in panic. Most joined them on their walk. Everyone transformed themselves by trying out and wearing the clothing popular ten years ago. It had a stunning, beyond startling effect. Carla and Ethel stood side by side in front of a large mirror, admiring themselves.

– I never was a part of the hippie scenery, Ethel remarked with distinct regret. – It would seem that I missed out.

– You look smashing, sweetie, Liz said, kissing her on the neck, feeling the power of the touch without trying, or trying very hard.

Ethel frowned briefly, before once again being caught in the quiet joy of the moment.

The large group of wanderers filled Wexler's to the brim. The evening, the long evening began. Ted walked to the bar with a huge smile on his face.

– You might want to hire more people and get more supplies for today and upcoming days, he said pleasantly. – We will sit down and wait patiently while you do so. We can also help out, if you should need it.

Wexler's was a big place, used to serve a large number of guests, but nothing like this influx, not this early. The wanderers put most of the tables together and sat down. They sat down and waited patiently for the beers to arrive. The glasses arrived, and they had a toast, and then it already felt like hours had passed, and it had turned dark outside.

Candles burned on the tables and cast shadows on sweaty faces. It felt very strange, very familiar, as if they had been sitting around a long table together, drinking together a thousand times before.

Liz and Ted were dancing together, dancing tight and slow, enjoying the moment.

– Look at them, she giggled. – They have never seen us both this powerful before. They sense us. Everyone does, on some level.

He nodded, not needing to really acknowledge her words. The power was tangible, potent, beyond potent.

– We should use it to do something, he said, – not letting it go to waste.

– I like the way you think, My Lord, she whispered in his ear.

She pulled back a little, enough for him to see all of her well.

– What else is new, she shrugged.

The grin spread to her entire face.

They danced, light on their feet, the happy buzz in their minds taking them further on their journey, their long walk. Others joined them on the large, polished floor, swarming around them like moths, and they burned, and the fire burned even stronger.

Jane came to them, touching them eagerly, willingly, giving herself. They felt her. She felt them, but didn't pull away.

The night fell. Wexler's became even more alive, approaching, even superseding old glory. The celebration spread to the street outside, and also to the surrounding buildings. There didn't seem to be any end to it. When closing time arrived, the establishment didn't close. The party quite simply continued. The songs from the Sixties kept flowing from the speakers, kept flooding people's ears.

– New York City is changing, Liz mused in frustration. – We are changing it, like we changed New Orleans, but not enough. We're just a pinprick on a giant bloated whore, unable to effect actual, lasting change.

There was solemn laughter and smiles. She smiled, too. The frustration persisted.

They felt it, felt it before two pairs of fireeyes started burning hotter.

The night ended, with more heated touch, with deep, content sleep.

The sun rose on the sky. They saw it while sleeping with their eyes closed.

Liz and Ted started crashing police patrol cars around noon.

The drivers in two cars rushing down Fifth Avenue suddenly lost control and crashed into an exclusive jewelry store, mowing down, killing and maiming most of the customers and staff. Shards of glass gutted police officers and cut their throats. Many people, hit by the runaway cars crouched on the street, dying by the numbers. Loud screams and wails echoed between the tall buildings. The area had suddenly, just like that become a slaughterhouse.

More patrol cars appeared, from several entry points this time. Ted and Liz had no trouble listening in on the hectic activity on the airwaves. The officers were heavily armed and primed for trouble. Liz and Ted pushed the gas pedal on all the cars through the floor and steered all of them at each other. More pedestrians were hit. The drivers let go of the gas pedal and desperately attempted to move the wheel in their hands, all in vain.

The cars met in a crash loud as thunder. At least two of them exploded and brought more secondary explosions. The slaughterhouse turned into an inferno. Screams of pain and pure terror filled what once, only minutes ago had been a fairly quiet, but busy luxurious area.

The midday sun had brightened the sidewalks, the road and the walls, and the flesh walking there, the metal beasts driving through it. Now, everything had been cast in Shadow.

Nothing moved, nothing breathed, at least nothing visible. People cooped up in their lush apartments didn't dare look out of the windows. They hardly dared doing anything, except crouching on the floor.

– I can feel their fear, Ethel told Liz and Ted in one of her lower apartments. – You do such great work!

– It feels like a dream, Liz mumbled with half closed eyes.

– It does, doesn't it? Ethel almost cried. – A lucid dream where you can control everything.

Her fireeyes twinkled even more in excitement.

Time passed slowly down there, in the heat and the thick haze. Nothing happened. Time stretched out. The first crows arrived, a bit hesitant at first, but then they began feeding off the still warm meat to their heart's content.

The police officers approached on foot. They advanced cautiously with drawn weapons. Those in front began firing at the crows, clearly agitated. Most of the bullets missed and hit the cooling flesh. The crows took off with loud shrieks.

Ravens arrived. They settled in the entire area. Ravens were fairly rare in New York City, but suddenly they were abundant on that particular stretch of Fifth Avenue. The police officers, clearly struggling already began ogling them. Sweat soaked already greasy hair and grew thick and beyond visible on their exposed skin.

Security guards protecting the wealthy and their property hid within the classy buildings. They shook so hard that they could hardly hold on to their guns, and made an effort to stay in hiding, to make themselves as inconspicuous as possible.

The police officers wore full riot gear and heavy arms. They moved their arms from left to right and back again, but there was no one to point at, nothing to fire at. No one moved but them in the entire avenue and adjacent streets. It was quiet like that everywhere. Even the ravens stayed quiet, evidently content with keeping an eye on the armored humans below.

Someone handled a gun. The unnatural metallic loud sound of a loading mechanism at work made everyone freeze in their position. Ted exposed his fangs. Liz giggled happily. The point man fired his machinegun at those in hiding. Everyone under his command followed him reducing the first floor in the building and everyone within to mashed meat.

Silence fell on the broad street yet again.

– We showed them, Sarge, an officer shouted in wild euphoria, sending off a few more rounds of bullets for good measure.

The sergeant frowned, staring at his still twitching finger as if it wasn't quite right. His shoulder hurt, as if it had been pulled hard in one particular direction without the body quite following.

Another security force opened fire at them from another building. Two more opened fire from other buildings. The policemen fell like dominoes. Some of them managed to return fire and reach cover. More flesh was relentlessly perforated. But the police officers were completely surrounded. They were taken out in crossfire until they had all joined the rest of the bodies in the insanely hot and humid Fifth Avenue.

– We did it, one of the private guards said from hiding. – We vanquished the insane, murderous bastards.

– We had no choice, a second man shaking hard said. – They would have taken us out without bothering with a trial.

– We're in deeep shit! A third choked.

– Remove all the surveillance tapes, the first barked, – and I mean all.

They went to work with an eager zeal they couldn't believe.

– LOOK!

It sounded more like a wail.

One man stood up out there. He was covered in blood and guts, and his clothes had been reduced to rags. Something didn't look right with him. The head rolled a bit on the shoulders, as if there were no muscles holding it up anymore. The gun dangled at the end of a dangling arm. He looked at them. The men hiding in what had once been a luxurious store ran seriously scared.

Then, the man jumped straight into the air and stayed there. All the tough guys within the building screamed.

What was obviously a dead body turned in the air, and started floating down the street.

Ted and Liz held hands. There were constant ghostly sparks emanating from them.

– I know who he is, Liz chuckled. – His name is, was Connor Blake. He received the Police Combat Cross a few days ago.

– What a great guy, Ted remarked.

He who had been Connor Blake floated a bit more through the air. The dead body floated away, leaving the immediate vicinity, clearly with a specific goal in mind. People stared at him and pointed, chilled to the bone in the pervasive heat.

The body landed, somewhat steady outside the twentieth precinct. He opened the door with his free hand and walked inside. The officers present didn't notice him at first. He grabbed the gun with both hands.

– Is that you, Connor? An officer frowned.

Blake shot in him the gut. The finger pulling the trigger did so with an eerie, uneven move. He fired the next bullet, shooting a female officer in the chest. People rushed for cover. They began returning fire. Blake fired his gun without changing his expression in any discernible way. The blood-filled eyes kept staring straight forward, seeing nothing at all. Bullets hit him. It ruined his… aim, made him miss the next target, but didn't have any discernible effect aside from that. Bullets kept striking him. He floated forward. The officers began screaming in a horrible fear. Some attempted to flee. They were shot in the back. His gun was empty. He let go of it. Another floated into his hand.

– Shoot at his feet, an officer shouted. – HIS FEET.

They did. It didn't help them any.

His feet, his body were shot to pieces. He kept hovering and firing. A bullet hit the gun. It slipped from the hand. It was back the next moment.

The firing pin hit another empty chamber. The gun fell from the hand. The body collapsed and dropped to the floor. The surviving officers stayed frozen on the floor for several heartbeats before they hesitatingly started moving. They had their eyes on Blake's unmoving body. Their stare didn't waver, and they didn't blink.

There was movement, something stirring in one heap of cooling flesh. It wasn't Blake, but Regina Johnson, one of those he had shot. She rose and stood straight, with the same empty eyes. They got the willies merely by looking at her. Several almost fired at her, but they managed to catch themselves just in time. She didn't hold a gun, but they knew by experience that could change anytime. Several took off, fled the fastest they possibly could, wailing like banshees. Those remaining kept their eyes locked on Johnson.

She raised a bloody hand and her index finger. Pay attention, she said, and they did.

They watched her relentlessly as she walked to the fairly unblemished wall. There were a few blood drops there, but not extensive amounts. She began writing with her bloodied index finger.

THIS IS NOT YOUR CITY. NEW YORK CITY BELONGS TO YOU NO LONGER. IF YOU MAKE ANY ATTEMPT AT REASSERTING YOUR AUTHORITY, YOU WILL SUFFER GREATLY. PASS IT ON.

Her arm fell. She fell, becoming just another lifeless husk on the floor. The open eyes kept staring at them. Slowly, only slowly, they managed to move, to take one step, two forward, not really feeling like they were in command of their limbs.

– Get the surveillance tapes, Captain Sanders squeaked. – Make certain never to let them out of your possession. Make copies. If we don't have them, we will most certainly be committed.

There was not much hope in his voice.

2

The Upper East Side was looted, every single exclusive store emptied of valuables and food. There were no cops to be seen anywhere. The various security details had fled from the area long ago. The bravest of the starving and homeless and most desperate came first. No cops stopped them from doing anything. Nothing bad happened to them. Others saw that. The deluge began.

Some of them attempted to leave again. Most of them were arrested the moment they reached an invisible demarcation line. The looters, the poor and homeless still within the no man's land that had been the Upper East Side remained and moved into abandoned buildings and apartments. They found the still functioning freezers and storage facilities for stores and restaurants where massive amounts of food and drink were still stored and took over the operation.

Officers from various more or less unaffected precincts formed an iron ring around what had been baptized «the afflicted area». Their hands clutched their guns. They pulled the trigger if the emerging looters as much as looked wrong at them.

The Lincoln Center and other notable buildings were occupied with the rest of them. The place was transformed in a matter of days into something alien and terrifying to those that worked there and lived near it.

Luciano Avrano stood at the top of his penthouse, surveying what had been his domain. He looked as haggard, as bad as the few of his aides and guards that still remained.

Liz and Ted recharged, touching briefly their friends and fellow warriors, filling themselves until they started feeling bloated, but no more. Everyone gave of themselves with eagerness and trust in their eyes.

Alex Horwath, another highly decorated officer began feeling uncomfortable. He began tripping back and forth. He felt like he was being touched and felt a powerful need to scratch himself. The others looked hard at him. He returned their stare with suspicion and anxiety. Suddenly, his firearm and arm and hand moved and pointed itself at another officer. Before he had properly acknowledged what was happening he had shot his colleague in the head. He fired again at the man standing next in line, and the next in line after that. Practically everyone standing close fired at Horwath. He disintegrated in the hail of bullets hitting him.

Then, several others began firing at them. Some of them fell. The rest returned the fire. Officers screamed in protest as their body failed to obey their thoughts. They died screaming. It spread across the entire iron wall. Grown men wet their pants and fled each other's company like scared children. Those fleeing being in even remotely close proximity fired at each other. Very few managed to get away.

Gun battles broke out in several precincts on Manhattan, both inside and outside the various stations. Officers fired at officers in wild panic and with a fear begging description.

Grinning zombies wrote on walls:

THIS IS NOT YOUR CITY. NEW YORK CITY BELONGS TO YOU NO LONGER. IF YOU MAKE ANY ATTEMPT AT REASSERTING YOUR AUTHORITY, YOU WILL SUFFER GREATLY. PASS IT ON.

The writing on the wall was heard... and understood. Fear, true, numb-striking fear filled all NYPD police officers' eyes.

All precincts on Manhattan were abandoned. It began as a trickle, and continued as a flood, until every single office was empty. Each officer sat alone in his or her apartment and shook in fear.

There had been no recorded incidents in the other boroughs yet, but the burgeoning panic was felt there as well. Officers stopped reporting for work and those doing so kept their contact to a minimum. NYPD, one of the most brutal and racist police departments in the world, ceased working as an effective organization.

Luciano Avrano took one look down on the crowded street and heard the loud choir of rage, and decided to stay a bit longer. He had tried to send for a chopper a couple of times. It suffered engine-trouble well before it could land on the roof, or come close enough to the roof for it to matter.

The Shadowwalkers walked through the untidy Manhattan streets. They were fully-armed. There were quite a few of them, more than sufficient numbers to discourage other fully-armed roaming groups. Those men and women stared at them, but were careful not to make any threatening moves.

People hiding in the shadows, in wet and humid apartments stared as well. Abby and most of the rest could not take their eyes of Liz and Ted, their awe and respect had not exactly diminished lately.

Carla looked relaxed, happy, not really moved beyond that at all. Ethel looked fresh and energetic. Patrick seemed bored. Lewis seemed beyond upbeat and astute, as if every moment brought new and exciting sensations. Linsey didn't seem to be there at all, not really. Jean towered above everyone.

Eric and Logan stared at Liz with worship in their eyes.

– I love how the guns are such total window dressing, Ethel chuckled. – We no longer need them beyond that, not in a million years.

A long, thick tail dangled behind them, a flock of breathing two-legged wolves with exposed fangs following the witches.

They reached the spot on Fifth Avenue, the tall building beset with ravens. Many others reached it as well. The gathering filled the width of the road and the sidewalks up and down the avenue. It seemed to go on for miles.

The place was packed.

Liz stepped forward to the microphone. The mood, starting off exuberant grew ecstatic.

– We gathered here some time ago, she cried. – The police stopped us from doing our inherent right of assembly and free speech. This time, no one will disturb or interrupt our meeting. It will keep going until *we* say it's done. We won't move an inch from this spot until the company in the building behind us commits to the right course of action in legally binding writing, fulfilling all the demands we have against it. These terms are non-negotiable and final.

The choir became a roar.

Liz stepped back. Ted stepped forward.

– The police are the tyrants' bullies, he shouted. – They protect and serve the rich and powerful and their property against those with little or nothing. If we want to end the injustice and inequality dominating current human society, we must deal with the police as well, and the very foundation of cops' existence. Lately, they have more than ever exposed themselves as the decease they are, but it is, in truth only a stronger manifestation of what they have always been; an insane part of human society.

Ted stepped back. Liz stepped forward.

– Let's not forget that the asshole company residing in the building behind us is just one of many. New York City is saying no to all of them, to all their oppressive ways.

The two of them stood there, side by side, watching the gathering, including those standing with them on the low stage.

– The company behind us has its hands in everything, Frances cried. – It's an amazing image of capitalism as a whole, of exploitation personified. It does slave trade, organizing enslavement both domestic and abroad. Is has earned many fortunes paying workers minimum wages and below or not paying them at all.

Faces shifted and blurred, growing older in their vision, their surroundings changing. Ted and Liz exchanged glances and knew what the visions told them.

The gathering stayed. There were more speeches, accompanied by singing and dancing. Everyone, or almost everyone had brought food. Those that hadn't were served. There was no lack of anything.

A chopper began descending towards the building. Everyone looked up. Then, they looked at the low stage, how relaxed everyone there was.

The chopper began having trouble, long before it reached its goal. It turned around. Its failing engine returned to full capacity almost immediately. It tried flying towards its destination again. The same engine failure resumed. It left.

Triumphant laughter echoed between the towers, filling this large segment of Fifth Avenue.

There was notable activity up there in the tower. Everyone noticed, or seemed to notice, only seconds after the members of The Janus Clan present at this particular spot in time and space did.

The elevator descended. Liz and Ted and the others with enhanced senses heard it move. The elevator stopped in the lobby. Its doors slid open. Luciano Avrano and his men and women stepped out. Liz and Ted and Ethel and Fallon matched their move from the other side. They gathered around a lone table by the entrance.

– These are our nonnegotiable terms, Liz stated calmly, going straight to the point.

An aide read it, turned pale and handed it to Avrano. They studied his calm features, how he gritted his teeth almost unnoticeable. He put it down on the table, grabbed a pen from his table and signed it. He was given copies to sign, and he did that as well and that was that.

Witnesses from both sides signed, signed all copies. Fallon nodded to Liz.

– You're getting off easy, Liz remarked. – Know that you will always be on our radar. We will most certainly get back to you.

Avrano didn't voice a reply. No one added more to the «conversation». Avrano and his people turned around and returned to the elevator.

Ted and Liz and the others returned to the crowd.

Liz stepped forward.

– Don't see this as a victory. It's too insignificant for that. Rejoice in the progress we have all made within and without recently. Know that this is merely the modest beginning.

Another roar rose from the assembly.

She stepped back. Ted stepped forward. Reality began flickering before his eyes.

He saw it in glimpses, in the familiar whirl of water and wind. A giant veil was torn down and he saw everything behind it in a clear, clear shadow. He looked at the people, all the people gathered before him, and saw each and every one of them changing by the tides. Most of the hundreds gathered here would be there, as well. He spoke to them in a distinct, deliberate voice.

– Yes, this is just the beginning, people. You shouldn't expect this particular thing we have here, great and satisfying as it is to last, but see it as an exercise of what's to come. This, if we had allowed it to continue wouldn't have led anywhere, but been yet another exercise in futility. Have fun while it lasts, but don't expect it to do so. You should think years, decades ahead, directing your attention at the point when the true rebellion begins. The upcoming weeks and months will tell us even more of what is possible, what we're truly capable of. Savor it. Never let it fade from your heart.

Liz and Ted stood side by side, their shadows mingling, interacting. Ethel stood a bit to the side, studying them with a faster breath, an elevated heart rhythm, a smile hot enough to melt ice.

3

The big fires began. The first skyscraper burned without anyone coming to its aid. Dark smoke covered a large part of the city.

Big city society broke down, dissolving like snow in the desert. People left Manhattan in droves, an even, uneven stream counting millions.

He saw himself stand by Jane's grave.

– I could have saved her, he choked. – I should have!

The sight faded like a mirage.

Jane stood vibrant, alive by his side.

They watched the long row of people crossing the Brooklyn Bridge.... and so did a score of ravens.

– I love those birds, she said. – I always have!

She had changed, too, as if something had touched her, transformed her, and the obvious truth of the matter... was that something had.

They pulled back into the depth of Manhattan Island. Their fast and powerful feet brought them vast distances through basically abandoned streets towards their own territory. They crossed other territories while doing so. Some consisted of only a few individuals. He sensed them scurrying behind closed curtains. The two of them stopped in the middle of the street.

– We can help you, he said aloud. – We have extensive plans how to survive the winter, and we're more than happy to share them with you.

There was no visible response. The two of them ran on. Sounds of the urban wilderness kept reaching them from high and low. The soundscape formed patterns in his head far more detailed then his eyesight did.

They reached an area with a fairly well-organized community, where stores were still open, and everything at least resembled normal. They were met and embraced just outside an open door.

Everyone stepped inside, into the pale shadows, into a store with quite a different selection of goods compared to only weeks ago.

– We appreciate everything you've done for us, Freddie said. – The fact is, we've never been this self-sufficient before.

Ted nodded to them, to himself. He and the others had shown people, all over town, had given them proof that they didn't need governments and/or corporations to run their lives, a beyond far-reaching realization.

– We will make it easily without the sick pressure from above, he declared quietly. – When we're done, you will know beyond words that you don't need that, in any way, know that it is, at best an unnecessary burden.

He felt the pleasant heat within, without, from himself, from them. It only grew when the travelers dined with the locals.

– You… run? A woman he had never met before asked him. – You actually run?

– We do, Rahne, he confirmed. – We could have used bicycles, I guess, but we love the sense of our feet touching the ground.

She studied him hard, like they had all done at first, wondering about him. All kinds of thoughts went through her head.

– It's such a great task we've set for ourselves, Connie marveled.

They had a toast around the table. They drank.

Ted and Jane said their goodbyes, and they were on their way again.

They passed through an area where all stores had been looted, where all dummies were naked and cold. Mist filled the air to a point where all the tall buildings seemed… gone, and only their naked bones remained. They ran on Broadway, approaching Times Square, and everything except the road, the path in front of them seemed to vanish to nothing.

The seething, vital community within and around the no longer empty warehouse appeared in their vision, captured by all their senses. Everyone welcomed them, welcomed them back from their brief absence. It felt like they had been away for ages, for a brief flare of a candle.

He felt their flesh and spirit in equal measure. He felt her, felt Liz. They were together, even when they were far apart.

The world changed around them, both close and far away. The events in New York City spread like uneven rings in the water, both subtle and obvious.

The writing on the wall appeared in Los Angeles, Toronto, London and elsewhere:

COPS ARE THE TYRANTS' BULLIES. IF YOU WANT TO KILL SOMEONE, BECOME A COP.

Every single country in the world eventually had variations of that on its walls.

Several more greenhouses had been made in Ted and Jane's absence and more was on their way. They had gathered many cans of petrol in and out of their territory. It would last easily through the winter. They had some makeshift batteries available, and could easily get more if they needed them. The roofs on the warehouse and also on quite a few neighboring buildings were already covered in soil and had begun turning green. Hydroponics reached from deep below the building and to its top. The outside walls, covered by growth well before they had moved in, hid the concrete completely during early autumn. The inside heat made the plants grow faster and stay green longer. Both domestic and wild animals roamed the ground floor with impunity.

– This is… Jane breathed, her voice failing her. – This is truly something!

Gerdie and Lynn and others welcomed them even more passionately than the rest. He felt them touch him long before they actually did.

– Urban farming is the future, Abby told Liz and Ted later. – A forest is a self-contained ecological system, and there is nothing keeping us from having one in the city, any city, from transforming all cities.

One flash, and they saw a city, not this one, covered in green. The green grew on buildings, roads and all open spaces. All concrete had been submerged in it. They walked on the trail where nothing grew. They climbed the Hill. They drifted through the whistling forest and saw the old house at the center of the lake, the Fire Lake.

And the dark fire in their eyes lit up the entire room, and the walls were covered by shifting images. Abby stared weak-kneed and transfixed at them.

– You see, she whispered, – see what's coming?

– And we made you see it as well? He wondered incredulous and notably excited.

She nodded, cat paralyzing her tongue.

They watched the display on the wall, watched as tall buildings crumbled and were covered in green. The green looked more like shadows, but it was more than distinct enough for them to understand the meaning of the shifting images and sensations assaulting them behind quivering eyelids.

Several others entered the room with wide eyes, with mouths they were unable to close. They got it, got the final embers of the fire, more than enough to leave them speechless.

An eternity passed as they stood there, frozen like insects in amber, and experienced the ages to come.

4

Many chose a life below the streets, in the darkness of the warm, warm sewers.

Others stayed above, in the icy wind and thick blanket of snow.

Packs of wild dogs roamed the streets. Wild animals returned surprisingly fast. Nature once again dominated what had been more or less lifeless concrete.

– It reminds me of the jungle, Liz cried pleased to her brethren. – There is no true difference, none that matters.

They stood at the top of the tall building and looked at a world completely covered by snow, a world without end.

Ethel looked at her with her ever-inquiring eyes. She didn't voice her comment, but still spoke volumes.

– I understand what you mean, Jean mused. – The cities have always been concrete jungles, but this is a step beyond that.

She was visibly pregnant, like all females except Liz. She and Patrick exchanged constant fond glances. They were obviously taken by each other.

– Manhattan has become a desolate place, Ted said, – like it is supposed to be.

– It's beautiful, Eloise breathed.

She stayed close to Liz and Ted, like Jane also did, never truly leaving their side, except when training with the sword, doing so harder than anyone else.

They heard and sensed her as moved and cut the air with her blade, and they visualized her various shapes in their head. That didn't prove difficult. That didn't either.

She returned to them, bowed down before them.

– Remember your lesson, Ted stressed. – Being too dedicated is just as dangerous as being lax.

– I will, Ror Ken, she swore. – I will never forget.

The name spoken aloud cut far deeper into him than the sword would have done.

Her story with them ran deep, even deeper than they had initially suspected.

Everyone except those on guard duty gathered in front of the fireplace in the great hall in the evening, the big fireplace brightening the entire room, casting everything in Shadow. The inside of the old, no longer dusty warehouse had been further transformed far beyond the modest beginning. This was one of several fireplaces. There was no trouble finding dry wood. They picked that up in a wide circle around the surrounding buildings. They hadn't had any encroachment on their territory for weeks, and the last hadn't really been very serious, hadn't felt like a threat at all. Manhattan had become so big, so very big. There was easily room enough for everyone, everyone left.

Ethel rubbed her belly, speaking to Liz.

– It's such a strange sensation, like something not really you at all growing within you, a strange being taking you over.

Goddesses become their daughters, Liz thought unprompted.

Ted and Liz ran across the island, patrolling an enormous area well outside their territory, well within their domain. They visited the other communities, making closer ties to most of them, getting to know its people intimately, joining yet another circle within a circle.

– It's quite amazing what has happened, a boy, a young man said with big, dreamy eyes. – What does the outside world make of it, I wonder.

– Is the outside world still there? Another chuckled amazed.

It certainly didn't feel like it just then, or almost all the time, but the dreams, the visions brought them closer to it, even though daily and nightly life did not. They had no trouble seeing beyond their current circumstances. The two of them ran on the edge of the island, all the way around it, feeding as they moved.

– Something is scratching my innards, he mused.

The almost formal language didn't fool her. She put a hand on his shoulder.

– You don't have to worry about me, he insisted.

She moved close to him, rubbing her lips seductively against his.

– I want us, the two of us to have children together, she said softly.

– I want that, too, he said.

– I can see him, she said, – see them.

One half closing of the eyes, and he could, too, pairs of happy and sinister fireeyes playing with other children.

– We know a bit more of what we're capable of, now, she mused. – We know more about our ultimate potential, and that we're not alone.

– It's amazing, isn't it, how Ethel and Patrick's powers fit each other like a glove? He said, a muse on her muse. – She sees long term and he short term, between the moments. Together they're…

– … a force to be reckoned with.

The thought brought both joy and dread.

They reached the Twin Towers. The buildings looked even more ghostly, ethereal than others they had passed. Lots of windows were missing from the lobby to the top. The two of them stepped inside, taking in both the mood and the physical properties of the place. One thought, and they moved faster. They ran up the stairs in the North Tower, testing their endurance. It was tested. They did feel tired, even exhausted after a while, but kept running. Their heart hammered so hard and fast in the chest that they feared it would burst, but they kept running. Their feet felt like jelly and a horrible metal taste filled their mouth. They kept running.

They Rose, and imagined it felt easier the further they ran, even as pieces of vomit erupted into their mouth. It felt, occasionally like their feet didn't even touch the steps. They were swaying in the wind at the Windows of the World restaurant at the top. She dried a bit of vomit from her lips and laughed heartily, looking at him with endearing eyes.

– That felt so good, she said.

Most of the windows were broken. It felt like they were standing outdoors. It didn't faze them. It did, on the contrary add to their enjoyment. He found himself join in on her laughter, and her joy, in turn grew even more pronounced.

She walked to him slowly, showing off for him, making absolutely no secret of her feelings. It didn't feel rushed or contrived in any way, but so very, very real.

He lifted her up and held her, held around her thighs.

– I feel like I'm flying, she cried.

She bent down and kissed him. He let go of her. She slid down his body until they stood face to face, close enough to burn.

They stood close to the edge, looking at Manhattan from various vantage points.

– One of the biggest cities on Earth has been brought to its knees, and no one in establishment circles have any idea how. People will never stop wondering about what happened here.

– Let them! Let them stay clueless.

The loud and defiant laughter spread across the quiet city, and also reached the Jersey side of the Hudson River where the hectic activity never seemed to cease. The heavy presence of troops, of military personnel was not hard for them to detect, not hard at all.

– Perhaps we should tell them, he said. – Perhaps we will eventually.

– That will be the day, she snickered.

She kept going for a considerable time… until she stopped and looked amazed at him with her big eyes. He saw the whirl of wind and water in her eyes.

They walked to the other three sides. One building had caught fire again. Some of the others were smoldering ruins. Others again looked pretty much unscathed, not visibly changed at all compared to months ago.

The tall buildings no longer seemed to pierce the sky, but appeared more like tiny sticks they could just grab and tear from the ground.

Smiles brightened their faces anew.

Chapter 17

Liz woke up afraid. Even all the warm bodies surrounding her could not chase the chill away. The dream lingered, stayed with her long after she had woken up.

Sometimes there were riders, in the early morning light, in the twilight of early evening.

– WHY? Why are you doing this to me? I've done nothing.

A boy that sometimes was a girl was chained to a post in the wilderness.

– WHY? ARE YOU REALLY THAT STUPID, ASKING THAT QUESTION? The voice of the city people, the voice with no form, no substance behind it snarled viciously at him. – WHY NOT?

The other faces filled her vision and didn't look real, and then she realized that they weren't. She walked among them like a specter, even as she slowly realized that they were the specters.

She woke up in Central Park alone, isolated, abandoned, shaking in fright. There were no other people there. She couldn't sense anyone anywhere. David Gidman's triumphant laughter thundered in her sore ears, and she imagined she glimpsed him in the mist not far away.

Lee woke up with a frown on his face, terror gnawing at his bones.

Liz stumbled through a ghostly landscape. No matter how hard she struggled, she couldn't walk right. She turned a corner, and the mist turned even more pronounced, even more solid. It felt like soup, like she could almost taste it.

She imagined she hung in chains in a cell, her captor staring at her with his patient predator eyes.

The image changed. Ted stood right in front of her, but he clearly didn't spot her, even though she did see how he turned restless and aware and noticed something. But she couldn't reach him, and she wondered why not, and anxiety, even panic broke through the surface of her eyes.

She stood frozen on an open road, free of chains, fearing they were still there. The scenery changed again. She found herself in a giant hall, standing in front of a man sitting on a throne, kneeling humbly before him. A flash rocked her. She recognized the man, the relative with the cold fireeyes.

Lee and Lydia woke up in a ghostly landscape on Times Square. They saw no people, no people anywhere. Lydia pulled closer to him, an instinctive move she instantly regretted and tried to amend. He attempted to comfort her, to convey that it didn't matter, but he wasn't very convincing.

They fought themselves on their feet, their wobbly feet.

– What has happened? She asked stricken, all the calm and confidence she had achieved lately gone. – How did we end up here?
– I don't know, he said slowly. – I don't remember.
He tried, searching for his last memory before this.
– We were at the… in the training hall, he said. – At least I think so.
The various clocks still on walls gave them no help. They had been frozen at a given time long ago. They hadn't used watches for months.
They started walking, doing so with growing urgency. Straining eyes searched for people, but they spotted no one, and they knew there were residents in this area.
– It's… empty, she said with numb lips.
He looked around, looked hard, not for people, but at the edges, noticing a distinct shimmering in the air. They began moving, without making the decision on a conscious level. When they rushed past the buildings, the buildings looked in glimpses… like they weren't there, or at least like they were transparent.
– Do you see it? He asked.
She nodded solemnly.
They closed in on what was supposed to be their home. There were only more empty streets, more emptiness in a place that only recently had been teeming with activity and life and fire and happiness and excitement and…
The two of them, holding, clutching hands turned the final corner. A gray, cold darkness met them. They had no trouble seeing. The darkness was easily penetrable, as if it wasn't darkness at all. Shadow and mist surrounded them. The road they walked seemed fluid, more air than solid ground, more ether than actual matter. They stepped into the main hall. Everything was there, all the furniture, all the setup, but no flesh and blood, no people. They felt an icy wind penetrate their flesh and freeze their bones.
She had dinner at some cafeteria somewhere, not certain if it was the past, present or future. On one level, it felt very real, felt rooted in the present, with all its scents, sights and sensations. On another… it didn't.
Looking outside, she saw something at the very least resembling a picturesque English town. A man entered a store at the other side of the street. She grabbed Ted's arm and pulled him on his feet.
– It's him, she insisted. – We're here!
They rushed outside and across the street, and into the other building. The man stood at the counter and spoke to an older man.
– No, not two-hundred and twenty-four, he said exasperated. – Two-hundred and twenty *dash* four. I wrote to you. My name is Isaiah Asteroth, and I wrote to you and described everything in detail.

A jolt of excitement surged through Liz, even as everything, including Ted faded away around her.

She realized she was adrift… in time, and wondered what had happened, what had caused it, if anything had. A woman imagining herself to be Elizabeth Warren, fearing she was not, cast long, anxious glanced around her, desperately attempting to catch it, catch its vicious flow.

The band played on in another large concert hall not too long into the future. She glimpsed Linsey standing there grinning, doing his thing, enjoying himself immensely.

– Oh, no, she mumbled, – you won't get away. Fate waits for no one, neither man nor god.

She raised her head, sniffing the air before she realized what she was doing. There was a scent, one she could remember, but not place. She reached out with her power, and got nothing but an eerie feeling, an echo baffling her. A second, more focused attempt and a third and a fourth brought no further illumination. The stench of her own sweat flooded her, and she shuddered in dismay, and didn't understand. Her own scent should not have bothered her. It never had, at least not since early childhood, before she had found her footing.

Eyes focused on one point in the room, at the coffee machine. It suddenly turned distinctly louder, its sound practically flooding her eardrums. It slipped away from her and appeared no more real than the prop it was.

She fought to catch herself, get her bearings, catch her breath. The thought alone was sufficient. Her breath became visible in the air, far more solid than the table where she rested her arms, and the chair where she rested her ass.

She began her preparations without really pondering the issue, putting herself in a light trance and concentrating on sharpening her focus. The first part of the spell flowed effortlessly from her lips. Her distress remained, but she didn't allow it to hold her back. The spell began growing her awareness and changing her surroundings, at the very least her perception of it, and she confirmed her growing suspicions.

The room and everything and everyone around her faded away, rearranging into something new. She found herself face to face with Lee and Lydia at what resembled the dusty warehouse. She watched them closely, and they did the same with her.

– Are you… real? Lydia asked with a brittle voice.

That made Liz smile. They stepped forward and touched each other. It felt solid, felt true.

– There *is* truth in flesh, Liz stated.

There were spirits, ghosts, revenants around them. She didn't have to strain herself to sense their presence. They held no threat to her.

But the wind whispered, brought danger, and she could not localize it or identify it.

– What happened? Lee asked anxiously.

– I… don't know, Liz replied.

There was a huge, vast abyss where her memory was. She could not recall what had happened. It was mundane dust, blowing in the wind.

– This looks like… it's all just… scenery, Lee said, – less real than a movie set.

– It's the shadow world, Lydia said startled, pulling the name from memory, from ancient life.

They both looked at Liz. The name itself brought a flow of memory, of acknowledgement to her.

– We should not be here, Liz said. – I don't know how we got here or how we can be here at all.

She felt it behind half closed eyes, but could not access it. Something… blocked her.

Her often spoken words echoed louder in the enclosed room that was not a room.

She struggled in vain to catch fleeting thoughts. All of them eluded her. Pain charged through her flesh. Thoughts hurt. Giant pearls of sweat formed on her brow.

– Things in the shadow world are incomplete copies, mirrors of those in the real world, she said slowly, – but not we, not human beings. We are complete or should be… should have been. If we're truly on the other side, we should have been bombarded with thought, with pure thought. Our Shadow is our eternal self, a vast, unrestrained being.

She sounded as timid and fearful as she felt. There was no hiding from the truth in this place not a place.

There was something… she couldn't, just couldn't grasp. She looked at her hand, the hand she was unable to close. It felt numb, almost dead, glowing in unhealthy colors. Something tightened around the wrist. It hurt. She choked. They looked astonished at her.

– Something is wrong, she sniffed. – Something is very wrong.

They attempted to comfort her, alleviate her rare distress.

– We stayed, didn't we? We stayed this time? We left early once, but not this time?

The prodded memories returned easily to her. She reexperienced the comradery, the growing community and fierce sense of common purpose. She and Ted had talked about leaving early, but they had never done more than talk. They had been pulled in, like the rest, into the vortex of radical thought and action. She knew they would never forget these months, no matter how distant they grew in time and space.

They nodded solemnly to her.

– You sure did, Lydia, responded empathically. – You taught us even more great things about the world and everything in it. I believed your teaching was complete the first month, but that was a mere appetizer compared to what was coming. And you have only just begun to teach humanity as a whole.

The girl's appreciation soothed Liz a bit, just a bit, enough for her to somewhat regain her bearings.

She once more reached out with her senses. Any attempt was returned to her tenfold, like a slap in the face, and she imagined she heard laughter, and she couldn't even assume that with any certainty. The chills kept flowing down her spine.

– We're caught in… in a prison, she stated. – Someone did this to us.

She felt the danger in every nerve. It was imminent and overwhelming.

– Take my hands!

They tried. Lee grabbed her right hand, and it was solid, but when Lydia tried grabbing the left, it passed straight through it. They looked stunned at her. Lydia tried grabbing higher up on the arm, but the entire limb was gone. It was only when she grabbed the shoulder, she was able to hold on.

The contact with them both strengthened her. It still felt hard, like walking through mud, but she started getting glimpses… beyond their immediate surroundings. The walls and buildings appeared increasingly like what they truly were, unreal props in a chaotic reality.

There was something else. Her arm… it didn't hurt. It felt… good. Power flowed through it. But she couldn't catch it. It flowed through her. She felt like a leak pipe, an open wound. It did hurt. She imagined a thousand knives were ripping her apart.

There was an echo, one growing stronger, not weaker, and she had not heard the original sound.

– This is insane, she mumbled. – This is…

She could not hold on to Lee and Lydia for long. At least she was not supposed to, without draining them of life. But that wasn't happening. The contact did strengthen her, but the transfer of power was slow, ineffective. She frowned and tilted her head.

– Do you hear that?

The other two shook their head.

She heard it, heard the screech of the ravens. First, there was only a remote, almost inaudible sound. Then, one moment, two later, she heard them loud and clear. Their… song penetrated her from toe to head, and joy filled her equally hard, and she realized she had been hearing it all the time without being aware of it.

Memory returned to her in piecemeal flashes, flashes within flashes. She remembered walking down the street with Abby, Lee and Lydia when everything turned into a jumble, a jigsaw puzzle making her bleed. A wind cold and dangerous was blowing. It felt like the threat was imminent and everywhere around her.

– Stop!

All her defense mechanisms kicked in simultaneously. Fear touched her. She grabbed Abby's hand, not truly conscious of the move at all.

Abby's power… touched the shadowland. With her power added to hers, Liz could, too.

A bubble embraced all four. Whatever the attack might be, it bounced harmlessly off the sizzling protective energy. Liz felt the power. It burned within her. Abby cried out in pain. Liz looked stunned at her as she faded away, first her body, then her arm. Liz cried out in pain. The energies shook her hard. Lee and Lydia remained within the bubble. It didn't fade, but grew in strength and size. The pain grew so bad that she feared her arm would be torn from her body. There was another burst of horrible pain, and her consciousness was blown out like a candle. Darkness followed darkness as she reexperienced her jaunting, or what felt like jaunting. She realized it was all in her mind, her powerful mind, and that she and the two children never had been more than a couple of steps away from each other.

They stood at the same spot where it had begun, mere moments ago. People's movement had first slowed down to a crawl, and then stopped altogether. A squeezed hand appeared in Liz's bigger hand, then the rest of Abby.

– Hold onto my hand, Abby shouted, as if she fought to be heard in a noisy storm. – Don't let go!

Her flimsy hand.

Lewis Warren's skin crackled with power. He soaked up the ambient energies as well.

Liz looked confused at Abby, finally comprehending what the other woman had shouted at her for ages.

It was over in a second or less. In a tiny moment, she felt godhood flood her and once again dissipate across time and space. That was all. In that moment was eternity.

The bubble dissolved around them. She sensed no threat anywhere,

anywhere close, and caught herself in wondering if there ever had been any. Fear touched her still.

Hand let go of hand. All strength left Liz's limbs. She dropped to the ground and lost consciousness long before she hit it. The fall felt endless, through a never-ending void.

2

Sweat burned her, soaked her. The legs on the bed had broken long ago. The bed had broken long ago. She rested on a mat.

Ted sat by her side.

She embraced him in fiery joy.

– I'm here? She choked. – I'm really here?

He did answer her in a manner of speaking, confirming what she already knew.

– I heard our song, heard it all the time. I was lost, so lost, but it led me back.

She still got flashes from time to time, but they were faint, unthreatening.

Now, she realized, now, she was rooted.

She felt it in every nerve, the pleasant calm, the quiet urgency, knowing it was temporary.

– My eyes, she mumbled, – my eyes are so big.

When she fell asleep again, the sweating had practically stopped, and she knew she would wake up fairly relaxed. She floated away in the great darkness with a smile on her face.

3

Growing bellies grew big. Snow fell again, then lots of rain, as winter turned to spring.

Winter had felt eternal, but now it felt like a dream, an enduring one, but a dream none the less.

Many small drums beat in various parts of the extended village called Manhattan.

People heard it, in the rest of New York and the world. Many others danced to its tune. Many in many cities were beaten up and arrested when the police attacked their peaceful dance, and many grew angry and fierce.

Tall fires rose against the heavens, the many heavens above, below. On the dark, moonless night without electricity anywhere, they felt to the gathered human beings like the sun itself had descended on them and kept them company.

People near and far sought to Central Park this night, this Great Darkness. It was pervasive, penetrating every synapse in their brain, every cell in their body. It more than resembled a migration. The ants dreaming they were the Universe, the universes dreaming they were ants arrived in groups and rows and as single beings. Everyone clearly had a set destination in mind. That stayed visible in their eyes and in every movement they made.

Ravens filled the sky, even the air. They stared at everyone with their black eyes, and the human beings returned their watch in fear and helpless fascination. The dark mass of flapping wings marked the spot more than anything else.

The overgrown lawns in Central Park were filled up with the migrants approaching a distinct area within the giant green place. They crossed Bow Bridge and entered The Ramble, the no longer so domesticated forest in droves.

The migrants, the walkers in the night settled, not settling within the area, removing the final pieces of fences, fitting it to their purpose, to nature.

The talks, the excited conversations began.

– The people of the world see us, Carla shouted in glee. – They know what we are doing, and they support us and our cause.

She burned in the attention of everyone present. Everyone noticed her the moment they arrived, noticed then what they had, in truth noticed and grown aware of long ago.

A giant drum beat somewhere, beat like a heart, the choir of every heart present.

Carla Wolf sat at the center of the wide circle, surrounded by rows upon rows of human beings.

She spoke. They heard her soft, powerful voice. She paused. They heard the drum.

– The Phoenix began as a small trickle at the top of a mountain far away and long ago, she began. – Sometimes it moves like a slow-moving river, sometimes like a waterfall, but it keeps floating downwards, towards the distant ocean, the vast, warm ocean that is both its destination and its path and origin. It might pause or slow down on that path, but it will never be stopped…

Round and round the broken circle went, turning an infinity both inwards and outwards, sideways and upwards and downwards. Everyone remained close to each other, like the dancing flames. Every tribal village on Manhattan Island early in the year nineteen-eighty became one that night, that Great Darkness lasting an eternity.

Food was made and served between the many trees, the denser forest that had grown without supervision for six months. The trees became part of the circle. The circle became part of the trees, of the deep, deep forest.

Caroline glanced at Rita again, looking away when she caught Liz's attention.

– I'm not…

– Don't be silly, sweetie. The way you look at her, leaves no doubt about what you're feeling.

Caroline bowed her head.

– My parents will never approve.

– You will never go home again, you know that, right? Your parents will never again decide what you will think and do. Embrace your true independence. Live it!

Caroline looked at Rita again, and this time she kept looking. She glanced at Liz, but Liz had turned away for a talk with Adrienne. Caroline's feet moved, rushed her towards Rita. Liz watched her as she engaged Rita, as she asked her for a dance, as determination flooded her as Rita smiled and accepted the invitation, as hormones kicked in and passion rose like a storm.

The Phoenix took one step forward, and they imagined they could glimpse its wings of fire and Shadow.

– You are here, Liz shouted, her soft voice cracking eardrums throughout the gathering. – The battle is won. You will always be here, even as you move on. You will remember in times of joy, in times of despair and sorrow and rage.

The Phoenix took one step back, one step forward.

– In spite of our visibility, Ted said with a quiet voice carrying far, – we're still like ghosts in the modern world, but that won't last.

He paused a bit, and everyone realized amazed that they held their breath.

His speech changed to become harsh, guttural.

– Witches are by nature agents of change, but the world has never seen anything like us.

They felt it, he knew they did, knew he was talking about all of them. Pride coursed through them. The good mood persisted when they gathered around the fire later with a thought they all experienced as real; that there was only one fire.

Excited minds communicated with small, excited thoughts. Ted heard one group talk, and he knew Carla and Liz and Ethel, and several others were listening in as well.

– It is weird, isn't it, the boy said to the girl, – that none of us believe there is a God? At the very least it's statistically unlikely.

– You're correct, the girl acknowledged willingly. – I haven't heard a single one of us declare belief in any god, and I'm convinced they would. It is weird.

– We know, of course, Ethel pointed out quite unnecessary, – know the stories, know what any god-fearing fool doesn't.

That slipped away like everything slipped away. Water, mercury flowed on any surface, any small and big rock or burning skin.

Liz relaxed in Ted's arms. It felt good to be there. The solemn smile stayed on her face.

– I can see us. We're together. Our reign will last a thousand years. We will have all the time in the world.

The fires warmed his back, his front, his sides, his almost smooth skin.

– It's a good night to be Liz and Ted Warren, a good night to be alive.

She knew his ambiguity, the one inevitably diminishing the good feeling.

– There are very few who can even begin to understand the hunger, the dark passions ruling us, she stated empathically, – but there are those who do, those sharing the path with us.

She included everyone in her embrace. They felt it, and their collective gasp made the fire grow further in intensity and size. It was an amazing sight.

– We're ancient beings, he said softly, everybody hearing him easily. – We're birds flying in the dark, the true agents of change finally knowing ourselves. We're the Janus Clan. We're the Shadowwalkers. World, behold our Wrath!

The two of them stood up and began putting clothes on. So did Jane and Eloise. It was a strange sight, even in their extensive experience of weird. It could have been an ending, but it didn't feel like that, didn't feel like that at all.

– They will want to tame you. Don't let them, let them make you forget, not intellectually, not emotionally what you've learned the last few months, but instead make it guide you for the rest of your life!

– For the rest of your life and beyond, Eloise cried with undiluted passion. – Never forget. Keep learning to remember.

There was silence, a strange and eerie sensation brought by the wind, cast further by the wind.

– Liz and Ted Warren returned to civilization to live it up, and they and their knights did, beyond any expectation, and will keep doing so. My friends, it may take five years, ten years, but we will be back.

Her dark grin burned everyone.

People in the gathering shared to a point their visions and sensations.

Loud and wild cheers echoed through the modest forest.

– We will take a swim, Ted remarked. – It's a great night for that. No one will object to us taking a refreshing nightly swim, right?

The quiet, pleasant and encouraging laughter followed the four as they turned and walked away. It followed them out of the park and through empty, ghostly city streets towards Hudson River. It didn't take them long to reach it, not long at all.

The long walk seemed like mere moments to them.

They remained with the others. They always would. There was no goodbye.

The two fireeyes glimpsed the hundreds still in the park, in the growing forest, and so, by default did the two traveling with them.

– I'm looking so much forward to watch people's reactions when you inadvertently share your visions with them. They will have no clue to what's happening, and fear they're going insane.

The chuckles echoed eerily at the slowly flowing surface.

They cast a brief look at the other side of the broad river, at the still insane activity.

– I imagine they don't sleep much over there, Jane mused. – Their nightmares give them no peace.

The good, exuberant mood persisted the last few steps to the waters. A shiver passed through the four, and it wasn't caused by the chill in the air. Ted and Liz grabbed each other's hands. The other two joined in. There was some transference of energy, but not enough to matter, to significantly drain them. It was like a kiss, a tender caress.

They jumped, and Hudson River kissed and caressed them, as they submerged themselves into its depths, and swam those depths with strong, enduring strokes. Liz and Ted took it easy, and Jane and Eloise had no trouble keeping up.

They reached The Dark River. It was very distinct, an easily identified moment. First, they glimpsed the bottom, then they saw it and the path ahead abundantly clear. The current took hold of them and didn't let go. They willingly submitted to its power. It brought them far away.

And beyond it all, beyond the path they pictured so vigorously in their head…

… awaited the Dragon.

Author's word

The past is with us, wherever we go, no matter how hard we try putting it to rest.

Yes, we remember places we've never been, events we've never experienced. We're taught to forget, no matter how much we need to remember.

Cities like New York are steeped in memories far older than the cities themselves. They don't forget, even if its people believe they do.

I started writing this story in my head more than forty years ago, like I did with all the books in the Janus Clan series. It has evolved a bit, but basically stayed the same. The scenery is basically a result of my visit in 1980, with a few blanks filled in later. My visit to York in England a few years later brought additional scenery to the story. I made the connection easily, in more ways than one. The story practically fledged out itself.

New York City didn't really make much of an impact on me, not compared to London and other cities later. Tall, giant spires have never impressed me, but have, on the contrary been a rather bland detail in a major city. Everything truly important, the way I see it, happens on street level, where people breathe and gasp and exist and live.

I always add something unplanned while I'm writing a given story, mostly details, but also broader strokes, and I did that here as well. I knew where to start, knew more than a bit of the middle and knew the end. Liz and Ted seek out long lost family members, while dealing with what they can never forget, and in the process meet quite a few people important to their past, present and future.

The tapestry is painted further with both broad and narrow strokes. We are halfway there, now, and the story pauses a bit, before moving on, gearing up for the end of the long walk. The first ten years or so have been told. The next thirty is waiting just around the corner, in the mist and the shadows far ahead.

And at the end of the long desert walk… awaits the dragon.

2018-12-12
Printed version ready 2019-01-13
Final proofreading complete March 5, 2019

The Werewolf of Locus Bradle

Three years have passed, three years of relative tranquility.

Wales and the southwestern parts of England, the misty hills, the wet moors, the Cornwall coast are steeped in legends and stories.

Somewhere there a beast is awakening, rising from its dark slumber, to visit its wrath upon the modern world. The city of Padstow is ravaged by death, a killer tearing to pieces its victims, leaving only parts of the body, enjoying human flesh. Fate has not been kind to Padstow and its inhabitants in recent years. The economy is in recession. The tourists, once the lifeblood of the area, are now staying away, far away.

Old friends call Liz and Ted Warren, paranormal investigators and adventurers, to the city. They arrive in a place paralyzed by fear and suspicion. Blood flows in Padstow. They can smell it, from the highest tower to the lowest cellar, as above so below. Many things, many people hide there, some they know, some they don't. But as they peel ever-thicker layers off the blanket hiding the town's secrets they're also closing in on their own riddles. They meet a man who can tell them everything, everything they've spent their lives wondering about. Fangs and claws of the Earth are tearing open the most confined of caskets.

Padstow is the world, and the world is the stage where they must wage their battle.

Other published and upcoming novels by **Amos Keppler** from **Midnight Fire Media**:

The Janus Clan - (ten chapters about the Wild Man in the modern world, a world balancing on a razor's edge):

The Defenseless
The Slaves
Birds Flying in the Dark
At the End of the Rainbow
Lewis of Modern York
The Werewolf of Locus Bradle
The Valley of Kings
Eye in the Sky
The Iron Cage
Phoenix Green Earth

The Defenseless

The two rivers meet and join in the city of Denver, becoming one...

The two dark brothers, growing up with their sister Linda in a mundane, average suburb, a place well entrenched in modern United States and the world, have since their moment of birth been at odds with the world... and with each other.

Mike and Ted Cousin are not who they are. There is a mystery here, one of birth and upbringing, one of fate. Violence and death, blood and fire follow them all the days of their lives. The fire is resting somewhere inside... waiting for the Spark.

Their parents know something, but are not telling it. The policeman Mark Stewart and their aunt Trudy do, too. Everybody knows something, pieces of the whole, but nobody knows the whole truth, nobody telling it.

The ancient power is returning to the world, a world massively suffering from physical and spiritual poison, on the brink of collapse and a collective tailspin suicide run without its like in human history.

Magick is returning from its long exile. Thus begins the story of the wild beasts rising from their ashes.

The Spark is struck, horrible and terrifying.

First book of ten in the Janus Clan series: Ten stories of the wild man in the modern world, forty years of wandering, before the Phoenix is rising from its ashes.

ISBN 978-82-91693-08-8

Earth and sky, day and Night, first story:

Season of the Witch

Lori is happily married. She and her husband of twenty years have three great children together. They have nice jobs and nice salaries, a nice house in a nice neighborhood. Life is good

Lori wakes up one morning, soaked in sweat after a particularly disturbing dream. Then she takes a good, hard look at herself in the mirror.

The world is no longer the same. She is no longer the same. The happy housewife and mother and company executive no longer exist. Suddenly familiar and pleasant surroundings are neither familiar nor pleasant. Increasingly disturbing events are pulling her ever further away from what she has known, confirming that the world has changed, that she has changed. She meets new people, people further opening her eyes to the world, to the world she has denied for so long. Perhaps her previous life and neighborhood and job and all weren't so great, after all?

Lori is cast brutally out of her world and headlong into the next. The people she encounters, both friend and foe are very much like herself a new breed, seekers in a world where seekers are frowned at, at best, and at worst hounded and hunted. Lori doesn't fit in in the old world anymore, and the new is still not quite there yet, emerging, like its people from the chrysalis, the dark corners and shadows of modern society.

They are the emerging Earth and Sky, Day and Night, and the world will never be the same.

ISBN 978-82-91693-22-4

EARTH AND SKY, DAY AND NIGHT

Existential horror.
(ten stand-alone, interrelated stories
about the beginning, the returned Power,
at the twilight of the modern world)
(novels, TV, Internet, serializing)

Season of the Witch
Resurrection Dreams
Burning in Gray
A Night in Hyde Park
Dead Woman Walking
The Twilight Storm
The Path of Shadows
The Returned Power
Winds of Change
(blowing wild)
The New Barbarians

ShadowWalk

The world is changing. They know this, in their core of cores, where everything moves and shifts. Night and fire have followed them all the days of their lives.

What they carry inside has always scared them, always intrigued them...

They have always felt different, apart from the crowd. And here, now, they get the confirmation they have always wanted, always yearned for, that they are truly different, a breed apart. The metamorphosis begins. Their minds, their bodies are changing in shocking and unpredictable ways, as what's on the inside is brought to the outside. And as they themselves are changing they are also changing the world.

Danger awaits them, Life awaits them, in the small, backward New England town. Magick and Mystery may be found beneath unturned stones.

People, young and old, are descending on the small, insignificant town of Northfield, New England.

Boys and girls, students at the school of Life, Seekers, yearning for what's different, what's hidden.

They're seeking within and without, high and low.

And here, in this dusty, remote place they're finding it, turning the stone, finding the strength within themselves to be themselves, to break out of confines, to the world beyond. And in time, after the initial, tentative steps, pushing down paths new and undreamed of.

And the present-day order sees them for what they are... Agents of Change, a threat to any establishment, any imposed reality. The heatwave, the worst in living memory, is nothing compared to the boiling within the human heart. The Indian Summer heralds the twilight of mankind.

ISBN 978-82-91693-12-5

Your Own Fate

From the Book of Fate:

In the Book of Fate there is everything. Every incident, all times, everything that has been, that is, that will ever be, everything that might be, everything that could have been.

But who is writing it? Who is penning it? Who is turning page by page, too many to be counted, blowing in the wind? Does it perhaps write itself, with a pen moving across the yellow sheets? Or is it a hand moving the pen, one unseen, one stretching back into the past, back to the time before everything was created, creating itself from nothing?

Timothy Joyce is an enigma, a man without a past, appearing from nowhere, to go on a rampage in an astonished world.

Jeremy Zahn is hunting Timothy Joyce. It seems like he has always been hunting him, from old London, from the island of angels, where it is said they met for the first time, to the city of angels, California, the new world.

Here, on this shaky ground, following confrontations spanning the globe, its time and space the two will fight for the last time.

And the world is watching, its people shivering in their frozen hearts.

ISBN 978-82-91693-05-7

Night on Earth

This is said to be the age of enlightenment and reason...
A culmination of thousands of years' development and illumination.

The hunters are dying off, they say. Their day is done, in favor of the new, enlightened time of neon lights, technology and civilization.

But a hunter is stalking the streets of London. A creature without form, eyes and skin. In a city on the brink of chaos, of social and economic collapse, it is stalking cops, killing them in ever more horrible ways. Sheila Watts is a hunter. She's a cop.

Sheila is lost, losing herself further by the second. She's losing herself, finding herself, as she's closing in on the creature of the night, as it is closing in on her.

Sheila Watts can taste the sweet blood in her mouth...

ISBN 978-82-91693-07-1

Dreams Belong to the Night

New, emerging urban rebel guerilla groups, freedom fighters, called terrorists by enraged authorities are overwhelming Europe.

What is, in truth terrorism? Who does it to whom?
How much can a human being take of bondage, injustice, degradation and destruction of spirit... before being fed up?

Present day society is a wound not closing.
In a modern world society destroying everything making life worth living there are those, who, through coincidence and fate, have decided not to take it anymore.
And as they are making that decision, together and as individuals, they are also starting on a journey, a journey back to humanity's roots.
Judith, Sivert, Kim, Willhelm, Anya and many more.
A handful of people against an entire world.

This is their story...

ISBN 978-82-91693-11-8

Experience the defeat of civilization, of tyranny, of anti-life in:

Thunder Road - Book One: Ice and Fire

Damon Terrill is the Storm Child. He is born into the life hostile civilization's last years, as humanity starts on its return to nature, return to Life.

It started with the need for Freedom, the passion of life, and went from there, in new and unforeseen directions, in one, final attempt to get it right.

– It's the human being's path through life, Anya told them. – What challenges, destroys and strengthens it.

The Thunder Road is making a turn. It always is. Burning Ice, Biting Flame...that is how life began. And that's how it will renew itself. No matter where humans are going. And now the blade is laid bare, ready to be tempered once more. Humanity's idiocy, their hubris has finally and fully been visited upon them. The End Time, the final hour, Ragnarok is here. The sea is rising, winds are increasing in strength. A thoroughly rotten society is collapsing under its own weight.

Humans are natural nomads. Now they become nomads anew, pulled together in small tribes once more, pulled into a fellowship of fate in a final, desperate attempt to survive, to live the life humans are born to live. Finally. Damon, Anya, Andrè, Myriam and many others have started on their way Home.

ISBN 978-82-91693-21-7

Alarums of reality

The end is the beginning. The beginning is the end…

The once so great Caine Manor has become a ruin, one only fit for carrion birds and revenants. No one but daring children and crazed souls dare breach its confines.

The proud and shiny Caine Manor is an outstanding example of renovated architecture at the heart of the city.

Looking at the building, the house, resembling a castle, hidden in a strange, illuminated mist, squinting your eyes, it's often hard to tell what's illusion and what's real. Reality shifts and burns around the Caine Manor, either ruin or proud house, reaching out with strands of night and fire to the surrounding areas and to existence at large. It is the center, or at least one center, in an ever-shifting world.

Is Chloe Webster dead or alive? Is Marion Dexter? Is Marlon Caine? Or David Fallon Somby? Are they perhaps both? Or neither? What is the world? Is it a brick, a hard, impenetrable wall or closer to something akin to mist and shadow? Existence might make sense, to us, to them, but only in glimpses, only in passing, beyond a corner somewhere ahead. They may wonder. They may die clueless. Because they don't know, don't know why terror strikes them and makes their heart beat like a sledgehammer in their chest.

From a place unbound by time and space alarums of reality are reaching out to touch and ultimately engulf them all.

ISBN 978-82-91693-13-2

FALLING

She can not rid herself of it, the sense of falling. It is lurking in her dreams, every time she looks at the world from the edge of her vision. The old, cruel oracle at the fair did not tell her anything she did not know.

Janet of the Blue Flame is born a sorcerer, one with powers of the mind and the body far exceeding those of most others, one in a line reaching far back in antiquity.

In this modern age she, like many others is virtually unaware of the potential resting in the murky parts of her being. She may know, deep down, but she is not aware… not until the day Malone the Sorcerer comes for her.

Malone is dark and powerful. His skills and might are unquestionable. His power speaks to her, to her murky depths, roaring in her consciousness like a storm. Janet is only Sweet Sixteen and is overwhelmed in Malone's presence. When he offers to train her, for her to become his apprentice she consents with an eagerness of a mule chasing the carrot. He is everything she is not, everything she has ever dreamed of being. She leaves her friends and family, leaves behind everything she knows and joins the mighty and enigmatic sorcerer on his quest. His harsh teaching takes her far away, into the nine realms and beyond.

He gives her her devoirs, gives her everything he promised and more, wishing her good luck, leaving her to pick up the pieces of her life.

Janet of the Blue Flame is ready for the world.

ISBN 978-82-91693-19-4

AFTERGLOW DUST

She has died a million times…

Someone is stalking her. She knows this, knows it at the edge of her vision, where nothing really is seen, only dreamed. Her nightmares give her no peace. She turns and looks behind her. There is nothing there her eyes can see. But in the wind, she can hear the wailing cry, the cry of Death. Sniffing that wind, she can smell the blood in her nostrils.

There is truth in flesh, they say… and there is truth in that. But there is also substance in what cannot be seen, cannot be touched. Claws and fangs cut ceaselessly through the night, looking for her. A silent cry is heard in the dark.

Someone… or something is stalking her.

She remembers a kind touch and a slap in the face, and hardly anything else.

Kathryn Caldwell is Afterglow, a woman of undetermined age, a strange creature wandering the dark corners of the world. Something happened to her once, something horrible, something she can never forget or put out of her mind. It is haunting her every second of her dark days, every moment of her pitiful sleep. She has become an empty shell, a pale imitation of the human being she once was. Long ago, as she measures time, she lost everything valuable in a human being, saw it fall through a crack, irreversible, never to be found again.

So she is wandering the darkened streets of the modern world, aimlessly, adrift, hardly ever seen, hardly ever there. People cannot see her, but she is there, present in their daily lives, an open wound that will never close.

No one is safe for Afterglow…

ISBN 978-82-91693-16-3

Black Dragon

One unexplainable, beyond mysterious event changed the world. In one moment, lasting an eternity the Earth and all its creatures was cast in shadow. The sun was blocked out in the sky, and people could only glimpse each other as flickering shapes in a seemingly endless night.

They called it the Great Darkness, and spent years and countless hours attempting to explain it, speculating in vain on its origin.

The results of the event weren't instantaneous, weren't obvious, but in the years to come many people transformed, and gained new and startling abilities, powers of the mind and body never before seen on this Earth.

Lady Grace, Flight Captain, Gimmick, Oracle, The Bowman, Raven Bird and many others rose from the sea of mankind, creatures straight from people's imagination, the fantastic writings of the world, crime fighters, vigilantes and master criminals similar to those previously described only in comic books living the life of their dreams.

The world changed, irrevocably, each new big and small dramatic event removing it further from what it had been, its status quo and social relations altered forever.

Unsettling dreams began haunting them, first at night, in their sleep, and then, slowly, spilling over into their days and waken lives. A creature, a terrifying nightmare rose from the primordial consciousness of them all.

They called it the Black Dragon…

ISBN 978-82-91693-18-7

Secrets

These are descriptions of what cannot be described.

These words within deal with the current world as it is, its prevalent and extensive alienation, inequality and injustice, its ongoing destruction of both spirit and flesh, of everything making life worth living.

But most of all it's about the Night, the great darkness, the dark passions ruling us all, what those in charge more than anything want to take away from us.

Words have power...

Contains 140 poems written from August 2003 to July 2013.

ISBN 978-82-91693-15-6

Red Shadow

Lawrence Watros is an ordinary man doing an ordinary office job. There s nothing exciting about it, nothing exciting at all. Each day is the same. Nothing ever changes. His existence is dominated by routine, by a regiment constantly repeating itself.

Larry's life sucks. He certainly thinks so and he has found no one disagreeing with him on that.

He has always looked at the patterns of his surroundings, never really making a production of it, but that is his forte, if anything is. Now, with one ingle event the pattern changes, is disrupted beyond recognition.

He meets the girl of his dreams, but she isn't exactly miss congeniality. The first thing she tells him is that he's in danger, in mortal danger.

It only grows weirder and more dangerous from there.

His life changes irrevocably and it keeps changing from that one, startling event. The mighty river of time is blocked and takes a completely different path.

From the anthology Red Shadow and Other Stories

ISBN 978-82-91693-23-1

www.ingramcontent.com/pod-product-compliance
Lightning Source LLC
Chambersburg PA
CBHW060605310726
48982CB00008B/1241/J

* 9 7 8 8 2 9 1 6 9 3 2 4 8 *